THE SINGING BLADE

BOOK I OF THE QUEEN OF SORROWS TRILOGY

MICAH CAMPBELL

THE SINGING BLADE

BOOK I OF THE QUEEN OF SORROWS TRILOGY

MICAH CAMPBELL

The Singing Blade

Book I of The Queen of Sorrows Trilogy

Copyright © 2025 Micah Campbell

Published by Micah Campbell

First Edition: December 2025

Printed in the United States of America

eISBN: 979-8-9856387-4-5

Paperback: 979-8-9856387-5-2

Hardcover: 979-8-9856387-6-9

Audiobook: 979-8-9856387-7-6

www.micahcampbell.com

Cover Design by Miblart

Editing by Busy Quill Press

Illia-Dara Illustration by Dalisacg

Interior Design and Formatting by Micah Campbell

This is a work of fiction. Names, characters, businesses, places, events, and incidents are either the products of the author's imagination or used in a fictitious manner. Any resemblance to actual persons, living or dead, or actual events is purely coincidental.

DEDICATION

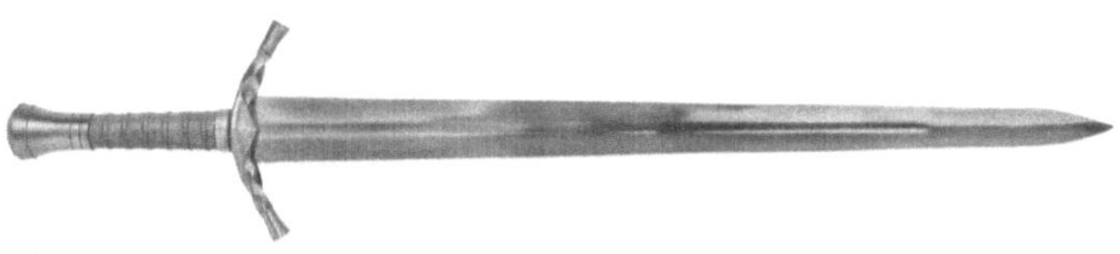

This story is a coalescence of many lives and many joys. Though not all life is pleasure, we persevere.

The whole of this story is dedicated to my children, Emma, Lily, and Declan. You are my light, my anchor, and my world.

The chapter titled, "Forever and Always" is dedicated to my wife, Amanda. That phrase, that mantra, has become a litany and a prayer. It, along with your lips, is tattooed on my neck and engraved upon my heart. I love you, "Forever and Always."

A special thank you to CD McKenna, JB Caine, and "The Bri/yans" for unwavering support and friendship.

A huge shoutout to the lovely people at Post Coffee. You learned my name (and my order) and gave me a place full of friends to finish this book – Beka, Zach, Elise, Kennady, Olivia, Logan, Kailee, Dottie, Marin, Anya, and Rachel – Thank you!

To the brave reader who chose this book,

Thank you for giving me a chance. Your decision to read The Singing Blade is a leap of faith, and it means the world to me. For so long, this story was a private dream, and your choice to open these pages is what finally brings it to life.

CONTENTS

PROLOGUE

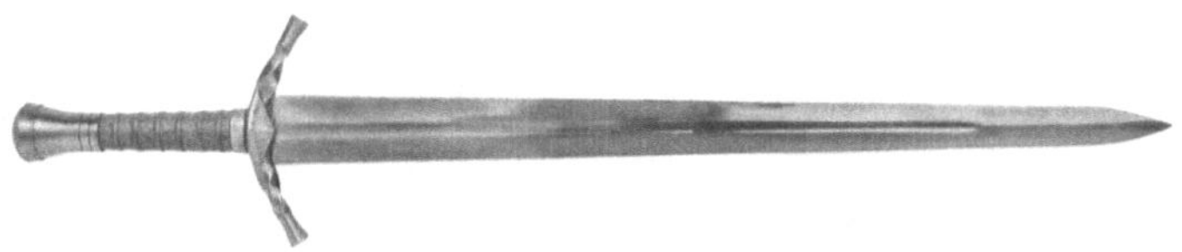

The first frayed thread of ruin was drawn on the night that Queen Cerceia died.

Two men stood cloaked and hooded over her naked body. Breath, white and heavy with condensation, had frozen to the fur lining of their hoods. The beauty of the ice crystals encircling their faces was the antithesis of hard eyes that peered from within. The moon threw silvers and blues across the morose scene as it wove down and around the skeletal canopy of towering trees and leafless branches—a frosted spotlight that seemed to limn this tragedy's ensemble in a milky glow. The stage had been set. The actors had known their marks and lines well. This was to have been the performance of a lifetime, centuries in the making. But none had accounted for the death of the star performer. For there she lay, bloodied and broken among a makeshift bed of leaves and branches on the cold forest floor, life taken from her even while in the very act of giving it.

Angry, red embers illuminated dark eyes as one of the men pulled deeply from his briarwood pipe. Smoke filled the drawn cowl of his cloak as he exhaled, the heat of smoldering berryroot weed and bitter-grass momentarily melting the crystalline splinters surrounding his face. His eyes were pinched, almost to closing, as much to protect them from the cold as to fight the tears that had frozen there. He scanned the forest depths for the telltale, hollow glow of voyeuristic eyes. They were deep in the recesses of the king's private wood, 300 acres of meticulously tended forest that was only accessible from a narrow egress that had been built centuries before when the Sunspire Citadel had been but a distant dream. At that time, all that occupied what was now the very soul of Y'ssara was little more than a blockhouse, a last line of defense for a burgeoning country that sat neatly between Stoneguard Pass and the Titan's Crown mountains. He knew they were well and surely alone, for he could sense no others about the place save for the wildlife that skittered and scampered about. But one could never be too cautious, especially regarding matters of this import.

The other kept his hands covered by long sleeves. They were clasped together in front of him, trembling. His tears ran freely in glacial channels, freezing and then flowing and then freezing again with every blink and every new sorrowful droplet. His body shook as he fought against the waves of sadness battering him as the dark tide of lament and grief grew stronger and more tempestuous with every ebb and swell within. His eyes were not scanning the dark hollows of the infinite shadows within his forest. His concern was not for the potential of spies or assassins or curious snoopers or busybodies. His gaze was solely fixed upon his wife, lying dead in the snow. His hands ached, covered in blood and amniotic fluid that had hardened into dark red gloves of bitter cold. His fingers burned, and he could not feel or move them. And he did not care. His wife was dead.

"Thank you for being at my side, Atamas," the trembling one said, though it was soft and broken as his chest quivered and tightened with involuntary convulsions, keeping his breath captive. "I don't know what I would do if you weren't here, my friend." He paused for a moment, then lifted his gaze from his dead lover to his dearest friend. "What am I going to d—" His voice failed him, and he began to sob openly, freely. The waves of misery had beaten through the last of his defenses, and he was now lost in a raging sea of pain and sorrow. Sanguine hands covered his face. Fresh tears, warm for but a moment, mingled with the blood of his wife and painted his cheeks. And he did not care. His wife was dead.

The other exhaled a cloud of smoke. The sweet scent of the berry-root mixed unfavorably with the stench of death and blood in this place. Under any other circumstance, the smell might have elicited some fond memories of the two of them sneaking out of the Sunspire, stealing some root weed from one of the garrison guard's lockers, and playing Bards and Bandits until far past their curfew, or gentle thoughts of the three of them squandering the entire day touring the alleyways of Y'ssara, Atamas invariably with his pipe and Onidine unfailingly swooning over Cerceia, always looking for some new way to impress her. Atamas smiled then, just for a moment, repining things that once were and never would be again. He raised a gloved and unsoiled hand to rest upon his oldest friend's heaving shoulder.

"Feel your sorrow," he said between draws. "Know your pain. But know, too, there will be time for mourning come 'morrow." Atamas pinched his pipe between his lips and placed both hands upon Onidine's shoulders, turning him so that their eyes met. Atamas blinked away surprise as he took into his friend's visage, broken and blood-streaked and hollow. "Mourn tomorrow, Onidine. And the next day. And the next, if you must. But for today, for right now, rejoice and be glad. Push aside your grief for a little while." He lifted his arms and patted Onidine's shoulders, feigning enthusiasm, for it was a hard thing to muster in this moment. "You have twin sons!"

And indeed, he did, for in the arms of the woman were two newborn babes, naked and squirming, suckling the very last of their mother's life force as she cradled them. They were content and at peace, warmed by the embrace of their dead mother, though that warmth was fast fading. Onidine had wrapped his wife's limp arms around her children in the last moments of her life. He had ensured that they latched to her and that she could feel their pull, their need for her as they nursed, as their small mouths pursued the life-giving milk that only a mother could provide. She had smiled at him, then, and thanked him. There was no fear in her eyes, only love—for him and for their children. And then she died.

"It seems even in death, Cerceia provides for her family," Atamas said. He looked from Onidine down to Cerceia's body and then to her newborn babes, the kingdom's past and future. "She truly was fairest in all of Y'ssildria."

Onidine smiled then, though it was not a happy smile.

"Queen Cerceia will be remembered throughout Y'ssara and the whole of Y'ssildria not only for the sacrifice she made this day but for the love and care that she lavished upon her people during her brief reign." Atamas pulled hard on his briarwood pipe, his cheeks filling and then exhaling. Images of Cerceia's coronation ceremony were called from the recesses of his memory. She had been beautiful and confident, not in herself, but in Onidine's love for her. He smiled, and his was a happy smile. "Her people, *your* people, loved her dearly, and they will love her children, their future, just as dearly and just as wholly."

Onidine, King of Y'ssildria, fell to his knees, breaking from Atamas' grasp. His strength had left him. His legs would no longer hold his burden. His knees ached as the cold and wet of the forest floor soaked into his pants. He could not feel his hands, though they grasped at the soil that the snow had made into mud. His knuckles cracked and bled as he gripped at the earth with all anger and despair. Broken twigs and fallen leaves stabbed and sliced at his palms as the muck and sludge seeped and squished around his fingers. He was bowed low and broken, genuflected before his bride and his newborn children. And after a time, his weeping turned to aught as he had no more tears to cry.

"Of course, you are right, dear Atamas," the king said after a moment, wiping stinging tears from his eyes. "It is such an odd sensation to be so heartbroken as my bride lay lifeless at my feet, yet so joyous and so in love with the gift that she has given me in her death."

"Onidine, my old friend," Atamas replied, extending his hand. The king accepted with a smile, and though it was a weak thing indeed, it was a genuine, hopeful smile. Linking forearms, Atamas heaved Onidine to his feet and brushed the snow and forest floor from his cloak. "It may be a dark day for the people of Y'ssildria, but the future is bright." He clapped Onidine on the back and embraced him. "You have an heir! Two of them, in fact! Let us go and bury your wife. We will put this dark day behind us and look on toward more glorious days to come!"

"Thank you, Atamas. I owe you mo—"

A cough, harmless by itself but accompanied by another, then another interrupted the silence.

Onidine knelt before his children.

"His flesh burns," he said as he placed his hand upon the coughing child's forehead. The babe's skin was fevered and damp. Onidine peeled his palm away and placed it on the other child's head. It was ordinary, distressingly so, as it accentuated the extremity of the other's malady.

He looked to his friend as he hoisted the child into his arms and wrapped it within the folds of his cloak, eyes wide and anxious, struck red with exhaustion and worry. The child coughed again and then again. It was a violent and croaking thing. Onidine could feel its chest rattle and rake as it drew breath, like a plow scraping across crushed rock. The breathing was labored, and when the child exhaled, it was throaty and thick. Onidine brought the child near, nuzzled it, and kissed it, not knowing what else to do. Fresh tears fell upon the child's head and face, though they were not tears of sadness this time, but of fear. Onidine had known fear, but the dread that now raged within him, the dread of a father helpless to save his child, was something altogether new to him. He stared into the eyes of his newborn son for the first time. He was beautiful, just like his mother. His skin was the shade of crushed almonds. His hair — oh, his hair! — wild and fiery. "Just as you will be, my son," Onidine whispered into his child's ear through a throat tight with worry. "Just as your mother was." And his eyes, his eyes were bright and intelligent, though they were distant and seeking. And they were unique in color, one to the other!

Atamas was there in a moment. He ripped his cloak from his back and tucked the other child tightly within. His gaze lingered, only for a moment, upon Cerceia's naked body, exposed now that the children had been removed. Maneuvering the child under one arm, carefully supporting its head and neck in these first hours of utmost fragility, Atamas removed the cowl from his head and swaddled the boy within its fur-lined womb. With a snap of his wrist, the cloak unbundled and extended to length. He covered his queen's body and turned his attention to Onidine and the sick child.

Atamas felt the child's forehead and chest, listening to its lungs as it labored to draw breath. His movements were calculated and confident, and his concentration was complete and undisturbed by Onidine's frantic and sporadic movements. He batted the king's hand away when Onidine reached to cover the child's exposed head. "Your duty now, my king, is to observe and assist if needed. Nothing else." Onidine's head bobbed in a single, sharp nod. "And I require no assistance in matters of healing." There was no malice or anger in Atamas' rebuke, nor did King Onidine take any offense. It was understood that they and their cause were one, and that was to save the boy.

Onidine's eyes strayed to his wife's body, only briefly. Still, the unintentional accusation impregnated the space between the two men in an instant—a combustion reaction like flame reaching gaseous fumes. The question that neither would ever ask but most likely would forever haunt them. Onidine looked back to Atamas, his eyes wide and pleading. He hoped that Atamas had missed the sidelong glance, but upon returning to his friend's eyes, he knew that was not the case.

"Atamas," he said. "I don't blame you for what transpired here this night. Labor is a dangerous and violent thing. There is a tax to be paid upon the giver of life. Always. And my dear Cerceia couldn't afford the tariff. Not with two ..." His voice broke, and he pulled his son close to his face, as much to bring warmth and love to the boy as to hide his tears.

The child's breath slowed and shallowed with each passing minute.

"He is sick, my friend," Atamas said at last. "He is dying."

He left Onidine's side and made his way over to Cerceia's body. His cloak still covered her, but it was now adorned with the slight sheen of diaphanous crystals. Snow had started to fall once again. He set the healthy child down atop its mother and began to lift the covering from her feet. He produced a blade from one of the many pockets sewn into his pants and began removing lengths of umbilical cord from between his dead queen's legs. Onidine turned away. He would not question his friend's actions or motives, as he knew them to be true, but neither would he gaze upon the butchering of his beloved.

The alcove seemed to blur and to darken, even as the first light of the morning reflected from the glassy calmness of Serrated Sea to the east and off the snowcapped peaks of the Titan's Crown to the north. This place was known well to him, but as he stared into the trees, squinting his eyes against the intrusive light, he was left to sift through myriad emotions and thoughts.

The trees, many of which were branded with the initials that he had carved into them as a child, bore scars from years of accepting strikes as the king—just a young prince at the time—had practiced his stances and thrusts and slashes with a dulled training sword, seemed suddenly foreign to him now, even hostile. They loomed and leered at him as he cried, as he held his dying son. They seemed to be taking measure of him as he stood beneath their menacing limbs, and he felt as if he was coming up very, very short. They knew him, of course. They knew him well. They had been here long before he and would most likely be here long after he departed this mortal coil. He was trapped in a vacuum of despair, betrayed by one of the most secure places he had ever known.

He ran his fingers across a deep gouge in the bark of an old dogwood. It was a crude-cut heart encompassing the letters *O* and *C*. He was taken back to the first day he and Cerceia had visited the wood. They had been young and, for the first time, alone, without their sullen and smoky friend beside them. Onidine had professed his love to her then, in the form of a promise ring that he had carved himself from the limb of this very tree. She had returned his declaration with a kiss, and they, together, had carved their initials into the trunk.

He could no longer smell the bouquet of berryroot weed burning within the briar bowl of Atamas' pipe. All he could smell was the iron and copper of blood, the mildew of wet, dead leaves smothered by snow against the forest floor, and excrement, both from his dead wife and his dying son.

"There must be something that we can do," Onidine said as he turned his back on his reverie, hearing sloshing footfalls of Atamas' return.

Atamas looked at the king, the child in one hand and an orb roughly the size of a walnut in the other. It was held together by mud and broken sticks. It was a bloody thing and was wrapped in strands of umbilical cord. It pulsed as if to the beat of a heart. Atamas' visage was one of dark and quiet things, secret things.

"There always is," he replied to his king.

The Road Beyond Knowing

Dusk surrendered its last rays of golden warmth to the gloom of night as the grim-cloaked riders swept across the vast fields of Greenfallow Downs and into the Western Wood. Their flight had been fierce. Even the fell winds of the north, sweeping down from the mountains in all the fury and ferocity of a harbinger of Wintertide, could not keep up with their steeds. Great haste was made by the two strangers who had visited young Heron just three days before. A blur of silvers and blacks painted the horizon as the riders raced to their home in Elimunthil. The sterling horses that carried the riders were none other than the magnificent creatures of the Herudime, blessed by the magic that saturates the mountains on the far side of the Wood—*the mountains that are not*—the mountains of Aetherfast. Herudime stallions were the swiftest and most graceful in all of Y'ssildria, even in all of Y'ssara. They would carry only riders such as these, riders of Illuminthil, though even these would never deign to tame the beasts, only cede to their power with reverence and hold tightly to the reigns.

The Western Wood was three days' journey from Heron's home in The Bairnbrand and the only territory separating The Downs from the mountains of The Herudime. It was so dense a population of elms, maples, and oaks that one could scarcely navigate its labyrinthian depths on foot, let alone on horseback. It had just one known cut path, and this led only halfway through the vast congregation of silent giants. The path was known as Deadlock Pass. The reason for the path's abrupt end was not common knowledge among those in The Downs or any surrounding areas. It was just a matter of fact that one did not venture further than Deadlock Pass—not that one could—for as the path ended, so too did the typical wooded environs of the region, giving way to a more coniferous sort as the shadows of the Hirudime mountains stretched out from high above. Black and white fir, jackpine, balsam, and tamarack crowded and fought for unoccupied space, of which there was very little left. Willows, poplars, and alders rose with the foothills, and in the understory, blueberry, cranberry, and berryroot bushes stretched and reached for whatever scraps of sunlight the trees left for them. To forward beyond the pass was not only a fool's errand, it was an impossibility. Y'ssildrians rarely traveled into the wood, even more seldom set foot on Deadlock Pass, for no one knew the recesses of its mysteries or terrors the forest held unseen. Even if they did—and were foolish enough to dare enter—there was no way to get through it.

The riders approached the entrance to the wood just as the moon reached its pinnacle, which was a boon for them and not at all by happenstance. They knew an apex moon was a powerful charm—and one would need powerful charms to cross the limens of Deadlock Pass.

"Illuminthil will not be pleased that we have returned without the boy," Atamas said as he lifted his staff before him. He whispered a series of phrases, causing the runestones fitted along the handle of the staff to glimmer with a brilliant blue glow. "We should have taken him, by force if the need presented itself—which I believe that it did—considering now that we, indeed, do not have him."

"He was not there, Atamas," the other rider responded. "What would you have us do, storm the Bairnbrand demanding to see for ourselves?"

"At least then we would know. Now we return to the council with nothing, just more questions."

The path before the riders began to sparkle, enchanted by the staff's radiance. Bellflowers awoke from their slumber, stretching and yawning, reaching their petals into the bespelled air. Beckoned by the unheard call of Atamas' staff and the lunar powers held there, they opened their bulbs and shone. The path glowed with soft reds and blues and pinks as the flowers to each side of the road came to life. Pollen, dust, and insects glittered and shimmered in the multi-colored lights that limned the way. What was once, only a moment before, a dark and dangerous road was now a well-lit, enchanted thing quite suited for wizards such as these.

"So quick to use magic and so quick to use force, yet so slow to use patience," the second said with a resigned sigh. "I truly hope that you are strong enough to succeed in your mastery of our ways, young Atamas." The rider urged his mount forward onto the path, continuing a practiced and oft-repeated admonition. "I do not share your lust for control, nor do any of your other brothers and sisters in Illuminthil. It is never wise to abuse the gift that Y'sa and The Aetherfast have bestowed upon us." He paused for a moment to wipe a cluster of widow-webs from his face. "It is more foolish, still, to oblige one's spirit to do the work for which one's hands are made."

The rider then produced a torch from within a well-worn, cross-stitched and patched satchel at his side and brought it to light with the click of a flame-fellow, a brass cylinder small enough to fit into one's palm that housed flint and steel on opposite gears. When the singular lever was struck with a thumb, it rotated the gears and produced spark enough to light dry tinder or a well-oiled torch. Shadows danced to and fro under the hold of the flame that bounced and swayed with the wind. Stren removed his hood. The light revealed a speckled beard and stern eyes, his face lined with strength and wisdom, and also concern.

"The road will be much easier to see with a bit of magic," the other replied with a smirk as he prompted his horse forward. He had shed his hood, following his master's lead, and beneath it was a bright-eyed young man, wearing neither the beard nor any evidence of the strength, wisdom, or concern that his master showed. "Always quick to use magic," he said, repeating his mentor's words and somber inflection, "because it is magic that gets the job done." He kicked at his mount's hindquarters then and leaped to the lead. "Come, teacher," he shouted back to Stren. "The hour is late, and *you* have a lot of explaining to do!"

Stren bowed his head and sighed deeply, coaxing his mighty stallion to follow.

"I pray, young Atamas, that you do not fall victim to the same desire for power that so many before you have," he said more to himself than to his charge. "So easily it is mistaken for the desire for peace. Peace comes with a great price, but power comes at a much more considerable toll." He raised his head and his voice then. "Do not be fooled by the evil that has presented itself to us this day. Evil rarely storms the gate. It walks through the front door, smiling, draped in the robes of righteousness." Stren's warning and wisdom both fell on deaf ears—as they had so often—for Atamas was deep into the Wood, growing farther and farther away from his master with every stride.

"Stay strong, dear Atamas."

OF FAE AND FUMBLEFOOT

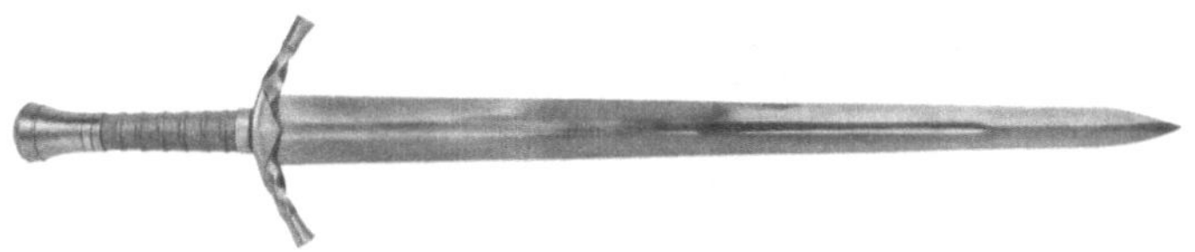

Even illumined by rudimentary flame and moon-harnessed magics, the path seemed threatening. The trees and brush were so closely connected that one could not see a horse's length into its foreboding sanctuary. Unbeknownst to the riders, *that* difficulty was theirs alone, for they could be seen perfectly well by those within the forest's hallow. Timber-Folk gazed intently upon the riders as they passed, following ever so quietly and communicating with one another in the telepathic manner common to dwellers of the mystical forest haven. Keeping the Western Wood was not the burden of any one race or group of peoples—for indeed the Wood had means of its own to dissuade ill-intentioned visitors—but the Timber-Folk took special pride as her self-proclaimed protectors and were very cautious of any who entered. The trees appreciated the respect that the woodland race showed toward the forest and, in return, allowed them to use powers of fellowship to stay in contact when words were dangerous.

Ere they Y'ssildrians, one questioned silently, the trees carrying his thoughts through bough and root.

Ere they a wishin' to herm the ferest, another responded with his own question.

Er Us, a third added.

Timber-Folk, also known as faeries, were a hearty and rotund people, almost as round as they were tall—which wasn't quite tall at all and was often a point of parody amongst children and acting troupes in the more civilized regions of Y'ssara. Faeries were hardened by aeons of working with their hands within the depths of the Wood. They were also brilliant gardeners. Faemen took the fiercest pride in two things in equal parts: the length of their beards, which came to just above their toes, and the callouses on their hands, known to be as hard and rough as the igneous rock that their forefathers mined from beneath the Crown.

It is said that in ages past, at the height of The Rending War and long before the Council of Rectitude, a faeman by the name of Fumblefoot led a most valiant advance against a stubborn and heavily-fortified regiment that had seized control of a small fishing village off the Summershine River's southern basin. So bold was Fumblefoot, so sharp his axe and so long his beard, that accounts of his thunderous charge continue to be told even today. It is said that he was more akin to a raging lion than a faeman that day, that his beard buffeted all around him like a mane, full of vengeance and promised violence. "Like prairie grass whipping in a windstorm," the storytellers would say. Fumblefoot was a catastrophe on two feet that day, the barreling ferocity of a fierce dragon defending its hoard. A fierce dragon with the beard of a long-forgotten god, that is.

The small force of villains that occupied the village trembled in fear and made ready to release their prisoners and plot their escape as Fumblefoot raced across the marsh, a roaring prayer to Y'sa on his lips and a blazing glint of bloodlust in his eyes.

Unfortunately for him and for all the doomed villagers he was trying so desperately to save, that was as far as poor Fumblefoot got before the wind shifted direction and blew his beard low. The warrior's whiskers went from framing his face in regal splendor to catching his feet in a tangle of tresses, bramble, and boots, all in the blink of a dumbfounded eye. Or rather, many dumbfounded eyes, as not only did Fumblefoot's band of freedom fighters look on in horror and disbelief, but so, too, did the invaders and the villagers. To a man, jaws fell, and gasps of bewilderment escaped gaping mouths as Fumblefoot lurched forward, beard over backside three times full, arms and legs outstretched and reaching, clawing and scrambling for purchase unfound until he dropped in a heap, a measure of four fully-grown men laid out end-to-end from where he started.

The villagers were slaughtered, men, women, and children all, and the fae battalion of would-be rescuers was routed, chased back to the woods by cackling invaders. Fumblefoot was left as carrion—a grim, gruesome, and bloated reminder to the fat faery people that they were better gardeners than warriors and that they should never, *ever* grow their magnificent beards past their toes or leave the safety of the Western Woods, no matter how many fishing villages were raided.

An' why would two men be travelin' the path at this time o' night, a fourth asked.

Er this time of the season, added a fifth.

Mayhaps they wish ter be *hermed*, a sixth chimed in with a chortle, although it sounded more akin to a series of syrupy coughs, as trees don't particularly have a sound for a *chortle*.

Silence. No response.

Martu. Is that you, the first asked.

Aye. It is, Martu responded after another moment of silence.

Yer no' even here, ye dolt! the third said, an air of exasperation in his voice.

Innit your night fer cleanin'? the first asked.

Aye, it is that! the fourth rang in. *An fer doin' the dishes besides.*

Wha'ye think I'm fer doin' now, ye flat-bellied snoffer, Martu shot back. *I know me place an' I'm knowin' it well. An fer tonight its dishes, but fer tomorrow its ter be fer kickin yer behind!*

A chorus of guffaws and cackles reverberated through the root systems of the many trees connecting Meritha Pol—the home of the Timber-Folk—to the hidden band watching the riders.

Bah! came the reply of too many voices to count.

Timber-Folk were not so different in appearance and attitude from their kin, the Stone-Folk, who dwelled within the subterranean grottos of the mountains to the north of Greenfallow Downs and the Western Wood. The Stone-Folk were the most prominent of the Wild Ones—humans that had forsaken the draw of comfort and contemporary advancement long ago in lieu of tradition and communion with the elements. All Wild Ones had adopted slight characteristics of the biomes which they inhabited. Stone-Folk were hearty, squat, and robust, reaching near the height of a grown man's waist. Millennia within caverns and under mountains had shortened and strengthened them and turned the pigment of their flesh dark and almost clay-like in tone.

Timber-folk, on the other hand, while similar in size and stature, were no longer accustomed to the hard work and grueling duties of their cave-dwelling kin. Their years were spent outside among the sun and trees, pruning and gardening. Thus, they had grown. Not upward, like the trees and vines to which they so meticulously ministered, but outward. Their bellies grew vast and soft and quite problematic for those who were inclined to cooking and sewing. And while they were no match for the Stone-Folk in strength and feat, they were more than equipped to tend and guard the forests they called their home in their own way.

Stone-Folk were rarely seen outside the mountainous ranges, preferring to live out their lives in the seclusion of rocky tunnels. Timber-folk, however, flourished in a variety of regions. Y'ssara was mostly forest, after all. Trees and streams, valleys and rivers, farmlands and lakes. It was a land of *life*. There were mountains and deserts and swamps, to be sure, but for the most part—three of four parts if one were to guess—Y'ssara was a land of trees.

It was said that when Y'sa created the sum of all things, he looked across the expanse of Y'ssara most favorably and bestowed upon her as many trees as were stars in the sky. And within the depths of these ageless forests dwell the Timber-folk, or the Fae, as they choose to refer to themselves.

The Fae were peaceful creatures, having just one desire and one love: Trees. They cared dearly for their lofty friends and would do anything to protect them. Being not at all knowledgeable in weapons and war, the fae had to rely on wit and reason to survive and to protect each other and the Wood. What little defense they did possess was in magic. Fae held the earth in such high esteem that she gave to them an understanding of natural magics in return. This is the power, or more appropriately, the right to summon the elements of the earth to aid in trials. This was not an offensive magic, but more a practical power. This was very taxing for the Timber-Folk, for it took a significant amount of their energy to summon the elements and an even more considerable amount of time for them to regain that loss.

We should n'er a brought the lad, came a thought from the line, though no one would claim responsibility for it. That was a problem of particularity with using the trees' telepathic properties to communicate; all thoughts went through the trees and into the heads of *all* others involved in the relay. The trees, loosely bound to their given position, would often let thoughts slip into the conversation, simply for entertainment, that the fae did not intend for public knowledge. For what else is a semi-bound being of ages to do? The five fae behind Thurdop just glanced around curiously, knowing good and well that the thought would forever remain anonymous unless the perpetrator chose to come forward.

He is too young fer such an impertent mission, ter be sure. This time the communication was claimed by Mergop, the most pessimistic and cantankerous of the party. *Just because he is yer kin. I donna think–*

His thought was cut short by a fierce and swift ring in their heads. Anger.

Ye donna think anything on this small journey, ye goat-arsed cow. All eyes were on Thurdop. And all of Thurdop's impressive—and silent—fury and rage was focused on Mergop. And impressive it was, for a half-man-sized fae hugging a tree with one hand and pointing a shaking, soundless finger at Mergop, as this communion within the wood was only achieved if the speaker was touching one of the trees.

Mergop replied, seemingly unimpressed with Thurdop's ire. *Ye know good an' proper that young Heron ain't who they be thinkin' he is, and ye know even more good and proper who actually is who they be thinkin' he is. And it ain't him! I know that yer thinkin' yer in cherge, an' ye may be fer the here an' now, but ye ain't ter be when we get back ter Meritha Pol! Yer to be planting an' seeding an' hervestin' with the rest of us. Yer just like the rest of us, 'cept ye got a bastard nerphew with no ma er pa that them stangers er wantin' an' we stole from 'em!*

An audible gasp sounded, and the silver rhythm of the insects and nightly creatures along the moonlit trail stilled. All eyes turned to Torin, a portly and oddly-dressed fae with thick, vine-thread spectacles and a pointy cap that was too small for his ample head. Both hands were removed from the tree that he had been clutching moments earlier, and were currently covering his mouth. His eyes, magnified by dense, round glass, were more akin to those of a barn owl that had just heard a most salacious and unseemly joke in the middle of a sacred assembly than those of a proud member of a clandestine team of spies.

Torin placed his hands back on the tree, though he wished he hadn't. He was assaulted with a symphony of curses and slander so foul that the bark of the trees in the vicinity seemed to take on the inflamed hue of the flowers glowing along the path. However, whether this was truly the case or Torin's own embarrassed remembrance was still debated among the wood-folk whenever stories of the end of all things were told.

Torin, ye derned fool, Thurdop chided. *Ye've the spine of a soggy loaf of bread and the wit of a troll mid-retch! If ye can't be fer bein' quiet yer fer bein' done with patrol. Fer tonight an' fer all the nights after. Ye'll be fer washing dishes aside Martu an' fer tuckin' the wee ones in besides!*

Torin recoiled at the admonition, more the latter than the former, as it was a well-established tradition that the fairer fae—that being the women-folk—were the ones who would see to the bairns and ensure that Meritha Pol was quiet and calm by a decent hour. The men of Meritha Pol handled the cleaning and the cooking and the dishes, as these were simple tasks. But the women tended to the children, as this was a monumental affair and one that required patience and grace, something that the faemen sorely lacked, as evidenced by the one ill-fated experiment by the tallest and yet shortest-lived chief of Meritha Pol.

Arissa was her name and she was fair, fairer by far than any of the other fae. It was said that she had stray blood in her, that is, that hers was mixed with the blood of outlanders, those outside of the family of Wild Ones. Arissa was fae, true enough though, and she was voted chief after her father, the most excellent chief of all Meritha Pol, passed suddenly in his sleep. Being his only heir, Arissa was the obvious choice to take her father's place, and being a progressive and forward-thinking people, not bound by the oligarchal chains of tradition, the fae of the Pol welcomed her with open arms. This quickly changed, though, as one of Arissa's first decrees was to reverse the long-standing tradition of roles within the clan.

"Fer far too long, the men of The Pol have taken advantage o' our love fer our wee ones an' fer them," she said. "They take advantage o' our kindness and our patience. We endure the pains of labor and bear them their children, an' they do nothin' but cook and clean and hunt! They provide for us, to be sure! But who's fer sayin' tha' we can'no be the ones fer doin' the huntin' an' they can be the ones fer bairn-rearin'?

The convocation enclave was full to bursting. Many stood on the outer rim as all the seats encircling the rostrum were taken. The enclave was just outside The Pol proper, and was a well-hidden copse of manicured forest floor surrounded by giant oaks. Fashioned brushery, trimmed and kept, of all the past chiefs, men and women alike, encircled and interwove throughout the assembly grounds. Fond faces, well-remembered and forever loved, stood out among the leaves and vines of the shrub sculptures, gazing upon their generational progeny in admiration and pride. Fallen trees, padded with the silky softness of mood moss, provided seating in the three inner circles, taking the natural shape of the thicket. All of Meritha Pol was in attendance. And all of Meritha Pol leaned forward in anticipation of Arissa's forthcoming ordinance, though most held onto their seats with trepidation.

"We be sittin' here among our ferefathers an' our feremothers an' I can'no help but wonder what they're thinkin' o' us now?"

This caused a ripple of movement and whispers among the attendees. A quiet reverberation like that of a low harp string strummed a third octave below middle C—a deep, resonating restless sound—moved throughout the gathering. However, there was a tension, too, as if it was a dominant note waiting for the resolve. The fae adjusted their positions. Some stood, as if it were uncomfortable to sit any longer, though the moss provided excellent cushion, and they had been sitting well under an hour's time. Questions of concern and confusion flitted and floated through the air, breathless and timid.

"I can see yer worries, friends. An' mer impertent, I can see yer hearts," Arissa said, hoping to quench the flames of doubt before they roared beyond the spark of suspicion. She raised her hands in a placating gesture as if patting the sky and continued. "Ye know me. Ye know me as ye knew me father. Ye been knowin' me from me birth, when me dear ma brought me to ye." She glanced around the copse slowly and deliberately, her eyes settling on the men and women throughout. "Armen," she said, eyes landing on an older fae with a checkered shirt and salty beard, "ye raised yer own darlin' Darfin to be a proud woman o' The Pol, did ye not? I know ye did, because I came up alongside her an' I'm fer knowin' it's true!"

Armen nodded slowly and lowered his gaze. His head disappeared beneath the mass of shoulders and beards as he sat back down.

"And Doris, ye, yer dern self told me not more than two hands ago that ye were itchin' ter get out there an' shoot yer bow! Ye telled me now that yer mister is gone, Y'sa rest his flame, ye been gettin' what's leftover from someone else's pot an' that it's been sand in yer slippers ere since his passin'." This time, she spoke to a young widow in the third circle, and same as the last, Doris looked away and sat down. On and on it went well into the morning, Arissa called on and called out the fae of Meritha Pol. And one by one, they sat, ceding to her charges.

And so it was that not only was Arissa, first and only daughter of Chief Orroban, named High Chief that night, but so too were the roles and responsibilities that had for eons past held The Pol thriving and prosperous, reassigned to better suit a more modern and advanced way of thinking. The faemen were tasked with the bairns, while the faewomen cleaned, cooked, and hunted. It lasted one night.

That following night, the faewomen returned from their hunting empty-handed, save for two scrawny—and squished—squirrels unlucky enough to cross paths with Arissa herself as she fell from her perch high atop a fledgling maple. She was not unfamiliar with a bow, nor was she a novice in climbing trees, but nocking an arrow whilst balancing across two limbs of questionable strength got the best of her. A gust of wind took to the leaves like a tempest catching the sail of a ship. It bent the branches low and stole poor Arissa's dubious foothold from beneath her. Hands occupied with bow and arrow, Arissa tumbled to the ground, managing to hit every branch on her descent and land directly onto two unsuspecting squirrels.

The faemen fared no better.

The hunting party returned to find Meritha Pol in a state of pandemonium. Fae children ran hither and yon, some wielding pots and pans and other such dinnerware as makeshift weapons in various versions of Gob-and-Smash, a game where one child is elected to play the part of a goblin, and the rest are valiant knights trying to tag them out. Tagging usually involved a slight tap or slap of the hand on one's shoulders, but this night, the tagging involved stew pots, frying pans, and a mess of bruised and crying bairns. The children were arrayed in all manner of makeshift armor, such as buckets for helmets and breadboards for chest pieces. However, many of them had abandoned their cloth diapers for a more natural option, as their diapers had become overloaded and soiled.

Most of the faemen were drunk and passed out or working diligently to reach such a state, as they had long ago given up on the assignment commissioned to them. The Pol was a cacophony of snores, shouts, crying, and laughing. Many of the fallen faemen had been unceremoniously rolled to the center of the camp, still clinging to empty tankards, and piled high by those who were well-passed sober but not entirely beyond consciousness. The bodies of the sleeping men were stacked and placed head to foot in cardinal directions to resemble, with some imagination, a fortress that the goblin could hide within. It was a safe zone for when the *smash* portion of the game became too much to take. When in the safe zone, the goblin could not be harmed.

The reign of High Chief Arissa Orroban of Meritha Pol ended that night. She was barred from all future council meetings and banned from entering Meritha Pol ever again. It is said that she lived out her days traveling Y'ssildria, peddling her enlightened philosophies as a self-proclaimed Luminary of Insightfulness. Meritha Pol was not the only city she was banned from. There is no shrub statue of her likeness to be found in the conclave.

Ye can'no do that, Torin replied, shock and anger evident on his face, if not in his words, as he had returned to tree-talk. *I'll be fer takin' up Martu's shifts afore I'll be—*

A soft, almost imperceivable sound interrupted the faemen. Almost imperceptible. It was nothing so notable as a twig snapping underfoot or even a faemen shouting out loud in the lull of midnight in a forgotten wood, no, it was breath, an exhalation, a sigh. The fae as one went silent, listening, looking. Even foolish Martu back at Meritha Pol, one hand still reaching out the kitchen window holding tight to his tree, the other mechanically scrubbing already clean dishes, stilled. All strained to hear, to see, to feel something, anything.

Then, a multicolored light shone forth. It was so vast a prism of luminance, so wide an angle of incidence, that the faemen couldn't help but fall back and cover their blinded eyes. They hit the ground hard and scrambled to the sounds of the others' shouting. Their purpose was singular: to reach each other, stand, and fight. To the death if they must. Their only hope was a united and defensible position. If they could link arms and form some kind of strategic bulwark they might have a chance. But that chance never came. And even if it did, the one who stood before them was too mighty a foe. They were no match for him.

First Loves and Old Friends

It wasn't the vast stretches of infinite fields or the tall and vibrant grey sage bowing in pious subjection to the subtle suggestions of the sea-kissed breeze wafting up and over the sheer cliffs of the Stoneguard that held him rapt in his reverie—though it was, indeed, beautiful. It wasn't the purples and blues and pinks and golds that speckled these fields in every possible combination of color imaginable, in every shade and pallet, every shape and size known to man or beast, as if the fair and fierce Maker of All Things Himself, had stretched an elegant hand high to the sun and extracted from within all of life and all of beauty in all its myriad forms and fashions and sprinkled them across the fields of dancing flowers that held Ixchel fast and frozen—though they were inspiring.

It wasn't the magnitude and might of the Titan's Crown Mountains that met at the pinnacle of Y'ssildria, at the northern and westernmost edge of what seemed to be all of existence, then careened hundreds of feet straight down to meet the Serrated Seas and then continue to the very depths of the ocean floor, or the Guard's monstrous gargoyle sentinels that keep watch over the stony pathways that had years ago been carved out by the sturdy and stout Pilgrims of Erilem that had Ixchel quaking where he stood in awe, unable to speak, unable even to draw breath—though they were awesome.

No, it was none of these things or anything else in all of creation that made him feel so completely taken by beauty, so inspired, so in awe, and so alive. It was her. It had always been and forever would be her. It was Illia-Dara. He was slain.

He had known her from a very early age. Ever since that day, 15 years ago tomorrow, when Stren had taken him to the Reaping Moon Festival, Ixchel knew that she was the one, his only one. She had been skipping alongside her adoptive mother amidst throngs of loyal patrons, both foreign and native. The streets were filled that day with more people in one place than Ixchel had ever seen before in his short life. More people than he had seen combined up to that point. But even among the crowd, even in the shadow of Queen Cerceia Cressedia, Illia-Dara stuck out like a sunflower among weeds, a majestic mountain among foothills. Her face was soft and kind. Her eyes, the color of spring laced with the golden sunset, were wide and inquisitive but not scared. Never scared. That was what caught Ixchel so. Her fearless curiosity. It was a stark contrast to his own horrified visage. Mouth agape and dark eyes as wide as two loaves of pan bread, he was anything but confident.

"Stay close to me, boy," Stren said as he tugged at Ixchel's sleeve, his voice rasping and raw from non-use. "There are many wonders to behold in Y'ssildria this time of year, but as with all things, you must remain vigilant. There are snakes in every garden, no matter how beautiful or well-kept. Remember that."

Ixchel tried to imagine an alternate reality, however impossible, where the beautiful young woman before him was anything but wholly good. He watched as she gracefully paused and nodded to passersby, acknowledging each and every one of them—whether dressed in regal attire fit for court or filthy makeshift coverings—as they knelt before her and her mother, offering gratitude and gifts and well-wishes. He watched her eyes. They were compassionate and honest and sparkled with a joy that reached to his soul. It was an infectious joy that began in his stomach and radiated up his chest and out to his limbs like a sip of fine and aged bourbon. He watched her mouth. There was no smirk there, no pity or patronizing. Her smile was true and pure. Her lips were wet and full and such a vivid shade of red as to be the very source of ember, like sweetheart cherries in early summer reflecting the shine of the sun. He had tasted sweetheart cherries once before, with his master on a journey through southern Y'ssara, and though they were delightful and sugary and held a hint of mischief and tartness, he knew in his very being that her lips were sweeter by far, full of warmth and wildness.

No, he told himself. *No, Master. In this, you are wrong. There is no snake here. There is only beauty.*

The strong stench of waste pulled Ixchel violently away from his reverie and back to the reality of his current situation: Chores.

Stren was a man of few friends and even fewer words. Ixchel often wondered if the latter encouraged the former or if it was because of his master's bleak outlook on people that they lived out in the hills of Mon Cree, an unremarkable and oft-forgotten hamlet far west of the city proper. He often found himself pondering this as they dined alone every evening, and then again as he woke every morning to the same hand-written note on crumpled yellow parchment.

Milk and eggs first.
Then straight to the barn with you.
Recitation and remembrance, next.
DO NOT AVOID YOUR SIGNS.
Crops, fruits, and nuts.
Dinner promptly at dusk.
One new dish and two new ingredients –
NO EXCEPTIONS
I will speak to you this evening.
–Stren
Postscriptum: Water

It was the same redundant routine every day. No visitors. No time for rest. No time for play. Ixchel was in a state of perpetual hope that Stren might loosen his grip, both figuratively and literally, on this most uncommon of days. But his grasp remained tight, and his hard eyes remained firm. This was not a day of leisure, not for him and not for his master. Why would he have thought any differently about today? There was never a day of leisure as far as Stren was concerned. He was a hard man and a hard master. He was kind, no doubt, but kindness does not equate to time off or the shirking of one's duties.

Ixchel had been busy transporting manure from the barn to the gardens when he heard his master's call. It was not an audible thing. There was no shout or shrill whistle. Instead, it was a light ringing in his head, a whisper, one word: *Come*. He threw the shovel aside and ran. It clanged loudly and toppled over the wheelbarrow that he had been using to move the dung. He was halfway up the cracked road before he skidded to a stop, stirring dried dust and dirt into a cloud of choking fog. Powder and rocks took flight as he pivoted. He ran back down the worn lane, righted the wheelbarrow, kicked the remaining contents around quickly in hopes of spreading it, set the shovel standing inside the barn, and took off again. His master rarely called him in the middle of chores. As a matter of truth, Ixchel could not recall any other time that his master had *ever* interrupted his chores.

A sense of urgency took hold. His stride increased, as did his heartbeat, as he ran in earnest. A dry and suffocating haze of rock dust rose and fell in his wake as he raced up the shatter-stone street that branched toward his home. It had been a hot and thirsty summer. The roads and fields alike were scorched and desiccated. Old ash stumps, strung with twisted wire for fencing, blurred by as he ran. Something compelled him to run, but he knew not what. He did not want to keep his master waiting, of course, but it was as if he knew nothing else save to return to him now, as if some invisible tether was pulling him, and he was just trying to keep up, to keep from stumbling and being dragged the rest of the way.

He slowed as he approached the old cottage at the forest's edge. The Elderfen, so named after the ancient sect of druidic hermits who settled Mon Cree after their sojourn from Erilem, stretched for miles and miles in all directions and remained lush and full despite the drought. Ixchel's lungs burned from labored sharp breaths. His eyes were red and angry from debris kicked up during his flight. His legs wobbled unsteadily as he willed them, unsuccessfully, to stop. He froze directly in front of the worn, horse-hair mat laid out on the doorstone of the only home he had ever known. It was a warm and welcoming place, if not rather small and cluttered now that he was older. His thighs shuddered as his momentum slowed and he tripped. His hands went up reflexively to guard his face.

Something was different. The old wooden half-door, painted the green of spring caladium—though it had been painted such for as long as Ixchel could remember and desperately needed a good sanding and repainting—was open at the top, just as it always was. But it was ajar at the bottom as well. It was never fully unlatched. Ixchel fell headlong through the threshold with a bang, both half-doors swinging in and crashing into the wall behind. The multicolored curtains that Stren used as rugs rushed to meet him in a not-so-friendly welcome as he hit the floor.

He sat motionless, listening, dreading Stren's rebuke, but it didn't come. The *new* curtains, which were the *old* blankets, were pulled back, allowing the sun to penetrate and illuminate the front rooms, just as they always were. Smoke came from the chimney, and the smell of sage and incense lilted in the air, as it always did. The fire was not for warmth but for cooking and binding. All was as it should be as Ixchel lifted himself off the floor with a groan. All was as it should be, but something felt off. There was an energy, a heaviness in the air. No, not in the air, but all around him. He was not breathing it. He was moving through it. It pressed upon him as if he were walking on the floor of a deep pool of water. The surrounding pressure intruded on him, made it hard to breathe, caused his steps and movements to slow. He was, of course, perfectly safe and could breathe just fine, but still, the pressure.

"Why is there dung on your shoes?"

"Er, what," Ixchel said, the question drawing him out of the resonant pressures of the pool and back into the present.

"Why is there dung on your shoes?" Stren repeated the question, slower this time and with a lower, less patient pitch.

"I," Ixchel remembered kicking the manure about frantically to heed his master's call most expeditiously. "I was cleaning the barn, master."

Stren's eyes narrowed, then closed. His shoulders slouched, and he exhaled a weighty and wordless breath. "Do you make a habit of cleaning the barn with your boots, Ixchel?" Stren straightened and turned his back, looking deeper into the old cottage. "Especially when we have company?"

Ixchel looked up to his master for a moment and then back down to his boots.

Not waiting for a response, Stren added, "Please make yourself presentable and join us. *Soon.*" He held out the last. It was not a request.

Ixchel could not help but grin as he pictured, only for the briefest of moments, his master as a lazy cow grazing out behind the barn *mooing. Mooooo. Mooooo. Sooooon.* He recovered quickly and dared a glance back up. Stren was staring at him. Ixchel brought a hand to his mouth and coughed, hoping to conceal any remnants or evidence of his thoughts or the accompanying smile. He failed.

"Now," Stren sighed as he turned and left Ixchel, disappearing down the hall and into the study.

Company, Ixchel thought. They had never had company, at least not inside, not even when King Onidine had visited years before. *Something is happening*.

He kicked his boots off and out onto the patio, eager to meet this unexpected guest. He looked at his hands as he closed the door. They were filthy. *He* was filthy! He soft-stepped down the hall toward his room. The small cottage was split into two parts by a long hallway adorned with all manner of paintings and trinkets from Stren's time at Council and from his many adventures. The hall darkened as it led further into the dwelling to the point that the back rooms on either side were nearly invisible from the front door. Stren's room was on the right-hand side at the back of the hall and the study closest to the front. Stren had said that this was so they could study with the natural light that the windows afforded them, though Ixchel thought that it was more likely the fact that Stren preferred his privacy. After all, they did the majority of their studies and lessons at night, by candlelight. That left Ixchel's room across from Stren's and the kitchen just ahead and across from the study.

He changed course. It only made sense that he would visit the kitchen before going to his bedroom to change clothes. His current state demanded a bit of attention. His hands and face were dirt-caked from a morning of chores and his race back home, but he did not smell too terribly bad, and what faint odors were coming off of him were quickly covered up by the smells of whatever his master had brewing in the fire. Having decided that a trip to the privy and adjoining washroom out back was not necessary, the kitchen it was. He tried to sneak a peek into the study as he turned, but the door was closed. He could hear two voices talking in low murmurs. Both were male. One was his master's, but he could not begin to imagine who the second voice belonged to. Leaving that mystery for later, he walked into the kitchen and realized how hungry he was. He needed to wash his hands and face, of course. If he happened to stumble across some delicious treat that Stren had prepared for their guest while in there, that would just be an added bonus.

Dust sparkled and drifted in and out of the rays of sunlight that peaked through the front window. Stren was well-kept and clean, and he maintained his house in much the same manner. Ixchel found it fascinating how much of the unseen can be exposed with the right light. He ran his hands through the shafts of gold. *Perspective is everything*, he thought. He shuffled slightly to his right, and the brilliant sparkles of dust disappeared. *Perspective* and *position*, he corrected.

He moved to the washbasin and poured fresh water—which he had collected earlier—into the funnel above the counter. The funnel was attached to a coil that ran down an iron rod and hung over the basin. There was a valve and stopper to avoid the contents spilling over and being wasted. As the water percolated, Ixchel struck the small flintstone affixed to the iron rod's bottom plate with a steel pin. This ignited the iron components of the tinderbox at the bottom of the heating rod. Stren would often chide Ixchel when he would take so much time and use up such valuable resources just to wash his hands, but Ixchel liked the warm water. It made him feel relaxed and cleaner than using cold water. Stren strictly forbade the use of magics in the mundane, so it was with cold water now or warm water later. Plus—and he would never admit this to his master—he just loved the simple efficiency of the whole thing. There was a much larger version of this water-warmer in the washroom behind the cottage, and Ixchel would often find himself becoming wrinkled and pruney as he would spend the longer side of an hour simply standing under the heated sprinkles of the captured rainwater, soaking and thinking. He had even helped Stren architect and install systems like this in neighboring villages. It was a system of Stren's own invention and a highly sought-after design.

Ixchel left the rod and water to warm and looked about the kitchen for something to eat. There were no cabinets, just shelving—and most of those were dedicated to herbs and medicinal plants. Vines and leaves grew out and about each other. It looked like an herbaceous mess, a small jungle of stems and roots, but Stren assured Ixchel that a healthy intermingling of the different herbs and oils would do far more for the whole of this small cultural environment than if he were to segregate them.

"All living things find their greatest purpose when they are both thriving and aiding the other," he had said when first introducing Ixchel to the herb garden. "Take, for example, this moonthistle leaf. You see how rich and green its healing leaves are?" He held a bundle of dark and dense green leaves gently in his hands. "These leaves have the power to cure, to heal, to extract that which is harming or even killing, but out in the wild, on their own, these leaves would become so heavy, so full of healing ointments, that they would weigh the whole of the plant down to the ground, to be suffocated and die under its own miraculous weight." He dropped the handful of leaves, but they did not weigh the plant down. Instead, they were held up by a red and black vine that had snaked its way throughout and around most of the kitchen.

"This venom-vine is angry and thorned, you see?"

Ixchel nodded and took a step back. He had seen his master get pricked by this vine before, had seen the vicious and violent infection that spread quickly from that minuscule little poke. He had witnessed, first-hand, the frantic, though not panicked, way his master had ripped and ground different leaves and roots from all around the vine to make a salve that he immediately applied to the wound.

"It has no other purpose in all the world except to kill," Stren continued. "More men have died clumsily or stupidly running across this vine out in the wild than in the last three wars combined. He laughed then, glancing down at his wrist, recalling the same memory that Ixchel had moments ago.

"Why would Y'sa make such a thing?" Ixchel had asked. "Why would Y'sa bring something so worthless and dangerous and," He struggled to reconcile his thoughts with his words. Ixchel was young then, not yet 10 years of age, "so evil?"

Stren smiled then and patted the boy on the shoulder. "Know this, boy, there is nothing in all of Y'sa's creation that was created with evil in mind, but has not the corruption of man manifested itself in all things? Look here," he drew Ixchel's attention back to the moonthistle. "You can see that the leaves have not fallen and, in fact, are thriving, even reaching upward, yes?"

"Yes," Ixchel tentatively agreed, though it sounded more like a question.

Stren carefully pulled back the leaves to reveal that the venom-vine had wound itself in and out of the stems and branches of the moonthistle plant, and that the leaves were not only being held aloft by the deadly vine but were being fed by it as well.

"The venom-vine on its own is deadly. Yes, it could and would thrive on its own, but its purpose would be only death, and what kind of life would that be? But that is only what is seen without seeing." He tapped his fingers against the side of his skull. "When we truly see that the vine's purpose is to protect and nurture the healing plants that Y'sa in his infinite wisdom has given us, we see the balance and the beauty in all that He has created."

Remembering this, it was with great caution that Ixchel reached across the plants and vines that monopolized the shelves to procure a pastry that was cooling high on a top shelf. So lost in his memories was he that he did not register the sounds of footsteps coming down the hall, nor did he notice the slight shift in the aroma that wafted into the room. He popped the pastry into his mouth and turned the valve on the tap to release the heated water. He washed his hands and splashed his face. He then smelled the faint scent of bitter-grass and berryroot weed. His hand patted the counters for a towel, eyes still closed.

"Here you are, young master," a voice that he did not recognize said.

He took the towel from the direction of the unknown voice and dried his face, patting the water from his eyes.

"Thank you, sir," Ixchel said.

As his sight returned to him and he focused on the stranger, he noticed two things. First, the man was tall, taller than Stren by at least a hand. The second thing he saw was the light, almost jovial, look in the man's eyes as he pulled deeply from an old briarwood pipe. The embers set his dark visage to blazing, and in that moment, Ixchel could see that he was much younger than his master, though still showing signs of age in the creases at the corner of his eyes and mouth.

"Please," he said with the slightest nod. "Your master calls me 'old friend.' You can call me Atamas."

THE LAST OAK OF BURSS

The study was quieter than usual, though not for lack of sound. Logs crackled in the hearth, wind whispered faintly through the windows, and the soft ticking of the old iron clock sounded from the mantel. Yet beneath it all, something else stirred—an unseen weight that pressed against the floorboards and pooled in the corners like darkened waters, grey and still but ever rising. Old books rested lazily on the shelves, leather-bound journals were splayed proudly over every inch of free space across the table, which acted as the centerpiece of the small room, and on the desk that took up residence against the window on the south wall. Scrolls upon scrolls nested securely in their cubbies rolled up tight and vying for space. A brass chandelier hung suspended above the table, unlit and unassuming, content to be nothing more than a spectator of the conversation taking place below. The only light was that of the hearth fire. The scent of burning hickory and cherry wood curled through the air like a hymn of smoke and spice, both ancient and strangely comforting.

Ixchel sat across from his master at the worn walnut table in the study. His fingers traced the intricate etchings along its edges. Recessed carvings of mountains and valleys unknown to him adorned the table's lip. All manner of land beasts were engraved there, and Ixchel often found himself lost in tracing them as he sat with his master late into the nights, hearing stories of Stren's past or reciting that day's lessons. However, in those instances, and all the cases prior to this one, his master sat at the head of the table in a chair that was more akin to a throne. All other chairs that surrounded the table were simple chairs made for sitting, but Stren's chair was made for something other. Crafted from blackened ashwood, so aged it bore the hue of old mists, the high-backed seat rose taller than a man. The wood bore the weight of years in its marbled grain and spoke of stories that predated even the stones below the house. Beneath it, the legs were carved into the likeness of fierce lion paws, planted firm against the floor, as though the chair refused to move for any save the one it recognized as master. Ixchel always thought his master fit into it perfectly, and even though it had been there since before he was born, in all his years, he had never once entertained the idea of sitting in it. Surely, he had never seen anyone but Stren occupy it. He had never been forbidden to sit there, but it was his master's chair.

Now, Stren sat opposite Ixchel. It was a view of his master that he hadn't seen before. Ixchel was in his usual chair, in his usual spot, at the right-hand side from the head. Stren, whose place had always been at the head of the table, sat facing him. The hooded stranger, called Atamas, sat at the head of the table. Ixchel did not like it, and had decided that he didn't much care for Atamas. His gaze shifted from his master to Atamas and then back again. He was trying to discern if there were some sort of tension or power struggle between the two. He had no reason to think that there should be, but something about this visitor, this guest in his master's home, sitting at his master's place grated on him. Not to mention that the dense pressure, like that of being submerged, surrounded by water or some thick, sticky substance, still hung in the air, heavy, solid, and nearly choking.

"And what about you, young master?" Atamas asked.

Ixchel blinked and shook his head to clear it of his contemplation. He had not been listening to the conversation. He had been occupied with finding ways to get this stranger out of his master's home, out of *his* home. He looked up from his hands that he had not realized had been stilled on a carving of a mighty winged beast that was raining fire on a doomed village. He shuddered and tore his hands away, placing them in his lap and wringing them as if to wash them clean of the image. It had never bothered him before, but sitting now, so near to this strange man who had somehow wormed his way into his master's seat like a serpent, quiet and sneaky and so obviously with malevolent intent, Ixchel was suddenly very uncomfortable with the image of the dragon. He looked up from his hands and away from the dragon to find both men staring at him expectantly.

"Um, I'm sorry," he said. "I wasn't listening."

Stren's eyes went hard, and he stretched his calloused hands on the table before him. They spread across the grain of the table, fingers splayed, as if the touch of the wood might keep him from unraveling. His knuckles sounded like twigs snapping underfoot as they protested the strain. His hands were scared from battles and years of grueling work, dark with decades of travel under the sun. Silver lines streaked across them in all manner of designs, a reminder that Stren had not always been a reclusive steward of an abandoned hamlet but had seen much hard labor and many fights in his long days.

"I meant I didn't hear what you... I, I just—"

Atamas laughed deeply and sincerely from somewhere beneath the shadow of his hood. He placed a hand on Ixchel's shoulder and patted it gently. "It's quite alright. It's alright," he said, amusement lingering in his voice.

Ixchel shuddered from the touch and fought the urge to pull away. The corner of his mouth tilted slightly into a flustered smile, but his eyes relayed no mirth.

"Your master and I were just discussing the strange happenings to our north," Atamas continued, drawing his hand back. "It seems that some malevolence is occurring high in the Crown. Some wicked weather. Dark clouds and rolling thunder for days on end."

He reached into some inner pocket of his cloak and produced an old leather pouch. It was folded three times and tied with a dark strap of soft leather. He dipped black-stained fingers into the pouch and pulled out a pinch of tobacco leaf. The scent was not known to Ixchel and yet, somehow familiar to him. It was a remnant, part of a dream that his subconscious recognized but that he did not remember.

He knew his master used to smoke a pipe, though he had never seen him do so. He had once found a worn black box, not much larger than a half-loaf when cleaning out the small compartment above the back rooms. It was not a livable area, only about two feet from deck to ceiling, but it crossed the span of the house and made for an excellent storage area. It also made for a fantastic hiding area, which is what Ixchel had been doing when he had come across the box.

It was old. That much was immediately clear. The finish had faded, and there were dark stains which Ixchel guessed came from of oils and tobacco. Inside was a completely different image altogether though. A deep green and gray fabric pulled tight along the edges. The bottom of the box was lifted slightly by some cushion or feathering, giving it an almost pillow-like interior. The material was soft and lustrous. It had to have been satin or silk. The top matched the bottom, except that it bore a crest or brand of some sort. Embroidered with golden thread was a circle that took up the whole of the center of the lid. Within that circle shone three more circles, intersecting and crossing each other. Each circle was perfectly round but not a perfect line. Ghost lines wove in and out of the main line of each circle, creating chaos within the calm of the image.

Ixchel knew the golden circles were expertly sewn. Even at his young age, he could tell that this must have taken hours, if not days of needlework. The circles were not whole, nor were they broken. Ixchel brought the box closer to inspect the intricacies of the crest. Lines broke off from one and seamlessly joined another. Ixchel traced the lines with his finger, much like he had always done with the images on the study table. There were, in fact, hundreds of different lines, all interwoven to make up the whole. There was no beginning and no end, yet there were three distinct circles within a larger one. In the box itself was a pipe. Its bit was worn from use, and the bowl, though still catching the dim light from the hallway on the stained exterior, was black and charred on the inside. Ixchel was tempted momentarily to place the bit between his teeth but thought better of it. The rank smell of ash was an unappealing thing. The pipe was made of black briar, rusticated and finished so that it fit snuggly in the webbing of his palm. Ixchel turned it over and noticed that the same circular emblem sewn into the underside of the tinderbox lid was embossed into the bottom of the pipe.

It lacked no intricacy or detail of the matching brand in the tinderbox. Fine gold lines weaved in and out of each other, connecting and dissecting one another in such a fluid and natural way that Ixchel's eyes tired from attempting to maintain sight of where one line ended and where another circle began. It almost seemed alive in its serpentine nature—a living, breathing, golden uroboros.

The only other contents of the box were a metal flame-fellow with flint and steel, much like the one used for the water heater, and a small opalescent stone. Ixchel picked up the stone and set it down again quickly. His pulse quickened, and he had begun to sweat. He swooned a bit and grabbed hold of the railing to keep from falling on his face or down the ladder to the hallway below. The stone had reacted to his touch, had rejected his touch, had rejected him. At the time, he was still early on in his training, but he had some knowledge of innate magics in abiotic materials.

"All things are subject to powers beyond this earthly tether," he remembered his master saying in one of his earliest lessons. "Remember this, young Ixchel. We may one day be silenced by fear or forgetfulness, but then even the rocks will cry out."

He had not understood what his master was saying, but it all made perfect sense when the small stone seemed to siphon his strength and will in a moment. It was an alive and sentient thing, inanimate though it was.

Ixchel would often revisit the loft above the back rooms. He was drawn to the small box and the pipe within, though he took great care not to touch the stone. He was intimately familiar with the intertwined circles of the golden emblem and was, therefore taken aback to see that the pipe that Atamas now held between his lips bore the same image.

The smell of sulfur filled the room as a match was struck. A harsh, bright light momentarily blinded Ixchel, as he was so transfixed on the golden emblem etched into the bottom of Atamas' pipe that he didn't even blink. Black spots swam amidst the white-hot light of the flame as his vision returned. The smell of sulfur retreated, chased away by a lovely bouquet of berryroot and bitter-grass.

That scent, Ixchel thought. *I know that scent.*

"It seems as if the watchers of the veil are once again trying to stir up untruths and superstitions where there are none," Atamas said as white puffs of sweet-smelling smoke billowed from his lips like the exhaust from a factory chimney and faded away into dancing wisps. "I, for one, tire of their ceaseless rhetoric."

"How can you so easily tire of something that you once held in so firm a faith?" Stren asked. "It wasn't so long ago that Atamas Antarius of the Ashahn line was the most ardent disciple of Y'sa and the prophecies of His champion."

"You needn't remind me of where I come from, Stren D'anyon, Last Oak of Burss."

Stren winced at this, ever so slightly. So minuscule was the movement, that to any save those closest to him, it would have gone unnoticed entirely, but it was enough for Ixchel to see. Much was hidden beneath the layered folds of his master's gray, woolen robes, but the shudder, the tensing of muscle, no matter how fleeting, was evident to the boy. Only for a moment, and then it was gone, like a memory or dream caught briefly and loosely in one's hand as one would attempt to catch a spring monarch—it fades and makes its escape as soon as one's hands are opened, leaving the catcher wondering if they'd imagined whole thing.

Atamas observed the flinch as well, Ixchel could tell. The man's posture shifted. His shoulders rose as he lifted his elbows from the table and sat back into the deep cushions of his chair, Stren's chair. He smiled beneath his hood, satisfaction evident in his piercing gaze, like a hunter knowing that his prey had just taken the bait and was already within the maw of a well-obscured trap.

A stillness began to take shape. A menacing and dark silence. A threatening silence. The weight of things unseen and unspoken. It was the weight of lies and secrets. It was the weight reserved for the closest of kin or the worst of enemies. Neither man moved to speak. They did not move at all. Ixchel wondered if the weight of this moment was being felt by the two men beside him, or if it was him alone.

"Why did you call him The Last Oak?" Ixchel asked, more to break the awkward silence than to get an answer. He could ask his master later, and would much prefer to hear it from him, but he had to say something.

Still, he didn't know *why* he said it. He looked from one to the other, eyes wide and apologetic. He let out a breath that he had not known he was holding and inhaled immediately, his lungs starving for air. His nostrils flared to take in the oxygen that he did not know he was lacking. He was out of breath and sweating. *How long have I been holding my breath?* he asked himself. *How long have we been sitting here in silence?*

"I hav—," Stren started to say, but was quickly cut off.

"He is so named because he is the one remaining sentinel of the old ways," Atamas said. "He is the last and lone oak in a forest long since burned to ash by the fires of progress." He produced an oblong stone, rounded and smooth, from the pouch and stamped the ashes of the pipe down, deeper into the bowl. He took a long moment to stare at the dull embers before relighting. "The roots of his society, once so embedded in conviction and tradition, were exposed by the shifting sands of complacency and set to rotting by the floods of compliance. One by one they relented until ..." Atamas paused, his eyes narrowing as he shifted his gaze from Ixchel to Stren. "... until all that remained was Stren." He paused for a moment, as if waiting for Stren to respond. When he did not speak, Atamas continued. "You *are* the only one left, are you not, *master*?" His voice dripped with contempt, like venom from a viper's fangs.

"I am," was all Stren said.

Atamas laughed then, not a wholesome and jovial laugh, but a bark, a single guffaw that made Ixchel jump in his seat. It was loud, like a powder keg explosion. The gravity, the pressure, that Ixchel had been feeling since he'd first arrived loosed. It released in a moment, a deluge of energy, like water bursting forth from a mighty dam. He was drenched with it, soaked to his very soul with the power and magnitude of it as it washed over him. It was such an attack on his senses, such an overload of power that he covered his ears and closed his eyes tight. There was no sound, nothing visible, but he didn't know what else to do. He was a child, a baby. He was helpless. He was utterly insignificant. He could not hold against it. And then it was gone. Ixchel looked to his master and found wet eyes staring back at him.

The innocuous black stone that Atamas had used to tamp his pipe seemed to writhe with some otherworldly energy. Small, near-translucent tendrils reached out from within it. Atamas palmed the stone quickly and placed it back within the pockets of his cloak.

Ixchel knew his master well. Stren was the only father he had ever known. He was kind, yet strict. He was quiet, yet commanded respect by his mere presence. He was humble, yet strong. Ixchel had seen him lift an entire cart pulled by a set of muscled labor-mules out of six inches of mud without so much as a grunt. He was powerful in the ways of magic. Until this very moment, Ixchel had thought him to be the most powerful wizard alive. Yet, he submitted to this Atamas, almost as if in reverence, almost as if in fear, and that unnerved Ixchel more than anything.

Atamas stood. Ixchel looked at him, shaking with anger and fear and hatred. He felt as if he had been violated. He felt empty and unclean. He hid his hands under the table. He could not still them. He placed them on his knees and pressed hard, trying to stop his legs from bouncing up and down. He was nervous and afraid. The conversation up to this point had been strained yet cordial. Ixchel had determined that there was history here that his master and this dark stranger were dodging, but now there was no cordiality, no semblance of old acquaintances catching up or a reunion of friends. No, this was a hostile encounter, an act of treason, or of war.

Atamas looked down upon Ixchel, all pageantry and parade abandoned. "Your master is a stalwart bulwark of convention, Ixchel. He is the only one left. The Lone Oak." Atamas nearly spat the last, his demeanor had gone from affable guest to malicious obtruder in mere moments. "You would do well to disembarrass yourself of his foolishness and seek guidance elsewhere. Perhaps," he paused and locked eyes with Stren, a wicked smile slithering across his mouth, "you'd want to travel with me back to Thar-Azhul where you could see firsthand the way of things to come—the way of the future your master so passionately fights against, no matter the futility."

"That's enough, Atamas."

The feet of Stren's chair scraped across the floor, a high-pitched and grating sound. The hearth fire behind him flickered and climbed to life as if following his lead as he rose. The dark and shadows that had moments earlier seemed oppressive and unnaturally ominous shrunk back and slithered away. Ixchel couldn't be sure, but it looked as if they were recoiling or retreating into Atamas' own shadow. Stren was standing now, though not to his full height. He was leaning on the table, hands flat against the lacquered finish. His head was down as if looking at his hands, taking in the measure of them. Ixchel wondered what he saw there, if his master saw the same strength and honor and loyalty and love that he saw. Or did he see only the scars and dirt and flaws that were on the surface?

"Because of our history, I have allowed you into my home," he said as he raised his head to look at the visitor. "Because of our bond, I have offered you the warmth of my fire and not just the comfort of a seat at my table, but *my* seat." He straightened. He looked taller now than Ixchel had remembered. "And because I once called you my own, I will let you leave. But if you threaten what is mine again—and know that this was a threat, Atamas—I will end you. I will not hesitate. I will not blink. I will take your fire from you, and I will quench it in the heart of the Vintermarrow. I will leave your body as rotting meat for vultures. And when they are done, I will grind your bones to dust and swallow you. I will consume you. There will be nothing left of Atamas Antarius. All will be as if it never was. All save your head. Your head I will send back to that accursed isle you now call home so that your minions may behold what it is to stand against me."

Ixchel stared stupidly at his master. He realized his mouth was agape and shut it quickly, too quickly, as there was an audible pop when his jaw snapped shut, and his lips met. He had never heard his master speak of such things. He had always seen his master as a loyal laborer, an inventor, a farmer, a father. He had never seen him as a lion, fangs like curved ivory daggers unsheathed and scythe-like claws poised for tearing.

"Then this is the end," Atamas said. He was clearly shaken. His countenance and confidence both had diminished, though not wholly. He stood tall and proud. He stood with one foot behind the other, balancing his weight as if ready to attack.

"Dear Atamas," Stren said in a cold, detached voice, "the end is a thing of the past. You and I both know that what you have done this day is the beginning."

When Even the Heavens Burn

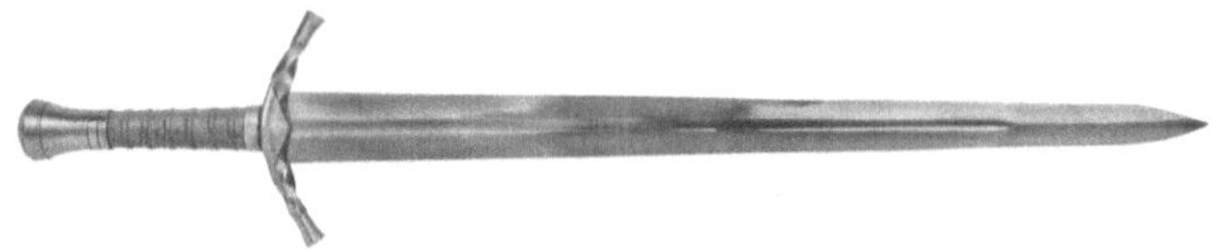

Though her feet were bare, her steps left no trace: no blood, no scar, no hesitation. Ten days and nights had passed since she first set foot upon the merciless crags of the Titan's Crown, yet fatigue dared not claim her, nor did the cruel terrain thwart her passage. Only the dust and stain of dirt upon her tattered robes spoke of the journey, a silent testament to the distance she had traveled. The wind howled through the jagged peaks of the mountain range, a symphony of thunder and stone, yet she moved as though untouched by the elements and unphased by the trial to come. She had traveled long, from beyond the celestial sphere, to reach the Crown. Her destination lay beyond these mountains, though, in Y'ssildria, the city of silver spires, of veiled intrigue, and of power. Her duty was clear, the path before her certain. And yet, unease had begun to crawl beneath her skin like a second shadow.

She placed a hand against the cold stone that surrounded her. The skin on her palm and fingertips constricted as steam hissed from the porous rock, a natural diametric response to the heat pulsing from her body. Hours earlier, when she first entered the crevasse, she had felt the reverberations. They had been faint and distant then, curious and timid, questioning, non-threatening—lying. Now, when she felt for them, they roared in response, like a rabid and malnourished dog reaching for meat teased but never given. The cavernous tunnel led her upward, and though every instinct, every voice screamed at her to turn back, she continued to climb. She knew he was waiting.

The wind was a living thing in the Crown and all across the Arcene mountain range, raging through cragged peaks, coiling through the shoulders and ridges, and finally flittering through the ravines below. It carried the scent of ice, sharp and clean, tinged with the ghost of old storms and even older, more ancient dangers. It stood as the final bastion, a stout-hearted sentry ever watchful and ever faithful. It was the last line of defense against the baleful torrent of the Vintermarrow, the shattered wasteland of ice and death far north of all living things.

Aoife slowed her pace, fingers brushing the stone. The air felt wrong. It was thick and heavy, as though something pressed against her unseen. It was a familiar weight, one she had felt before and one she knew well, but it did not belong here. It belonged in places where black roots wound deep, and the sun was but a memory. It belonged below, not above. The mountains had been silent for days. Too silent, too quiet, too still, as if the world itself were holding its breath. And now it roared with anticipation.

Her steps halted. A flicker of movement at the edge of her vision. Her muscles tensed. She exited the cave system slowly, cautiously, and entered a forgotten alcove of long-dead trees. The stream that had once carried life from the snow-covered peaks had stalled and dried up ages ago and was now little more than a crumbing and cracked fissure. The trees were ancient, their bark knotted with time, turned gray from lack of drink. They leaned inward now, their branches trembling without wind, away from the old stream and toward Aofie. The entire grove seemed to be listening, *waiting*. Then came the whisper. Not from behind her, not from above, but from everywhere and nowhere all at once.

"Starborn. Flesh and fire. Daughter of the Cradle. You do not belong here. You are not welcome here."

Aoife turned sharply and went low, a flaming sword appearing in her hand in a single flick of motion. Her stance was one of fleeing, not fighting, for she knew who spoke to her. The steel caught what little light pierced the spaces of the dense rocks that surrounded her in this small space, and then the light was gone. Darkness moved. The shadows cast from the decrepit trees and overhanging jags coalesced, sewn together in a slithering, snake-like motion, slow, intentional, and sure. It bled into the world. The shadows thickened, pooling together, stretching as ink spilled into water.

From the depths of that consuming blackness, it came. A towering silhouette, a shifting mass of shadow and hunger. The thing had no face, yet faces *lived* within it. Dozens, perhaps hundreds of horrified visages flickered across its shifting form, their mouths locked in silent screams. Aoife's grip tightened on her sword. A Soul Stealer. An abhorrence. An echo of something ancient and wrong, a predator not of this world but something that had slipped between the cracks of existence.

"You are light," it crooned, its voice an abomination of many discordant and pained voices, overlapping and harsh. "And I am the end of light."

It moved.

Aoife barely dodged in time as the Soul Stealer lashed out, its clawed hand slicing through the air where she had stood a heartbeat before. The very stone beneath her feet cracked and crumbled. Shards of rock exploded outward, cutting into her skin as she twisted away, sword raised.

She struck. The blade carved a clean arc through the darkness, the holy steel biting deep, and yet, there was no blood. The creature *rippled*, its form shuddering, recoiling, before snapping forward again with relentless hunger. It had taken its corporeal form, out of shadow and into a mass of muscled flesh. Its red and blistered skin glistened with cursed energy. Black, leathery wings extended out from its spine, their span fully the length of the entire coppice. Any and all light from above, from the sun, that peeked through the rocks, was now extinguished. Boarish and spiraling horns reached skyward from its malformed and caprine skull.

This was no mindless beast, no enemy of flesh and bone. Nature's laws did not bind a Soul Stealer. It did not bleed or tire. It devoured entirely. Aofie stole a glance at her enemy's chest. It glowed white and hot. Orbs of fire darted about within. They were the source of its power, she knew. And this one was powerful. Hundreds of souls, victims of the creature, raged and screamed and cried for release, for rescue. Collected over the ages, each soul taken, each life devoured strengthened the demon—men, women, and children defiled and damned for all eternity.

She would not let it take her. She reached inside herself, into the fire that had been granted to her in her genesis, to her very essence. She prayed to Y'sa for strength and for courage. She knew well that she faced death here, and she was at peace with that, but the fear of spending all eternity imprisoned within the black gaol of Baelgorak, who stood before her now, was too much to bear. If she was to die this day, so too would the demon. She set herself within the faith of her maker and prayed for starfire.

The celestial blaze roared to life in her palm, a radiant white inferno that swallowed the darkness in its glow. Streams of silver and gold careened from the heavens and into her outstretched hands. Flames blazed to life behind her, and the cavern to her back filled with hot light as wings of pure fire burst forth from her shoulders. She rose, her toes just scraping the rock below her. She was an inferno. She was fire. She was a Star Speaker. With a wordless snarl, she gathered the remaining energy of holy light swirling about her and hurled it forward in a blast that shook the Crown to its core.

The impact was instantaneous. Flames engulfed the Soul Stealer, its abyssal body convulsing as the celestial fire licked around and through it. The faces inside it writhed, twisting in agony, their silent screams stretching through Aofie's conscience and into eternity. The edges of its fibrous, bat-like wings smoldered and curled like parchment held to a candle. A living atlas of searing embers burnt away the hair and fibers as the flame worked its way across the demon's flesh.

Baelgorak shuddered but did not fall.

Aoife's breath came fast, her chest rising and falling in measured heaves. She descended slowly, her feet finding purchase as she prepared for the coming assault. It would take some time before she was ready for another attack of that magnitude. Defense was her priority now. She gripped her sword with both hands and pointed it at the beast.

"Bring your worst, demon," she snarled.

The Soul Stealer struck again, moving faster than before. This time, its claws found their mark. Pain exploded across Aoife's shoulder as the talons raked through her flesh. Blood sprayed, dark against the bright glow of her fire. She staggered back, her vision swimming for a moment. She weakened and fell to her knees. The creature had not simply wounded her—it had *fed* on her. It had taken some small part of her. Another blow came, not a hungry, penetrating strike, but a blunt and battering attack, one made for crushing, like the iron hammer of a siege engine created for ruin. Aofie was not quick enough. The demon's mighty, curled fist crashed into her, rocketing her backward as if dragged by a hundred frightened horses. Her body flew through the cavern through which she had entered. She bounced and crashed into stone walls as she hurled uncontrollably. She was thrown between rocky formations like an arrow with no flight path, guided only by stalagmites and stalactites that sent her to and fro in a violent ricochet until there was no shape left but pain. She landed in a heap of bruises and lacerations.

"Starborn," it whispered, its voice slithering into her fractured bones. "I will savor you."

"No," she said through gritted teeth, as much to herself as to the demon. She would not fall here, not to this thing, not to this void made flesh. "You are known to me, Baelgorak, Black Flame Unbound, Breaker of Oaths, Lord of Lies." She could see him, though only as a silhouette glowing with the trapped spirits, standing at the breach of the cavern. His chest heaved in slow cadence, his arms at his sides, though not resting. They were taut, all sinew and muscle rippling with energy waiting to explode. Aofie pushed herself up, one hand on the ground and the other on bent and broken knee. "I know you for what you are, betrayer, *brother*." She spat the last with vehemence and blood. She began walking toward him, toward her fate, toward her doom. She was running out of time, she knew. Her fire alone would not destroy it. Her sword could not kill what did not live. There was only one way to end this.

"Come, Aoife Oohna," he said, gesturing *welcome* with his clawed and monstrous hands. "Come and let us have our reunion." He laughed low then. His abyssal voice rumbled through the rocky floor, causing pebbles and dust to spill around her from the tunnel ceiling. "I am eager to taste you."

She increased her pace as the stiffness of her injuries faded from her consciousness. One bare and bloodied foot in front of the other, she began to run. She could see the reflection of trapped souls gleaming on the ground near the demon's hoofed feet—her sword. She must have dropped it when he hit her. She lowered her head and rushed forward. Her wings, nearly extinguished by the earlier impact, flickered and sparked. And she reached.

Baelgorak stepped back and smiled. His lips peeled back to show rotted and porous teeth, yellow with decay and wet with saliva. He was hungry, and he was ready. He would give her enough room to exit the cavern. He did not cherish the thought of bending low and folding his wing around himself to fit into the tight corridors of that small space.

"Come, sister," Baelgorak teased.

She obliged.

Aoife dove forward at full speed and tucked into a ball. She did not dive toward Baelgorak, instead she leaped for her sword. She caught up the blade moments before she threw her legs forward. She completed the roll and was on her feet in an instant. Blade in hand, she ran, momentum and determination unphased. She ran with composure and acceptance. She knew what she must do.

The demon's eyes went wide, not from fear but from true bewilderment. This fragile, broken woman must know she could not win. She must know what horrors awaited her within his prison. *If she does not*, he mused darkly, *she will. She will know what pain is. She will know fear.* He reached for her, arms going out in a great bear hug. He would consume her whole.

Inches from the demon, she leaped. She did not duck or dodge his grasp. So close was she that as he lunged, she placed a foot on his forward knee, using it as a springboard, and soared through his closing arms. His bulbous head acted as the second perch in her ascent. She kicked off his skull with all her might and stretched her arms to the sky. Her gaze lifted to the heavens, which had always been her ally. Her fingers curled into the empty air as she grasped for the invisible. Far above, beyond the mortal plane, the stars stirred, and the world shook.

A distant hum reverberated through the mountains, a pull stronger than gravity. The very mountains began to tremble. The Soul Stealer sensed it. It twisted, shrieking, its form unraveling in agitation. It lunged skyward. Anger was replaced by desperation when the realization of the Star Speaker's intent became apparent and the heavens tore open.

Aoife continued to ascend. Her wings burst to life and pulsed her still upward. She was a Valkyrie of fire, a blaze of verdict and retribution. She lifted her sword. It became a sentient thing, full of life and thought. It knew its purpose and shot forth a brilliant burst of energy that pierced the sky and left it rent, a starfield of purples and blues. A meteor, wreathed in celestial flame, plunged from the heavens. It fell like a star unmoored, like the fierce gavel of a judicator, judgment made manifest. The Soul Stealer shrieked, its true voice this time, raw and filled with something it had never known, fear. Its eyes grew, black pupils dilating, and within them was reflected the wrath of Y'sa Himself, in the form of the great falling star.

The explosion shattered the cosmos. Aoife barely registered the force of it as it threw her back, her body weightless for a breathless, endless moment before the ground slammed into her. She was lost in descent as her body tumbled lifelessly down the side of the mountain. Her form was lost in an avalanche of dirt and boulders and clouds of dust and debris.

Then darkness.

She did not know how long she lay there. Smoke coiled into the sky, mingling with the scent of scorched earth. The land was ruin, the trees leveled, the very mountains forever more moved and scarred by the ethereal outrage she had unleashed. She tried to move, but only pain answered. Her limbs felt like lead. Her body screamed in protest. The Soul Stealer was gone. Nothing but ash remained. And yet, she had paid a price. The world tilted, her vision blurring. She heard the wind again, the faint crackle of dying embers—then, footsteps.

Voices, rough and wary with uncertainty, came from somewhere in the distance.

"What in all the hells is she," one voice said.

"Does it *matter*? She's dying," another voice responded.

"And what do you suggest we do, Cante? That blast could be seen in all of Y'ssara. We don't need trouble."

"Trouble's already here, brother. She's breathing. That makes her our problem now."

Two shadows combined into one and loomed over her, blurred and indistinct. Aoife tried to speak, tried to move, but the void swallowed her whole. The last thing she saw before the darkness took her once again was two pairs of unfamiliar hands reaching for her.

The Calm Before the Crown

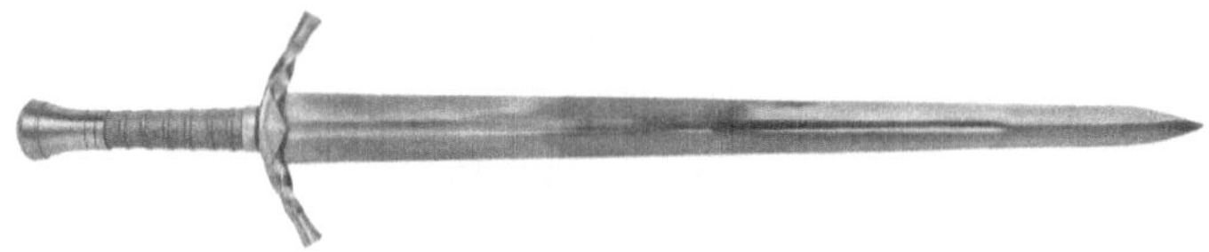

The morning sun blazed through the stained-glass windows like a kaleidoscopic prism, illuminating the king's chambers in color and warmth. It cast muted reds, purples, and blues across the worn map of Y'ssara that lay in wait on the marble table. Hewn from a single slab of deep-veined marble, the table shimmered in the golden light. Its surface had been worn smooth by decades of sleepless nights, clandestine council meetings, and the weight of war. Streaks of silver traced the veins like rivers. The old map was unfurled and anchored at the corners with bronze weights cast into the shapes of the old houses, the recognized houses of royalty across the lands. The vellum had yellowed with time, its edges curled and frayed, and lines once inked in precision now bled and faded. It was marked with decades of annotations bearing witness, not merely to the realm as it was but to what it had been and what it might yet become.

The two stood on opposite sides of the Y'ssaran diagram. Both had their arms crossed, and both looked like men with too much responsibility and far too little time. They stared intently at the map as if waiting for it to speak or to move, to offer some insight or advice. It did not. Artificial bloodstains blotted the southern regions, while freshly inked markers indicated new boundaries. It was an ever-evolving, living thing, but it would not speak to them. It remained silent, offering only what they already knew—and what they knew, they did not like.

King Onidine broke the silence, drawing the other from his brooding. "The prince will be crowned on Vaelorae, Stren. I am ready. And more importantly, he is ready. I trust that I have your full support and that he will have your loyalty, just as I have all these years."

"You say that as if it changes what must come after." Stren did not blink. He did not move. He was a statue of stoic disapproval.

King Onidine's jaw tightened. "It does change things. Especially after the grievous news you brought me concerning Atamas."

"You speak as though the ceremony grants him wisdom," Stren said. He lowered his arms to rest at his sides. It had always been a complex thing to navigate negotiations with royalty, especially with the king of all of Y'ssara. Stren was the captain of a sea vessel, and Onidine was the waves, the wind, the squall, the hurricane, and the rocks that could appear from the dark waters to penetrate, puncture, and drive the ship to the depths. Stren was the tidewarden, but King Onidine was the sea itself. "It does not," Stren continued, more softly. "I see the weight of this burden upon you. I see how it has hunched your shoulders and weakened your legs. Your hair has whitened, and your sight has faltered." Stren reached out a hand and placed it on his king's shoulder. "You are still a strong man, a wonderful father, and a righteous king, but all you have given has also taken much from you. Do you truly wish that weight to be heaved upon Endryll?'

"He is stronger than you give him credit for," Onidine replied, though with less conviction than before. "He is the rightful King of Y'ssara."

"He is a boy."

"He is a king," Onidine growled, anger flaring within him. "He is my son, and he has come of age. He is my only heir." He stepped away from Stren's touch then and walked to the window overlooking Y'ssildria. "You saw to that when you sent Atamas in your stead that night so long ago. That dreadful and damned night." He spun fast on his heels, arm stretched long, and finger extended accusingly. "You saw to that when you let my wife die. You were off on one of your wild pursuits when you knew we needed you. Your thirst for knowledge cost me my bride and my second-born!"

Stren held the king's gaze, unflinching. "You see what you want to see, my friend. And you speak out of anger. Though not out of turn," he added quickly, seeing Onidine's eyebrow raised in a warning arch. "I loved Cerceia like my own sister and I have always loved you like my own brother. Atamas loved you and *called* you brother. His love for you and for Cerceia was never a question." Stren once again softened his gaze and his tone. "Atamas did everything he could for her. You know this. And he saved your son. Without him, Endryll would be an only child."

"He is an only child now! He has no knowledge of his brother, and Atamas ensured that he never will." King Onidine exhaled sharply, turning his back on Stren and pacing toward the nearest door to the balcony. Outside and far below, the city hummed with celebration and excitement. Wagons and carts of all sizes lined the streets, their drivers and hired hands moving contents and cargo to and fro on wheeled handcarts. The rhythmic tapping of hammers and the heave-ho harmony of men hoisting heavy tarps up heavier poles could be heard even from Ondine's perch. Vendors and townsfolk alike were raising small cloth tents and building makeshift booths. Children ran along the winding streets. Banners and streamers of green and gold flitted and flapped in their wake as they adorned the streets and squares with the colors of King Cressedia and of Y'ssildira.

Stren's voice came quiet behind him. "They adore you, truly."

King Onidine's tight grip on the railing loosened as he let out a gentle laugh. "They adored *her*," he said in a wistful tone. "They tolerate me." Silence stretched between them, but it was no longer a strained thing.

Finally, the king spoke again. "I miss her, Stren," he said as he turned to his oldest and dearest friend. "I miss her so much."

"We all do. She was the First Light of Y'ssildria, and Y'ssara is a darker place in her absence." King Onidine did not answer. He could not. His gray eyes glistened in the morning sun, wet with tears. He pinched his lips tight to keep them from quivering, so Stren continued. "I am a stubborn old man, Onidine. I am fearful of what might happen to Endryll in the days and years to come."

The king sighed, shaking his head. "We cannot keep them bound forever, Stren. It's not fair to Endryll. And it's not fair to—"

Onidine and Stren turned as one to the mighty Titan's Crown, far off to the north and west of Y'ssildria. The dark clouds of mountain storms separated like logs split by a woodsman's great axe. The very heavens rent and tore, separating and spiraling away in cardinal directions. A chasm of blackest night, of infinite emptiness, remained as the skies fled. A pillar of fire shot forth skyward from deep within the peaks of the Crown as golden light sped from the cosmos to intercept it. The two powers collided in an astral maelstrom. The shockwave surged down the mountainside and across the foothills and valleys, felling thousand-year-old trees, tossing livestock and wildlife, and disintegrating farmhouses in its wake. King Onidine and Stren were thrown from their feet to crash against the castle walls, which rattled and splintered from the billowing front of the blast.

Y'ssildria was a city of weights and counterweights, checks and balances. It was a thriving metropolis where all manner of peoples were welcome and where, indeed, all manner of peoples lived. It was a sprawling network of interconnected streets and alleys, highways and byways, cottages, houses, strongholds, and castles. There were markets for fish and meats and breads and vegetables, salves and tonics, weapons and farming tools. There were apothecaries and libraries, schools and churches, and factories and factions, laborers and lords. Y'ssildria and her people wanted for nothing and were unafraid. The capital city was built into and around the easternmost rocks of the Crown, fully protected by the mountains from the back. To the south and east and far below raged the Serrated Sea. The city was only accessible by the west, and even there, Y'ssara guarded her, for any visitors would have to make the trek up and through the Stoneguard, a long and winding cliff road that led from the open plains of the Whistle Wilds to the front gates of Y'ssildria with sheer rock on either side. Carved throughout the rock were the Guardians, huge, gargoyleish monstrosities of stone who once stood, animated and ready for battle.

Beyond the city walls, where the cliffs dropped into the sea, three figures lay lazily in the lush green grass of the Wilds, watching as the sky shifted from indigo to gold to blue. The field grass whipped around them, stirred by the briny breeze of the shoreline of the Serrated Sea. Gulls screamed, sharp and shrill, from high above as they circled. The birds climbed high into the sky and then raced to the surface to return moments later with breakfast, dripping wet and entirely too proud of themselves.

Endryll Cressedia, prince of Y'ssildria, let out a slow breath, arms behind his head, his gaze fixed on the birds above. He was a handsome boy on the verge of manhood. His sun-kissed skin complimented his light eyes. His straw-colored hair, made lighter because of his penchant for being outside with his friends, playing pranks on cranky shop owners or having cliffside duels with dummy swords instead of being indoors studying or practicing etiquette, was cut fashionably to brush his broad shoulders. The loose natural curls hid its true length, though, as it fell far past his shoulders when wet. He was, every part of him, the complete princely package.

Illia-Dara lay beside him, her fingers idly twining through loose strands of her hair. It billowed out beneath her like waves of scarlet silk. The greens of the grass contrasted the dark reds of her hair yet bled into the shining jade of her eyes, making them stand out even more than usual. She was beautiful. She was a kiss of dew on moonlit heather, a breath between worlds, untamed, untouched, yet delicate and unforgettable. She turned her head toward him. "Do you feel different yet?" she asked, lifting one hand to shade her eyes from the bright morning sun.

"Should I?" he responded, still following the birds and their frantic flight for morning sustenance.

"I think so," she said. She rolled over and laid her chest on his, forcing him to look at her. The rest of her body still lay on the grass, her toes wriggling into the soft earth. Her hair cascaded down around him, covering their faces. It took a moment for his eyes to adjust. She stared at him under an auburn blanket of privacy. "Are you scared, my love?"

"I am," he said. "Not for the coronation celebration or becoming king or anything like that." He was silent for a moment, still as a startled rabbit. He was lost in her eyes, in the beauty of them, in the vast galaxies swirling with stars that he would never be able to name but would spend his lifetime chasing. "I am scared that, for a moment, I was more interested in the goings on of sea-fowl than in the wonder that is you." He kissed her then, and she returned it in kind.

"You are sweet, my prince," she said. Then she lowered her mouth to his ear and whispered. "My husband." Her breath was warm and sweet with the scent of passion and promise.

"And I, you, my wife," he whispered back to her, kissing her earlobe. "My bride. My Illi— "

"Will you two get a room!" a voice groaned loudly.

Illia-Dara was at once pulled from her lover's embrace by her ankles and sent unceremoniously rolling through the pasturage. Ixchel replaced her atop Endryll's chest, but instead of showering him with affection, he reigned down blow upon blow upon blow, to his stomach first. Then, when Endryll rolled over to protect his ever-reddening belly, Ixchel went to work on his backside and legs. Endryll's cries of protest were soon muffled as Illia-Dara joined in, stuffing a handkerchief into his mouth and tickling him anywhere her fingers could find flesh.

"I yield! I yield," he cried through fits of laughter. "Ouch! I said I yield!"

Endryll sat up as soon as he was allowed. His hair was a mess of tangles and grass, and his face was flushed with exertion. He began massaging his legs in an attempt to work the cramping out of them. He spat the handkerchief from his mouth, wadded it up, and threw it toward a still-laughing Illia-Dara. It was thick with saliva and hung loosely on her cheek before falling into her hands.

"Eww! It's wet!"

"Of course, it's wet! I was choking on it while being beaten to within an inch of my life," he said in mock outrage. "I could have you both arrested for the attempted assassination of the new king of Y'ssildria!"

"You're not the king yet," Ixchel shouted. He had fled to a safe distance from Endryll after letting him up. He now stood far off from them and deep into the taller grass of the Wilds. "You won't be king until Vaelorae! That means I still have four days to beat on you!"

Endryll laughed and stood, brushing the grass and dirt from his shirt and pants. "I think I could just as easily have you arrested for the attempted assassination of the only heir to the throne, you fiend." He reached a hand to Illia-Dara, who was still sitting awkwardly where she had landed when he had eventually bucked her off. Her hair was no better off than his, and her dress was grass-stained and wrinkled. "Come, my sweet. Allow me to assist you."

"Why, thank you, dear husband," she said as she clasped her hand in his. She was halfway up when he loosed his grip and took off toward Ixchel. She fell back down with a thump and a shout, but Endryll didn't hear her.

The chase was on. He had an assassin to catch. "Idiots," she muttered as she pushed herself up and followed behind. "Wait for me!"

She caught up to them just as the sun reached its zenith. Endryll was without his shirt. *Not an all-too-terrible view*, she thought as her mouth tilted to a half grin. His muscles tensed and stretched under golden skin as he wrung his shirt out before him. He was still wet from whatever horseplay he and Ixchel had gotten up to before her arrival. Beads of water dripped from him, leaving rivulets of pearl in their wake from his soaked hair down to the line of his pants, where it pooled and darkened the olive-stained fabric to a ring of black around his slim and muscled waist. His hair was straight and shades darker. It reached to the middle of his back and sent droplets of water crawling unhurriedly down his spine.

Ixchel was also topless, though he did not strike such a captivating pose as Endryll. If Endryll was the complete princely package, Ixchel was the **Return to Sender** note slapped on the side. He was shorter than Endryll by a head and had hair akin to a dandelion ready to seed. It was fluffed and unkempt, creating an aura effect around his head. Illia-Dara had tried on more than one occasion to tame the woolly ball of brown knots to no avail. It wasn't a style choice. It was just him. He was small, not only in height but also in musculature. He was roughly the same age as Endryll but showed none of the signs of growth and strength that the prince had over the last year. That's not to say that Ixchel wasn't strong. He was. Working the fields and gardens and with livestock under Stren all his life had hardened him and given him a strength often unattainable to those unaccustomed to working with their hands. There are vanity muscles that are good for looking at, and there are stiff, strong muscles suitable for plowing, farming, and shoveling manure. Ixchel bore the latter.

"What in all that is wrong with this picture did you two do while I was left to fend for myself in the Wilds," she asked playfully, unable to keep the laughter from her voice.

"I caught our would-be assassin, my love," Endryll responded proudly with a mocking gesture to Ixchel. "Oh, he was a wily one and stronger than you'd think! But, in the end, your prince prevailed." His teeth shone white and straight through his broad smile.

"I see that," she chuckled. "But what I am concerned with is the state of undress that I find you both in. What is a new bride to think when she comes upon her husband and the stable b—"

"I'm more than a stable boy, you wicked woman," Ixchel interjected. "I also tend your gardens and see to your plumbing!" He wasn't looking at them. Instead, he was in his third battle of the morning, though this time it wasn't with his oldest and dearest friend but rather with a stubborn twig that had somehow gotten itself so integrated into the frizzy mop atop his head that he was losing strands of hair just trying to pull it out. Eventually, he just gave up, resigned to the fact that the stick was now a permanent fixture. Noticing the silence, he looked up at his two friends. They were just staring at him. Illia-Dara had one hand covering her mouth and the other on her husband's shoulder. Endryll's hands were clasped in front of him, his elbows perched on his knees. "At least now maybe the birds will have a place to rest after their breakfast?"

The three of them laughed then. Endryll stood and pulled his shirt over his head. Ixchel moved to follow suit, but he was left wanting after a brief search for his own. His eyes went to Endryll and saw him holding the missing shirt in one hand, high above his head. His other was extended and gesturing for Ixchel to approach.

"This is my trophy," he said triumphantly. "I claim it as victor of our impromptu river battle, and it is also proof of your failed attempt on my life." He paused for a moment, a playful glint in his eye. "Unless you'd like to try and win it back?"

Ixchel sighed. "You can have it. I think I've had enough fighting for one day. Plus, I'd hate to whoop you in front of your lovely wife." A sound halfway between a gasp and a cackle came from where Illia-Dara was standing, though she was quick to cover it with a feigned cough. Ixchel glowered at her, putting on his most menacing face. "Don't think I won't come for you when I'm done with him," he said. "I have no issue with beating on a recent widow."

She smiled warmly at him. "Oh dear, Ixchel," she said as she walked toward him. "You would take issue with beating on a rogue wasp even as it stung you." She stood by him and ran her fingers through his hair or tried to, at least. "You are my dove in a world of hawks." She bent low to kiss his forehead. "And that is why I cherish you."

Ixchel looked up at her. A breeze tugged at her auburn hair, and in the shifting light that passed through the bouquet of leaves that they sat under, she was radiant. She was the most beautiful creation in all of Y'ssara, a goddess of ages past, in a time before time, before men, before war, or strife, or famine, or fealty, or pain, or worry. She was a glimpse of Y'sa's perfect plan. He had loved her since the first day he saw her in the market square all those years ago, and he would continue to love her until his dying day. She was Endyll's, he knew, and Endryll was hers, wholly and completely, and that pained him. But in that moment, under the trees in the vast expanse of the Wilds' western fields, Illia-Dara and Endryll Cressedia by his side, he knew all was right. All was as it should be. All was as it *must* be. He would live to love these friends of his, and he would die to protect them.

Ixchel turned his gaze away, out to the endless oceans of the Serrated Sea. A silence had stretched between them like a cat warming itself under the sun, uncoiling and arching in comfortable and easy movements. Endryll was there, one arm around his wife and the other on Ixchel's shoulder. They all looked across the expanse of waters, and though their thoughts were their own, this time and this moment they shared together.

Finally, Ixchel exhaled. "It won't change, you know."

Illia-Dara glanced at him. "What won't?"

"This." Ixchel gestured to the sky, the sea, and then to them. "No matter what happens on Vaelorae, this will always be ours."

"A noble sentiment," Endryll said and squeezed his shoulder tight.

Ixchel grinned, not looking up. "I have my moments."

The day sank into dusk, and the stars began to blink into being. The moon faded into the sky as if by the stroke of a master painter adding layer upon layer of soft color until it was a bright and bold orb of light. The insects and nocturnal creatures of the Wilds took their cue and counted in their harmonious chorus of chirps and howls with a few experimental notes. Then, all the Wilds rose in symphonic accord. Night had come to Y'ssildria, and it was good. Because in that moment, they were not a prince, a betrothed, and a farmhand. They were not husband and wife and stable boy, they were not a future king, queen, and mage.

They were simply Endryll, Illia-Dara, and Ixchel.

THE BINDING OF EARTH AND FIRE

The air was thick with early morning warmth as Stren stepped into the castle gardens. The scent of freshly-turned earth mingling with the salt-kissed breeze rolling in from the south greeted him fondly. Y'ssildria's great castle stood tall and proud behind him, its spires spearing the sky, its walls gleaming in the golden light of the rising sun. He had been granted all the accommodations that his king could provide—a soft and full bed filled with down, covered in lavish blankets and pillows of all shapes and sizes and firmness, all the food he could want, and all the wine he could drink. He did not accept any of it, save the wine. Not out of spite or a higher sense of nobility, but because comfort felt awkward there. To rest in silks and bathe in tubs made of copper filled with fragrant soaps and lathers was to betray all his sensibilities. He was a simple man, and he preferred the comfort of the outdoors, among the trees and vegetation. And so, he slept in the outer courtyard behind the castle.

Stren surveyed the field before him, taking slow, deliberate steps. He was stiff from his night on a bench in the plaza. He could hear the murmur of the palace servants preparing for not only the morning, but for the days ahead. There were the familiar sounds of chefs cooking and maids cleaning, but there was also the clatter of wooden stalls being erected, the rhythmic pounding of mallets driving stakes deep into the soil, and just a general sense of anticipation. The wedding of Prince Endryll to the Lady Illia-Dara would be an event unlike any the kingdom had seen in decades, and it would be topped off by Endryll's coronation. It was for this reason that Stren was here. He closed his eyes and knelt. He sank his fingers deep into the ground. The land had been restless and unsteady since yesterday's events in the mountains, as if it sensed something was coming. He exhaled, let the tension drain from his body, and called upon his magic.

The earth answered. The soil beneath his feet and around his fingers stirred, shifting and moving at his call. He reached deeper, listening to the land, feeling its strength and vitality. Roots buried beneath the surface, old but strong, drank from the power as the gardens awoke. The ground trembled. The vines stretched upward, thickening and braiding into sturdy archways adorned with emerald leaves. Flowers bloomed in an instant, spirals of violet and gold unfurling from the greenery as if awakened from a dream. The wedding grounds were taking shape. This was his domain. Earthen art was more than mere magic, it was balance, creation, the binding force of all things. And it was Stren's to command.

Ixchel stood just beyond the line of trees, watching. He had seen his master's powers before, but that did not make it any less a spectacle. He could feel Stren's magic through the tree he was pressed against. It echoed such a force that, for a moment, Ixchel had to remove himself from the rough bark of the tree's trunk lest he be made sick and brought low by the disorienting waves. He stepped on a small fallen branch. It made nary a sound, but it was enough to be heard by his master's keen ears.

Stren wiped the sweat from his brow and turned to face the young man. Ixchel thrust his hands into his pockets and shuffled out from the cover of the old tree. His dark eyes darted away quickly, shifting to the castle's high walls as if he hadn't been caught staring and just happened to be taking an early morning stroll through the gardens. He pursed his lips to pick up a whistling tune midway through, hoping to cement his ruse further. It didn't work.

"Don't even start to whistle," Stren said. "You're not good at it, and my headache is bad enough already without your tuneless warbling adding to it." Stren straightened. "How long have you been standing there?"

Ixchel shrugged, dragging the toe of his boot against the dirt in a small, semi-circular fashion. "Long enough to know I'll never be able to do anything like that."

Stren sighed. He had always known that Ixchel wrestled with his own magic. He flailed and grasped for it like a babe reaching for its rattle, awkward and unfamiliar with its own body. Unlike Endryll, who had inherited the strength and precision of a warrior, or Stren's own innate grasp of the Aetherfast, harnessed and controlled with years of practice, Ixchel's gifts were far more elusive, far less tangible. His magic was not of the earth nor steel but something far more delicate. His powers were of illusion, artistry, the bending of light and perception. To Ixchel, it had always seemed a lesser thing, a worthless thing.

Stren studied the boy carefully. "And what is it you think you lack?"

Ixchel took his hands from his pockets and crossed his arms. "Usefulness."

"That's an odd word for a wizard to use. Magic is useful in any form, Ixchel. You just have to discover what that use is."

"Not mine," Ixchel muttered, his voice tight with frustration. "What can I do that would make any difference, wave my arms and make candles flicker? It'd be just as easy to blow them out."

The words stung—not because they were untrue but because they echoed Stren's own private fears. He had raised Ixchel since he was a child, taking him in when he was little more than a half-starved babe. He had trained him, taught him discipline, and cultivated his talents with the same care as he would have his own son, as he had once with Atamas. And yet, he had failed. No matter how much Stren reassured Ixchel or how many times he told him that advancing in magic was not a contest or race, the boy still measured himself against Endryll. And it was not just his skill that Ixchel envied. Stren had seen the way Ixchel looked at Illia-Dara. The glances that lingered too long, the quiet ache beneath his words whenever her name was mentioned. It was a jealousy he would never voice aloud, and a war against his heart that he would never win.

"Your magic is more than you know," Stren said. "It is the sum of your parts. You do not see the full potential of what you wield because you see it as something to catch and tame rather than something that is already inside you."

"Show me," Ixchel said, trying to keep from sounding as if he were pleading. But he *was* pleading. His chest felt like it would burst. The agony of being so small, so ineffective, so powerless for so long raked at his insides like a caged beast. He felt like a hurricane trapped in a jar. "Please."

It was an oft repeated request, and one that Stren had grown tired of attempting. Ixchel fought against the magic. He tried too hard to reign it in, to conquer it, instead of letting it lead him. Nothing Stren had tried over the years seemed to get the boy anywhere closer to seeing that, in fact, he seemed to stray farther and farther the more he tried.

Stren hesitated. It was a dangerous request. Ixchel was headstrong, stubborn, and filled with a resentment he did not understand and could hardly control. Stren could push him, force him into something beyond his comfort, and wake that slumbering part of him where his magic dwelt. But would it help? Or would it only drive him deeper into his doubts? He had focused on history and mathematics, herbology and rune-lore, astronomy, and agriculture because these things were tangible. They were easily grasped and mastered, especially for one of Ixchel's cognitive abilities. Magic was a vapor to Ixchel. No matter how many times or how hard he reached for it, it slipped through his fingers like smoke. Still, he would not waste the moment. He could not. Ixchel had not sought him out in this for years. He would try again.

"Fine," Stren said, brushing the dirt from his hands. "Let's test your theory."

"Right now?" Ixchel's voice cracked. "Here?" He looked around him. Castle staff were milling about the courtyard, running this way and that, carrying on tasks that ran the gamut from mundane daily chores to the grand and frantic preparations for the prince's wedding and coronation.

Stren nodded. "You want to know what your magic is worth? I'll show you."

Ixchel swallowed hard, but he squared his shoulders. "What do I do?"

Stren took a step back and motioned to the open gardens behind them. "Use what you know," Stren said. "Defend yourself. Show me your worth."

"Defend myself? What d—" Ixchel began to protest, but it was too late. Something erupted from the ground behind him and swept out his legs from under him before he could finish his sentence.

He landed on his back. Dirt and clay and even the creeping, crawling things of the earth rained down on him. An earthworm that had been otherwise unconcerned with the goings on of the things above suddenly found itself within an inch of Ixchel's gaping mouth. It slithered away as Ixchel spat and coughed. He tried to catch his breath while simultaneously wiping the falling dirt from his face. It was then that he noticed the cause of not only his current prostrate position but also the falling debris. A massive root swayed erect above him. It twisted and turned, looking more like a colossal sea serpent ready to wrap itself around the hull of a ship than the appendage of a garden tree. Then it descended.

He rolled to the left and was tossed high into the air. It had missed him, but he was caught in the wake of the collision meant for him. The earth rippled like water absorbing a stone tossed from a bridge. The giant root buried itself deep and sank below the surface, but the splash sent waves upon waves of soft earth up and out from its center of impact. In flight, Ixchel caught a brief, disorienting glimpse of his master. He was smiling. Then, the garden floor rushed to greet him. Ixchel had little choice in the matter, so he tucked into as tight of a ball as he could manage and accepted the shock, though not without some trepidation. Stren had trained him well in many different forms of martial combat, and much of that training had more to do with avoiding blows and, if that wasn't possible, taking as little damage as possible from them. He hit the ground with his right shoulder leading, allowing momentum to tire itself before extending both hands, palm down, and slapping hard. He uncoiled and sprang off his hands to land in a tripedal stance, facing his master.

He held the pose. His breathing was shallow and sharp as his lungs fought to replenish their exhausted reservoirs. He blinked away the dirt and sweat from his eyes. He focused on his master, watching, waiting, trying to discern or anticipate his next move. Stren gave nothing away. His hands were clasped together in front of him. His warden-gray robes billowed around him like storm clouds. Ixchel shuddered. It was a bright and calm summer morning, not a cloud in the sky and no breeze to speak of. Yet, his master's robes danced as if he stood amid a hurricane. And maybe he did. Ixchel knew Stren was powerful but also knew that he had never seen the full extent of his master's will or his command over it.

"I said, 'defend yourself,' Ixchel," Stren said, and though they stood within talking distance, and his master was never one to shout, his voice came as thunder. It boomed around him. It crashed in him and through him like the voice of a god. "Not avoid or run." Stren extended his arms then and began to sign. His fingers split the air in front of him with golden lashes. He traced ancient runes known only to the Illuminthil. They blinked to life in an instant and then vanished, leaving trace outlines of sparks in their stead. "I have taught you everything I can in this matter, yet your mind refuses to awaken to it. If you truly believe that you are incomplete, that you are somehow lesser without your flame, then I will draw it from you one way or another." His eyes narrowed, his casting complete. "Even if that means that you die this day!"

He threw forth his hands, pushing, willing his runic spell forward. The trees blew apart around him, brought low by the force of his powers loosed. A great pachyderm materialized before him. It came from the misted edge of the Aetherfast, a mountain draped in flesh and frenzy, its skin as thick as old bark and lashed with scars that spoke of war and violence. Its jagged and yellowed tusks split the air as it bellowed a cry that promised pain. Its ears, wide as war banners, flared and beat against the wind, and its eyes, small, bright ember-coals buried in battle-furrowed wrinkles, glinted with rage.

"Die?" Ixchel shouted in disbelief.

The giant elephant charged with the force of an earthquake. Dust erupted beneath it. Trees snapped like matchsticks. Each step pounded the earth as if hammering out the rhythm of fate itself. It had appeared at full speed, already charging, unstoppable and unyielding, a living siege engine of vapor and wrath.

Ixchel blinked as the monstrosity approached. He blinked again, hoping it would disappear as quickly as it had materialized. It didn't. It closed the gap in an instant. Ixchel had no time to react. It was barreling straight for him. Was Stren *really* going to kill him? Images of Illia-Dara flashed across his vision. Images of that first day he had seen her and every day after that. Then he saw Endryll, his dearest friend. He saw them together. He saw their love blossom and take shape. Pictures of his life with them glimmered into existence and then faded, only to be replaced by another, then another. And he saw images of himself, in the background, always there, always waiting. *For what*, he thought. *FOR WHAT*, his mind screamed at him. He watched the elephant approach. He wouldn't hesitate. Not now. Not anymore. He closed his eyes and exhaled. Lifting his hands, fingers curling into practiced shapes, he called forth his power. He didn't know what he was doing, but he knew *how* to do it. His head had known for years, but his heart never had. Not before this very moment, faced with the very real possibility that he could die within a matter of seconds. He wasn't necessarily concerned with his own death, for he had convinced himself that he was disposable, invisible, but facing a reality of never seeing Illia-Dara again, that he could not do. Something woke within him. The air around him flickered, light stretched, and time itself warped, bent to his will.

Stren felt the shift immediately. The world blurred. He considered briefly calling back his attacker. He could never truly hurt Ixchel, no more than his secrets already had. It even pained him that Ixchel *believed* he was capable of harming him. The elephant was an indestructible juggernaut of singular purpose, a being of the Aetherfast that only knew destruction, as evidenced by the broken trees and torn earth. But he had to convince his pupil that he was in real danger, that his life was on the line. There was no other way to coax his dormant powers than to show Ixchel a threat so sure that failure would mean death. Stren saw the despair in his young student's eyes. He felt Ixchel's fear in his heart. And there was regret, too, like a dense blanket of fog rolling through Ixchel's subconsciousness. It was a persistent and accusing thing. It was a poisonous cloud, suffocating Ixchel's spirit, smothering his burgeoning flame. Stren began tracing the runes to return his conjuring to the Aetherfast. Then Ixchel was gone.

A flicker.

A glint.

A surge of blueish energy like a star exploding across a cloudless horizon, and suddenly, three Ixchels stood where there had just been one. All were perfectly calm, perfectly unafraid. They breathed as one. None were entirely solid, nor were they all together translucent. Each moved just a heartbeat apart from the others, one blinking, one tilting his head, one smiling, and the other following a moment later. They were refractions of the whole. No, not refractions, they were reflections. It was impossible to determine the lead or order of actions among them, so identical and reactive were they to one another, so in sync.

Stren narrowed his eyes and stopped his casting. He watched as his creation rushed through all three Ixchels. It lowered its head, tusks digging deep into the ground, then raised it with such ferocity as it met its target that Stren looked away. A shower of torn earth burst forth as the tusks breached. He tensed his shoulders and looked behind him, unable to bring himself to watch the carnage. His adopted son would be decimated if there were even the slightest chance that one of those illusory beings was the real Ixchel. And that was something that Stren could not bear to watch.

The triumvirate Ixchel burst apart in glittering shards of ethereal glass. The elephant roared its victory in a triumphant shout. It pressed up hard, moving the earth beneath it as it rose high into the air. Its front legs reached, and its trunk stretched. It stood on its hind legs and strained to the sky. Its call was that of a trumpet, so clear and bright that it pierced the very fabric of existence and pulled on the threads of reality. A veil was torn into being, an extraplanar window momentarily connecting this world to the world of the Aetherfast. Its task was completed, its target was destroyed, and it did not need to wait for Stren to order it to return home. Indeed, it would not, for Stren commanded it no longer. Only the call of its ancestral plain governed it now. It lumbered through the portal and vanished just as quickly as it had appeared.

"I did it!"

Stren startled and spun. Behind him stood Ixchel. He was smiling, looking almost manic. His teeth were bared and his lips spread thin across them. His hair, ever the erratic tuft of chestnut tangles, stuck out in all directions. It swayed unnaturally, for the forest had calmed, and there was no breeze. His eyes were wild and shone with a glint of gold speckled throughout his otherwise hazel irises. He trembled slightly as if a fever had taken him, as if he had journeyed through the Vintermarrow and returned frostbound.

"I did it," he said again. "I don't know what I did, exactly, but I know I did it! Did you see me, master?"

"I did," Stren replied with a sigh of relief and roll of laughter. "I did, indeed." He neared his student and bent to look into his eyes. He cupped Ixchel's face and drew him nearer still. "How do you feel?"

"I, I can't stop shaking. S-sh-shivering," he said through chattering teeth. "I feel tired, but like I could climb the Stoneguard. Barefoot. Backward! With a pig on my shoulders!" He raised his hands to each side and began flapping his arms wildly. "I feel like I can fly, master! I feel like I can do anything!"

"You can't," Stren said dryly. "You can barely stand."

Ixchel stopped flapping and embraced Stren the same way so that each held the other's face. He looked deeply into his master's eyes. "Have you always looked so ..." he considered his words. He bit his lip and closed his eyes for a moment, as if working out some sort of arithmetic or equation in his mind. He opened his eyes. "... old? You are *old*, old. I mean, look at how many lines are on your face. Master, are you dying? Why wouldn't you tell me? You can't leave me now!" Ixchel became more excited and more unstable, his voice high and irritated.

"Ixchel, steady yourself," Stren interjected. It seemed as if Ixchel would have continued indefinitely had he not. "I will answer all your questions soon, but right now, I need to get you into a hot bath and then a warm bed. You've been across the veil. You have found your powers, or more accurately, your powers have found you." He studied him closely. "You're hearing more than you should. Seeing more than what's there. Your senses are stretched thin. You are not meant to live in that place, not yet. You are veildrunk, and you need time to recover. Also," he paused for a moment, "you are quite naked."

Ixchel's face was placid, and though he looked more like a crazed jester than a student of a powerful magician, he took the news with a calm detachedness. His eyebrows arched slightly, but nothing so cartoonish as what was already plastered across his face from his trip to the veil. He looked down and surveyed his current state of undress. "Hmph," he said. "So I am." He then fell limply into Stren's waiting arms, the veildrunkenness ushering him to sleep.

Warm water coursed around him, carrying the scent of cedar and elderflower. The natural flow of the mountain-fed headwater caused the currents to lick and caress his skin as it ran toward the high cliffs overlooking the Serrated Sea, where it spilled into the infinite abyss of the ocean far below. Ixchel would have been freezing, had the stone basin, hollowed out and placed into the center of the stream, not been fixed directly over a hot spring that fed into the meander as it snaked its way downhill. The bath was deep, built into the earth at the rear of the castle gardens where they met the foothills of the Crown. This had been done at Stren's request years ago when he had spent much more time in Y'ssildria, when Cerceia had still been with them. Even then, he preferred a natural spring bath that trickled fresh mountain rain in a soft, melodic gurgle to the stillness and staleness of the castle baths. Ixchel sat submerged to his chest, arms flung unceremoniously over either side of the stone. He was barely conscious, his breath shallow but steady. His skin was colorless, drained from effort, and a soft sheen of sweat glistened on his brow. Stren knelt beside the pool, waist-deep in rushing water, sleeves rolled up to his elbows as he gently ladled water over the boy's shoulders.

"Why didn't you stop me?" Ixchel murmured sluggishly. "If you knew it was dangerous, why did you let me do it?"

Stren didn't answer right away. He scooped another clay-full of water and poured it over Ixchel's neck, following the spilling water with his other hand, gently and soothingly, with all the care a father would have bathing his newborn son. "Because I couldn't," he said finally. "I couldn't allow my fear, my concern for your safety and comfort, to hold you back. Not anymore." Stren placed the clay pot on the lip of the stone tub and began to lather Ixchel's hair with ointment. The scent of vanilla and lavender filled the space between them as the rushing waters filled the silence. Stren felt his student relax, lowering himself deeper into the bath. His eyes were closed, but Stren knew that he was listening. "Power isn't taught," he continued. "It is *claimed*. And besides," he said, his mouth turning up to a slight grin, "you asked me to."

Ixchel turned his head slowly to look at his master. His movements were lethargic. His eyelids were heavy from exhaustion. "You *were* trying to kill me?" he asked as his head rolled to hang awkwardly over the back of the tub's edge.

Stren chuckled under his breath. "No. I was trying to make you *choose* to live."

A bird chirped somewhere beyond the garden gate, its call echoing off the castle walls. The day was still young, but Stren knew that Ixchel was young no longer. He had grown from a boy to a man in mere moments. Faced with danger unto death, he had found his flame and claimed it. He owned it. It was his now.

"Is that what this was?" Ixchel asked, his voice hoarse. "Some lesson?"

"No," Stren said. "Not a lesson. A moment in time. A choice. One that only you could make."

Ixchel exhaled. "It felt like I was dying."

"In a way, you were. You *did*. When your flame responded to your call, it consumed you. It drew you into the Aetherfast. And there you were engulfed by it, wholly and completely. You and your flame became one. You were consumed by it, brought to ash. And from that ash, you rose." Ixchel was tiring, he knew. He would soon be asleep and remain bound to his recovery for many hours. But he persisted, knowing that while his mind was in this lucid realm, caught halfway between the here-and-now and the Aetherfast, it would be more open, more susceptible to higher contemplation. "Do you know what you did, how your powers helped you? Could you do it again?"

"I think so," he replied. "I don't understand *how* I did it, but I know *what* I did. When I saw the elephant coming, I honestly thought that you meant to kill me. I can't say why. I couldn't reconcile the betrayal I felt, but knew at that moment it was true." He closed his eyes and mouth as Stren poured a fresh pot of water over his hair and began massaging the lather. "I just reacted. I knew I had to get away. I closed my eyes and pictured myself behind you. But then everything went still. The elephant stopped where it was, mid-run. I saw trees half-fallen from its charge, just hanging there, suspended in motion. Even the leaves and grass that had been spinning and flying all around moments before were just frozen." He wiped at his eyes to get the water out. "Then I was in quicksand. I was moving, but it was difficult, like pushing through a me-sized-spiderweb. Everything around me flickered and flashed in and out of my vision, there one moment and then gone the next."

"You were veilmelding," Stren interjected. "Your mortal mind and your ethereal mind, your flame, were merging. It is typically not so jarring, but most with the gift meld far earlier than you did. Their powers are naturally lesser, because their *minds* are lesser, younger. But you refused to meld. No matter how I explained it to you, you refused to understand. Your mind rejected it. So, your flame expanded in power over the years, but it had nowhere to go. It was just trapped in the Aetherfast growing, straining to break free. But your flame is yours alone, no one else's. No one else could free it or claim it. When you finally entered the Aetherfast, your flame was eager. It ravaged you. Our flames are jealous and desire only to be one with their master."

"So, you're saying it won't be so bad the next time I call on it?"

Stren laughed as he shook the last droplets of water from Ixchel's hair. "I dare say that next time you call on your flame, instead of wading through webs, you will soar the very heights of Y'ssara."

"I like that idea."

"As do I, Ixchel. As do I." Stren rose and stretched. He was waterlogged from the waist down. He gathered the soaps and tonics and placed them into the clay pot.

"Master," Ixchel said. "What of the three illusions? I knew I needed to distract the elephant so I could escape, but I didn't conjure them. I didn't call them or create them. They just *appeared*."

Stren dried himself off with a towel and then threw it to Ixchel. He caught it with one hand and began scrubbing his hair dry. "Those are your Echoborn. They are echoes of your soul, your flame, born from the depths of the Aetherfast. They are a part of you, though not wholly. They are also a part of the larger spirit of Y'ssara, woven into you through the Aetherfast. It is what makes your flame unique. You may call on them in necessity or want, and they will respond, but they may appear of their own accord when needed. They are reflections of you, not as Y'ssara sees you, but as you see yourself."

Ixchel squinted against the noonday sun. "So, you're saying they won't always look like me?" He moved to stand, and Stren was there to hold his arm. He stepped from the basin and into the flow of the stream. He swayed as he adjusted to the surge. "Why didn't they appear as mighty warriors clad in battle armor and lay waste to the creature, or at least challenge it?"

"Ah," Stren replied, "do you see yourself as a battle-ready warrior, able to fell a raging behemoth, Ixchel?"

Ixchel laughed this time, though he held his hands to his head and groaned afterward. "I suppose I don't. Before today, I didn't see myself as much of anything."

"Though it saddens me to hear that, I am glad your paradigm has shifted." He placed an arm around Ixchel's shoulder and escorted him across the stream. "Maybe one day you will see yourself as that mighty warrior."

"Maybe."

The grass was thick and lush, cushioning Ixchel's wrinkled toes as they stepped out of the water. They walked in silent reflection, the castle looming before them, casting shadows far over them and into the Titan's Crown. Ixchel, still being supported by his master, looked at the castle and its many rising and twisting towers. He followed one high into the sky, stopping on a shaded window. Curtains blew out and whipped in the wind high above Y'ssildira. They were Illia-Dara's rooms.

"You know they married in secret last night, don't you," he asked. A quiver of sadness caused his breath to catch. "It was just me and the priest there."

"There are no secrets kept from me, Ixchel. Only truths that have not been discovered."

"I figured you knew."

"You figured correctly." Stren stopped, pulling Ixchel back with him. He looked at his student, his adopted son. "Does this pain you?"

"Yes," he said. Ixchel wouldn't meet his eyes. He pretended as if the sun was too bright to look up. He brought a hand up to block the light and to cover his face from his master. "But not in a bitter way. I am happy for her. And I am happy for Endryll. I love them both very much."

"But you love her differently," Stren pressed.

"I do."

"I knew that, too," Stren said, bringing Ixchel close and hugging him tightly. "Come," he said as they began to walk again, "we have quite the celebration to prepare for."

"Master," Ixchel said after a moment.

"Yes, Ixchel."

"Why was I naked?"

STRAKK THE DOG

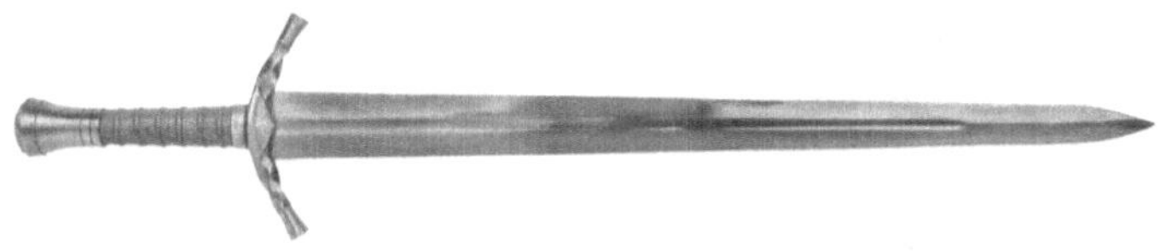

The other darklings called him a runt. He was shorter than the rest, weaker, frailer. He was fragile, not only in constitution, but in character and ego, too. He knew this. He knew this is what they thought of him, but it didn't bother him. He was small, even by darkling standards—his frame wiry, his black fur speckled with gray from too many nights spent huddled in dark corners of darker alleys, no protection from the ruthless elements of the Drossfang Barrens. His teeth, sharp and yellowed, peaked out from snarling lips. His eyes, black as the ink of a thal'ziruun, reflected the ruin of the Barrens in glossy precision as he looked over his dwelling. His fingers, elongated and clawed, dug deeply into the stone lip of the cracked well that he perched upon as he watched. They called him *Strakk the Dog* because he was a creature too weak to fight and too cowardly to claw. Again, he didn't mind. Let them think what they wished. Everyone knew that dogs lived longer than wolves. And this dog could, indeed, bite if he wished.

The Drossfang Barrens stretched out beneath a sky of perpetual ash, its desolate hills rolling like the ribs of a desiccated and long-dead beast across plains of burnt and blistered soil. No tree took root here and had not for ages. There were no plants to offer support or shade, no waters to sate or sustain life. The land was gnarled by ancient evils, the soil dry and fractured by an angry and fiery mountain that belched forth flame and damnation. It was a place forgotten by kings, abandoned by good, and ruled by those the world called vermin. It was here, among the crumbling remains of the lost city of Vaelthwyn, a spectre of the world's indifference, that the darklings made their home.

Vaelthwyn had been a glorious city of marble towers and gypsum stone streets. It had once been the sister city of Y'ssildria, far to the south and west, across the Whistle Wilds along the coast of the Emberwake Bay, and outshone her in radiance and wealth. Lord Tansys of Vaelthwyn was a good man and an honest ruler, but his hunger for splendor was voracious. His lust for riches drove him mad, searching ever deeper into the bowels of the mountains and into the darkest recesses of the seas ... searching for more. Gildrot festered and grew in his mind, corrupting his soul and consuming his thoughts. The sickness drove his people from him. Even his wife and daughter fled his frenzied crusade, seeking a new life far to the north, to Y'ssildria. Those who remained were poisoned and diseased by Tansys's greed, devoured by avarice and transformed into something other, something gruesome. They were shaped into the nightmare of all goodly races.

Now, they were something else entirely. They had traded bargains and bartering for bloodshed, families and full bellies for subterfuge, tools of trade and honest work for blades and backstabbing. Darklings were the corrupted remnants of a once-prosperous city, the villainous vapor left behind after the caustic crash of a civilization. Now, the towers, once shimmering monuments to vanity, lay in heaps of broken rubble. The streets, once white and warm with families and fare, spilled into burned and broken homes and shops, displaced by mighty quakes and the unceasing assault of molten slag.

And Strakk preferred it that way. Most darklings seethed in their hate, stewed and simmered in the memories of their lives before and the loved ones who abandoned them during the fall of Vaelthwyn. They poached life and color and breath from the Barrens with rampant abandon, killing their neighbors for any perceived slight, then loathing and lamenting their station in life. The blame for their plight never fell on their corruption, their violence or blackness of soul—it was always laid squarely on those who had abandoned them.

But Strakk didn't see it that way. He acknowledged the decisions that he had made all those years before. He wasn't so narcissistic, so vainglorious to assume that all of his problems were someone else's fault. He remembered the reason for the destruction of Vaelthwyn and knew well that he had played a hand in it, as had all the others who had stayed.

He sat at the edge of the dried and tumbletorn well, gnawing on a grey strip of something that might have been rabbit or squirrel, or it may have been something altogether less savory. He liked being above things. He was able to be alone with his contemplations. He was free to wander and explore. When he was above things he was alone. He would play sketching games on the walls of uninhabited buildings, where one player would mark a square with an X and the other would mark an O. They would do this on a 3x3 grid until one or the other matched three in a row. He, of course, had to pull dual roles, as no one else would play with him. No one else in the Barrens even remembered the game. It had been wiped away, tossed from their consciousness like the rind of a fruit to the compost. But he remembered.

He had once found a ball that had miraculously survived the destruction of Vaelthwyn. Oh, how he marveled as it bounced, how he joyed when he threw it against the wall and it returned to him! It was as if he had finally found a companion to play with. He hadn't wanted to be alone, not at first. He was thrilled when he finally found something to reciprocate, to react, to interact. He named it Seridwyn, after his loving wife. She had been lost to him in the fall of Vaelthwyn. She had chosen to flee to Y'ssildria with their children. He didn't blame her. He loved and cherished Seridwyn then, and he loved and cherished her now. But his respite didn't last long. One day, scavengers from the Below had seen him playing catch with his new friend.

"Look at the dog," one croaked in a mocking tone. "No one to play fetch with, aye, mutt?"

The others joined in with jeers, shouting taunts and slurs with slobbering maws as they encircled him. There were three, and they were big, strong, well-armed, and armored all. They carried the glaives of the Vaelthwyn army, long poles made of wood and capped with a vicious two-sided blade. The lengths of the shafts were reinforced with iron ingots that had been stretched and folded many times over in the flame and forge of the once-famed Forgemaster of Vaelthwyn, Brannoc the Ashwright. They were then gilded with the purest gold. A round of gold leaf bearing the image of Lord Tansys adorned the hilt, and from it hung braided tassels of deep reds and blacks. More red and black cord was wrapped in intricate knots where the blade was fixed to the handle. The blades were half the full length of the shaft and weighed twice that. They were infused with the lava stone that had once been a recondite and sacred treasure of Vaelthwyn, but now rained down perpetually from Mount Vorthul'kai's gurgling depths within the Helwyr Peaks. It is said that when the blade of a Vaelthwyn glaive found purchase, the victim wouldn't bleed, as the searing heat from the lava stone would cauterize the wound even before the blade was withdrawn. In a past life, these three were loyal members of the royal guard. Now, they were a brutish militia of lawless wolf-men.

"Strakk the Dog," another said. "Have you taken a moment away from itching your fleas to chase balls?"

Strakk cowered. What other recourse did he have? He clung tightly to his red leather ball and lowered himself before the three. He bowed his head, showing his fear and fealty. "I'm sorry," he said, and then coughed hard. It had been too long since he had spoken aloud. The vibration of his vocal cords felt like grit paper being dragged along his gullet. He coughed again, and this time spat a large globulous ball of phlegm to clear his throat. "I meant no harm, no disrespect."

"We don't care at all for your meaning," one replied. "We care that you are here at all. What concerns us is why you exist, you waste of flesh and fur." Smiles drenched with the promise of violence spread across the mouths of the three as their circle continued to close around poor Strakk.

"I care that he has stolen my ball, Gravok," the one to the left of Strakk said. "What a miserable wretch to steal from his own kin." The other two nodded in unison, growling their agreement from flared nostrils.

"Is it true that you have stolen this ball from your brother, Vetch," the one called Gravok asked Strakk. "Even a whelp like you who prefers to spend his days Above knows the rules," he paused, ensuring that he had Strakk's full attention, "and the consequences for breaking them." His voice turned lascivious and low as he finished. He closed his eyes and smelled the air. "I can taste your fear, Strakk the Dog. Fear is something of which the innocent know nothing."

"I—I didn't," Strakk said quickly. "I found it, just over there. I promise!" He raised one shaking hand to point over the ruins of an old market to what used to be a park. Cheerful families and young lovers once ran and played together there. Children would skip and sing and play with leather balls and make chalk drawings. Strakk's eyes went distant for a moment as he remembered those times. The laughs of the children came back to him like a phantom song. The melody of happy voices wafted through his memory and brought a smile to his mouth.

That smile was replaced by a grimace of white-hot pain, the song replaced by a howl of agony, as Gravok's glaive sliced the air in an upward bow. The blade split the air with a shrill scream and cut through flesh and fur and bone as Strakk's still-pointing hand was removed from his arm. No blood followed the trajectory of his severed hand as it arched through the air, the Vaelthwyn blade living up to its reputation and stemming the flow immediately. Strakk raised his limb to his eyes. It was still smoking from where the lava stone had done its work. The smoke danced and twisted in cryptic tendrils in front of him before it dissolved in a golden flash as the hilt of Gravok's weapon rushed through and battered Strakk across his face. He fell to the ground like a sack of wheat tossed from the shoulder of a grocer.

He never lost consciousness, but his faculties fled and left him a weak and whimpering thing. He clung to his throbbing limb with the arm that remained whole, and both clung to Seridwyn the Ball in a trembling hug. He squeezed so tightly that his shoulders ached with the pressure. His breathing was shallow from the force of the ball being driven into his chest. His eyes were shut, and his chin and knees were tucked around Seridwyn, as well. He lay curled in fetal form, shaking and crying. This was no longer merely a ball, no longer a simple plaything made of leather and filled with air. This was his tether to humanity. This was his wife, his anchor. This was his Seridwyn.

"Strakk the Dog," Gravok said. "You have been judged for the crime of theft. Your sentence has been handed out and paid in full." He barked a cruel laugh then and turned to leave.

"Not entirely paid," Vetch said, stopping Gravok short. "He has been tried and judged for theft, yes, but there is still the matter of my stolen property."

"Ah, yes. Threnhal," Gravok said, addressing the third without turning around. "See to the retrieval of Vetch's stolen property."

Threnhal nodded, though Gravok had already continued on his way. He strode to where Strakk lay clutching his ball. His shadow crawled over

Strakk like a rainstorm over a valley, dark and menacing. He stood above him, glaive in hand, and said, "Give me the ball, Dog."

"Please," Strakk pled. "Please don't take her from me." His voice was a desperate and broken thing. "Please. She is all I have left. I am nothing witho—"

Thernhal plunged his blade deep into the ball and wrenched it from frail arms. Strakk's sobs could be heard even over the whoosh of air as the ball deflated, its form melting around the edges of Threnhal's steel. He held his glaive out long toward the waiting Vetch. Threnhal's arms did not shake, even with the weight of the long polearm fully extended.

"Your ball," he said, his tone callous and casual. "Though I may have damaged it," he laughed, and then the glaive did dip a bit.

Vetch tore the mound of red-stained flesh from the blade and looked at it thoughtfully. "Oh, dear," he said. It seems I have made a mistake." He turned the ruined thing around in his knotted and scarred hands, the fur running down his clawed fingers, blowing about with the last breaths of the diminishing ball. "Mine was blue." He tossed it down to land at Strakk's side.

Strakk's consciousness faded then. The last thing he remembered was wicked laughter and his own soft voice whispering, "Seridwyn" over and over, until at last, he remembered no more.

That was a lifetime ago. It had taken two lifetimes for Strakk to reach his current state in life, one of indifference, one of base survival, one where he cared for no one and nothing, not even himself. Sitting on the stone water-throat, chewing his meat and thinking sinful thoughts of darkling things, he laughed. He spat a piece of gristle he had been working out of his cracked fangs. He shook his head in disgust at the pathetic, weak creature he was back then. A thin and jagged hook of three tines protruded from his right arm. Its tang had been driven deep into the misshapen mound of flesh and fixed to the bone of his arm with bolts and screws that shot grotesquely out of either side of his forearm. The shanks were barbed and sharpened to fine and lethal points. He scraped the last bits of fat from the bone of his meal with one of the prongs. It dug deep grooves into the bone as it shredded the grey flesh away. He shivered. The wind had picked up, blowing his threadbare black garments, and the sun had lowered behind the Helwyr Peaks. It was getting dark. Just the way he liked it.

The wind did no favors for the one who approached from somewhere far behind him. Strakk had smelled the stranger hours ago, when he had first crossed into the Barrens from the East. He knew that scent and hated it. It was the scent of a Y'ssildrian, the scent of a human. He knew, too, that he was not the only darkling in the Above who was aware of the visitor's presence. He hopped from his ledge and landed softly, quietly, though he landed on loose pebbles and gravel that were eager to move under his weight. Strakk threw the bone down the well and took off at full sprint. Though he had just eaten, he couldn't give up the opportunity to dine on human flesh.

It seemed Strakk arrived just moments too late. As he took the bend into an old cart lane that had once been a bustling byway for merchants and farmers carting their wares and goods to and from one of the many market squares, he saw that three darklings had already cornered the man in an ambush. They were closing in on the doomed stranger from all angles, forming a circle, wickedly-bladed staffs leading the way. Strakk threw himself against the wall opposite the group, again not making a sound. His breathing stilled, and he listened.

"You are a long way from home, Y'ssildrian."

Strakk knew that voice. The sound of it struck him like a warhammer. What little breath he was holding in his lungs escaped him, and he was left gasping silently for air. He looked around for a better vantage point, somewhere higher. There was a wall brought low by time and decay. Its scattered bricks made for an ideal staircase leading to the roof above. *Maybe not perfect*, he thought, *but easy enough for me*. He launched himself up the stones with his left foot, right foot, left foot, and then leaped with his right. He extended his arm and caught the roof's edge with his hooked hand. He pulled himself up easily and gracefully, his muscled back rippling through his matted fur.

Hovering high above and out of sight, he was able to relax. He drank deeply of the putrid and ashen air, allowing it to circulate in his blackened lungs. He took long breaths in through his nose and then exhaled quickly through his mouth. He willed himself to a state of calm. Then he watched. He had missed a few moments of conversation, though he knew well that these darklings only feigned interest in any honest discussion. They were biding their time and toying with their prey. A brief scan of the area confirmed what his keen senses already told him, they were alone. Though surely other darklings had picked up on the stranger's scent, no others had come out to investigate. Strakk nodded his approval.

It had been many years since Gravok and his entourage had disfigured and humiliated him, and he had not been idle during the intervening years. The first days and weeks after the confrontation bled together in a wash of lament and anger. He wandered aimlessly on the Above, simply avoiding the various and random patrols of the darklings, specifically Gravok's. It was easy to get lost in the Barrens and quite difficult to be found, and for the most part, Strakk had little trouble evading his fellow fallen, but when he scented or saw any sign that Gravok, Vetch, or Thernhal were anywhere about, he ran. He ran to the very edges of the Barrens until he couldn't run anymore, until his legs ached and cramped and refused to run any further, until his chest heaved to bursting and his lungs felt like a forge fire with a monstrous wendrigal, a lair troll, at the bellows, until his vision blurred and went dark. And then one day his legs stopped aching. His chest stopped heaving. His eyes stopped failing. Strakk had conditioned himself through cowardice to withstand and even overcome the natural limitations of his kind, unintentionally making himself faster and stronger than any darkling or natural predator in all Drossfang. So, he had stopped running and began hunting.

He developed a mind for sabotage, an understanding of close-quarters battle, and an eye for potential traps and ambushes. He honed these skills mercilessly, leading unsuspecting darklings, those he used to call kin and friends, into sunless corners of abandoned streets. He learned to choose his targets and anticipate their reactions and movements well before his victims knew he was there. By playing the encounter out in his mind ahead of time, he could move, strike, and kill before others even registered the attack. So, he watched and waited.

The visitor had been fully encircled. His attempted backpedaling was thwarted by the tip of Vetch's glaive. He wore no hat or beard, though his collar was pulled up high and tied tight, obscuring his mouth. He wore an ankle-length traveling cloak, thick and coated with wax to deflect the rain, though it would do little to deflect a stab from one of those razor-sharp blades. The robe was cinched tight around the waist by a double-wound cord of leather. Strakk could see no weapons beneath the stranger's garb. There was no print of sword, dagger, or crossbow showing through, yet he did not seem particularly intimidated by his predicament. Strakk envied him for a moment. How would things have differed if he had had that courage the last time he and Grovak met? Was it courage, or was it stupidity, or naivete?

"I'll ask you again, stranger," Grovak said in a low growl, "and know that this is the last time. What are you doing here in Drossfang? We don't like visitors, and we don't like your kind."

"You reek of sunshine and green grass," Thernhal said as he sniffed in the stranger's direction. "You don't belong here."

"I told you," the stranger replied, "I seek the one-handed darkling. He is known as Strakk."

Strakk leaned closer. *How did this man know his name?* Strakk was the name he had taken after the end of things, after the dust and ash had settled on what once had been. No one in his previous life would know him now. He closed his eyes, as they were little help in identifying the Y'ssildrian, and opened his other senses wide. He listened to the voice and searched the recesses of his mind to find some recognition. He smelled and tasted the air. He had never been in close proximity of this man before. If he had, he would remember.

"The dog?" Grovak asked with a laugh. "Surely, there are much prettier puppies for you to take home to your children." He stretched his arms out wide and spun slowly. The tip of his glaive scraped sluggishly against a far wall, leaving crooked white lines etched in the stone as he turned. "You are in the Drossfang Barrens, stranger! You will find nothing here save vermin and low-lifes. You are in the land of villains and castawa—"

Grovak's eyes widened in surprise mid-sentence and mid-turn, as halfway through his rotation, he was met head-on by a soaring dog-faced humanoid in tattered clothing, his tri-hook, devilish and barbed, leading his descent. Two of the hooks found purchase in the wide eyes of the larger darkling even before Strakk landed. Grovak shrieked and stumbled to the ground as Strakk ripped the curved prongs from his target's skull. His eyes, mangled and misshapen on the spiny metal shafts, came out of his skull with a sucking and sickening pop. Strakk left Grovak screaming and clutching blindly at his empty eye sockets. He strode forward to his next target before the other two fully comprehended what was happening.

Vetch was first. Strakk had already calculated the possible scenarios, the variables, and the outcomes. Vetch was closer and more aggressive. He would attack. Thernhal was a bully in the most literal sense. He was big and mean, but he would run when faced with real danger without backup. He would run, he would beg, and he would die. They would all die this day. Strakk continued his approach, calm and poised to strike, a tiger stalking its prey. Grovak continued to wail behind him.

Vetch lunged forward, stabbing his glaive once, twice, then a third time before pulling it back close, shifting his wrists, and sending it into a sweeping arc, first low and then, using its weight and momentum, a second time high. The air sang with vibration as the blade sliced this way and that. Strakk stepped back, then dodged right, then left. The first three attacks were sloppy and telegraphed, easily avoided. He leaped high and landed low into a deep stretch, all in one fluid motion, to avoid the arcs. He extended his leg into a spinning kick near the ground and swept Vetch's feet from under him. Vetch loosed his grip on the glaive in order to free up his hands to absorb some of the impact. Strakk rocked back, his shoulders hitting the ground. He placed his hands behind his ears and kicked up, landing deftly on the balls of his feet and breaking into a sprint. He leaped over Vetch, snatched the still-falling glaive in its descent, turned the blade downward, and plunged it into Vetch's chest, using the shaft to assist in his vault. Vetch coughed up blood and clasped the blade, but it was buried deep into the ground beneath him. Strakk landed and walked on, leaving his second victim to suffocate and die in his own gore, now spilling freely down his throat.

Thernhal was already backing away. He had dropped his weapon, and his hands were clasped in front of him. He interlaced his clawed fingers as if praying. Spittle dripped and spewed from trembling lips as he muttered and begged in indecipherable tongues. Mucilage hung from his white whiskers in tiny quaking droplets. He continued to backpedal. Then his heels hit solid rock. He turned to see that he had backed into a corner. He was trapped. High stone walls rose behind him and to each side, and death advanced from the front. Strakk was all teeth. His canines stuck to his top lip, stretching his smile thin, even as they protruded menacingly far beyond his bottom lip. He was no longer Strakk the Dog. He was Strakk the Hunter.

"Please." Thernhal dropped to his knees and extended his still-clasped hands. "Please."

"Please, what?" Strakk hissed. He was standing in front of Thernhal now. His tri-hooked right hand swung level with Thernhal's gaze. The trapped darkling cowered and bit back a yelp as he gazed into his defeated leader's eyes, still dangling from Strakk's hooks. Detached and bulbous, bloody and bursting, they stared at him. They were shocked and accusing. "Please don't kill you? Please make it quick? What would you ask of me, Thernhal?" He stared down hard at the groveling darkling. He was sickened by his weakness, by his spinelessness. It reminded Strakk too much of himself, of what he used to be, of what he was when he was just a dog.

"Please don't kill me," Thernhal begged. He tore his eyes away from the butchery dangling off the hooks and looked into Strakk's narrowed eyes. "Please don't kill me," he said again. "I'll leave. I'll go Below, and you'll never see me again. I promise."

Strakk was quiet for a long moment. He looked across the small corner square. Thernhal dropped his head and began to weep softly. Vetch had expired, a pool of blood and other liquids still pooling around him. Grovak was squirming and trying to find his way, clawing ahead on his belly and getting nowhere. He looked at the stranger. For a moment, he was surprised. He had forgotten the man was there. The stranger had moved back into a broken doorway carved into one of the walls and was watching and waiting. It had taken less than a minute. Less than one minute to inflict maximum carnage on the three darklings that had brutalized him and haunted his memory for years. Then Strakk stepped aside. The sudden movement of pebbles beneath his feet broke the silence.

"Go," he said.

Thernhal looked up. His eyes were shot red with tears. His mouth gaped.

"Do not say a word, or I will take your tongue as a complement to Grovak's eyes. Just go."

Thernhal rose. He was slow and deliberate, keeping Strakk in his peripheral vision as long as he could, until he was well behind him. He walked warily away, past Vetch, past Grovak. He didn't even look down at his compatriots. He just kept walking.

He didn't look back.

If he had, he would have seen the hunter approaching quickly and quietly. Strakk held one side of a band of red leather in his left hand, and the other was pierced and wrapped around his hooked hand. He pulled it taught and raised it over Thernhal's head. Then he snapped back hard.

The darkling gasped as Strakk drew him in, the strap just below his chin. Thernhal's hands went instinctively to his throat, his fingers clawing to get under the leather. But it was too tight. Strakk's grip was too firm. The red leather was too thick and too stiff against his flesh. His eyes bulged as he began to convulse. He dropped his weight and wriggled, trying to loosen the grip and free himself. Air, he needed air, just the briefest respite, just a single life-saving gulp would clear the fog, would restore his strength. But it wasn't just air of which he was deprived. Strakk had ensured the makeshift garrote covered the full width of his enemy's neck, and around behind the ears. He was not only cutting off Thernhal's oxygen supply, but also his blood supply. Soon enough, it was over. Thernhal's lifeless body collapsed into Strakk's arms. His face, some amalgamation of human and canine, was bloated and blue. His eyes were swollen and convex, bellying out of his skull like jellyfish. His ears and nose ran with dark, viscous ichor, and he breathed no more.

Strakk dropped the body where he stood. He marched over to Grovak, who had found his way to a wall and set his back against it. He was breathing rapidly. His cries had turned to a sorrowful and simpering moan. Strakk tore out the glaive, still protruding from Vetch's chest. It came forth with the snap of ribs and the ripping of flesh. He heaved it into Grovak's pitiful, eyeless face as he passed—the blade of the glaive buried well into the stone behind his skull. He was still clutching the deflated red leather ball that he had just used to end Thernhal's life as he reached the doorframe where the stranger stood.

"What is it?" Strakk had asked, his eyes narrowed in suspicion.

"It is your invitation to Prince Endryll's coronation and wedding."

"You're joking," he said, his sharp-toothed maw stretching wide in a mirthless grin.

"I assure you, this is no joke," the man had said stiffly. He did not laugh. He held the enclosed letter out to Strakk. It was of heavy stock and enveloped in fine parchment. A green and golden glob of wax sealed the folds, and pressed into it was the insignia of a dogwood in bloom, the king's seal, the seal of Y'ssildria. "The invitation is genuine," he continued. "The king has called for envoys of all free peoples of the land to witness his son's ascension."

Strakk scoffed, tossing a peel of bark from a dried log into the fire around which they now sat. The flames licked at the wood and engulfed it immediately, ravenous for more. Three bodies lay piled and burning in the middle of the bonfire. Bone had been exposed by melting flesh as smoke rose high and black into the starless night. Neither man showed any signs of disgust or repulsion by the sweet scent of cooking flesh or the rancid smell of bursting innards as the fire made quick work of the dead darklings. Strakk had even helped himself to a few choice cuts over the course of their introductions.

"All the free peoples? That's rich," he snorted. "Last I checked, we darklings and all other creatures of the Drossfang weren't free. We're tolerated. There's a difference."

"The king watches over all his kingdom. Even the forgotten places. Even the sewers and the Barrens."

"What do you know of the sewers, Y'ssildrian?" The glow from the fire flickered across Strakk's furry face, warping his already misshapen head into a malleable and moving grimace of anger. "What does your king know of the Barrens? I was born in the gutter of the world and told I was lesser. We were forgotten, abandoned. No one watches the gutters. No one pays any heed to the sewers until the floods come—and by then, it is too late."

The stranger sighed and lowered his hand, still holding the king's letter. "The king extends his hand in peace, Strakk. He is well aware of your kin's fondness of shadow and seclusion. He would never deign steal that from you. But your kind and ours were once bonded. We were once brothers and sisters, mothers and fathers. He would simply like to bring you under the shade of Y'ssildria, so that you may again be with your people."

Strakk spat onto the cracked, dry ground. "Tell the king to keep his token of peace. It doesn't spend well in the Barrens."

The stranger's mouth tightened, but he said nothing more. He tucked the letter into an inner pocket and brushed the ash from his cloak as he stood. Then he simply turned and left, his silhouette slowly fading into the night.

Strakk watched as the dust settled from the stranger's retreating footsteps, his sharp nails tapping against the stone he sat on. He hated the Y'ssarians and their self-righteousness. He hated their smiles and their skin. He hated their children and their laughter. He hated them more deeply than he had hated Grovak, Vetch, and Thernhal. But more than that, he hated how much he wished things were different.

The second visitor came as Strakk was at home and preparing for sleep. He had doused the fire and collected the bones, buckles, and weapons from among the cinders. Ash from Vorthul'kai would cover from curious eyes all traces of the fight, all footsteps, and anything else he may have missed. He buried the remains under his box-straw bed and flattened the disturbed earth with an old shovel that was used for foraging and finding treasures of the old world. Strakk felt the presence before he saw it, a power that did not belong. Then, the figure stepped from the gloom into the faint light of Strakk's single burning candle. He was tall and grim and cloaked in a gloom that seemed to drink the light. The scent of berryroot weed clung to him. A deep hood obscured his face, but the glowing embers of his pipe illuminated his eyes. They were dark and hollow, distant. They were dangerous. His voice was iron wrapped in velvet when he spoke.

"You will go to the coronation," the figure said. "And you will deliver a gift to the prince's chamber."

The air grew colder. Strakk found himself holding his arms across his chest to stifle a shiver. He recognized his posture at once and forced his arms back down to his sides. He was Strakk the Hunter now. He did not cower. He would not be intimidated. This man was just like any other man. He would bleed and he would die. Strakk forced himself to remain where he was, chewing lazily on what looked to be a singed sliver of bone. "Will I, now?"

"You will." The figure did not move. Did not breathe. Strakk couldn't even be sure if the man standing on his threshold had spoken. But he heard him either way. "You will attend the coronation, and you will deliver the gift to Prince Endryll's private chamber," the figure repeated. "You will do this because it is asked of you. You will do this because it is your duty."

"My duty," Strakk scoffed. "I owe fealty to no one. My only duty is to myself." He pushed himself off the old rain barrel he had been leaning on and tossed the bone aside. The barrel creaked under the pressure and rocked back and forth before settling. It was empty, of course, as there was little rain in Drossfang. He made his way to the man, his hook digging into a blackened and rotting table that was barely standing. Grooves formed in its wake as wood splintered and tore. "I already told your errand boy that I was not interested in the games of the high court." Strakk raised his hooks to the stranger's face. The steel shone in the candlelight, as did the crusty remnants of blood and gore from his recent fight. "He left in one piece. I suggest you follow, or you may not be so lucky."

The stranger pulled on his pipe, again lighting his face beneath the cowl. Strakk gasped and stepped back.

"It is not the King who asks for this service, Olanfar Auren," the stranger whispered. "It is I."

Strakk reeled, his hand going to his head. His hook caught the table as he began to falter, catching the edge before he fell to the floor. No one had called him Olanfar since before the cataclysm. He had been Olanfar Auren once. He had been happy and whole once. He had been married to Seridwyn Auren. He'd had children! Memories came crashing into him in tsunamic waves. He cried out, though he couldn't be sure if it was aloud or in his battered mind. In his head, he was alone in a torrent. He was far out at sea, being tossed about by the breakers of remembrance. The salty spume of angry waves slammed into him. The undertow of a forgotten life pulled him deeper and deeper down. Images blinked through his mind's eye faster than he could see them. He tried to catch them. He tried to hold on, but they were too fast, too slippery. He didn't know which images were real and which were figments of his tortured imagination. The last image was of Seridwyn and his children reaching down from above the tempest, reaching, stretching, trying to take hold. He pushed with every ounce of strength he had. His muscles ripped, his bones shifted under taut skin. His spine tore, and his ribs cracked. Still, he reached, but it wasn't enough.

"You remember," the stranger said.

Strakk was gulping for air that wouldn't come. He willed his lungs to work, but they were full already. He was hyperventilating and feared he would soon lose consciousness. Just as quickly as he had been ushered into the drowning depths of recollection, he was back in the present moment. The return was jarring. He was on his knees, head buried deep in his arms, and sobbing. He looked to the stranger, his face black with ash and streaked with tears. "What do you know?"

"I know that your children live. I know that they miss their mother," he paused for a moment, "and their father."

"No."

"Yes, Olanfar. They live, but they live in squalor. They live in poverty."

"No."

"They live in the Bairnbrand."

"No." Strakk's head fell to the dirt floor once again, and his sobs began anew. "No. No. No." His shoulders shook, and his voice cracked. "How can this be? How could I have forgotten?"

"You are not who or what you once were, Olanfar. Your body transformed, and also your mind and soul, your very flame, was deformed and corrupted." The stranger stepped across the threshold and approached Strakk, slowly, cautiously, and placed a hand on his trembling shoulder. "But not all that is damaged is lost. You remember."

Strakk looked to the stranger, eyes wet and wild with lament. "I cannot," he said. "I am a monster. I am a twisted and evil thing."

"Look at your hand, Olanfar."

Strakk held his hand to the candle. The flame hopped about nervously as his movements disturbed the air around it. His eyes went wide as he saw not his tri-hook, grotesque and stained, barbed and bloody, but instead he saw his right hand, whole and without blemish. He moved his fingers gingerly, wriggling them. He opened and closed his hand and turned it to different angles in the light. It was not his darkling hand. It was not marred and knotted. There was no fur or claw. It was a human hand. It was *his* human hand, devoid of any metal or bolts or hooks.

"How?"

"Like I said, you are not lost, not nearly." The stranger removed his hand from Strakk's shoulder and returned the way he had come. "Do this for me, Olanfar, and I will make you whole. I will restore you to your old self, and you will be the man you once were. You will be the father you once were and could be again."

Strakk stood, pushing off his knee. He flinched in pain as the razors of his hooks bit into the flesh of his leg. He shot the stranger a look of pure contempt. "You betray me!"

"No. You will do my bidding. Then, and only then, will I restore you."

"I will do ..." Strakk leaned heavily on the old table, which shook and groaned under his weight. The candle flickered and threatened to go out. "... whatever you would have me do."

"I know," the stranger replied. "Your invitation is on the table, as is the prince's gift. I will meet you there and give you further instructions." With that, the stranger left, disappearing into the night.

"Wait," Strakk called out. "What do I call you?"

"You may call me Atamas."

The invitation, the same one the first stranger had held out to him hours before, appeared on the table. Next to it, a package appeared, small and slowly pulsating. Then there was a small box, black as the void, its surface covered in runes that pulsed like a dying heartbeat. Strakk's stomach twisted. He didn't need to be a scholar to recognize cursed magic. His fingers itched as he reached for the box. The dark wood was cold, impossibly cold. He stared at the box for long moments. He could run. He could disappear. No. His children. His children needed him. And he needed them. With a heavy sigh, Strakk took hold of the box. It was ice, the very breath of the Vintermarrow. He tucked the box into a pocket, its weight like a stone pressing against his ribs. Then, without another word, he turned toward Y'ssildria. Toward the prince. Toward the coronation. Toward whatever damnation awaited him.

WHERE FELL THE FROST

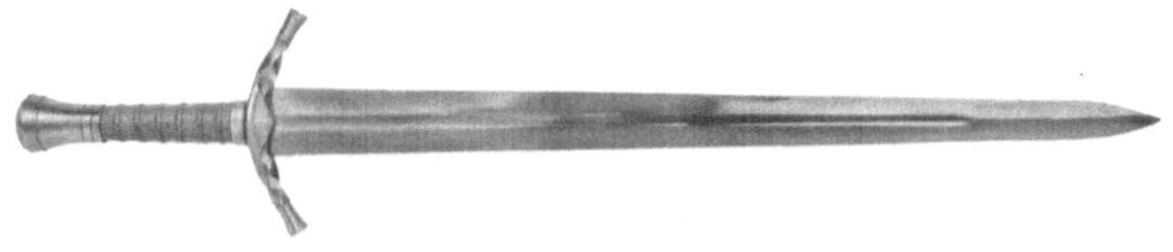

The wagon creaked and groaned as it rolled along the uneven ground. The two mules, Murrow and Bitter by name, snorted in irritation as they pulled their burden over the foothills of the Crown. The explosion had scorched the land, leaving patches of charred earth and shattered stone strewn across the narrow paths, making it a difficult trek for the beasts and wagon both. The wagon was covered with a purple pokebonnett that whipped about in the volatile winds created by the cold, northern climate of the Arcene Mountain Range and the warmer breeze of the Wilds to the south. It was fixed to the wagon with golden tassels tied through iron grommets along the frame that peaked to preformed bows, giving the wagon a regal acme. The hand-stitched likeness of two short, fat, and balding men embracing and raising frothing mugs was embroidered on the front-facing portion of the fabric with the words, *The Brothers Rand: Bobbles, Gallipots, Thumblejacks, and Fixsmiths*. The wagon's contents rattled and clanked as the well-worn wheels hiccupped and bounced over pebbles and into divots that pocked the road.

"Well," Feste said, scratching at his unshaven jaw, causing flakes and leftovers of yesterday's breakfast to crumble out and settle on his generous belly. "That ain't somethin' you see every day."

"Sure ain't," Cante agreed, taking a charitable bite of chewing tobacco from a hard-packed brick. "Think that was natural?"

Feste turned his head back to the mountains. The outline of a giant mushroom cloud could still be seen as an echo, even the morning after. Whole crags and peaks still glowed a fiery red in the distance, like embers from a blazing fire. Reverberations of the destruction had followed them down from the Crown and could still be felt in the slight tremors beneath their wagon. "Dunno. It might'a been a dragon. It might be an omen."

Cante nodded his agreement. "Might be both."

The brothers sat in silence, digesting that profoundly terrifying thought.

Then, after a long, contemplative chew, Cante spat and said, "Think we oughta check on her?"

The Rand brothers had not expected to find anyone alive when they came upon the rubble of the avalanche, but they had found Aoife. The woman had been barely breathing, her skin ghostly pale, her clothing burned away to smoking threads. Blood had soaked into the ground around her, and if she had spoken when they first found her, neither of them had heard it. Her flesh was torn, and though they were not physicians, they knew that many of her bones were splintered and broken. They had done what any well-meaning, questionably competent men would do. They bandaged her up the best they could and loaded her into the back of their wagon.

The wagon lurched violently then as both men turned to look at their unconscious passenger, Cante temporarily forgetting that he held the reins. "Whoa, whoa there," he shouted as he pulled tight on the leather straps. "Whoooaaaa!"

"Cante, you darned fool, you nearly threw the young lass out the back!"

The wagon tottered to a stop. Both brothers leaped from their seats and hurried to the back of the wagon. The sun had risen, but black smoke from the mountains had followed them down and seemed to be settling heavily across the plains, casting shadows amid the spears of light. Tall green grass that grew in thick tufts whipped at their ankles. They were low in the piedmont, surrounded by miles and miles of open field.

They each took a cane bolt and slid it clear of the brackets to each side of the wagon's tailgate. The gate dropped heavily and swung below the wagon from sturdy iron hinges. On the inner side of the swinging gate was a set of rungs attached to chain links and fixed with bolts. Feste loosed the small pin holding the ladder, and it spilled down, the slack collecting in a neat pool at their feet. The wagon wasn't particularly large or tall, it was pulled by mules, after all, but the Rands were not significant men. They were short, almost half-men, and thus they had to work in certain contrivances to accommodate their stature.

One after the other, they hoisted themselves up the ladder and into the wagon. The woman lay there between shelves, cabinets, and chests, all secured firmly to the wagon by straps and bolts, locked up tight and secure with deadbolts and cipher locks. They had made do with what was available to them to give her the most comfortable ride possible. Both men had emptied their chests of clothing, blankets, and pillows and piled them high on the wagon floor. They had encircled her body with pillows, elevating her head, arms, and legs, and they had covered her with light sheets, so as not to overwhelm her in her fever. It had only been a few hours since they had started from where they'd found her, but it already looked like some of the color was returning to her, and though the sheets were soaked through, her brow no longer glistened with sweat.

"Flame and feather," she moaned, taking a slow and careful stretch, "Must you hit every damned hole in the road?"

Feste and Cante startled. They hadn't realized that she was awake.

"Now, lady," Feste said, removing his wide-brimmed straw hat and bowing so low that his nose left a slight swoosh in the dust of the wagon's floor. "If we avoided all the holes, we'd never get where we're going!"

Cante, who stood beside Feste, quickly followed suit, removed his matching hat, and bowing low, though he drew up short, having seen the dark smudge on his brother's nose. "Sometimes, you just gotta let the road take ya where it will, dear lady."

"And it seems that this bumpy and holey road took us to you," Feste added. "And now it's taking us to Y'ssildria!"

"We are the brothers Rand," Cante said as he pointed his straw hat toward his brother. "This is Feste, and I am Cante. And we are at your service." They both bowed again and swept their hats out wide in a well-rehearsed routine.

She stifled a painful laugh as she took in the pair. Their bows were elegant and courtly, yet their clothing and demeanor betrayed their station. Not to mention that royalty would never be caught dead in such a common wagon or on such a common road. Aoife closed her eyes and exhaled sharply, lowering her head back to the nest of pillows.

"I am Aoife," she said at last, eyes still closed. "It is a pleasure to meet you." She looked at them again, lifting herself to her elbows. "And thank you. For saving me."

"It is and was our greatest pleasure, Lady Aoife," Feste said.

"Aoife is fine, master Feste. I am no lady of the court, and am of no higher station than yourselves."

"You may not be courtly, miss, but you are surely a lady, and as long as you remain in our care, you are *our* lady."

"Lady Aoife of," Cante said, but did not finish. "Where are you from, my lady?"

"Ha! Oh..." This time, Aoife could not suppress her laugh. She cringed and sucked in air that stung her. She held her side softly. Her ribs were tender to the touch, and she felt like she had taken a kick from a warhorse. "I am from very, very far away, master Cante."

"Are you from Myrr Caelun, lady?"

"No. No, not that far," she paused for a moment, her eyebrows furrowing. "Or maybe further still. I, I don't quite recall at the moment, kind Cante. But I know that it is far away, indeed."

The brothers exchanged glances.

"Well then," Cante said. "Lady Aoife of Further Still or Not Quite So Far as That, we welcome you to ride with us as we make our way to the capital city of Y'ssildria, where we will celebrate Prince Endryll's anointing and also his wedding to the lovely Lady Illia-Dara. There will be dancing and drinking aplenty, and enough merriment to mend all your aches and pains!"

"And we can find you a proper healer," Feste added with a wink. "If the alcohol and dancing don't do the trick."

"Well," Aoife said with another painful laugh, "while I'm not sure that I'm quite up for imbibing and frolicking about, a healer sounds divine. I accept your invitation, masters Rand, and I thank you again for your hospitality." She moved the sheets to one side and started to rise. "But now I must stand and stretch. I am slowly turning into a board, lying here so stiff and cramped."

Two yelps, high and loud, caused Aoife to pause mid-movement. Both brothers were backing away, clumsily feeling for the gate and ladder behind them with one hand, the other was holding their hats flat against blushing faces. Feste knocked over a box of glass bottles with his blindly flailing elbow and sent the elixirs crashing to the floor to shatter and spill between the cracks of the wood planking. Cante fell backward out of the wagon and landed hard on his rump into the field below with a whoop of air and a groan. Feste didn't hesitate. He leaped out after his brother. He landed on his feet, but so short and stocky were his legs, that he still wound up in an awkward somersault ending with him on his backside, feet resting on Cante's stomach. Both still held one hand tight to their hats, which were still pressed firmly against their faces.

"What on earth are you silly little men on about?" Aoife asked as she bent through the rear of the wagon to look at them.

"You are near naked, Lady!" It was Cante who spoke. The brothers had covered Aoife with a sheet quickly and blindly when they had found her and had administered aid to her with carefully averted eyes. Both had loving wives back in Thimbleglean Vale and many young children between them. They had not let their eyes wander out of respect for the unconscious woman and the vows that they had made. It made for tedious work and more than a few guesses as to where and how to apply the salves and bandages, but it had worked out in the end, Aoife's honor and the brothers' consciouses intact.

"I am not!" Aoife protested with a giggle. "I borrowed some of your clothes when you two were drifting off to sleep and running this wagon into every pothole in Y'ssara! Now get up before the eagles mistake you for a pair of flipped turtles that can't right themselves and try to carry you off."

"Eagles," Cante exclaimed, shoving his brother's legs off and climbing to his feet. "Where?" He was looking up, scanning the sky. His hat was still blocking his view of Aoife.

Feste rose as well. "There are no eagles, brother," he said. "The lady was just having a little fun at our expense." He looked at Aoife. She was clothed in a clean white button-down shirt. It would have been too scandalous to wear alone, except that it was fitted for the brothers specifically and had been let out to allow for their ample guts. As it was, it hung to just below Aoife's knees and looked more like a sleeping gown than a shirt. The shirt covered her arms, exposing only the lower parts of her legs and bare feet. Her legs were scarred and bruised, though the wounds were paler in shade and less angry than they had been the previous night. "She is covered, Cante," he said. "And she appears to be healing quite well."

"I'll say," Cante replied. He had ventured a wary look and, once determined that it was okay to open his eyes, could plainly see that Aoife had healed weeks' worth in a matter of hours. "How?" he asked. "How are you even standing?"

It felt good to be sitting in the driver's box. It was cramped, as there was a Rand to either side of her, but still, it was better than lying on her back and getting tossed around like loose baggage. Her hair was unrestrained and without braid or barrette. It waved freely behind her, brilliant streamers of copper and rose clashing and beating against the royal purple of the wagon cover. She smiled as she brushed away Feste's beard from her face. The brothers had little more than wisps on their shining skulls, but their beards were full and long and caught the wind in much the same way her hair did. She liked the Rands, Cante and Feste both. They were honest. They were oddly capable and fiercely loyal. She had learned this more from how their eyes shone with pride and their chest swelled with passion as they told her of their families back home than the actual stories they shared. And she liked how they called her *Lady*. It had been a long time since she had been anything but a warrior, anything more than a weapon.

"Feelin' better, are ya?" Feste stole a glimpse at Aoife out of his peripheral and noticed her smile.

"Much better," she replied as she flung her arms out wide and threw her head back, making herself a bigger target for the southern breeze, reveling in the caress of warmth that washed over her.

Cante chuckled. "I still don't know how you went from within an inch of Y'sa's glorious halls to riding up here with such a smile on your face that all of Y'ssildria will know we're coming, what with all them pearly whites bouncing the sun back at 'em."

She brought her hands close to her again. Her smile faded, though not completely. She shook her head. "I am sure some already know that I'm coming," she said softly.

"What do you mean?"

Aoife didn't reply. Her gaze was far off and wandering. She had beaten Baelgorak, the Black Flame Unbound. She had survived the calamity of pure impartial destruction when she called down the comet from the heavens. She had seen many battles and faced many enemies—man, monster, and demon all. She had even survived a night in the back of a ruddy wagon led by a team of sassy mules and their blind drivers. Still, her heart trembled, anxious and fearful, for what awaited her in Y'ssildria.

"Lady Aoife?"

"Hmmm?"

Cante looked across her to Feste and raised a bushy and twisted eyebrow, the follicles pointing this way and that, all seeming quite as confused as he was.

Aoife shook her head as if clearing her thoughts. "I'm sorry," she said. "I was just thinking."

"Looked more like you were worrying to me," Feste pointed out, his voice carrying a soft tiptoe of a lilt.

"No. I'm fine. I'm fine." Her stomach growled then. She held it and rocked back to push it out as far as she could, though she couldn't come close to reaching the extent of her new friends' round bellies. "I'm fine and I'm hungry! Do you think we could stop soon for a bite to eat?"

Cante threw the handbrake forward and pulled back on the reins so quickly that all three rocked forward. Murrow and Bitter huffed and kicked at the abrupt halt, tossing sidelong glances back at their driver. "Oh, calm yourselves down, you ungrateful, miserable asses," Cante chided. "You know you'll be eating, too." He hung the reins on an iron spring ring affixed to the nearest upright tang of the wagon's frame. He wrapped it around three times and yanked it tight. "Sorry for the sharp stop," he said to the others, "but I've been waiting hours for someone else to bring up lunch!"

Aoife laughed, despite her annoyance at being jostled about. "You'd think I'd be used to your driving by now, Master Rand, seeing as I received the same treatment in the back of your wagon."

"It's not me, my lady," Cante said in defense. "It's these blasted mules! They're loyal to a fault, but ornery as..." he thought for a moment, "ornery as asses!" He harrumphed then, quite pleased with himself, and stepped off the riding bench to retrieve two feeding sacks from a side compartment next to the front wheel. "These two put themselves in front of me and my brother when our fire died out, and the wolves got a bit too curious just a few nights back." He patted Murrow's behind as he reached the front axle where the two were harnessed. "They kicked and screamed and sent those wolfies howling back to their den so quick they didn't know what hit 'em." He scratched at Bitter's ears, which had perked up and twitched as Cante told the story of their heroics. "Isn't that right, you stupid, ornery, lovable, wonderful ass?" He kissed them both on the snouts, unlatched the yolk, and snapped their feeding bags in place.

Feste emerged from behind the wagon with a large, checkered quilt, a basket, and a bottle of wine. "They were part of a deal gone bad," he said, flicking the quilt out wide. It caught the wind and unfolded easily. He then lowered it and, standing on one corner, reached around to find sufficiently-sized rocks and placed them on the four corners, his being last.

"Or a deal gone right," Cante corrected from within the wagon. He came out moments later with three narrow, fluted glasses and a cutting board.

"Right, right," Feste nodded. "Point is, they weren't ours, and then they were, and now they won't leave."

Cante grinned. "I think they like us."

Aoife dropped easily from the high bench, foregoing the steps and landing gracefully in the tall grass. "Have you considered that they hate you and simply wish to torment you until your deaths and that those wolves were trying to steal the kill that they are plotting?"

Feste tilted his head toward the sun. "That *is* a real possibility," he said with a chuckle.

"Absolutely," Cante agreed. "That'd explain a lot."

"Well, could you please tell them that I am not part of this traveling circus and would be quite content to stay out of whatever dastardly plans they have for you both?" Aoife smiled as she joined the brothers on the cloth.

"Oh, that wouldn't do any good, lady," Feste said as he drew a slender dagger from his belt and began cutting fruits and cheese on the board. "I'm afraid they just don't listen to us."

The Crownfields stretched all around them, a vast and lush land dotted with verdure of every species, and often creating new hybrids as natural seeding and pollination ran their course over the years. All manner of wildlife made their homes here. The stag and hind, creatures vulpine in nature, coney and nutkin, and even the elusive shadewright and dawnstalker all found ample resources and refuge in the Crownfields' many forests, lakes, and streams along the northern road to Y'ssildria. Once called the Gloamway, now simply referred to as The Old King's Highway, this was the most well-kept northern road leading from Y'ssildria to the infinite stretches of Y'ssara. It was long and could be dangerous, but it was regularly patrolled and traveled.

The spires of the capital rose in the distance, gleaming beneath the sun. Beyond that, the Serrated Sea sprawled out in infinite white-capped waves. The hills rose gently against the shimmering sky, the grass licking around them as the sea winds carried salt and brine from far, far south. From this height, Y'ssildria was a master artist's opus painting, her banners lashing against the battlements in a green and gold flurry. No one knew what, if anything, lay beyond the sea. Expeditions had once been commissioned regularly and never suffered from a lack of enthusiastic volunteers or supporters, at least in the early, burgeoning years of the great city. But that soon changed as none of the expeditions ever returned. The entire city would gather on the docks below the Stoneguard in anticipation of their loved ones' return, but cheers and calls of welcome would ever turn into songs of lament and sorrow as the sun set, leaving the harbor still and empty.

The three travelers sat in silence, their lunch and wine consumed. Murrow and Bitter had been brushed down and led to a stream to soak and drink, their bridles loosened. It was a silence of contemplation, easy and calm, but swollen with things unnamed and unseen, heavy as the hush before a breaking storm. Cante and Feste sat cross-legged a few paces from Aoife. The quiet hung over them—not the easy quiet of friends at rest, but something more profound, older, as if the land itself was holding its breath.

"Feste can carry a fine tune," Cante blurted out, shattering the silence like a ball peen hammer to a sheet of crystal.

The others stirred, brought out of their reverie by Cante's proclamation. Aoife twisted at the waist and leaned on one arm to see the little man better, adjusting her hair to the other shoulder and out of her eyes, amusement clear on her porcelain face. Feste stared daggers at his brother, his mouth pinched, and brows creased in low arcs. Neither of them said a word.

"If we're needing something to fill the quiet," Cante said quickly, his face reddening as he spoke, "He could … er … he might be willing to sing a bit, if you'd like."

He realized too late that the words had come out far louder than intended, ricocheting off the peaceful slopes and rolling hills like a war horn. His ears burned, matching the deepening shades crawling up his cheeks, first a bashful pink, then a more determined red, until at last he was flushed so violently that he looked like he had taken a fever. He tugged at the collar of his tunic as if loosening the threadbare cloth might staunch the flood of color racing across his face and neck. He gave an awkward cough and glanced between them, his eyes begging for some form of rescue.

For a moment, no one spoke. Aoife merely smiled into her sleeve. Feste closed his eyes, slowly and heavily, as if praying. Cante cleared his throat again, another useless effort to reclaim his lost dignity, and muttered, "Or, or we can just go back to staring at the grass, if that's preferred."

Aoife set her gaze back out across the wild plains toward the gleaming city beyond, her soft features hardened by memories. Her eyes, usually so bright, had grown misted and distant. Feste blinked moisture into his dry eyes caused by the humidity of a southern zephyr. His lips parted, but no words came, and he closed them again, bowing his head. His thumb worried the frayed hem of his cloak. Cante, somber as his brother, peeled apart the husk of a rushreed he had plucked while seeing to the mules near the stream, the soft, white seeds floating away around them.

It was Aoife who broke the next silence, not with words, but with song. Her voice was an innuendo, soft and delicate, threading through the serenity like a needle through fabric. No bard's flourish, no lavish performance, just her voice, raw and clear, bearing a grief older than memory.

Where fell the frost, no roses grow,
The wind blows soft through flesh and bone.
The crown was lost in hoarfrost's hold,
The First Light's flame left alone.

The words drifted, almost too fragile for the air, much like the rushreed seeds, yet they remained. Cante lifted his head. Feste stilled. They knew the melody.

She sang *Where Fell the Frost*, an ode to Queen Cerceia, known to few and reserved for fewer still. The aria, old and worn and achingly familiar, was the ancient tune of *O'er Seydra's Starlit Barrow*, a ballad once sung around hearths and on lovers' partings, its origin lost to time. But in times of deepest sorrow, it was this melody that bore the words of lamentation, words murmured over the dead, sung for kings and queens and the light of all things lost. It was the melody sung of old, at the harbor and in many other times and many other occasions where words alone were not enough.

No harp may play, no horn may call,
Where silent cries wear a name.
We bury her light beneath the hill—
And still, the dark remains.

Aoife's voice did not waver. Her hands, resting on her knees, tightened slightly, as though holding back tremors that had little to do with the evening air. Her knuckles whitened and her spine stiffened. The Rand brothers listened, silent save for the hitching of their breath.

Most in Y'ssildria knew only the first verse of this version, written in the shadow of the Queen's passing and sung in broad mourning when anniversary bells tolled. But Aoife knew the older verse, the secret one, sung only by the royal line, or by those who had stood closest to the First Light's pyre. Soft as falling snow, she sang it.

The silver road remembers her tread,
Y'sa's gates we dare not close.
Her cloak still stirs in ancient halls,
Where no moonlight or star now goes.

A long moment stretched after the last note fled into the fields, chasing invisible wisps of current. It seemed that this somber time of song had ended. And then Feste began, a harsh baritone against Aoife's tenor, as he gave the refrain its due:

O let her name be carried low,
Where none may speak, yet all must know.
O let her flame forever more,
Where none may speak, yet all must know.

When he finished, all was utterly still. No bird called. No breeze stirred, and without the breeze, even the grass seemed to bow its head. Cante's face was streaked with tears he made no effort to hide. His chest rose and fell in uneven breaths, his broad shoulders trembling. Feste sat with both hands over his mouth, his body shaking with silent sobs, the kind that come not from the mind, but from somewhere deeper within, from the marrow, from the soul. Neither brother spoke. There was nothing to say. Only the sound of their weeping, and beyond it, the slow, inexorable hush of the waning light.

Aoife sat still, her hands resting quietly in her lap, her eyes tracing the thin golden thread of the distant city's fading lights. She did not weep. She dared not. For if she gave herself to sadness, she feared she would never find her way back. Instead, she closed her eyes against the sting behind them and bowed her head, carrying their grief and her own like a secret torch cupped close against the dark. Soon enough, she feared, they would have grief aplenty.

THE STORMS OF PORTION

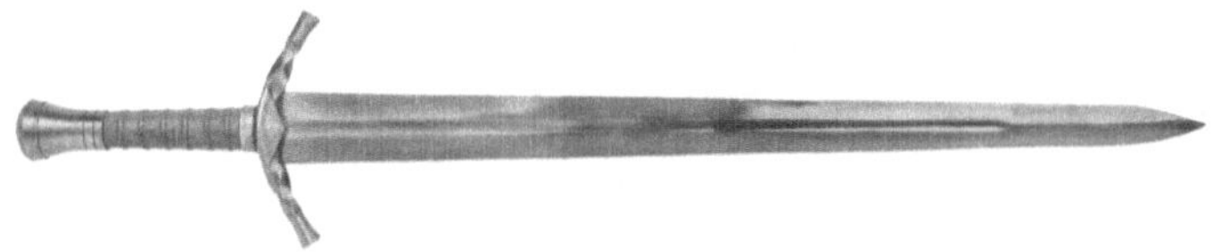

"Well," Endryll muttered, gripping the edge of the short stone wall, "there's no turning back now." It was warm to his touch, even though the sun had set hours ago. The balcony was narrow but elegant, crowned with wrought-iron filigree sprouting up from the smooth stone and overgrown with trailing moonvine, its blossoms already beginning to open to the night. He stood high above the city, overlooking his kingdom from the terrace of his rooms, which faced south and took in the warmest parts of the day. The high grounds of the Sunspire Citadel had always been a place of solitude, of respite, a place to stand above the world and watch it move and breathe and thrive. He'd always felt connected to the people of Y'ssildria, yet never one of them. How could he be one of them when he had never endured their struggles, ploughed their fields, or toiled for hours on end, day in and day out, to sustain their simple lives? He felt he was a part of Y'ssildria, but not a part of her being. He was an adornment, a shining stone fixed to a silver chain swinging lazily from her neck, or a fanciful hat embellished with silks and plumage. He was a part of what made Y'ssildria, but he was not a part of her body. He was a final corner piece to the puzzle, to be sure, he helped complete the whole, but brought no genuine intrinsic value, save for filling an unnecessary and largely ceremonial role. "That all changes tomorrow," he said to himself.

"What changes tomorrow, my love?"

Endryll started and turned to see his bride gliding toward him across the tiger-striped marble floors of his sitting room. Illi wore an evening dress of soft, single-cut, leaf-green silks. It swayed with her as she walked and clung as if it were a part of her. His smile widened as she approached. And how could it not? She was a shining opal in a quarry of rock, she was the warm roof and soft bed to the road-worn traveler, she was the lighthouse in the raging night sea, she was the rain from heaven to the desiccated lands in drought. She slipped her arm through the curve of his and covered his hand with hers. She interwove their fingers and felt the warm stone beneath. They were a perfectly natural fit as they looked over the city. The high parapets gave them a magnificent view of the kingdom's splendor, of banners and flags catching the wind, of nobles and emissaries flooding through the golden and guarded gates, of merchant ships cutting through the Serrated Sea toward the harbor.

"Good evening," Endryll said as he kissed her head. He lingered there, taking in the scent of her. She smelled of wild heather, of sun-warmed petals and the silvered mist of meadows at dawn. There was a trace of sea salt, faint and clean. It was like distant tides hidden beneath fields of green. Her hair carried the memory of the day's sunlight, of laughter chased through hills, and of firsts—first rains, first loves, and first steps of dawn when the world was young. It was a scent that unraveled him, and he could no more resist breathing her in than he could will his own heart to stop beating.

"Good evening, husband," she replied, rolling her neck and exhaling softly. "What troubles you?"

He laughed and rested his cheek where his lips had been as she lay her head against his shoulder. "Oh, darling, nothing now. Nothing at all."

"It couldn't be that tomorrow instead of going away on your honeymoon, you're being crowned king, and you have to have a fake wedding, and waste the day away accepting lavish gifts and praises from all your adoring subjects, would it?" Ixchel clapped Endryll on the back as he approached the side opposite Illia-Dara and wrapped an arm around the prince. "It couldn't be that tomorrow all of this," he made a flat, semi-circular and sweeping motion with his other hand, indicating the majestic city and beyond, "will be yours, could it?" His smile was wide and innocent, his tousled hair just as untamed as it always was, tickling Endryll's ear.

"That could have something to do with it."

"It wouldn't have anything to do with the fact that you are grossly underprepared for taking on the most thriving metropolis this side of the Western Wood, or that you will never, under any circumstances, ever measure up to King Ondine in their eyes?" He squeezed Endryll's shoulder then, and added, "I'm just playing around! Ouch! I said I was kidding," when he felt sharp nails pinch the flesh of his ribs and twist hard. "I said I was kidding," he screamed as he tried to get out of the headlock Endryll had put him in and the death grip that Illi currently had on his side.

"You are an evil, wicked little thing, Ixchel Osvaldo," Illi said through a concealed laugh as she continued her snakebite-like hold. "I will be telling Stren about you and your foolish talk first thing tomorrow!"

"I said I was kidd—"

"There will be no tomorrow for this wretch," Endryll grunted as he grabbed hold of Ixchel's pants in a hurried clump of fabric and flesh and hoisted him high over his shoulders, his other hand a vice grip around his neck. Ixchel choked out a startled cry as he went parallel to the ground far below. Endryll made a few faux tosses, swinging him from side to side, threatening to launch him over the balcony wall. "I don't need subjects like this one!"

Illia-Dara gasped, made a noise halfway between a laugh and a scream, and disappeared into the tower at a sprint. The slapping of her bare feet could be heard across the marble, even over the boys' tussle. She reappeared moments later holding a broomstick and playfully swinging at Ixchel, not hard enough to injure, but hard enough to cause light bruising.

"I'm sorry," he cried. "I'm sorry! You're twice the—ouch!—man your father will ever be! Pleeaasssee, put me—OUCH!—down!"

Endryll set Ixchel down gently and then placed his hands on his own knees. He breathed heavily, his bare chest red from exertion, but his smile was wide and true. Ixchel fell to the ground in an exaggerated collapse, the backside of one hand going to his forehead while the other absorbed the impact of the fall. Illi ran to them then. Ixchel straightened and gave her a most pitiful groan, his face set in grimaced agony. She cast the broom handle at him and embraced Endryll in a wide hug. The broom handle clattered to the ground, but not before striking Ixchel sidelong across the face.

"Ow!"

"It serves you right," Illia said, looking over her husband in mock concern. Her hands slid from his face to his shoulders, trying to find wounds that were not there. "Not only do you insult my husband on the eve of his coronation, but you attack him as well?"

"He attacked me," Ixchel protested, leaping to his feet and brushing off his mangled pants. "I, for one, do not desire a king who cannot tame his temper." He paused, as if considering his next words. "Your father would never have behaved so childishly!"

"Childishly?" Endryll and Illia all but shouted together.

"You're the one who—" Endryll began, but was interrupted.

"It was a joke," Ixchel said with a laugh. He was backing away from the couple, his hands patting the air as if playing a children's clapping game alone. "I was joking, brother! You know I believe you will be the greatest king Y'ssildria has ever known. You will be the greatest king Y'ssara has ever known!" Once safely inside the sitting rooms and far away from his friends, he lowered his placating hands. "Besides, I burn hot with a hundred roaring infernos of jealousy over your crowning."

He sat on an ottoman near the terrace doors and sank deeply into the Calidene velvet of the down-stuffed cushions. "I should be king," he continued, lifting his shirt over his head. "I would be a marvelous ruler." He hung his shirt over the end table that butted against the ottoman. It was made of oak and lacquered to a near-reflective sheen. Its arced and beveled legs were inlaid with brass buttons and thick, polished iron bands. His common cotton shirt of muted fawn looked very out of place resting atop it. Of course, he looked quite out of place, too, next to his elegant and regal friends.

The room, made for sitting and sipping and quiet conversations, was more furnished than his and Stren's entire house. There were matching ottomans like the one he occupied, taller and larger versions that could sit three or four, upholstered in the same emerald Calidene velvet and stitched with silver thread so fine that it shimmered like spider silk. The couches and chairs formed a crescent around a low-burning hearth inset into the wall, where scented logs of ocean-borne driftwood crackled gently, releasing a soft fragrance of the sea that was so integral a part of Y'ssildrian life. The hearth was the visage of a screaming griffon's head, expertly crafted of pewter. The curved beak stretched wide as it broke out from the wall and seemed to swallow the flames burning within. Such detail was carved into the image so that one could count the individual feathers starting from the comb and moving down the head to where the bust melted into the wall. Above the mantle hung a triptych of painted panels, each depicting a different season over the city of Y'ssildria, one in bloom, one in snow, one in golden autumn fire, all viewed from the same vantage point, high in the Crownfields.

The marble floor was almost entirely hidden beneath an expansive hand-woven rug from the mystic weavers of northern Tassarith, dyed in sunset hues and braided so densely that Ixchel doubted even time could unravel it. Along the far wall, an etched bookcase made of torch-burned cedar held precisely placed volumes of histories, epics, poems, and treaties, none of which looked as if they'd ever been opened. Between its shelves sat ornamental hourglasses, crystal orbs, and half-burned candles of milky white.

The ceiling arched high above, coffered and painted in sapphire blue with pinpricks of gold leaf shaped like constellations of the twelve Prophets of Y'sa, not the ones in the sky above, but the legendary ones from the old stories, handed down in verse and song. And to Ixchel's right, just beyond the terrace doors, the city stretched out in grades of flickering torchlight. He looked down at himself, bare-chested, dusty, and with many welts beginning to pock his alabaster skin in angry red marks, and chuckled. "Yes," he muttered, glancing around at the lavish room, "I'd make a magnificent king."

"You'd make a magnificent trophy to be hung in my halls," Endryll snarked as he and Illia entered, hand in hand, "and nothing more."

"I would not," he objected. "I'm far too pretty to be hung on these vanglorious walls. If you were to mount me anywhere, it would be the great courtroom, where all the peasants and peons would wither under my accusatory gaze as they grovel for mercy!"

"Ha!" Endryll barked. He released Illia's hand and dashed toward Ixchel but was slowed by Illia wrapping her arms around his waist. Ixchel rose and scampered away, jumping to stand on the couch across the room. He bent low, arms outstretched and ready for the incoming assault.

"Enough, you two," she ordered, and though she had planted her feet and thrown her weight opposite Endryll's, she was still dragged a few paces across the floor. "I'll not have my lover's face tarnished and bruised at his coronation tomorrow. And I won't have my dearest friend beaten to within an inch of his life and miss the whole thing!"

Endryll stopped short, and Illia skittered to a stop, bumping into his back. Ixchel lowered his arms to rest on his waist and stood straight, a comically heroic pose, as he was shirtless and splotched.

"True enough, my love," Endryll said. "About the latter, at least." He hung an arm around her and kissed her lightly on the cheek. "Though I doubt I would come away with so much as a scratch should we ever come to blows. Isn't that right, Ixchel?"

"First off," Ixchel said as he sprawled across the couch, kicking his boots off before resting his feet. "While our games often involve a bit of rough-housing, I don't see us ever taking it much further than that." He bowed slightly to Endryll's nod of agreement. "However," he said, raising a finger to trace the constellations in the ceiling. "I happened to have bested my master in a battle of magics early yesterday in the gardens." He looked to his friends expectantly and was disappointed in their expressions.

While he was anticipating looks of shock and awe and maybe even admiration, what he saw instead was skepticism and pity. "I'm not lying!" He bolted to a sitting position and continued, "I beat Stren in the gardens! I found my flame!"

"Ixchel," Illia-Dara said, "you can hardly manage a simple conjuration of smoke or cause a sapling to leaf. You honestly expect us to believe that you beat Stren in magics that he has known and mastered over decades?" She leaned forward with her elbows on her knees, her hands flat against each other, and pointed toward him. "I know that you don't truly harbor any jealousy toward Endryll, but I think that maybe you are feeling a little left out or underappreciated in the wake of all that is happening."

Ixchel flushed and adjusted his position, equally uncomfortable with the former comment on his lack of jealousy as with the latter on the reasons for his story. But he remained silent. He could not interrupt her. Not now. For this moment in time, she was solely focused on him. It didn't matter that she didn't believe him. She would, in time. All that mattered to Ixchel was that right here, right now, was that their eyes were locked. He didn't have to steal a glance when Endryll wasn't looking. He didn't have to make an excuse when he was caught.

He didn't lust for her. He would never betray Endryll or Illia by acting on momentary impulses or desires, but he loved her. He couldn't deny that. She cared for him, too. He knew that. He cherished that knowledge and held it, locked it away in the most secure vaults of his heart.

"You know that we love you, and that no matter what happens, neither Endryll nor I will ever let you escape our lives." She tilted her head, the curtains of her hair shifting and falling in layers of softest frame around her face. "You know that, don't you?"

"I know," he replied, "but I beat him. He'll tell you." He recounted the morning with Stren in the gardens. He told them of the whipping vines, the colossal behemoth full of rage and horn, and the three Echoborn that came to his subconscious call. He told them everything, omitting no detail, small or large. When he finished, he realized he was standing and out of breath. He had somehow made his way across the room and now stood near the doors to the rest of the wing. He looked to his friends and was surprised to see their faces locked in stunned amazement. His face lit with pride, and he straightened, lifting his shoulders. "Well?"

"Why were you naked?" Endryll asked. Illia's mouth moved as if to ask her own question, but no words came out.

Ixchel deflated a bit, his shoulders slumping over. "Stren said it was the blaze of the Aetherfast," he answered. "He told me that in the future it shouldn't happen, but that my flame was so famished that it took to me a bit to eagerly."

"It *shouldn't* happen again?" Endryll was grinning widely. "But it *could*?"

"If you are picturing me naked, please stop," Ixchel snapped. "Is that all you're taking away from this?"

Illia blinked rapidly and shook her head, apparently drawn from her trance by the mention of Ixchel's nudity. "You *beat* him?"

Ixchel nodded slowly.

"How?"

"Illi, who cares how? He was *naked*!"

"Stop it," she said, slapping Endryll's arm. "Ixchel, how?"

"I honestly don't know," he said as he walked over to where they sat on the ottoman he had first been sitting on. He pulled over a three-legged stool from near the hearth and sat in front of them. "Stren said that it had been welling up in me for a long time, a dam to bursting, and when he loosed his elephant on me, I just reacted."

"Could you do it again?" Endryll's voice was more earnest and somber than before.

"I think so. I can feel it inside me now." Ixchel shook his head and placed a hand to his chest. "I can't explain it, but it feels like a part of me. Like it'd be as natural as breathing."

"Show us," came the reply in unison. Both Endryll and Illi had eager smiles on their faces. They leaned forward, fully rapt and keen for a display. Ixchel was taken aback by this sudden shift. There was no mocking lift of the eyebrow, no tilt at the corner of their mouths, no taunt in their tone. Endryll brushed a hand through his wavy, sand-colored hair and moved forward in his seat. Illi gave a nod of encouragement. They were entirely and wholly his.

He closed his eyes and exhaled long, emptying his lungs and his mind. He concentrated, all conscious thought fading away. He imagined the Aetherfast. He saw the swirling storms of amethyst energy pulsing around and through him. He saw the black silhouettes of ancient statues and towers blur in and out of focus like a mirage. He imagined himself among the throngs of aetherbeasts, shadewrights and dawnstalkers and brindlequills. He felt his whole body tremor and shake, the reverberations from his visions bleeding into reality. His heart beat fast and faster still, his pulse thundering in his ears like a thousand naval cannons being fired one after the other in rapid succession. He brought his hands to his head and screamed a silent scream. And then he was gone.

"Ixchel," Illi ran to where Ixchel had been just a moment before. "Ixchel!"

"I'm here," he said from the balcony doors.

"No, I'm here," another Ixchel announced in a sing-song voice, as it straddled the griffon's head above the hearth.

"No, you silly prince! I'm over here," a third chimed in from behind Endryll. It was sitting on a bookshelf and swinging its feet.

Illia and Endryll whipped their heads this way and that as the Echoborn Ixchels disappeared and reappeared elsewhere around the room with declarations of, "I'm here!" and "No. Over here!" Illi found her way back to

Endryll and they held each other close, tracking the ghost-like images of their friend as they bounced about.

"Here I am."

"Over here!"

Finally, the last blinked away, and none more appeared.

"Where did he go?" Illi wondered, more to the room than to Endryll, for surely, he knew no better than she.

"Where did *they* go?" he added.

"I'm right here," Ixchel answered, his voice eerily similar to his Echoborn. His fingers were laced behind his head, his legs were crossed, and his feet rocked back and forth as he stretched out comfortably and lazily in a reclined position on the large couch. His smile practically oozed with satisfaction and pride. "I told you."

"I can't believe our little Ixchel is all grown up," Illi said, hours later, as they lounged around the hearth fire. She passed the bowl of grapes they had been sharing back to Ixchel as she spoke. It was made of glass and etched with many fine ghostly lines. "What does it feel like," she asked, "when you, well, how did you put it, cross over?"

"I don't know if that's the official name for it," Ixchel said, nodding his understanding. "I don't even know if there *is* a proper name for it, but that's the best way I have to describe it."

"So, you really just have to think about the Aetherfast, and then you're there?"

"What's it like?" Endryll interjected before Ixchel could answer Illi's question. "The Aetherfast, I mean."

Ixchel threw a few more grapes than necessary into his mouth and began to chew. He did this partially because he was famished after his demonstration, and partly because he was not happy to have been interrupted when conversing with Illia-Dara. This was the most attention she had given him since she and Endryll had wed, and he would take every bit of her attention she would offer. Endryll could wait until he was done chewing.

"Well," Illi said, waving her hands toward herself and prompting Ixchel along. "What's it like?"

"It's li–" Ixchel stopped suddenly and retrieved his shirt from the table, not to cover himself, but to catch the streams of juice and saliva that escaped from the sides of his mouth as he spoke. He swallowed, coughed, and wiped his mouth clean. "Sorry. It's like I'm already there," he continued. "The Aetherfast is all around us," he waved his arms about in large circles, indicating the entirety of the room. "Think of it like a second world, not on top or below ours, but *in* ours, or maybe ours is within it." The confused look they gave him had not changed. Their eyes were glazed over, and their faces were even and still.

"Ok," he said, ripping the bowl of grapes from Endryll's hand, ignoring his surprised protestations. "Say this bowl is the Aetherfast." He held it before them like a priceless artifact or a babe presented for christening. He then dumped the remaining grapes to the floor and lifted the pitcher of water that they had been using to refill their glasses. He poured the water into the bowl until it threatened to flow over the sides. He placed it on the end table, careful not to spill any. "The water is us, is this." Again, he waved his arms in wide circles. "Two different elements occupying the same space. They are singularly individual, but together they become one whole."

The two were silent for a moment, then Endryll said, "That's not a very good explanation. They are *not* occupying the same space. The water is occupying the space that the bowl creates."

"Exactly!" Ixchel slapped the floor hard with both hands and came to his knees excitedly. "I couldn't have said it better myself!"

"You didn't," Endryll started to say, but was hushed quickly by Illi.

"The Aetherfast is a shell," Ixchel said, ignoring him. "Or a rind. No, not a rind." He shook his head and pinched the bridge of his nose between his fingers. He stayed there for a long moment. Illia and Endryll exchanged looks, and Illi shrugged.

"I've got it!" Ixchel's shout caused them both to jump where they sat. He ran out of the sitting room and into an adjoining room off the main hall, opposite the balcony. There was a clatter of clays and ceramics and metals as dishes and cutlery crashed to the floor. He emerged from the kitchens holding a knife. The light from the many burning candles and the hearth fire caught the blade's edge and rode it from hilt to point.

"What are you doing with th—" Endryll began.

"No!" His question was cut short by Illi's shout, but it was too late.

Ixchel stood over the bowl of water, knife held in one hand. He had the look of a lunatic. His smile was all teeth, his eyes were wide, and his hair stood on end. In one fluid motion, he drew the knife across his palm, from top to bottom. He wrapped his hand around the blade and squeezed. The knife was sharp and the cut was clean. He didn't even feel it, not at first. Drops of dark, thick blood splashed into the water below, causing pink ripples to expand from their impact. Then, he freed his hand from the knife and squeezed. It was an unnatural amount of blood. It poured from his wound like stream waters over stones after a thaw. The drops and splashes turned into a continuous current. The blood dove below the surface and lingered in slow-motion movements, like dancers in a ballet. It curled and coiled in graceful spirals, ribbons of crimson unfurling through the clear waters like ink. Some of it clung to itself in thick strands, some stretched thin, translucent, and delicate, like silk unraveling in a tender breeze. The pink had deepened to red, the red to black, and still blood poured, pulsing outward in rhythm with his heartbeat, forming spires and sigils that seemed not to disperse but to *form*.

"Do you see it?" he asked.

Illia had covered her mouth with her hands and stood back from the two men. Endryll was still on the floor, but had crawled close to the bowl. He watched as blood mixed with water, his reflection a darker and streaked version of himself.

"Two elements occupying the same space!"

Endryll nodded dumbly, staring at the blood as it formed, reformed, and separated.

"Ixchel, tie off your hand," Illi said as she threw his shirt to him.

He caught it and opened his palm. The pain came then. It was hot and furious. The cut was much wider than he had meant it to be, and it continued to bleed. The flesh where the knife had cut was ghostly pale and peeling back, as if trying to get as far away, one side from the other, as it could. He tied the shirt around his hand. The wound burned and bit him. He looked at Illia-Dara. "Do you have a needle and gut?" he asked.

She rolled her eyes and let out an exasperated sigh. "Just sit there," she said, pointing to the nearest chair. "And don't get any blood on *anything*." She left toward the back rooms, where the bedrooms were.

"You get it, though, right?" he asked Endryll, leaning down to peer at him through the other side of the bowl.

Endryll recoiled as he looked up and was met with a round-faced and exaggerated liquid portrait of Ixchel swimming back at him. It didn't help that the liquid was quickly becoming translucent again, as the blood pooled near the bottom of the bowl.

"What about that?" he asked, pointing to the dark, pooling mass.

"I thought of that," Ixchel said excitedly. "You see, in the Aetherfast, the winds are always blowing and shifting. It's always moving!" He thrust his injured hand into the bowl and began to stir. The blood followed the motion of his fingers and was soon part of the same space once again. "See? The Aetherfast is always moving, it keeps the blood, us, moving with it until we become one with it!"

He stood and dried his hand on his leg. The olive color of his pants stained to a dark, black splotch where the water soaked in. Endryll stood to join him just as Illi entered, carrying a tack box and folds of clean white cloth. She stopped and took in the scene. Both men were standing shirtless around the bowl of still swirling bloody water. They were talking in hushed excitement and both smiling like children. They *were* children, she decided as she joined them.

"You're an idiot, Ixchel," she said. "Sit down and show me your hand."

He did as he was told, resuming his position on the couch. "But you *get* it right?"

"I do," she responded. "The whole of the Spire probably gets it, given how noisily you two were gabbing on about it." She took hold of his injured hand and unwrapped the bloody shirt to reveal a garish opening that stuck and pulled at the cloth as she removed it. He jerked his hand back instinctively, but she pulled it roughly toward herself and slapped him on the top of his head. "Don't move."

"What was that for?" he asked, blinking away the surprise.

"That was for slicing yourself open in my sitting room to prove a silly point." She wasn't looking at him. She was applying a cold liquid to his palm by way of a squeeze bulb. It was a single-molded ball made of eel bladder with a hollow extension on one side. The bulb could be squeezed and the nub submerged in liquid, then upon release of the bulb, the liquid would be sucked into the belly for later administration. She applied minimal pressure to the bulb with only her fingertips, and a milky substance dripped lethargically onto his palm and even directly into the gash. Ixchel squirmed and started to pull away, but froze immediately, as Illi fixed him with a scowl so fierce that he feared she would open the wound further just to teach him a lesson.

"What are you putting on it?" Endryll asked from over Illi's shoulder. "It smells almost sweet."

"Milk of moonthistle," Ixchel answered before Illia had a chance. "It is a healing agent that also draws out things like poison or dirt or infection. Though th—Ow!"

"Be quiet and hold still," Illia said, her head still bowed over Ixchel's hand, her brow furrowed in concentration. "Though the sweet smell is from mellisong leaf." Illi looked up at Ixchel, giving him a playful grin, knowing how much he loved showing off his herbalogics.

"It's the same leaf used in honey mead," Ixchel spat out quickly. "Mel means honey." He had just enough time to steal the end of the lesson from Illi and smile smugly back at her before she jabbed the hook needle into his flesh. Her eyes never left his.

"OW!"

It was well into the morning hours, and they were all well into their mellisong mead. Endryll had never sampled the sweet drink, so after Illi had finished her ministrations on Ixchel, he had suggested that he wake poor old Carvin, the night captain of the Citadel kitchens, to brew a few fresh pots of the liquor and bring it to them. They had even invited him in to join them in their debauchery, but he politely declined.

"You must stay, Carvin!" Endryll said, holding the door wide and stepping aside for the third time. "It won't be the same without you. And besides, this is the last time you'll ever be able to drink with me as a prince."

"I cannot, your majesty," he said, bowing. Carvin was an unassuming man with a humble posture. His white hair formed a semicircle around his otherwise naked head. He had removed his nightcap and was ringing it nervously in his hands. His sleeping robe was faded stripes of blues and grays. His slippers were the only evidence of his station. He wore soft leather shoes, conditioned and oiled to the texture of silk. Tufts of exotic and spotted furs poked out around his ankles. "The king would have my hide if I were anything besides perfectly on my point tomorrow for your majesty's coronation and ..." he looked to Illia-Dara standing behind her husband, looking more than a little embarrassed, "... and your wedding," he finished, bowing even lower.

"Ah, but there's where we find ourselves a loophole," Endryll said, raising his finger toward Carvin. "Tomorrow, I will be king! And I make my first royal decree to you, Sir Carvin, here and now, that you shall be free from all duties on the morrow so long as you imbibe with us tonight!"

Carvin's eyes went wide at Endryll's proclamation. He was silent for a moment, contemplating his options. Then he scanned the room. The two men were shirtless, and the wild one was splotchy and bruised, his hand wrapped in fresh gauze. Illia-Dara was wiping her red-stained hands on a bloody towel. There was torn gut splayed out along the floor, and what looked to be a fishbowl full of some clotted, crimson wine in the middle of it all.

"I fear I must retire," he said, slowly backing away from the open door and down the hall. "If there's nothing else, sire?"

"Oh, go on, then," Endryll said, disappointment heavy in his voice. "I shall just have to drink your portion as well." He waved Carvin away and shut the door behind him.

"Goodnight, young prince," Carvin said through the closed door. "And to you, Lady Illia-Dara."

That had been two hours and many, many drinks ago.

"It's too bad old Carvin couldn't join us," Endryll said. "I've always liked that little man."

"You're lucky he didn't tell your father," Illi replied. "Can you imagine what this must have looked like to him?"

"A good time?" Ixchel offered, his head lolling as he closed his eyes.

"Ha!" Endryll chortled. "The best of times, with the best of friends." He lifted his cup high, and the other two met it with their own. They had moved to the kitchen and sat across from each other at a small stone-topped table, jars of millisong mead, two of them empty, acted as the centerpiece.

"Cheers," rang the chorus as the cups clinked together.

"I am proud of you, Ixchel," Illia said, her voice taking on a more somber, though not sober, note. "It is no small feat what you have done, and I know that you will only grow in your command over it." She leaned in her chair, arching her back and stretching her shoulders. The chair's back groaned under the movement. "Imagine that an orphan would grow up to be a queen." She leaned forward and reached out to Endryll and to Ixchel and clasped their hands, one in each. "That my husband would be the finest swordsman in all of Y'ssildria and my dearest friend would become a most powerful sorcerer."

Endryll took Ixchel's free hand in his, completing the circle. "Together," he said, "we will rule this kingdom."

"You will rule this kingdom," Ixchel said, all mirth and drunkenness missing from his face. "You will stand tall as king of Y'ssildria." He looked at Illi and squeezed her hand. "And you will guide him with all the wisdom, strength, and patience that made him love you. Your people will love you, and they will follow you." He looked to each of them in turn. "And I will protect you. On my life, I will never fail you. As Stren was to King Onidine and Queen Cerceia, so I pledge now I will be to you." He stood then, and said, "My strength is your shield, my breath, your barrier, and my life, the last gate." He kneeled before them and bowed his head.

"It's a bit early for pageantry, isn't it, Ixchel?" Endryll said dryly. "You won't be taking your oaths until after the coronation."

Ixchel raised his head slightly. "You rushed your wedding. Are you really going to talk to me about jumping the line?"

Illi and Endryll sighed. Still holding hands, they rose and repeated their part of the most sacred and ancient vow Ixchel had just pledged. "And we are safe behind the gate."

"I'm sorry for dampening the festivities," he said with a chuckle as he rose and embraced his friends. "I have been wanting to do that since news of your coronation, but ..." he shrugged and went silent.

"Even before you found your powers, I would have no one else beside me as my Crownward but you, Ixchel," Illia said.

"You act like you had a choice in the matter," Endryll said, his embrace tightening around the two. "We were just waiting for you to finally say it." He pushed Ixchel back and ran his hand roughly through the scraggly mop of Ixchel's hair. "Illi thought you'd never do it, but I knew better!"

"I did not doubt him," Illi protested. There were tears in her eyes. "You are and always were our Crownward, whether you ever formally pledged it or not."

Ixchel wiped a tear from her cheek with his thumb and held her face in his palm. He placed the other on Endryll's shoulder. "Before I knew you, I was yours. Forever and always." His lips were quivering and his hands shaking. "Endryll will be the strength of Y'ssildria, but you will be its heart."

Illi pressed into Ixchel's hand and closed her eyes. "I don't know if I can walk in the shadow left by Queen Cerceia." She drew Endryll close to her, tears beginning anew.

The first blades of the morning sun cut through the darkness of the small kitchen in lancing beams of promise and potential. The candles had burned out long ago. Peals of thunder rolled across the Serrated Sea, booming and crashing with a contingent of dark clouds from the east. Winds of fate, storms of portion, began to blow. A new day was upon them. The day that Endryll would be crowned King of Y'ssildria, the day that Illia-Dara would be made queen, the day that all the world would see them as husband and wife. It was a day of new beginnings, of joy and uncertainty braided together in a cord of destiny under the banners of Y'ssildira and before her people. It was a day of celebration and portent, of ceremony and somber vows.

"It is not a shadow that my mother left for you," Endryll said, looking from the raging sea to his lover. "It was a path, and one that you will undoubtedly follow to the end, where you will then make your own," he kissed her lovingly then, "and I will be forever by your side."

"As will I," Ixchel said. "Forever and always."

Minnows and Monsters

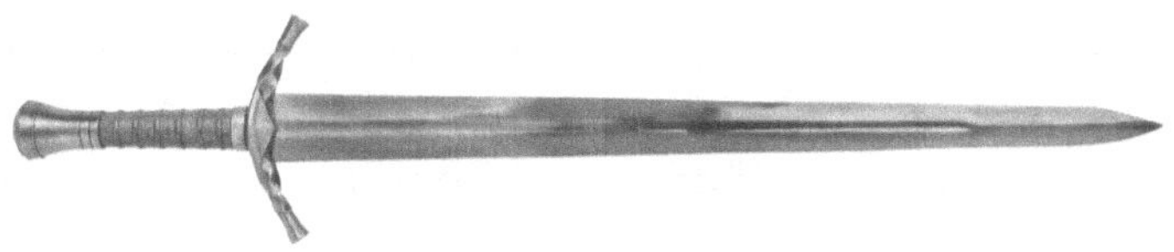

King Onidine watched as the clouds darkened the sky. The storms came in from the south and east, which was enough to cause concern. Winds, and therefore storms, typically blew in from the west. An easterly storm heralded ill tidings. The last time a storm had blown through Y'ssildria from the east, King Onidine had been made a widower. The storm's direc-tion only added to his mounting anxieties. Today was the most important day of Y'ssildrian history since that dreadful day. He had accounted for everything. He'd had the final word, from the flowers to the silverware to the musicians, the arrangement of the tables, the placement of every noble house within the Great Hall, everything. He had overseen the writ-ing of every oath, the casting of every ring, and even the forging of the crown itself. Every step of the coronation procession had been measured, rehearsed, and refined beneath his scrutinizing eye. Nothing had been left to chance. And yet, as he stared into the spinning darkness gathering about the Stoneguard, he felt the uneasy truth settle deep in his bones: No amount of preparation could keep this storm from coming.

"Of all the cursed luck," he said to Stren as he paced the length of the expansive south-facing windows that overlooked the Stoneguard from his study. The ornamental muntin that separated the windows in elegant cursive designs cast faint, elongated shadows across the smoky ashwood floors as he passed. When lightning rent the sky, however, those faint shadows burst into black lines that seemed to burn indecipherable words, runes, and glyphs into the grain of the floor, only to blink away moments later.

Stren was still as the stone behemoths below him. He was so close to the glass of the bay windows that his breath appeared in phantasmal chimera and then vanished in cadence with his breathing. His thumb, blackened and ash-stained, stoppered the opening of his briarwood churchwarden, which he held to his lips but did not draw from. The stem was the length of his beard, a full hand, from thumb to small finger, from his chin, and bent down steeply to a rusticated and well-lacquered bowl. He had replaced his loose and tatty gray robes with a much more fitted gown of deep greens and brilliant golds, the colors of Y'ssildria. A wide sash draped from his right shoulder and was clasped to the left side of his waist with a pin and brooch of bronze, fashioned in the shape of three interconnected rings. From this hung a scabbard of white and gold, molded to fit the Sword of the Crownward.

In all of Y'ssildria, there was only one such sword, and Sylvandralis was its name. Forged in the scorching breath of Brannoc the Ashwright's ancient kiln and quenched in the sacred tears of Auralys, the lost waterfall that is said to run with the sadness of Y'sa's mourning. Its blade was slender steel with a slight arc, pale as moonlight, etched down its fuller with a line of ancient glyphs whose meaning had been gleaned from the Witches of the Aetherfast. The glyphs were inlaid with lava stone melted down and blessed by the Erilem Pilgrims. The hilt was wrapped in midnight leather, bound by three interwoven bands of bronze, gold, and iron, the Threefold Binding, a symbol of oath, crown, and courage. Its guard curved downward from the chappe like a pair of outstretched wings, simple but elegant, feathered but strong, and its pommel bore a single stone of deep green, flecked with golden veins. Sylvandralis was no mere weapon. It was a symbol, a covenant passed from protector to protector, each bearer sworn not only to the king but also to the kingdom.

What made this sword unique was not its one-of-a-kind craftsmanship but the interplay of machinery and magic within. Inside the scabbard, on both sides of the locket, were a series of small gears and wheels on rotating pins. The wheels were made of flint and grindstone and angled in such a way as to accept Sylvandralis's blade and sharpen it as it was sheathed, guaranteeing a razor's edge on every strike. That was enough to elevate this sword above all others, but the real magic happened when the sword was removed from the scabbard, for when the sword was drawn, the gears and wheels would reverse direction, and the flint would ignite the lava stone worked into the glyphs. The sword would blaze to life with the fires of Mount Vorthul'kai. If the glaives of Vaelthwyn were Brannoc's metier, then Sylvandralis was his masterpiece.

"I thought you quit smoking years ago," the king said as he paced past the old wizard.

"It is a new day, old friend," Stren responded with a mirthless chuckle. "The storm is still far out over the waters," Stren continued, changing the subject quickly. "It will be hours yet before it makes landfall. It is still far beyond the Skelter Cay. But once it is upon us—"

"Once it is upon us," King Onidine interjected, raising his arms and waving them wildly above his head as he continued to pace. "We will all be running around like soaked rats on a sinking ship!"

Stren stifled a laugh. "Yes, well," he coughed in an effort to hide his gaiety. There was nothing funny about the impending storm, he knew, but the sight of the king of Y'ssildria throwing a tantrum at something so far out of his control plucked such a merry note inside him that he all but laughed out loud. "Erhumph," he coughed again. "My apologies. I must have caught a bit of a tickle in my throat from sleeping in the gardens."

The king glowered at him but said nothing as his marching brought him near and then away again with a sharp spin of his heel.

"We have plenty of rooms in the castle," Stren continued. "And Maddelwyn Borinbarrel has already offered every available room she has, as well." He put his hand out, palm forward, to catch the king as he came around. Onidine nearly pushed straight through, but Stren held his footing, his hand on his king's heart. Onidine's chest was warm, almost hot, as it pounded nervously. "All will be well, dear friend," he said, his voice low and soft, steady and sure. The king's heartbeat slowed under Stren's gentle touch. "Rest in me," he told his king as he touched his forehead to Onidine's. "Your son will surely require your strong shoulder this day. So, you may lay your encumbrances on me."

King Onidine let out a breath, and as he exhaled, he released all of his anxieties, all of his worries, all of the unknown things that had been biting at him like a ravenous swarm of needle-hawks for weeks on end. Needle-hawks, minuscule, mosquito-like insects with sharp and powerful siphonous beaks, could milk the very life from their victims if given half a chance. Onidine did not wish to see himself in any such state. "My worry has so weakened me," he sighed. "It will be good to rid myself of it." He clasped the back of Stren's neck and pressed their foreheads together. His hand shook. "Thank you, Stren, for all you have done."

Stren nodded as he stepped back. "Ixchel found his flame," he said with a final clap to Onidine's back as he returned to the windows. The docks were filling. Flags from all across Y'ssara whipped violently in the storm's front. "He will, no doubt, take up the mantle of Crownward for young Endryll." His gaze scanned the harbor, and he began to silently take count of arrivals.

The port was alive with clamor and creaking wood. Masts stabbed skyward like a listing, living forest of splintery steeples. Ships sat anchored in proud procession, each bearing the mark of distant realms. The vessels from Sindrelis were long and lean, their hulls painted deep teal with gilded filigree curling along the prow like seafoam frozen in flight. Their sails bore the split golden sun, bisected by a black diagonal slash, snapping sharp and defiant in the salt wind. Beside those loomed the flagships of Edravein, broader and heavier, hulls clad in brass plates that caught the flashes of lightning in molten flares. Scarlet pennants trailed from their rigging, and from the center masts hung the banner of the coiled golden serpent wrapped around a merchant's scale, both glinting against a field of crimson. The third envoy was a single vessel, darker and lower in the water. Its timbers were scorched black along the waterline as if it had passed through fire to reach the shores, upon its sail stretched the stark emblem of a black scorpion poised above a withered crown, the banner of Zevarath rippling like a wound against the darkening sky. Even at rest, it seemed a predator lying in wait. All together, they made the harbor look and feel much smaller.

"He will make a fine Crownward, Stren. You have taught him well. He has your passion and your mercy. And he loves my son and his wife very much."

"His wife?"

"Oh," Onidine said with a slight chuckle. "You didn't think you were the only one with your finger on the pulse of unspoken things, did you?"

"I, well—" Stren started to respond, bewildered and a bit perturbed at his discovery that not all his secrets remained so.

"I only jest, dear friend." Onidine joined him in overseeing the nautical arrivals. He rested an arm around Stren's shoulder. "Illi came to me yestermorn. She was quite convinced I would be angry but said I needed to know before the ceremony. She is strong, that one."

"And were you," Stren asked, "angry?"

A flash of lightning lit up their gray faces. For just a moment, the reflection of two men, old and tired, stared back at them from the glass of the windows, eyes sunken and hollow, skin loose and sagging, wrinkles and sunspots evidencing their age and the passing of time. And with the passage of time came the passing of responsibility, they both knew. It was a fleeting image in the fleeting strike, there and then not. Their old eyes again focused on the disembarkation en masse far below at the docks. Hundreds of workers and sailors, and soldiers ran about wildly, throwing and tying thick strands of seaweed-covered rope, straining against salt-rusted downhauls as they worked to drop sails, and carrying chests and arks full of lavish gifts up and down gangplanks and toward the waiting carriages.

"No. Not at all. She reminds me so much of my Cerceia, her unyielding strength, her unquenchable ardor, her unshakable love. She is lovely, and she is wholly principled."

"She will make your wife proud."

"She already has, my friend. She already has."

Dockside was not the only Y'ssildrian entry point experiencing an influx of visitants this Vaelorae morn. Hours before dawn, the Royal Guard had begun hastily checking invitations and escorting honored guests to the Spire grounds. The Stoneguard portcullis had been raised while most of Y'ssildria was still fast asleep, though the creaking and rain-rusted chains grinding noisily to hoist the laden mass of thick timbers and iron bands and bolts caused such a racket that most of the citizens had a much shorter night than they would have preferred. None were complaining, though, as once they were awake, they were too anxious and excited for the day's festivities to entertain the idea of returning to their slumber. Today was the day of Prince Endryll's coronation!

Amid the throng of travelling caravans and royal processions from all across Y'ssara making their way up the Stoneguard pass, a small apothecary wagon rode in the wake, a minnow swimming amongst leviathans. Its violet canvas was weighed down to the point of bursting with rains coming in off the stirring coast of the Serrated Sea and leaking into the quickly filling bed. A young woman, wading in ankle-deep waters that sloshed and splashed to nip and soak the cuffs of her rolled-up pants, and had hidden her boots in a covered shelf that was strapped tight against the sideboards, ran barefoot from corner to corner of the wagon and heaved the concave pillows full of rain water up and over the crossbars, splashing their contents into the mud and puddles and ruts of the trodden and wheel-gultched road leading to the city square.

The tiny man alongside her wasn't much help, as he couldn't reach the canvas even with the weight of the water pulling it down. Instead, he scooped bucketful after bucketful out and over the sides. He was soaked to the bone, from head to foot. Every breath he took filled his mouth with water. His eyes stung. His muscles ached. And still he scooped. The wagoneer pulled the reins hard left, then right, then left again, trying to keep the two struggling mules on course. His wide-brimmed straw hat had fallen limply across his eyes miles ago, and he had to strain his neck skyward to see the spattering road before him.

"I'm not good for much more, brother," Cante shouted over the deluge. "My legs are like soggy bread and barely holdin' me up!"

The storm had come on in full force and fury in a very short time just after daybreak. There was no preemptory sprinkle or warning of any kind. The dark clouds took shape over the Skelter Cay and Thar-Azhul Isles and then arrived on the shores of Y'ssildria within hours. Just as the multitude of travelers entered the Stoneguard pass.

"I can see the gate," came the response. "Just a little while yet," Feste said, braving a look back and into the wagon. He could see the gates, but that was still miles yet from where they were, and the condition of the road was deteriorating in exponential strides.

"No!" he exclaimed as he returned his eyes to the road just in time to see a giant black wagon race alongside them.

The wheels alone dwarfed Murrow and Bitter as they skittered to the left, away from the encroaching vehicle. This took the wagon up and over the ruts it had been following and into foreign territory. The wagon lurched and came down hard. Both brothers went airborne. Cante splashed back down in a mess of floating bottles, jars, and herbs, the waters covering him to his waist as he sat dazed. Feste was launched from the jockey box, his grip slipping from the reins as he flew first up and then backward with a yelp and surely would have been crushed under the wheels of the wagon that had just cut them off if it weren't for Aiofe.

From within, Aiofe reached out and caught the flailing little man by the belt of his drenched trousers. He hit the side of the cart with an "oof." The road thundered angrily beneath him. Feste wiped his face furiously as he was assailed by mud and small pebbles kicked up from the wheels. His hat tore from his head and whipped past his reaching arms. It disappeared under the stampede of hooves and wheels behind him. Aoife's right arm strained to hold on as her left gripped the drop pole in the center of the wagon. Her aching muscles tore, and her joints popped and groaned, as she had not fully healed from her mountain-top battle. "Climb up, you fool," she shouted through gritted teeth. "I can't hold you forever!"

Feste did what he was told. He wrapped first his hands, then his arms, past the lip of the wagon and, with Aoife's help, pulled himself over. Cante let go of his bear-hug hold on Aiofe's arm and the center pole and raced to the jockey box.

Murrow and Bitter, for all their obstinacy, were not bad mules. On the contrary, they were excellent and obedient beasts. Their whirlwind flight was not one of insubordination but of necessity, of survival. Nor were the myriad other wagons and chariots trying to trample them. It was as if a large boulder had been loosed atop a steep mountain, slowly gaining speed on its descent. But soon enough, it roars down a path not made, but of its own making. The velocity becomes a thing unto itself, and everything in its wake must keep up the precedent set or be overrun.

So, it was with the procession of Y'ssarian envoys. The race to beat the storm to the gates of Y'ssildra began as a soft, hushed snap of reins, a gentle prod to increase the pace ever so slightly. But just as the boulder gathers an army of tumbling trees and rolling rocks in its wake, so too did the first wagon spur the others to pursuit. And soon, it was a stampede, not one against another, but all against the velocity of the boulder and its avalanche. Murrow and Bitter just happened to be the shortest and smallest trees caught up in the barrage. They were running for their very lives, and the lives of their passengers.

"I can't see the reins," Cante called back as he searched desperately for a way to bring Murrow and Bitter back under control. The wagon continued to veer left and was coming dangerously close to the solid and jagged stone walls of the Stoneguard. "We're going to have to jump!"

The Stoneguard was a mountainous canyon that ran from the very gates of Y'ssildria to the shores of the Serrated Sea on the south side and to the fields of the Wilds on the north side. It was a colossal funnel of pure rock and earth reaching skyward, and the only way in or out of Y'ssildria that didn't involve either diving hundreds of feet into crashing waves or scaling leagues of mountain cliffs. The high walls offered the perfect offensive perch for Y'ssildrian archers and the perfect defensive bulwark against attacks. It also provided no escape from an onslaught of speeding chariots pulled by teams of strong horses.

"Jump where?" The others shouted as one, holding tight to each other and to the strong centerpost.

Aoife's stance was wide and low, her muscled and well-honed legs absorbing the chaotic and unpredictable jolts and bounces of the wagon's tear. Feste was strong. His body was built by hard labor in the fields of Thimbleglean Vale. He was a farmer before he was a rootminder and salver, but he was no warrior. He was airborne as often as he was grounded, jostled and tossed about by the whiplash movements. His squat form lacked the length and agility to absorb the trampoline-like effect of the bouncing wagon.

Cante scanned the shifting scene before him. Murrow and Bitter were rapidly losing all sense of direction. They were simply running. Eyes wide and panicked, mouths frothed and foaming, coats slick with sweat and latherin, they bolted this way and that, cut off by the Stoneguard walls on the left and the careening procession to the right. Desperation coursed into Cante's voice as he replied softly, "I don't know."

"Jump!"

The call came not from any of the three within the cart, but from a wagoneer perched atop a massive silver shuttle that had come alongside them and was keeping pace with the quickly tiring mules. This wagon was not pulled by a team of strong horses but instead propelled by a team of fierce wolf-like creatures, their course kept true by sharp and powerful claws that dug deep into the mud and found the purchase of clay and stone beneath. Ivory-white fangs, kept clean of the filth of the splashing road by wagging, licking tongues, seemed to glow in the storm-darkened morn. Eyes, sharp with intelligence and full of rage, blinked away rain and debris. The lupine foursome pulled hard and tirelessly against thick shoulder harnesses, the grain and emblems etched within the leather strained and elongated from the weight of the coach they towed. It was a lavish and gaudy thing, lined in gold and jewels and emblazoned with the forgotten crest of fallen Vaelthwyn. "Jump!" The command came again, followed by an outstretched hand covered in fur and scars.

Cante looked back to his brother. Feste nodded, eyes hysterical and wide, mouth a line of firm resolve and acceptance. With one final, sorrowful look to Murrow and Bitter, Cante jumped. Or, started to jump, for as he planted his feet and loaded the weight of his dense form to spring, his foot slipped on the rain-slicked seat. His leap turned to a miserable hop as he fell, arms raised high and eyes squeezed tight. He did not want to see his end coming.

His descent ended as abruptly as it had begun, as a massive, clawed hand enveloped his. He pumped his tiny legs instinctively, though they were inches from the ground. He looked like a soaked puppy held above a bath, legs moving as if already in the water and swimming. Then he began to rise. "Grab the handle," his rescuer shouted. "Open the door and help your friends, you imbecile!"

Cante looked up, through the pouring deluge and, in a crackle of brilliant blue lightning, saw his savior. What stared back at him was no man. The face above was twisted and monstrous with cheekbones like sharpened stone, eyes like molten coin, burning even in the dark. Jagged teeth jutted from a maw stretched too wide, too unnatural, and the rain hissed as it struck the heat of his breath. Brindle and mottled fur shone in the storm light beneath a dark cloak and hood.

Cante's stomach dropped. He nearly let go. He nearly screamed.

But then the claw tightened on his wrist and the voice boomed again, low and fierce. "Climb! Or they die."

Cante climbed. He gripped the cuff of the rider's sleeve with his free hand and planted his scrambling feet against the sidewall of the coach. He set one foot firmly against the frame of a low window near the driver's box. The other he sent out along the length of the wall to the handle of the wagon's door. The tip of his boot touched the handle, but he was just shy of putting any weight behind it. "I need to get further out," he called to the driver. "I can't rea—ahhh!"

Strakk threw his left arm back and released his grip, summarily releasing poor Cante. He gripped the reins with both hands and pulled to the right, narrowly avoiding a wagon that had just lost a wheel. The wolves were temporarily blinded as splinters and pieces of wood flew into their eyes and faces. The wagon in front of them lurched to one side, the axle, now devoid of a wheel, dug into the ground and pulled the vehicle hard to the left. It exploded from the center as the axle, anchored in place, ripped from the undercarriage. Shrapnel flew out of the bisected wagon as the rear portion flipped directly in front of Murrow and Bitter, the front of the wagon, and its poor occupants bounced ahead and crashed in a heap of splinters and lost luggage. The waggoneer cut the harnesses and reins from his two-horse team, climbed atop one, and kicked. He was off, out of harm's way and back into the flow of traffic in moments. The remaining occupants, a man and a woman dressed in modest Doradalden attire, were not so lucky. As Murrow and Bitter cut left and Strakk and his team cut right, a royal carriage from Braadeth emerged between the newly created canal. The driver had no choice, no chance to move. The collision was instant and brutal. The Braadethian team barreled into the remnants of the Doradalden envoy. Horses leaped and crumbled. The chariot flipped end over end, over the horses, over the rubble, and landed directly on the confused and terrified couple.

The two carriages met on the other side of the carnage. Strakk once again brought his team parallel to the Rand's wagon. Murrow and Bitter reeled from the sight of the encroaching monsters, edging dangerously close to Stoneguard's unforgiving cliff face. The small apothecary wagon slammed into the Stoneguard and then bounced away, leaving bits and pieces of wheel and wood paneling behind. Aiofe, poised and ready on the edge of the cart, held fast to the pokebonnet bow with one hand, her other hand clung tightly to Feste. She held him close. Her warrior instincts had kicked in, and she was wholly prepared to die trying to save this little man who had saved her only nights before.

As Strakk wheeled around, both Aiofe and Feste gasped in awe, for there swinging from a now-opened carriage, hanging by a single hand to the handle of the door, was Cante. His body whipped and jolted in the wind like one of the majestic banners of the Sunspire. He swung out, the door oscillating wide on its hinges as Strakk pulled up alongside the wayward wagon, only to slam hard against the sidewall of the carriage once his trajectory was set. Cante's face was one of abject horror blended with wide-eyed astonishment. His mouth was stretched broadly into a wild grin.

"Is he smili—" Feste's question was left behind and carried away in the rushing wind as Aiofe jumped. She maneuvered Feste to her front in midflight, pulled her knees up to her stomach, and then kicked out. Feste flew away from her in a jumble of flailing limbs and curses. He soared through the open door and crashed in a heap at the far side of the floor. Aiofe alighted on the iron threshold of Strakk's wagon, knees bent, arms wide, hair darkened by the storm plastered to her cheeks by wind and rain. Her bare feet skidded but held firm on the slick surface. She didn't falter. She caught herself in a low crouch, already reaching. Cante was slipping. His fingers, already numb from the cold, were peeling away from the edge of the door. His legs kicked, searching for footing that wasn't there. The only thing between him and the road was a single weak hand and sheer, desperate luck.

Aiofe lunged. She seized the back of his cloak just as his grip gave out. With a grunt of effort and sheer determination, and a single strained pull, she hauled him up and in, flinging him across the floor like an armful of laundry. He tumbled past her into the wagon, landing in a wet sprawl beside his brother, who hadn't yet managed to uncurl from his own awkward heap. Without pause, Aoife stepped fully inside, slammed the door behind them, and turned, as if expecting death to follow them through. But all she heard was the sound of their wagon disintegrating behind them and the mournful, pained cries of Murrow and Bitter.

High above the tumult, high above the chaos and wreckage, high atop the Stoneguard stood Atamas. He was among the throng of visitors who had already arrived and chosen to endure the rain and wind to watch the drama unfold below. It wasn't that those caught in the flume were ill-intentioned, rather, it was the unprecedented deluge during an otherwise dry season, turning the steep climb of the Stoneguard pass into a sluiceway that caused the frantic and deadly flight. The audience was not a barbaric gathering of bloodthirsty onlookers in the rafters of a theater, cheering on the kill and carnage, rather, they were friends and family and neighbors, frightened and concerned for their fellow man. All save Atamas shared this worry. Atamas was concerned only for one, the darkling.

He squinted his eyes in an attempt to ward off the rain and better see what was happening below. An audible gasp arose and quickly turned into shouts of terror as a trio far below made a daring high-speed escape from a doomed wagon. The small wagon had rutted and pitched a near-perfect right angle at the exact moment the woman had leaped. The poor mules pulling the cart were yanked back by their tether and lost within the ruin of the crash. Then, the pile of wood and reins that only moments before had been a small apothecary wagon exploded in a fiery ball of reds and whites and yellows as whatever concoctions and brews and compounds rattling about within finally collided with one another. The flames roared up the side of the Stoneguard, casting a portion of the wall in pitch and soot and temporarily blinding those who watched from the high ground.

"Strakk, you fool," Atamas whispered. "You just placed the eyes of all Y'ssildria upon you and, too, your clandestine mission." He wiped the wetness from his brow and pulled his hood low. "Fool," he said again as he walked away, pushing his way through the growing crowd, head low and face concealed.

"The lightning's getting worse, Ma," came the call from the crow's nest. Poor Estor had been trapped high atop the mainmast for hours, ever since the storm rolled in, or more appropriately, ever since *The Lass o' No Virtue* had sailed *into* the storm. He was clinging to the giant and splintered oak mast that shot through the nest box like his life depended on it, and it very much did, if one were to ask anyone besides Tam-Ma.

Tam-Ma's eyes were wide with exuberance beneath her coal-black goggles as she bit the bound leather strap that held her braid of coal-colored hair tight while she yanked a lever overhead with both hands. The airship groaned in response from somewhere deep within its bowels, as if protesting the abuse. A fresh hiss of steam burst from the vent pipes lining the quarterdeck, followed by the rhythmic chugs of the portside engine finally catching its breath again.

"Lightning's just the sky gettin' nervous, Estor!" she shouted through the wind. "We done worse than this on one sail and half a balloon! Now, quit cowerin' up there in yer little birdie-box and get yer arse down here where I'm needin' ya!"

The storm had long ago dislodged the heavy nails that held the rope ladder climbing the mainmast in place. It waved frantically about. True enough, it was still secured to the porthole at Estor's feet, but the rest was a lost and drunken thing, cast this way and that at the whim of an uncertain and certainly furious storm. If he tried to descend, he'd be lost to the sky and then the sea in short order, so he chose to stay where he was, no matter how it rubbed his captain.

The Lass creaked and snarled through the heavens like an old boozer in a street fight, held aloft by a patchwork of rusting copper turbines, enchanted lift-ballasts stitched with reinforced cloth, and at least one boiler that ran more on prayer than fuel. The ship bucked violently as a crosswind hammered into the port bow, and a dozen crewmen cursed in harmony as they clung to rigging and wheel and whatever luck remained in their breeches. Her sails were black as oil and laced with shimmering veins of Aether filament that pulsed like the lightning splitting the sky. Balloon pods strapped to the cannon ports by heavy chains and thick brass straps and stitched with a dozen years of mismatched canvas groaned against the wind. Her figurehead, a horned warrioress carved of charred wood and grinning like she had just outsinned a sailor, split the storm as though daring the skies to retaliate. Behind her, a contrail of smoke curled in stylized spirals from the exhaust stacks. This was Tam-Ma's signature flourish, and somewhere, below deck, the pipe-organ-horn let out a warbled sea shanty that no one could remember the words to, but everyone suspected was naughty and irreverent.

"She's coming in over the Stoneguard!" someone cried from within the safety and relative sobriety of one of the many pop-up pavilions littering the Spire's front gardens, their voice a mingling of awe and horror.

And come in she did.

All in the vicinity turned to witness the arrival of Tam-Ma. A phantom at the forefront of a perpetually darkening sky, *The Lass*, having kept level with the Stoneguard and invisible to those gathered above, breached the plain of the jagged peaks like a shark on the hunt, ripping through water and sky to catch its fleeing prey. The slack-jawed observers couldn't be certain if it was coincidence or a well-timed act of theatrical grandeur, but bright flashes of blinding white lightning screamed across the horizon at the very moment of *The Lass's* reveal. To this day, the story goes both ways, and be sure that whichever way it is told, it is told as a spectacular thing.

The Lass sliced a jagged path through the thunderclouds like a rusting dagger dragged across the blackest parchment. Noble courtiers who were gathered under silken canopies to await Prince Endryll's coronation looked up with expressions ranging from distaste to outright despair. A fat, frilly woman dropped her champagne flute onto the flagstone floor. It shattered into a thousand pieces of crystal, and its contents spilled across the ground, getting lost in the quagmire of the already soaked earth. A steward was there in an instant to replace the lost beverage and ensure the woman was okay. "Not her again," he muttered while looking to the sky and the airship, as if invoking a curse. Then he knelt to collect the broken glass.

But the people, the commoners, the everyman, crowded on rooftops and terraces, soaked in rain, cheered. Loudly and gleefully, they shouted the airship captain's name like a rebel hymn, their voices rough with cold and laughter, their joy unpolished but true. Children waved kerchiefs from windows. Hard-working and hard-living men grinned through rain-slicked beards. Housewives bent to their little ones, pointed to the sky, and told stories by way of introduction to those who had not yet heard. A stableboy near the lower causeway climbed a stone carving of King Onidine, cape frozen in motion, crown high atop his head, scepter outstretched, to get a better view. No one stopped him.

"Tam-Ma!" they called, over and over, until it became rhythm, a chant, and a dare.

All knew of Tam-Ma and *The Lass O' No Virtue*. The captain wasn't a noble. She wasn't clean. She was a pirate through and true. She'd never been caught. She'd never been tried. But all knew who and what Tam-Ma was. She was a thief, but a thief who stole from higher society and gave back to the people.

She was the story that parents told their children on nights when the hearth burned low, not because warmth wasn't necessary, but because there was no wood to burn. She was the hero of the common folk, the bane of the aristocracy, and the symbol of rebellion. And as her ship wheezed and whistled above them, steam and rain curling in its wake, the people of Y'ssildria lifted their arms and howled for her in reverence.

The Lass began her descent like a falling god, flames licking from her exhausts, tattered banners snapping in the wind, and lightning playing tag along her rigging. She spiraled once, for flair, tipping slightly starboard so that her hull caught the city's light and reflected it in shimmering, rain-streaked waves across the wet gleam of the royal plaza. Gaslights flickered across the main deck as she drew near. *The Lass* roared over the plaza. Chains clinked, gears snapped into place, and massive clawed grappling hooks unfurled from the belly of the ship, latching onto old landing moorings built into the Stoneguard, long unused, as airships were a rare thing, indeed. Sparks burst from where the iron of the anchors met the stone of the Guard, and for a moment, it looked like the chains would break apart. Instead, *The Lass* lurched into place, anchoring herself still twenty feet above the clifftop. In complete and glorious grandeur, she hovered there, high above the heads of nobles, knights, clergy, and commoners.

Then, from one of the side booms, a length of slick rope uncoiled like a serpent and down she came. Tam-Ma lowered herself, neither royalty nor entirely rebel, but something entirely of her own making. She gripped the rope in fingerless gloves, boots squealing in the heat of descent, a long, slow-burning cigarette of parchment filled with herb clenched between her teeth, a brass-buckled coat flaring like wings, and a wide-brimmed hat tucked low over one eye. The moment her boots touched stone, the tension atop the Guard broke like glass, like a champagne flute dropped and forgotten.

She tipped her head up toward the watching court. "Apologies for the theatrics," she called, voice rough and tinged with amusement. "Yer party was looking a little lonely." She took the cigarette from her mouth and blew a perfect smoke ring into the air, which caught the wind and shattered like the breaking of a charm.

For a moment, there was only silence, the kind that follows a thunder-clap or the breath held before a blade is drawn. Then the crowd erupted in cheer.

THE SILENCE BETWEEN HEARTBEATS

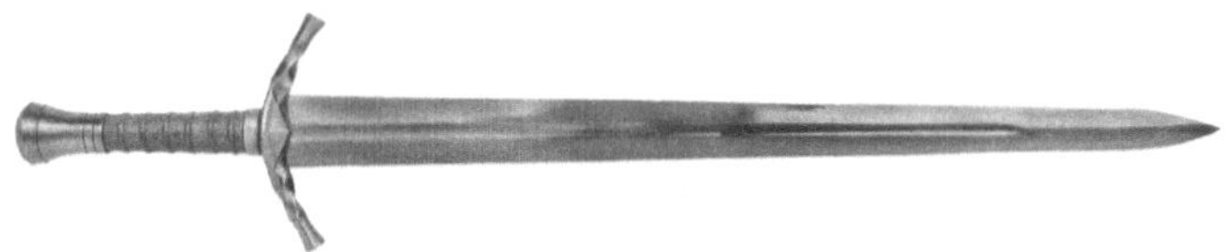

The air was thick with warmth inside despite the dampness and cold of the day. It was also dense with the lingering traces of passion. The faint scent of sandalwood and spice wafted from candles burned low near the bedside, as the silence between heartbeats spoke volumes. The heavy velvet curtains billowed sluggishly in the storm's breeze that seeped in through the open window, stirring the silken sheets that lay tangled around Endryll and Illia-Dara. Endryll traced lazy circles along the bare skin of her shoulder, his fingers rough with the calluses of training, but his touch gentle and adoring. His other arm remained curled beneath his head, exhaustion pressing down on him. He was not tired from the previous night, never that. His heart was heavy for what was to come.

"I can hear you thinking," Illia-Dara murmured against his chest, her voice hushed and thick with waking.

He exhaled a quiet chuckle, shifting just enough to press a kiss to the crown of his beloved's head. He cherished the warmth of her skin against his lips. "What does it say about me that my thoughts are loud enough for you to hear, my love?"

"It says that you are worried, dear prince." She tilted her face upward so that her eyes met his. "And it says that you don't want to tell me why."

The storm raged just beyond the threshold of their rooms. Outside, rains and winds howled, rolling clouds darkened the sky, multitudes of guests arrived, scrambling for cover and to confirm accommodations. Maids and stewards rushed about to ensure everything was ready for the festivities, but within this chamber, this sanctuary, there was no chaos, no race or rush. Within these walls was only adoration, only love, only husband and wife, only Endryll and Illia-Dara.

He hesitated. Not because he wished to keep secrets from his lover, but because he didn't know what to say. How did he say that the weight of his own name threatened to crush him? That the very idea of the crown upon his head made him feel like a prisoner in his own skin? That the longer he held her, the less he wanted to let go? He would never let go.

Instead, Endryll tightened his hold on her, fingers slipping through her red-gold hair, threading into the locks that had reminded him of a bonfire caught in the wind on the day he met her. "I love you," he murmured.

"And?" Illia prompted, nuzzling deeper into the crook of his arm and chest. His flesh flared hot where her cheek now rested. "You're not getting away that easily."

Endryll sighed. "And ... I am not the only one."

Illia-Dara stilled. Her breathing remained even, but the subtle shift in her muscles, the way her fingers paused against his chest, told Endryll that his words had found their mark.

"Ixchel," Illia-Dara said at last, softer than hush.

Endryll nodded. "Ixchel."

Illia-Dara turned onto her back, her gaze fixed on the carved wooden ceiling beams above them, her expression unreadable. Endryll watched her, waiting, giving her the time she needed. He didn't know why he had brought this up. Why now? It had always been there, under the surface, but never had it been spoken. Ixchel was their dearest friend, a brother to them both, loyal and without blame. Was he deflecting attention so as not to speak of his true fears? Or was this a small seed of fear that had taken root and now sprouted into something more? Jealousy?

"I have known Ixchel since we were children," Illia-Dara muttered finally. "Since before I understood what love meant or was supposed to mean. He was always there, always watching, always waiting. He has always loved me. And he has always been one step behind you."

"He still is."

A flicker of something—guilt, sorrow, understanding—flashed across Illia-Dara's face before she closed her eyes. "Ixchel never said anything. Not once." She was silent for a moment. "Not ever."

"He never had to," Endryll replied, his voice solemn.

She turned her head to him, a frown tugging at her lips, her gold-speckled and emerald eyes glistening with wetness. "And you think that means I owe him something?"

Endryll's jaw tightened. "That isn't what I said."

"But do I?" she pressed. "Do we? Do you think that because he has loved me in silence, I should say something about it? That I should—"

"That you should not hurt him more than necessary," Endryll interrupted, his voice quiet but firm.

Illia-Dara inhaled deeply, closing her eyes for a brief moment before exhaling. "I never wanted this. Any of it."

Endryll reached out, brushing his knuckles along the curve of her jaw. "I know."

The space between them was quiet, contemplative but not uncomfortable, and the anticipation of words not spoken ebbed and flowed all around them.

"And now?" Endryll asked after a moment.

Illia-Dara's lips parted, as if she had an answer, but she said nothing.

"Ixchel loves you," Endryll said, running his fingers lightly over the curve of Illia-Dara's bare shoulder. "He always has, but he would never betray you. He would never betray me."

Illia-Dara turned onto her side. "I know," she whispered. "Instead, he will live out his life alongside us. Watching, as always. He will see our love grow. He will see our children grow. He will see the only life he ever wanted, lived by another." She stifled a cry and went silent.

Endryll closed his eyes against the ache in his chest, for his wife and for Ixchel. "He will be the greatest Crownward Y'ssildria has ever known. And the greatest friend. And the greatest uncle to our children."

"But will he ever be happy, truly?" she asked through glistening tears.

"I have to hope so," Endryll said. "I pray he is, or that he will be one day."

Illi smiled then, wiping away the tears that had finally fallen, soaking her silken sheets. "He is already our greatest friend," she said as she drifted off, back to sleep.

Illia-Dara moved to sit up, reaching for the robe draped over the edge of the bed. Though it was late in the morning, the sky had darkened. The curtains no longer swayed languidly. They bulged and surged, caught fully in the wake of the storm. Endryll caught her wrist, his grip gentle but unyielding. She turned to her husband.

"Stay," he whispered.

Illia-Dara hesitated. Not because she wanted to leave, but because she had to. "You have to prepare," she reminded him.

"I will prepare later," Endryll countered.

"You say that as if the world will wait," Illia-Dara chided, smiling faintly. "As if duty does not lie in wait outside that door, eager to take you from me."

Endryll sat up and moved to her side of the bed. He rested his forehead against her bare stomach. It was strong and powerful, just as she was.

"It feels wrong," Endryll admitted, "letting you go right now. Something about today—" He stopped, shaking his head. "I can't explain it."

Illia-Dara pressed a kiss to his head. "It is only nerves, my love."
He did not look convinced, but he let her go, his hand sliding across hers as she walked away. He exhaled slowly, releasing her wrist fully, though his fingers lingered as long as they could before falling.

"I will see you at the feast," Illia-Dara promised.

Illia slipped the robe over her shoulders, tying the sash with practiced ease. The air felt cool against her skin as she moved toward the door. She shuttered the chill away and walked toward the baths.

"Illia," Endryll called.

She turned back.

"I love you."

Illia-Dara studied him, taking in the sharp lines of his face, the intensity in his eyes.

"I know," she answered softly. "And I, you."
And then she was gone.

"I know," she answered softly. "And I, you."
And then she was gone.

THE RIGHTEOUS RANDS

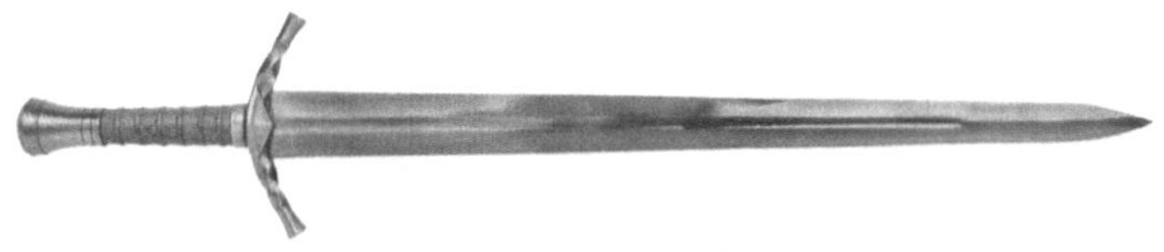

The rain beat mercilessly against the stained-glass clerestories above, transforming what little light there was outside into watery smears of color that spilled across the marble floor in shifting hues. The storms had turned the world beyond into a mire, dreary and soggy, and what had been planned as a grand outdoor festival beneath the open sky was now being hurriedly and haphazardly resurrected within the vaulted hall of the Sunrise Citadel. Tables were dragged across the floor by red-faced squires and apprentices who barked at one another over the clatter of pewter and chair legs. Bakers from the Low Rise shouted about crushed pastries and re-iced cakes. Vendors in mismatched cloaks stumbled through puddles that had found their way in through archways, clutching bolts of silk, spiced skewers, and delicate glasswork wrapped in shawls. And, soaked through, trailing mud and looking like indentured vagrants of a forgotten nation, came Aoife, Cante, and Feste Rand.

They *shouldn't* have been here. They *should* have been in a broken wagon by the roadside, trampled and dead, like poor Murrow and Bitter. But they had been saved. Cante still felt the air whip past him as he dangled from Strakk's clawed hand, legs kicking, helpless. He glanced at his brother. They were both so tired. Feste met Cante's eyes and smiled a sad smile.

"We'll go back for them," he said, wrapping an arm around his brother. "We'll find'em and we'll give them a proper burial. One meant for family."

"No," Cante replied. "Not one meant for family. One meant for warriors." His eyes were like granite as he spoke. "They fought for us back there. They fought and died for us, brother." His breath caught in his heaving chest as he said the last.

"True enough," Feste said. "If it weren't for them fool donkeys giving every last bit they had, we'd be just as dead."

"A warrior's burial, then?"

"The finest burial a warrior has ever received, brother."

"Remind me to never accept a simple supply run again," Cante said with a maudlin laugh.

"You're the one who called it 'easy coin,'" Feste replied, wincing as he took his arm away, flexing his bruised shoulder.

Aoife strode forward, chin high. Her torn pants tangled about her ankles, leaving puddles at her feet, ignoring the whispers and stares. The image of Strakk's face, bathed in rain and lightning, loomed in her mind, the feral gleam in his eyes, the monstrous lines of his jaw. She felt no fear when she thought of him, only a gnawing curiosity. He had saved them. *Why? Why would a darkling care for the lives of three strangers? Why would a darkling care for anyone or anything but himself? Also, and maybe most importantly, why would a darkling be invited to a coronation and wedding in Y'ssildira at all?*

Why, indeed.

"What are you boys going to do now that all your wares have been lost?" she asked as the Brothers Rand sidled up beside her.

"Eat," Cante answered excitedly, taking in the banquet laid out before them.

Tables stretched nearly the entire length of the Sunrise Citadel's grand hall, each covered in cloth-of-gold and lit by candelabras wrought of pewter in the shapes of cloaked harpists and blossoming lilies. The feast was a grand display of colors and aromas. Silver trays gleamed with roasted pheasant glazed in honey and elderflower. There were platters of fresh-caught river trout stuffed with lemon and wild herbs, and towers of sugared fruits, dripping with syrup and dusted with crushed almonds. There were loaves of steaming bread thick with salted butters and spreads, braided with rosemary and thyme, wheels of soft white cheese laced with honeycomb, and bottomless bowls of spiced carrot and barley stew, rich and savory, the scent of cumin and coriander wafting in inviting waves.

Golden goblets brimming with wine so dark it was almost black lined the tables and rode steadily on golden trays carried by skillful servers. Crystalline decanters sparkled with ciders, cordials, and mulled juices that steamed in the cool hall. Along the far end, an entire wild boar sat at attention, its hide lacquered and glistening, an apple clenched between its teeth and garlands of thyme and laurel woven about its tusks. And sweets! Rows upon rows of tiny pastries glazed in lavender sugar, honeyed figs wrapped in candied almond bark, and flutes of clear jelly layered with crushed berries and cream.

Cante's mouth was open wide. He nudged Feste sharply in the ribs.

"If this is what the nobles eat every coronation, I'll kiss a king's boots for an invitation next time," Feste whispered.

"Forget kissing boots," Cante said. "I'll kiss his pretty lips."

Aoife snorted, barely disguising her laughter.

"Come on," she said, "before you two embarrass yourselves by drooling on the royal carpets."

She tugged them forward, weaving through the throng with ease. While most guests clustered at the nearest tables, elbows brushing, hands darting toward platters like hawks, Aoife steered them toward the quieter far end of the banquet, where the servers had just finished arranging a fresh spread.

The scent of freshly-baked bread and roasting meat thickened the air. Cante was practically floating by the time they reached a table piled high with crispy herbed flatbreads, small roasted game hens glazed in spiced plum sauce, and bowls of shimmering pearl onions braised in dark wine.

"This—" Cante began, reaching for a steaming hen. A hand darted out and smacked his away from the temptation of the feast.

"Try not to look like you've never seen food before," came a dry voice from across the table.

The three froze.

A severe man stood before them, the plate in his hand neatly piled with a modest sampling. He wore robes of black and deep green, simple in cut but impeccably kept, the fabric catching the candlelight in muted gleams. At his collar, embroidered in thread so dark it barely caught the eye, was a trio of interlocked rings. His hair, silvered at the temples, framed a face lined not with age but with the quiet gravity of one who had seen much and survived it. His eyes, sharp and glinting like frost over dark water, missed nothing as they scanned the three newcomers. At his hip hung a sword. Its hilt was wrapped in dark leather and bound with silver bands. The blade itself, though mostly hidden in its sheath, seemed to hum with a power all its own, a slender, moon-pale arc of steel. He shifted slightly, adjusting the lay of his cloak over his shoulder to cover the blade.

Aoife's lips tightened. "We're not here to cause trouble," she said flatly.

The man tilted his head slightly, studying her, then the brothers. His mouth curled into something that was not quite a smile.

"No," he replied with a wink. "Not yet."

Cante swallowed hard.

Feste, ever the diplomat, cleared his throat and managed a stiff half-bow.

The man nodded, seemingly satisfied, and turned his attention back to arranging his plate. For a moment, they thought he might simply dismiss them, let them fade back into the crowd. But as he plucked a handful of almonds from an ornate dish, he added, almost conversationally, "Be careful who you brush shoulders with today. Some stains are impossible to scrub clean." Then he walked away, vanishing into the shifting sea of silks and armor.

Aoife let out a slow breath. "Charming," she muttered. "I miss when banquets only had to worry about poisoned wine."

"Who was that?" Feste whispered.

Aoife shook her head. "That was Stren D'anyon."

"And, er ... Who's that?" Cante asked.

"He is the Last Oak of Burss," Aiofe replied quietly, almost reverently. "Crownward of Y'ssildria. Warden of Sylvandralis. And a powerful practitioner of the Aether Arts."

"Ohhhh," the brothers said together.

"He sounds impressive," Cante said.

"He sounds *important*," Feste corrected.

She grabbed a handful of flatbread, shoved it into Cante's arms, and spun on her heel, guiding them away from the food tables and back toward the less-crowded edges of the hall. "Eat quickly," she said. "And stay sharp."

Feste glanced down at the toasted, still-warm bread in his hands and sighed. "I miss when I only had to worry about my plate."

They crossed the wide mosaic floor toward the outskirts of the crowd, dodging harried pages and noble guests, as well as all their dirty looks. The

Sunrise Citadel was a hive of frantic excitement, and they were the only ones seemingly moving with any purpose. Aiofe's eyes never stayed in one place, even as they moved toward her destination. She scrutinized every person, every corner, every balcony.

Then she stopped.

There, beyond the rush of servants, the gossip of frail lordlings, and the clatter of goblets, stood Illia-Dara.

She was radiant, standing tall in a gown of shimmering green and silver. Light pooled around her as if the sun itself had wrestled its way through the gloom of the storm just to bow at her feet. Her hair, woven with strands of thistle and silver, crowned her head like fire gilded in morning dew. Her eyes flicked, just for a moment, toward Aoife, and then back to her audience of well-wishers.

Aoife's breath hitched. She hadn't seen her in years, not truly. And now, now she was something more than she had been so long ago.

Aoife watched as Illia-Dara continued to oblige those around her, play-ing the perfect hostess. She nodded gracefully, laughed with raised hand to cover her mouth when appropriate, and yet, she often blinked and looked away, directly toward the three. Aofie noticed a faint recognition as it flickered in Illia-Dara's gaze, but knew that no name surfaced. The Star Speaker continued to observe, as Illia-Dara turned slightly toward her, stepping from the circle of subjects and betters, both, and made her way slowly, cautiously to where she and the Rand brothers stood.

The brothers sat placated at a table, enjoying the commodities. Cante, mid-bite into a hen that he had managed to swipe without Aoife seeing, froze with his mouth open, the massive bite, far too large, shoved halfway down his gullet. Feste blinked slowly as though not trusting his eyes, the goblet in his hand tilting due to lack of concentration and spilling steaming cider to the floor.

"That's her," Cante choked out, still having not removed his bite.

"I *know* it's her," Feste whispered back, hastily wiping his hands on his filthy shirt.

Panic seized them both as Illia-Dara arrived.

Cante tried to salvage the moment, shoving the rest of the hen not onto the table, but into his mouth and stumbling to his feet. Feste mirrored him a beat later, not returning his drink to the table, but instead chugging it down in one messy, noisy gulp. They exchanged a quick, helpless look, wiped each other's faces with greasy cloths, then bowed low.

Too low.

Cante's forehead thudded against the edge of the table with a dull *clunk*.

Feste wobbled, overcompensated, and nearly pitched face-first into a platter of sugared figs, the immediacy of his libation affecting his balance more than he had anticipated.

"What'd they put in that cider?" he asked shakily.

Illia-Dara paused, a polite smile flickering at the corner of her mouth. She said nothing, only dipped her chin in graceful acknowledgment as the brothers scrambled to recover what little dignity they had left.

"Your Majesty," Feste croaked, wincing as he straightened.

"She's not queen yet," Cante muttered under his breath, elbowing his brother with one arm while rubbing a reddening knot on his forehead with his other hand.

Illia-Dara allowed herself a small, amused breath, but her attention had already moved past them to Aoife.

Aoife dipped her head in a shallow, respectful nod and stepped forward.

"My Lady Illia-Dara," she said reverently. "It is an honor to meet you."

Their eyes met fully. Illia-Dara squinted as if trying to grasp the memory. She felt certain that she had never met this woman. She had never seen her before, at least not to her knowledge, and yet …

Up close, the woman was smaller than Illia-Dara had first thought, but there was nothing diminished about her. She stood with the stillness of someone used to being overlooked, or trying to be, and using it to her advantage. Her dark hair, damp from the storm, clung in unruly waves to her temples and the nape of her neck, and a loose braid hung over one shoulder, the end frayed and uneven. Her eyes met Illia's without flinching, clear and crisp. They missed nothing, those eyes. They measured, weighed, and *knew* more than they said. She wore simple leathers, faded whites and browns scuffed and muddied from long travel. A gray cloak hung carelessly back over her shoulders. Not a stitch of finery touched her, yet she stood proud and confident. And though she stood still, she was vibrating with potential motion—lean, wiry, coiled as if ready to vanish or strike, whichever the moment demanded.

"Are you lost, my lady?" Illia-Dara asked, her voice warm but edged with formality, her posture stiff, but whether that was to keep up regal appearances or because she was uncomfortable, only she knew.

Aoife smiled, a small, secret smile, and shook her head. "No," she said, voice cordial. "Just finding my place."

Illia-Dara nodded, as if this made perfect sense. "You know my name," she said, "but I'm sorry to say that I don't know yours."

"Wrenloch," Aoife said, not taking her eyes from the future queen. "Aiofe Wrenloch."

The world was silent for a moment. Illia-Dara searched every corner of her memory, listening to the voice that seemed to be screaming from the depths of her subconscious that she *knew* this woman, this Aiofe Wrenloch. But how?

Cante belched, loudly though unintentionally.

"And these," Aiofe said, looking away from Illia-Dara for the first time since greeting her, "are the brothers Rand, Cante and Feste." She pointed to each with a flattened palm as she said their names.

"My Lady," they said together. They bowed again, though not as low and with a much less tragic outcome than before.

Aoife rolled her eyes. "They are fine and noble men from Thimbleglean Vale and traveled all this way to wish you and Prince Endryll the most happy of unions, and a long and prosperous reign."

The brothers stood taller then, pride spread wide across their faces at Aiofe's words.

"They also came bearing gifts and trinkets to be sold during your celebration, but all was lost along with our cart and our poor mules in the mad flight up the Stoneguard."

The countenance of Feste and Cante fell as they were reminded of their loss. Their shoulders lost all strength and rolled forward as they lowered their heads.

"I am truly sorry for your troubles, Brothers Rand," Illi said, "and for your loss. I will speak to my future husband, and we will see what can be done to recover or replace what has been lost."

"Thank you, my lady," Feste began. "But we would never as—"

"You didn't ask," Illi interrupted, not unkindly. "I offered."

Feste bowed. "Thank you, Lady."

"You are quite welcome, Master Rand. Now, I am sure that you did not intend to attend my wedding and Prince Endryll's coronation dressed like beggars. At least I hope you didn't, because that would entirely change my first impression of you." She smiled and turned, waving an arm wide toward one set of the dual spiraling staircases to either side of them. "Come," she ordered. "The world is about to change. You wouldn't want to miss it, but you must clean yourselves up. Please, bathe, rest, and my servants will tend to you and bring you something to wear."

"You're too kind, My Lady," Aiofe replied with a bow.

"I am," Illi said back with a smile, "but I think that you and I have more to learn from each other than names. And I can't do that with every guard in the Citadel watching you like they'd love nothing more than for me to order them to throw you out."

"True enough. I look forward to our next meeting."

"As do I, Aiofe Wrenloch."

Illia-Dara waved to her girls-in-waiting and gave them instructions concerning her guests.

Aoife gestured for Cante and Feste to follow the young girls up and around the stairs. They fell into step behind her, eyes wide. The brothers climbed the staircase, a marvel of pale marble, flowing stone, and intricate ironwork. Twin spirals coiled upward toward the vaulted ceilings and split off at the upper levels of the Spire's main quarters. Along the balustrades, gold-leafed vines and blossoms curled and twisted, catching the dancing light from nearby candles in dazzling glints of orange glow. Cante and Feste lagged behind, gaping openly at the grandeur. Feste's hand trailed lightly along the carved rail, sanded, stained, and waxed to a shine, while Cante craned his neck so far back to stare at the ceiling frescoes that he nearly missed a step. He caught himself on Feste's shoulder.

"Steady," Aoife murmured without turning, a small smirk tugging at her mouth. She had only known these men for a short time but knew enough about them to know that they had never stepped foot in such a place as the Sunspire Citadel. She wondered how they would react if she were to escort them through the icy halls of Caerlinth in the Cloudmire Highlands, or the enchanted gardens of Edravein along the Gilded Gulf coast. Her smile widened as she imagined Cante amid the elven royalty of Edravein. She would take them there, she determined, if they survived the day.

Above them, the girls-in-waiting moved like actors in a well-rehearsed play, handing off scented silks and expertly-cut cloth, and communicating through carefully measured glances. They led the way through a wide archway into a quieter wing of the citadel. Here, the noise of the banquet and the clamor of conversation faded, replaced by the soft hush of woven carpets and the faint scent of rosewater and vanilla.

A pair of double doors stood open, and beyond them lay a suite that could have housed both Feste and Cante's entire farmsteads. High-backed chairs upholstered in green and gold sat before a massive hearth where a fire crackled softly. Baths had already been drawn in porcelain tubs clawed with polished iron, steam curling listlessly into the air around them. Stacks of plush white towels, linens finer than anything the Rand brothers had ever touched, and mannequins draped with formal tunics and gowns awaited them.

Cante whistled low under his breath. "You sure we're not being fattened for a sacrifice?"

Feste elbowed him sharply, but his own eyes were wide, drinking in the finery, the glitter of sparkling mirrors, the glint of gold-threaded arrases, the crystal carafes filled with pale wine and costly perfumes.

One of the girls-in-waiting stepped forward from the doorway. She was younger than Aoife, perhaps sixteen, seventeen at most, but carried herself with a practiced grace that made her seem older. Her gown was a soft blush of peach and cream, simple in cut but heavy with brocade embroidery at the hems. A narrow circlet of woven gold was tied loosely in her dark hair, which was pinned back from a face still untouched by worry or suspicion. She dipped into a careful curtsey, crisp and exact, and lifted her head, eyes the color of early dusk locking briefly onto each of them with measured calm. She commanded much for her young years.

"Baths have been prepared," she said softly, her voice trained into politeness but not stripped of warmth. "Clothing has been laid out. Please, allow us to assist you."

"Assist us with what?" Cante blurted out, his voice shrill and panicked.

The girl blinked, unfazed. "With your preparations, Master Rand. Bathing, dressing—"

"No, no, no," Cante said quickly, waving his hands as if shooing away a swarm of angry wasps. "No assistance needed. None at all. We're married men. Very, *very* married."

Beside him, Feste coughed and adjusted the collar of his muddy tunic, his face rapidly turning the color of boiled beets. "Happily married," he said, a little too loudly, his voice squeaking. "Very much attached. Vows and all."

"We're capable of washing ourselves," Cante added, backing toward the nearest tub as if it might defend him. "Have been for years. Lifelong skill, really."

The girl said nothing, only regarded them with the serene patience one might afford a pair of stubborn goats.

Aoife smirked, folding her arms across her chest.

"I'm sure your wives would be proud," the girl said at last, her lips twitching ever so slightly. "But I assure you, sirs, our duties are merely to provide assistance if requested. Many find the buttons on the formal attire... taxing."

"*Buttons?*" Cante repeated warily.

Feste muttered something more about vows and drowning himself in the nearest tub.

Aoife shook her head and stepped forward, peeling her soaked cloak from her shoulders. "We can manage," she said, giving the girl a slight smile. "Thank you."

The girl curtseyed again, a little deeper this time, and withdrew with her entourage, their footsteps fading as they departed.

As soon as they were gone, Cante sagged against the side of the tub, clutching at his chest. "Thought I was about to be disrobed by a stranger and have to explain it to my beloved."

Feste was already pulling off his boots, grumbling. "Imagine the songs they'd write about us. The Randy Rands or some such."

"The Righteous Rands?" Aoife offered dryly.

Cante nodded solemnly. "Better righteous than divorced."

"Better righteous than dead," Feste countered with a shudder.

"Well," Cante said, already shrugging out of his rain-soaked cloak, "I suppose if we're going to be dressed like lords, we might as well start smelling like them." He was already unbuckling his muddied belt, eyeing the tubs like a starving man eyes a roast.

Aoife hesitated only a moment longer before tugging loose the cords of her own sodden cloak and stepping behind a curtained wall to her own bath. She would allow this, the baths, the silks, the soft linen. She would cede to this momentary respite, more for the sake of her companions than herself. She couldn't help but smile again, though this time it was no joyous thing. It was a small and secret thing as she thought of Illia-Dara's words, *the world is about to change.*

"It already has," she said quietly as she stepped into the steaming water.

A Whisper in the Dark

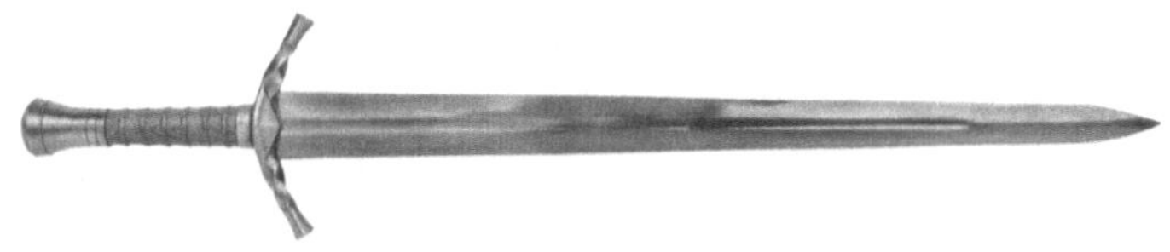

Illia-Dara moved through the crowded hall like a folded paper boat through a rocky stream. She was graceful despite the swirl around her, her fine emerald gown catching glances with every step. The fabric clung to her in all the right places, elegant and sculpted, its bodice cinched with golden thread in a rising spiral, the symbol of Y'sa's light ascending. She'd spent more time dressing than she'd meant to, but the gown made her feel grounded. She needed to know that this was happening and that she was *meant* to be here. She loved Endryll and knew that she belonged next to him, in his arms, but who was she to ascend to Queen of Y'ssildria? She was no one! She was an orphan from a shattered kingdom, the daughter of a dead soldier and a lost family. The dress helped her to at least pretend that she belonged here, to play the part of queen-to-be.

"Lady Illia, oh, stars above, watch out!" A boy no older than ten, face smeared with dried paints and fear for just shouting at his future queen, ducked past her with a dripping banner meant for the dais. "Sorry, Lady Illia-Dara," he belted as he ran on.

To her left, two noblewomen argued loudly with a knight who had mistaken their assigned seats. To her right, a trio of enchanters stood on chairs and muttered frustrated incantations at the ceiling, where floating orbs of flame sputtered in the damp air. A goat bleated somewhere, but she didn't look. The Sunrise Citadel's grand hall, meant for solemnity and ceremony, had been turned into a riotous river market. The dais, once a reserved platform of polished stone, was now half-buried under tangled garlands, drooping pennants, and crates of decor being arranged and rearranged by red-faced stewards. Musicians bickered at the foot of the steps, struggling to find a dry corner for their lutes and harps. A cask of cider had burst near the eastern pillars, and a small lake of sweet-smelling slop now puddled there, roping around the boots of oblivious guests. In the midst of it all, the court's best-dressed nobility fanned themselves, tutted, barked orders and apologies in equal measure.

And everywhere she turned, they looked at her.

She met their stares with what poise she could summon, dipping her chin in acknowledgment, letting the gown and the gold thread carry her where her confidence might falter. But inside, she was a taut wire, a cord stretched too thin. She moved through the multitude, each step measured, every breath calculated, and though she smiled, though she laughed where she must and answered where she should, she could not quiet the thundering in her chest.

I am not ready.

A heavy garland swung down from an overburdened beam above, brushing her hair. She kept walking. Near the dais, she caught a glimpse of King Onidine speaking in low tones with Stren. The old king, whether stooped by time or the stress of the past days, leaned heavily on his staff, the deep folds of his robes brushing the floor. At his side, Stren stood solid and unmoving.

Stren's eyes met hers briefly, impassive, steady. He was a man carved from loyalty and duty. He nodded at her and gave her a reassuring smile, but his eyes spoke of something else.

She inclined her head in respect and moved on.

Farther along, she glimpsed Ixchel threading his way through the churning waters of the growing crowd, chuckling as he caught a toppled tray before it could crash to the floor. He spotted her a moment later and offered a quick, irreverent salute before disappearing into the masses. Somehow, seeing him eased the iron band tightening around her chest.

She reached the far end of the hall where the preparations thinned and the noise dulled to a more bearable level. Here, the polished floor reflected her image back at her in hazy observation. Illia-Dara closed her eyes for the briefest of moments, centering herself. *This is happening. You are happening.* She opened them to the great bells of the citadel tower tolling, slow and sonorous, calling all to witness the coronation of a new king, and the crowning of a new queen. She turned in place slowly, unsure if she was meant to be at the inner stair or the Crownward antechamber, or ...

"Illia!"

The voice, clear and sharp and utterly familiar sliced through the din.

She turned too quickly and nearly collided with a servant hauling a rack of goblets over his shoulder. "Forgive me," she said automatically, eyes scanning the crowd.

"Illia! Over here, by the pillar. Yes! Here!"

She found him then, Ixchel, arm raised, half-cloaked in shadow beneath one of the massive stone-carved columns near the western portico. His wild curls were damp with sweat or rain, or both. His sleeves were rolled high, and he was breathing heavily. He was wearing a toothy smile and waving frantically to her. And he was the loveliest thing she had seen all day.

"You have to see what they've done to the dais," he said as she approached, weaving through groups of guests and staff. "They've put the flower arch where the musicians were meant to be, and the musicians are where the altar was until someone moved it and someone thought it a fine idea to hang Endryll's crown directly above the boar's head and that had to have been a joke, right? And then the—"

Illia embraced him. She held him close and hugged him so tightly that he struggled to breathe.

"Wha—? What's all this?" he asked, though he didn't push her away.

"Just —" she started, "Just, thank you." She held him back at arm's length. "Thank you for being you, Ixchel. Thank you for being here."

"Where else would I be, Illi?" he asked. "I'll always be here, with you and Endryll."

Illia-Dara blinked away a tear, hoping Ixchel didn't notice. "I know you will. I just really needed someone right now and you were, well, you were exactly that someone I needed. With Endryll off signing papers and getting ready, I just felt so alone, so lost."

Ixchel reached out his hand, which she seized immediately.

"You'll never be alone again, Illi. Not with Endryll and me at your side." Then he spun her around and pointed to the podium at the far end of the halls. "Now look at that mess!" He was smiling a gaping, goofy, childish smile, eyes bright with disbelief and merriment. "It's chaos. Absolute, brilliant chaos!"

She laughed despite herself, unreasonably grateful for him in that moment.

"Show me," she said.

Ixchel offered his hand again, without ceremony, and she took it without hesitation. His palm was warm, and it grounded her more than any regal dress could. Together, they slipped between a pair of pageboys discussing the optimal location for the wreath that hung between them and into the western corridor where the inner pavilion narrowed. She had been here moments before, and so much had already changed since then.

The great golden doors at the entrance end of the hall, meant to part with measured grandeur before the coronation, were wide open to usher in more chairs. A trio of sweaty servers passed by them, muttering about missing corks and broken tongs.

"The canopy was supposed to hang here," Ixchel said, gesturing with a sweep of his arm. "But they forgot to account for the harpists. So now, the canopy's been lowered, *lowered*, and tied to the musicians' riser. Look."

Illia squinted.

And there it was, the ceremonial canopy of Y'ssildria, draped crookedly across a scaffolding of chairs, ropes knotted in haste, sagging in the middle as though mourning its own precarious predicament. Beneath it, a red-faced harpist sat tuning furiously, glaring upward as if daring the whole thing to collapse on his head. To one side of the dais, the royal standards, proud green and gold banners embroidered with the sunburst and spiraling vine of Y'sa, had been propped against the wall, forgotten and slightly askew, one half-folded onto itself.

The throne, Endryll's throne, meant to be the centerpiece of the ceremony, stood off-center by several paces, a crooked monarch among the wreckage. Hers stood forgotten behind it. Her crown sat unassumingly on the seat. Someone had tried to move her throne earlier, leaving a series of heavy scuff marks across the polished flooring like scars that refused to heal. A scattering of flower petals was strewn across the steps leading up to the dais, but most of them had been trampled underfoot, now nothing more than bruised smears of color against the white stone. Off to the side, a knot of court magicians argued in agitated tones, glancing up at the canopy, muttering under their breath. Wisps of magic drifted from their fingers, but none dared risk a complete incantation to stabilize the sagging disaster overhead.

"I think it's charming," Ixchel said, crossing his arms with mock solemnity.

Illia shot him a look. "It's a catastrophe."

He smiled. "A very *Y'ssildrian* catastrophe, though. We're nothing if not committed to making grand disasters look dignified."

She pressed her lips together, torn between laughter and despair.

Her gaze drifted to the thrones again, to the seat she would be called to share, to the crown that waited there, heavy and golden, and once worn by Queen Cerceia. That thought added more weight to the crown than any metal or jewel ever could. *It's only a chair,* she told herself. *It's only a crown.*

Her heart thudded traitorously in her chest.

"Come on," Ixchel said quietly. "Let's get you to the back before someone ties a banner to you and calls it a day. They'll have it fixed in time."

She let him steer her away from the dais, away from the sagging canopy and the skewed thrones, away from the noise and the mounting pressure. They weaved through the rivers of people toward the calm of the antechamber. The bells were still tolling, slow and deep, and with each heavy chime, the halls filled with more and more of Y'ssildria's lords and ladies, merchants and soldiers, scholars and seers, all of them come to see history made.

She turned back once more, before exiting and brought a hand to her mouth, eyes wide. "Oh," she whispered. "It can't stay like this."

"I told them," Ixchel said playfully. "But you know how it is. 'We've no time, Master Ixchel! We've no time!' As if I'm the one who conjured a storm just to test their improvisational prowess."

"Perhaps you did," she said, glancing at him sidelong.

"Only the lightning," he said, winking. "The thunder is all Endryll's snoring ... and the wind is his—"

She laughed then, truly laughed, the sound startling a passing servant.

They stood like that for a breath, just the two of them, half-hidden in the antechamber as the Citadel buzzed with frantic life. Still holding hands. Still connected.

Then Ixchel's voice softened. "You look radiant, by the way."

Illia turned her head slightly, as if unsure he was speaking to her.

"Green suits you," he continued, more gently. "It always has. You look like you belong in this madness."

"I feel like a stitch come loose," she replied. "I don't know where I'm supposed to stand, or wait, or speak. I can't find Endryll. Everyone's running and shouting, and I—" She stopped and exhaled. "I feel like the storm followed me inside."

Ixchel studied her face for a long moment. "Then we'll find your footing," he asserted. "Together."

She nodded, though she couldn't quite meet his eyes.

Behind them, someone dropped a tray with a crash, followed by a string of angry curses and muttered apologies. From above, the fire orbs finally flared to life in uneven bursts, casting patches of firelight and shadow across the hall. Somewhere down the corridor, the court herald could be heard bellowing instructions, his voice already hoarse. Before either could speak again, a voice interrupted, smooth, measured, and strangely calm amid the clamor.

"Lady Illia. Master Ixchel."

Both turned in unison.

Atamas stood before them, flanked by no one, as if the crowd had been bent around him, stretched and arched, moved and made malleable by his very presence. He was untouched by rain or worry, unsmeared by flour or ash. His deep violet coat, stitched in precise black thread, bore the emblem of the Thar-Azhul across his shoulder, a blackened spiral of three interlocking arcs, their thorn-notched edges coiling toward a void at the center, all encircled by a broken ring split into seven uneven shards. In the center lay an empty eye, the Eye of Azhul, symbolizing unseen truths, forbidden knowledge, and the promise of rebirth. The symbol was stark, geometric, and unsettling in its imperfect symmetry. It was a directed response and antithesis to the golden rings of the Crownward. He bowed, the motion exact and without warmth.

Illi's eyes lingered on the symbol. She'd noticed that Atamas had been wearing it more as of late, whether emblazoned on some piece of clothing or hanging from a chain around his neck. She didn't know what it meant, but she had seen Atamas and Stren arguing in dark corners more than once and wondered if it had something to do with his new choice of emblem. She shuddered as Atamas rose from his bow. She did not nod, nor did she smile, except for when she felt Ixchel squeeze her hand, and even then it was a small thing, meant only for him, not for Atamas.

"Forgive the intrusion," Atamas said. "I would not interrupt if it weren't of the utmost import." His eyes settled on Illia-Dara, not lingering, but too direct, too obvious to be polite.

She straightened, schooling her features. "Of course, Commander."

"Only Atamas today," he said, with a tight smile. "It's a celebration, after all."

Ixchel stepped half a pace closer to the dangerous man, positioning himself just slightly between Illi and Atamas, subtly, but the movement didn't go unnoticed. Atamas flicked him a glance, then returned to Illia-Dara.

"I only wished to offer my congratulations. The city has never looked more resplendent." He gestured vaguely around them, where a server had just tripped on a lute and scattered a bowl of sugared treats across the floor. "Even in catastrophe, you seem to shine." He reached for her hand, not with the customary grace of courtly etiquette, but with something more deliberate, and took it gently in his own. "Your courage, Lady Illia, is the kind that echoes through halls long after the banners have fallen." His thumb brushed her knuckles. "May your reign be long."

He released her hand, and as he did, she felt it, a shift, the faintest drag of fabric against fabric. The weight was imperceptible at first, but her instincts caught it like a thorn in silk. Something had been slipped into the pocket sewn into the side of her gown.

Her breath caught.

Ixchel noticed. His shoulders tensed. He set one foot slightly behind the other and out to the side, giving himself a more stable stance. He let go of Illi's hand and began to focus on the Aether, drawing it in, calling to it softly from within.

Atamas turned then to him. "And you, Master Ixchel. I expect your talents will be ... invaluable, in the days to come." His voice never changed, still gracious, still formal, but something behind the words gleamed like the edge of a hidden blade.

Ixchel tilted his head. "My *usefulness* may come when least expected."

Atamas smiled, slow and cold, his eyes locked with Ixchel's. "Indeed," he said. "Perhaps not even by choice." With that, he stepped back, bowed once more, and vanished into the crowd with the quiet certainty of a man who feared nothing and expected everything.

Illia-Dara's fingers slipped discreetly into her pocket. The object was small and cold. The fabric was rectangular and coarse. She closed her hand around the cloth wrapping and felt the object within. It was too heavy to be a token or gem, too light and small to be a weapon. A folded note, perhaps? She didn't remove it from her pocket. She didn't want to look at it, not with Ixchel here.

"I don't like him," Ixchel said, voice tight as a drawn bowstring.

"You're not supposed to," she replied, her heart suddenly louder in her chest. "That's how men like him work."

Strakk the Fool

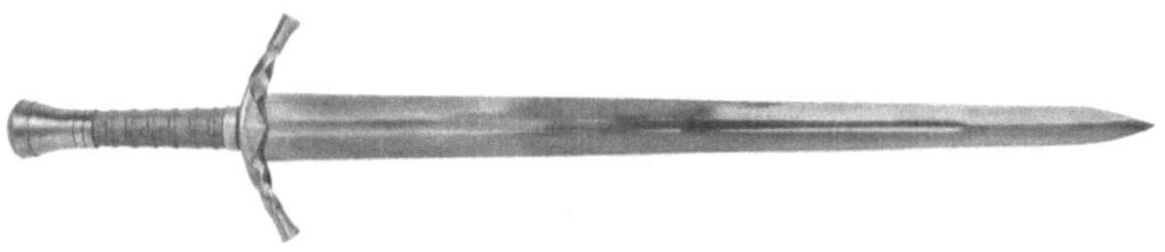

The halls beneath the Sunspire Citadel's ceremonial levels were older and rougher and untouched by the polish and pageantry above. Here, under the great hall and the royal gardens, the stones sweated with the humid breath of the earth. The walls, carved centuries before, bore the ghosts of once-bright murals now faded to the color of old bone, their stories lost beneath creeping moss and the cracks of long, slow ruin. The air was harder to breathe, a mingling of damp mortar, ancient crypts, and the dry, metallic tang of ash. The scent of old fires lingered, though no flames had burned here in years. It was a place where sound carried strangely, swallowed by the stone, turning footsteps into murmurs and voices into flat mutters.

No one visited unless duty demanded it. Even the bravest scurried through by necessity, kept their heads low and their feet quick. No one lingered once their errands, illicit or proper, were done, and those who dared speak of it above did so in the hush of superstition. The lower keep was where the castle remembered things forgotten by the living. The corridors narrowed as they wound deeper, the walls tightening like a hungry snake around a sunken and hollow chest. Torches burned low and infrequently, their light creating shallow pools of flickering shine on the flagstone, leaving everything beyond in a thick, waiting darkness. Iron sconces spotted the walls, rusted through and crusted with the wax of a thousand years of spent candles.

"I thought I told you to keep your presence unknown," Atamas said, emerging from the shadows.

Strakk's yellow eyes narrowed beneath his hood. "You told me to deliver the package. I did."

"No. You hurled yourself between wagons and revealed yourself to all of Y'ssildria. You became a spectacle when your sole missive was to get the envelope and box through the gates unnoticed."

Strakk shifted, rising to his full, unnatural height. His broad and muscled shoulders cast dark shadows over Atamas as he unfurled. "They were about to die," he growled.

"Yes," Atamas said, his voice a whip crack of anger, unfazed by Strakk's imposing stature, "and had they died, their bodies would've been mourned, buried, and forgotten, quietly. Instead, *you*, the most conspicuous thing this side of the Western Wood, decided to play hero."

Something in Strakk's chest rumbled up and through his throat. "I wasn't going to let them die."

Atamas stepped closer. "Do not forget, *dog*, that though you have been promised restoration, it is upon successful completion of your tasks. And you would do well to remember, as well, that this is a future thing. You are nothing but a beast. Worry yourself only with your duties and not with the lives of those who don't concern you."

They stood there in silence, the tension between them thick as mortar dust.

Then Atamas sighed. He unclenched his fists and adjusted the sleeves of his robe.

"Still, you got the package through the gate." He allowed himself a small smile. "That's more than I expected."

Strakk said nothing.

"It's in her pocket now," Atamas said, his voice dipping into something almost delighted. He stepped even closer, until the light from the single lantern reflected in his eyes. "You see? Even dogs have their uses."

Strakk's jaw flexed, but he didn't speak.

Atamas's tone softened, just slightly. "I haven't forgotten our arrangement, Strakk. Have you? I will restore you to your former self and to your family. You have my word on this."

Strakk remained still.

"You have the box?" Atamas asked.

Strakk nodded.

"Good. Deliver it to the prince's chambers and be gone from this place. I will find you."

Strakk turned his head just slightly as if listening to or for something.

"What do you hear?"

"It's starting."

"Go. Do not fail me."

Strakk growled again. "You do not fail me," he hissed through the guttural rumbling.

Atamas leaned in, voice all velvets and poisons. "You'll be whole. No more claws. No more hunger. No more hiding from the light. You'll see your children again, Strakk. You'll hold them in arms that won't make them scream in terror."

Strakk looked away as Atamas disappeared back into the shadows.

OATHS AND THE END OF ALL THINGS

The transformation was complete. Gone was the clamor, the chaos, the rushing feet, and shouted orders. The great inner hall of the Sunrise Citadel had become an enchanted kingdom of candlelight. Draperies of dawn-colored silks hung from the buttresses, catching the flicker of fire-orbs above. Music spilled from harp and flute, soft and reverent. The floor flashed with new polish, and fresh petals lined the central aisle in gentle curls of violet, blue, and crimson. The thrones, the banners, the crowns, the musicians, the decor, were all in their proper places.

The guests had all arrived, and there thrummed an expectant hush of a thousand held breaths. Every noble seat was filled. Lords and ladies were arrayed in their house colors of golds and greens, sapphires and silvers, crimsons and coals, all gleaming like a field of bejeweled flowers beneath the high chandeliers. Common folk clustered along the lower benches, their faces open and eager. Laughter and murmurs rippled through the chamber like a river in the spring.

At the far end of the hall, on the dais, King Onidine stood resplendent in robes of deep forest green, his crown of oak and silver resting loosely on his brow. Beside him, Stren, regal in his formal greens and bronze sash, stood straight-backed and unmoving, his hand resting on the hilt of Sylvandralis, the Sword of the Crownward, now visible to all. His face was chisled in solemnity, but his eyes, when they found his king, softened almost imperceptibly. The moment waited, poised on the bated breath of all in attendance.

In the wings, just beyond the colonnade where lightning pierced the high windows, Illia-Dara stood with Ixchel. She looked radiant. The green gown shimmered like fresh spring leaves in sunlight, each embroidered gold stitch a quiet ray of hope. Her hair was braided in the triple-knot of queenship, threaded with silver and thistle blossoms, a crown made not of jewels, but of endurance and patience. Her eyes shone with wonder and restraint, as though caught between joy and fright.

Ixchel stood at her side in a fitted dark coat, his sleeves now unrolled, his usual grin softened by something deeper. His hair was tamed into a tight bun on the back of his head, though wayward and rogue strands had escaped and curled around his eyes. He leaned toward her, voice hushed so only she could hear.

"Remember when you said they would never accept you as queen?"

Illia smiled, barely. "I said they'd laugh me out of the room."

"They didn't," he said, eyes holding hers. "Look at them now." He gestured to the staff and late-comers who had eyes only for her. "They're staring because you're the only one here who looks like she belongs on a throne."

She turned and kissed him on the head. "Thank you."

"For what?"

"For seeing me, even when I didn't. All those years ago."

He opened his mouth, but the music swelled, as the herald stepped forward and raised his hands. The silence was immediate and all-encompassing. The moment had arrived. Illia drew a breath. Her hand trembled. Ixchel took it and squeezed it gently, without pressure or question.

"You're ready," he whispered.

She nodded. "I suppose I am."

The great doors at the end of the hall swung open. A collective gasp rose from the gathered crowd as Illia-Dara stepped forward, alone now, bathed in the fractured light of the high windows. There was a shuffle of movement as all in attendance rose to their feet. She moved slowly and deliberately down the petal-strewn aisle. She felt every gaze, the hush of admiration and scrutiny, the dreams and doubts stitched together in the breathless silence. She met the eyes of friends and foreigners alike.

Among the common folk, Cante and Feste Rand stood stiffly in their newly tailored coats of dark blue and silver trim, their hair neatly combed, their boots polished so brightly they seemed out of place on their usually dust-worn feet. They shifted awkwardly under the grandeur, but even they could not help but stare as Illia-Dara passed, open awe on their faces. Beside them, Aoife, dressed now in a simple gown of cream and coffee with an understated obsidian clasp at her shoulder, watched with a more measured gaze. She saw not the finery, but the strength beneath it, the girl she had known and the queen she would become.

High on one of the side balconies, leaning against the carved stone railing with a roguish grin, Tam-Ma watched the proceedings with the detached amusement of someone used to slipping past such ceremonies rather than attending them. She twirled a small silver coin between her fingers, one boot propped lazily on the rail. Her pirate entourage, caught up in the elegance and splendor of the red-haired beauty below them, simply stared, mesmerized and entranced.

On the dais, Endryll stood waiting. He wore a tunic of green and gold, the colors of Y'ssildria, stitched with a pattern of the rising sun and the ancient dogwood so special to his family. His cloak, pinned with a brooch of jade and pearl, hung perfectly across his shoulders. But none of it mattered. When he saw Illia-Dara, the weight of the crown, the eyes of the court, the gravity of what was to come, all of it vanished. He saw only her. And he smiled the pure, unguarded smile of a boy who had loved her before the world knew her name. He glanced at his father, King of Y'ssildria, and saw that he was weeping openly, his chest heaving as he tried to control the torrent of emotions welling within him. Endryll turned back to his bride. He blinked away his own tears as she approached.

As she reached the steps of the dais, Stren stepped forward. He withdrew Sylvandralis from its sheath with a sound like wind over ice, the blade coming to life with the fires of the embedded magic stones within, casting brilliant arcs across the hall. Murmurs and gasps arose from those in the gathering. All had heard rumors and lore of the magnificent Crownward blade, but few had ever seen it in all its magic and majesty.

The murmurs stilled as Stren, with a slow, solemn motion, offered the sword to Illia-Dara. She took hold of the hilt, wary of the hungry flames licking about the foible. She held it in her right hand. It was heavy, but not cumbersome. It seemed to adjust to her grip. It felt comfortable. It was no burden. The harpists shifted, and a new melody filled the hall, grave, yearning, the Song of First Light, a hymn sung only at the crowning of monarchs.

"Who do you call as Crownward, Lady?" Stren asked, loud enough for all to hear.

"I call upon Ixchel Osvaldo," she responded.

"Ixchel Osvaldo, come forward and take your pledge."

From the edge of the gathering, Ixchel stepped forward, each footfall calculated and counted. He had shed the easy smile he often wore like armor. His face was solemn with the oath he was about to swear. He wore the same dark coat, but now his chest gleamed with a new clasp, the Crownward sigil, three interlocking rings in golden thread. He approached Illia-Dara and knelt, one knee to the polished marble, head bowed. The light of Sylvandralis cast an ethereal glow across his wild hair and the clean lines of his shoulders.

Illia-Dara extended the sword, the point angled down, the hilt toward him. It was not an offer. It was a command. And one he was glad to accept. He could feel the heat of the flames upon his face as he lifted his eyes to meet hers and laid his right hand over his heart. His voice, when he spoke, was clear and unwavering, each word rising into the vaulted ceiling and beyond.

"My strength is your shield, my breath, your barrier, and my life, the last gate."

The hall was utterly still. Everyone leaned in to listen, rapt with the significance of what was being said.

Illia-Dara did not hesitate. She spoke the ancient response, her voice steady. "And I am safe behind the gate."

Ixchel rose to his feet and reached for Sylvandralis. His fingers closed around the hilt, firm and unflinching. At his touch, the sword stirred. The flames at the foible pulsed once, bright and sharp, a moment of heat, then flared outward, casting a ripple of light that swept across the dais, across the floor, across the upturned faces of all who watched. The fire twisted, shimmered, and then fell still, folding inward as if drawing breath.

Then the sword began to change. No longer did it curve like a crescent of pale moonlight. The lava stone set in its fuller darkened, sinking into the steel as though some unseen tide had swallowed it. The cross guard, once outstretched like wings, folded and reformed to a sleeker, narrower, more direct shape, shedding its old form like a serpent discards its skin.

The black wyvern leather of the grip unraveled, sloughing away into threads, and in its place rose deep-stained oak, dark and gleaming, polished until it caught the light like a mirror. Over this, a soft, silver-gray hide was bound, etched subtly with spirals of old Y'ssildrian script, blessings and burdens woven into the leather. The cross guard and pommel flared once in a last gasp of flame, and when the light receded, they gleamed as if newly born of pure gold, unsullied and unadorned. The blade was no longer moonlight pale, but white as the first snows of winter, forged anew in that single breath, both terrible and beautiful. It thrummed softly in the stillness, a song only the worthy could hear. Sylvandralis sang a new song to Ixchel, and it awakened him as if he had slept through long ages, waiting for this very moment. Ixchel stepped back, next to Stren, and lowered the blade to his side.

"I am proud of you, my son," Stren whispered through strained vocal cords.

Illia-Dara ascended the steps, her pulse a drumbeat in her chest, and stood beside Endryll. He reached for her hand, and when their fingers touched, it was not the world that shook, but the future, re-shaped by the simple, undeniable power of two souls entwining. She lowered her head to his shoulder. She fell into him completely, and he into her. She felt his warmth, his strength, his sure and steady breath, and she lingered there, safe, secure, at peace. She was home here in his arms.

On the dais, King Onidine stepped forward, his every motion steeped in ceremony. He carried on his head the crown of Y'ssildria, its edges shaped like rising sunbursts and entwined vines. Endryll stood waiting, his brow bare, his shoulders square. The old king removed the crown with trembling hands, not from weakness, but from the sheer gravity of what he was about to do. He lifted it high, the torchlight catching in the intricate weave of gold, sending a thousand gleaming threads of light across the chamber. He looked upon his son, no longer a boy, no longer the wild-hearted youth who had raced horses through the valleys of Y'ssildria, but a man who would bear the hopes of a kingdom.

"By the light of Y'sa," King Onidine said, voice rough with age but clear with purpose, "and by the blood of our fathers, by the stone and sun and sword, I name you, Endryll, son of Onidine, King of Y'ssildria." He lowered the crown carefully, placing it upon Endryll's brow. As the circlet settled, it seemed as if the hall itself exhaled a held breath. "Now, greet your people as king so we can get you married," he said with a wink.

Endryll turned to face the gathering, one hand lifting to rest briefly atop the crown, grounding himself in the feel of it. His other still grasped Illia-Dara's. His smile was not one of pride, but of solemn gratitude. Illia-Dara advanced in step with him, her gown of shimmering green flowing behind her. Together, they faced the hall, and Endryll raised his arm, fingers still entwined with his lover's, and presented himself to his subjects, side by side with their future queen.

A beat of silence.

Then the hall erupted.

Cheers thundered against the vaulted ceilings and high walls, a rolling wave of joy and devotion that shook the banners and rattled the vast vault beams overhead. Flowers rained down from the balconies, hands clapped, voices shouted, and the great hall became a testament to what the kingdom of Y'ssildria truly was.

"Long live King Endryll!" someone cried.

"Long live Queen Illia-Dara!" shouted another.

The words echoed, caught, and carried, swelling into a chorus that rose like the tide, vast and uncontainable.

"Long live the King and Queen of Y'ssildria!"

Endryll and Illia-Dara stood together in the center of it all, two hearts, one crown, one kingdom, bathed in the warmth of their people's love.

Across the hall, Ixchel watched, his mouth smiling but his eyes distant. Near the rear on the second floor, Strakk, hooded and still, lurked, unseen. High in the rafters, where no one ever looked, Tam-Ma flipped her silver coin, caught it, and laughed a bright, joyous laugh. The music soared. The people cheered. It was the *perfect moment*, a moment that would be remembered forever.

Stren stepped forward, hands raised, patting the air in an attempt to quiet the roaring hall.

"Y'ssildrians! Friends! Neighbors!" he called, his voice magnified by the hall's high arches. "Let's get to the wedding!"

A fresh chorus of cheers came then, louder than the first, hungrier than before. Shouts and laughter rang with renewed vigor. Fathers hoisted their children onto their shoulders, little hands waving bright green and gold flags, confetti and petals raining down in a brilliant, careless storm of color. Someone threw a hand-stitched wreath of yarn toward the dais, a crocheted replica of the crown, a tiny symbol of the love and hope of this gathering.

It hung in the air, spinning slowly.

And then a flash of silver.

A glaive, one of the terrible, famed glaives of fallen Vaelthwyn, whistled through the space, high above the attendance, slicing the yarn wreath into a flutter of shredded green and gold strands. The blade struck King Onidine squarely in the chest, buried so deeply that the impact knocked the old king backward against the throne. He sagged without a sound, held up awkwardly as the glaive pinned him to the throne, blood blooming darkly around the jagged blade and spreading across his royal coats. For a heartbeat, the hall was frozen, a painting of horror trapped in the moment before it screamed.

The massive double doors at the far end of the hall, opposite the dais, burst inward. The wood didn't crack, it exploded, reduced to splinters and shards, a cannon blast of shrapnel that cut through the unsuspecting crowd. Joy turned to terror in an instant. Laughter became shrieks. Applause became cries as black-clad soldiers poured through the rubble, their faces hidden behind black masks and soot-smeared helms. Glaives, spears, and cruel, serrated swords flashed in their hands, poised for bloodshed.

The first wave hit the crowd before most could even move. Men, women, and children, the blades did not discriminate. They *carved*. They culled. They slaughtered.

A woman clutching a garland stumbled backward, her mouth frozen in a silent cry as a spear tore through her ribs. A boy in festival green was trampled under the panicked crush. A father reached out, trying to pull his daughter free, but a black glaive took him through the back, snapping rib and spine in one brutal thrust. The white marble floor turned red, petals and confetti swirling into the pools of blood like fallen leaves in muddy puddles after a rain.

From the dais, Stren roared words lost beneath the screams and drew Sylvandralis, or would have, except that Sylvandralis was his no longer.

Endryll shoved Illia-Dara behind him, his face pale but set. Ixchel was already moving, vaulting the low bannisters, his hands glowing faintly as he reached for the Aetherfast, summoning power with a grim, sharp breath. High above, Tam-Ma's smile dropped. She tucked her coin away and reached for the strange flintlock at her hip, muttering a curse as she swung down from the rafters, coat billowing behind her. And in the chaos, the black tide kept pouring through the shattered doors, endless and merciless, as if the night itself had come to claim Y'ssildria. And, indeed, it had, as Atamas stepped casually through the ruined doors and over corpses, a smile wide across his face.

The Bastard of Bairnbrand

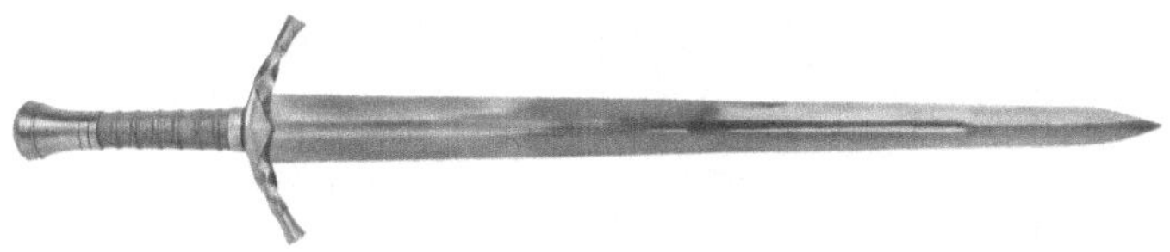

The rain clawed at the tattered cloaks of the Timber-Folk as they strained against the incline of the Stoneguard Pass. Driven by the gale as it lashed at their faces, stung their eyes and plastered their long, tangled beards to their chins, every breath was a painful gasp of wet air, tasting of damp stone and distant, acrid smoke. Their short legs, accustomed to the soft loam of the Western Wood, ached with the unyielding demands of the ascent, each step forward was owed only to their stubborn determination. If it weren't for their ancestral heritage, that of the Stone-Folk, they would have given up long ago.

Mergop, his usually booming voice reduced to a thin, reedy whine, stumbled on a loose, rain-slicked cobble. His curses, a string of colorful and inventive insults aimed at the weather, the road, and the universe in general, were ripped from his lips and scattered to the winds before they could fully form. "Blast and botheration, Thurdop!" he wheezed, shaking a fist at the churning, leaden sky overhead. "I told ye, this were a fool's errand! A cursed journey for cursed times, it is! M'toes are frozen numb, and I can'no feel m'beard past m'face!"

Thurdop lumbered on ahead, his broad back a solid shield against the wind. He merely grunted in response, the sound a rumble from deep within his chest. "Yer complainin' is more of a botheration than this road, Mergop. Keep yer breath fer walkin', an' not whinin'. We'll be there when we're there, and no sooner for any o' yer belly-achin'."

"Whinin', is it?" Mergop sputtered, scrambling to catch up, his round belly jiggling with each frantic step. "I'm jus' observin' the facts, is all! We should've ne'er agreed to that old man's whims. Sending us all the way to the Bairnbrand for the lad, when the skies themselves are weepin' floodwaters and the mountains are shaking apart!" He gestured wildly with his free hand toward the Titan's Crown, its jagged peaks barely discernible through the swirling mist and rain. A faint, angry glow, a ghostly ember from some celestial forge, still pulsed high among the crags, a stark and terrifying reminder of the cataclysm that had ripped through the world just days prior.

A collective shudder, like a ripple through a patch of wind-struck weeds, ran through the small band of Timber-Folk. The memory of the earth's shriek and the sky's sundering was fresh in their minds, and gnawed at the edges of their courage.

"His whims, ye call 'em?" piped Torin, who's thick, vine-thread spectacles were perpetually fogged with damp and exertion, making his eyes seem enormous and bewildered. He pushed them up his nose with a muddy thumb. "He's the Crownward, ye dolt! An' a powerful one, at that! Ye saw what he did to the path in the Western Wood! Not a twig snapped when he wished it not to, and flowers blooming in the dead of night, like he pulled them from Y'sa's own arse!"

"Aye," Mergop grumbled, his voice laced with grudging concession, "and speaking o' that, why didn't he just 'magic' us a ride to the Bairnbrand, then? Or fly us on one o' his blasted Aetherfast beasties? He's got magic enough to make the very road sparkle like a baby's toy, but not enough to spare our poor feet the sufferin o' this infernal trek?"

"Because," Thurdop interjected, his voice carrying surprising clarity and weight above the howl, "some flights require footfalls, ye harpie. Some things're callin' fer the sweat of honest labor an' not the flick o' the wrist. He said as much. Said it was important that we walk this path. I'm not fer knowin' why." Thurdop paused, his gaze sweeping over the bedraggled figures of his kin. "Maybe he needed to be knowin' that our loyalty was true, an' not ter be swayed by comfort or convenience."

"He said 'go to the Bairnbrand and retrieve the boy,'" Torin recited, his voice taking on the cadence of remembered instruction. "'Be prepared to bring him to Y'ssildria, on the day I come to you again. For he has a part to play in this story.'"

"An' tha' was dern near 15 years ago!" Mergop seemed to have found his bluster once again now that the conversation had come back to the lunacy of this march. "A part in the story, indeed!" He scoffed. "What story?" He forgot his cap and waved his hands wildly all around. "More like a headache an' no more, if ye ask me. The boy has been on the outside o' things er' since we retrieved him from that Matron woman's grip all those years ago. An' now an almost-man, an' he's still fer being an outsider! And why the rush? Why all this secrecy? Why now? Derned Stren." Mergop's hat caught the wind and leaped from his head as if it were trying to escape him. It twisted in the wind like a tassel, spinning this way and that and climbing an updraft until it reached the top of the Stoneguard and flitted out of sight.

Mergop watched it go in stunned disbelief, eyes blinking rapidly and jaw wide. His hands were twitching at his sides. "An' there goes me derned hat!" he finally announced angrily.

The others held in their laughter and seemed suddenly very interested in the small rivers of rushing water at their feet. No one said a thing, for fear of exacerbating the already riled faeman.

The name "Stren" hung in the air, not at all molested by the gale. The tall, stern man, who was power and wisdom and held secrets only known to scribes and ancients, had met them at the entrance to Deadlock Pass, his briarwood pipe glowing, his runestone-fitted staff glimmering with brilliant blue light. He was the one who had commanded them. He was the one they had chosen to obey, despite their misgivings about the mission's suddenness and secrecy.

"He said ... er, he said the boy had a connection Lady Illia-Dara," put in a quiet voice from the back of the group, one of the younger fae, barely more than a sapling, who had been mostly silent throughout the arduous trek. Krumble was his name. His wide, innocent eyes, usually filled with childlike wonder, were now darkened by a burgeoning understanding of the world's harsh realities outside the confines and comforts of the Western

Wood. "And that he was of 'divided blood. Like a river splitting but still connected at the source.'"

Thurdop nodded grimly, the raindrops washing over his stoic face. "Aye. 'Divided blood.' That's what stuck in m' craw. An' the way he looked when he said it, like it was a burdensome thing that he carried himself, heavy as a stone in his own heart." He paused, looking out over the mudslide, the gates still far, far away. "He spoke of a choice. A choice made long ago, and its shadow fallin' across this generation."

"Wha' could a bastard o' Bairnbrand possibly have to do with the Crown of Y'ssildria?" Mergop continued, oblivious to the deeper currents of the conversation. His mind was more concerned with practicalities than prophecies. "An' why did Stren pick *us*? Why not his own kind, those Illuminthil folk he's fer ridin' with, with their fancy cloaks and their glowing sticks? Why not send one o' them ter fetch a boy?"

"Don't ye git it, ye idjit?" Thurdop replied, glancing meaningfully at the dense thicket of water-logged debris they had just passed, their branches swaying and groaning in the wind. "This is why he asked us ter nab him all them years ago! We're the watchers o' the Wood, the keepers o' its secrets. An' this boy, m' dearly departed sister's boy, Stren said he was a secret o' the Wood, too. An' tha' we were ter be hidin' him away."

The argument, a familiar rhythm between Mergop's stubborn skepticism and Thurdop's obstinate stoicism, was abruptly cut short by a faint, mournful bray that was nearly unheard in the storm. In fact, it would have gone unheard, except that the fae were well attuned to nature, and, indeed, it was a cry from nature, herself. It was close and laced with desperate urgency. It was a sound that struck a chord of poignant familiarity in their hearts, a sound that spoke of hardship and resilience.

"What in the blazes was that?" Mergop exclaimed, straining his small, keen ears against the din of the storm. "Sounds like a badger caught in a snare, but bigger."

"Sounds like ... mules?" Torin ventured, pushing his spectacles higher up his nose, his wide eyes attempting to pierce the blurry gloom ahead. "Aye, a pair o' them, by the sound. And they ain't too happy, at that."

They pressed forward with renewed urgency, the road growing slicker and more treacherous as they climbed. The mud sucked at their boots with each determined step. The wind, a banshee wail through the jagged peaks, continued to assault them, making their progress that much harder, but their focus was forward, toward the cries of the animals, and eventually, the Sunrise Citadel. Then, around a sharp bend in the narrowing pass, they saw them. Two bedraggled, mud-splattered mules, their coats dark with rain and mud, and even blood. Their heads were low, their bodies trembling with a mixture of fear, exhaustion, and the faint, almost extinguished spark of hope at seeing the fae.

The beasts were no longer pulling a wagon but milling about the wreckage of what had once been a small cart, its violet canvas ripped to shreds, contents spilled and scattered across the sodden road. Jars lay shattered, their pungent elixirs bleeding into the churned earth, and splintered wood mingled with the broken glass. A single, broken wheel lay detached, its spokes splayed like the bones of a long-dead creature. Amidst the ruin, the mules stumbled, their ears laid back, their eyes wide and rolling, reflecting the dim light of the storm-darkened sky.

The mules lifted their heads, their long ears twitching, and let out another series of sad brays. They hobbled toward the fae, jostling each other as if seeking comfort, their heavy hooves splashing through the puddles.

"Would ye look a' that," Thurdop muttered, his demeanor softening as he reached out a hand to stroke Murrow's wet snout. "Seems someone else had a rougher journey tha' us. An' here we thought we were the only fools out in this storm."

Mergop knelt in the mud without a second thought, his earlier complaints forgotten in the face of the bedraggled beasts. He began gently rubbing Bitter's flank, murmuring reassurances to the trembling animal. "Poor beasties. Look at 'em. Musta come through the thick of it. The very thick of it."

As if to punctuate his words, a distant boom, far louder and more resonant than any thunderclap, echoed through the mountains, followed by a faint, metallic clang. The air crackled with a strange, unnatural energy, wicked and sharp, that made the faes' beards prickle and sent shivers down their spines.

"Tha's no thunder," Torin said, his gaze fixed on the looming silhouette of the Stoneguard gates far ahead of them, dimly visible through the driving rain and darkened sky.

"Aye," Thurdop said, gazing up to the Spire. "Tha's a battle."

A terrible realization struck them, chilling them far more effectively than the biting wind and relentless rain. The air around them vibrated with a deep, resonant pinch that was not of nature, but of raw, unleashed power. This was no mere atmospheric disturbance. The thunderous roar, a sound that cracked through the mountains and echoed down the pass, was accompanied by flashes of blinding light that flared with an unnatural intensity, too sharp and too violent, too unnatural to be lightning. The earth beneath their soggy feet trembled with a rhythmic shaking, a vibration that spoke of immense force and impact. And then, through the wail of the wind, came the distant cries. They were not the cries of animals caught in a tempest, nor the desolate sigh of the wind through stone, they were sharp, desperate, and undeniably human. It was war. And it was happening inside the impenetrable walls of Y'ssildria!

"To the gates!" Thurdop commanded, his voice suddenly fierce and urgent. "Somethin's gone bad in the city an' it looks like we got here just in time for the show."

Clutching the reins of Murrow and Bitter, whose earlier grievances were now forgotten in the face of the unfolding horror, the Timber-Folk marched. As they drew nearer to the grand Stoneguard archway, the air itself seemed to thicken with the roar of conflict. The clang of steel on steel ripped through the pass, a brutal chorus of violence. Guttural shouts, raw and desperate, mingled with terrible, primal shrieks. Through the gloom, past the shattered and burning remnants of a dozen or more wagons and overturned carts, strewn aside like discarded toys, they saw it. The Sunspire Citadel, always the beacon of silver light and unwavering hope, now ablaze like a ghastly, flickering inferno. A lurid red and orange pulsed against the purple of the twilight sky, painting the clouds with the grim hues of destruction. Figures in black, indistinct but menacing, moved within its grand hall, their glaives flashing like predatory teeth. It was carnage. It was awful. And the Timber-Folk, the humble gardeners of the Western Wood, were running right into it.

"By the beard o' tha fool, Fumblefoot," Mergop muttered, his earlier complaints replaced by a stunned awe that silenced even his endless grumbling, "they're fer killin' each other in there."

Thurdop said nothing, his eyes narrowing as he scanned the scene with grim intensity. He had seen battle before, in the faded drawings of old stories and heard legends around winter fires. But this was different. This was not the orderly clash of armies on a field, but a visceral, bloody thing erupting within the very heart of civilization. He saw the shattered portcullis, rent as if by a giant's fist, the guards lying broken amid the rubble. He saw the gleam of weapons that were too black, too hungry, to be of any earthly forge. And then he saw them. Scores of them, pouring into the citadel like a tidal wave of black insects, their snarling faces illuminated by the eerie glow of fires within the hall.

"Darklings," Torin breathed, his voice trembling with a mixture of fear and academic fascination. "So far from the Barrens. So," he paused, searching for a word that escaped him as he remembered everything he had read about the fallen peoples, "organized."

"Aye," Thurdop agreed, his hand unconsciously dropping to the small, well-worn axe at his belt. He sighed, knowing that it was a blade made for work and not war. "But there's no honor in this. No sense. No reason."

They crouched behind a pile of splintered stone, the scent of burnt wood and something metallic stinging their nostrils. The screams from within the citadel were torturous and pitiful things, slicing through the squall like an arrow. They could see scores of dark, wolf-like figures crawling up the enceinte walls and across battlements, slipping through broken stained-glass windows, and even more marching through the main gate.

"What do we do?" the younger fae whispered, clinging to Thurdop's leg, his face pale and wide-eyed. "We were sent to bring the cross-blood. Not to fight."

Thurdop's gaze shifted from the brutal scene to the frightened faces of his kin. They were gardeners, not warriors. Their hands were made for tending roots and coaxing blossoms, not for wielding steel against such unbridled savagery. Yet, they had come this far. They had been given a mission by the Crownward himself. The stories of doomed old Fumblefoot flashed across his thoughts. There was a reason they didn't fight. There was a reason they stayed quieted away in Meritha Pol and the Western Wood. But there was also a reason Fumblefoot did what he did. For what man could call himself a man if he didn't rise to the defense of the innocent, if he stood idly by while darkness consumed the light, or if he allowed fear to shackle his heart when justice cried out for a champion?

"We find Stren," Thurdop stated, his voice unwavering, leaving no room for argument. "That was our charge. And if he is within those walls, then we go to him. And we bring the lad to him."

"But how?" Mergop asked, his usual bluster replaced by a genuine fear that drew lines into his round face. "We can barely see our own feet in this muck, let alone navigate a battle. And those, those things." He gestured vaguely toward the darklings.

"The Wood protects its own," Thurdop murmured, more to himself than to them, his eyes sweeping over the rain-lashed stone of the Spire. "An' we're fer being' children o' the Wood, ain't we? We will find a way." He looked to the bairn at his side, kneeling and taking hold of both his small shoulders.

"Krumble, I want you to ride back with Torin. Take the mules and go back to Meritha Pol an' tell'em wha' ye seen." He stood and turned to Torin. The scholarly faeman wore a fierce frown of disapproval as Thurdop continued. "Torin, see young Krumble back to the safety o' the Wood. Yer fer knowin' tha' this init me gettin' rid o' ye. But ye're less a fighter than me or Mergop, an' Mergop wouldn't be fer leavin' anyhow. It init a small task I'm askin' o' ye, an' it's one I'm trustin' to ye."

"But I can't be fer leavin' m'boys," Torin said, his voice quivering with dueling emotions of fear and anger.

"Yer not leavin' us, brother. Yer doin' yer part to keep us an Meritha Pol safe." Thurdop patted his shoulder then, firm and sure. "Er'yone here an er'yone back home knows that yer never fer leavin' yer family."

Torin nodded solemnly. "C'mon then, Krumble," he said to the sapling. "Pick ye a mule an' let's get ter ridin'. It's a long way back, an' there are folks needin' to know what we're knowin'."

The two faemen, proud timber-folk of Meritha Pol, set off, exchanging whispers of luck and safety as they began their descent back down the pass. Murrow and Bitter, though reluctant to leave their masters who were somewhere in the Citadel, obliged, glad to be led away from the pandemonium of the battle. They seemed to know what was at stake. Their ears were low to their heads, and their heads were low to the ground, as they found the safest and quickest way down the pass. They carried their wards proudly, only looking back occasionally, sad eyes scanning the ever-receding image of the castle for any sign of their masters.

Thurdop watched them fade away. When they were out of sight, his gaze fixed on a section of the wall far down the pass, where the ancient, gargoyle-like sentinels of the Stoneguard stood in silent vigil, their stone faces carved with eternal vigilance. These were the Guardians of Y'ssildria, hulking monstrosities of rock that had once been animated, brought to life by powerful magic to defend the kingdom. Now, they were merely statues, weathered and worn, symbols of a bygone era. Yet, as Thurdop looked, he saw something else. The faint, swirling lines of Aether, usually invisible to all but the most sensitive eyes, pulsed faintly around the ancient carvings. Then he remembered Stren's words when he commissioned him as the leader of this expedition, his voice as grave and ancient as the mountain itself.

He reached out a hand, pressing his palm against the cold and damp stone of the massive rock wall that formed the base of one side of the Stoneguard. He closed his eyes, drawing a slow, deep breath, and sent his awareness out, reaching, probing, seeking the deep currents of the earth that were his birthright. The stone responded, a low thrumming reverberating through his hand, a pulse that matched the frantic beat of the battle within. It was a language he knew, a song of earth and stone, of deep roots and unyielding patience. The power of the mountains flowed into him, carried through the deep roots all the way from the Western Wood.

"Hold to the stone," he commanded, his voice a low growl that seemed to come from somewhere deeper within him. "Feel the mountain. Let it hide you. Let it guide you."

"You, too, boy," Mergop said to the young man who had been thus far primarily ignored, content to walk in the shadows of the shorter and stockier faemen.

Heron stepped forward and placed his hand next to the others on the rock. His hands were smaller and less meaty than Thurdop's or Mergop's. There were no callouses, no scars there. His fingers were long and narrow, just as he was. His lithe form looked more akin to a tall pine tree than a sturdy boulder like Mergop and Thurdop, as they hunched low together in their communion.

One by one, their eyes squeezed shut in concentration. A faint, earthy glow, almost imperceptible, rippled around them, a subtle shift in the air, a blending with the very essence of the mountain, and deeper still, the Wood. They were not invisible, not truly. But they were less seen, less felt, their presence muted, their forms blurring against the rain-swept stone.

"Now," Thurdop said, opening his eyes. They glowed faintly with a deep, earthy green. "We go."

They moved as one, a shadowy, silent procession, slipping through the shattered gates of the Stoneguard, past the mangled corpses of guards and nobles, past the twisted metal of the abandoned and burning carriages, and into the heart of the raging battle. The transition was abrupt and jarring. The relative quiet of the outer pass gave way to a deafening cacophony of screams and clashing steel. The roars of darklings and the crackle of arcane energies were all around them. The air was a swirling miasma, thick with the scent of blood, Aether, and burnt hair that clawed at their throats.

Mergop gagged, his hand flying to his mouth, but Thurdop merely tightened his grip on his axe, his eyes darting from shadow to shadow, assessing and calculating. He saw noble knights, gleaming in their plate armor, fighting with desperate courage, but they were being overwhelmed by the sheer numbers of the black-clad invaders. The darklings moved with brutal efficiency, their lava-stone-infused glaives searing flesh and bone and armor with every strike. Wine ran with blood across the stained floors, tables were overturned and splintered, and foodstuffs littered every inch of the hall. A savage darkling, frothing and howling, ran directly in front of them, his wicked glaive leading the charge. He didn't see them, but he did see a helpless maid standing still as stone, hands held to her mouth, eyes wide. She was shaking, trying to cry, trying to scream, trying to run, but her body would do none of these things. The darkling ran her through without slowing down and tossed her lifeless form from the glaive's blade with a quick whip of his muscled arm.

"This way," Thurdop whispered, his voice strained with anger and fear. "Stay low. Keep ter the shadows. Remember ar reasonin' fer bein' here."

"Are we just going to slither by in the dark, while the rest of these peo—" Heron began to ask. He had even begun to act, drawing the first few inches of steel from the scabbard at his waist, before he was interrupted and rebuked.

"Ye quiet yerself an' stay yer blade, idjit boy," Thurdop said as quietly as he could while still conveying the command. "Ya ain't said but two words this whole journey, an' that w'jus fine wit' me, but now, in the middle o' all hells, ye choose to wake up?"

"But we need —"

"But nothin'," Mergop insisted. "Ye listen ter yer betters an' that be that. What we're fer needin' is to find Stren and get ye to 'im. An' that's all that's needin' ter be said."

Heron returned the length of blade that he'd drawn back to its home with a snap of his wrist. He glared at the two faemen. His eyes smoldered as he calculated his next move. He didn't owe these two anything. Yes, his mother was a fae, but he never knew her, and he most certainly didn't know this Mergop or Thrudop. He was taken to the Bairnbrand when he was still wrapped in cloth and crawling, and there he was raised, in squalor and servitude, reminded every day that he was alone and would always be. Until these two ferried him away when he was little more than a child.

The Bairnbrand was a squat, sprawling orphanage carved from the ancient, wind-gnarled oaks at the edge of the Greenfallow Downs. Heron had known no other home than the rambling orphanage for his first years of remembering. His days were a ceaseless cycle of scrubbing pots until his knuckles ached, mending threadbare tunics by the dim light of sputtering tallow candles, and hauling endless buckets of water from the perpetually creaking and leaking well. The Matron, a woman whose smile was as thin and sharp as an icicle, delighted in reminding him of his unfortunate circumstance, a phrase that always carried the unspoken meaning of *unwanted* and *unclaimed*. He was just another mouth to feed, a body to put to work, and his singular, striking appearance, his fiery red hair, only set him further apart in a place where conformity was the only comfort.

He'd lived his whole childhood in the Bairnbrand, and while it wasn't anything special, it was, indeed, all he knew. That is, until a few days before his eighth birthday, when four rough-shodden and suspicious-looking faemen came and demanded that he go with them by order of someone named Stren. Their brief exchange with The Matron went from curt and crude insults, to bribes and jingling purses, and nearly to fisticuffs, when one of the fae, a faemen by the name of Mergop, not-so-politely told her that her face could curdle milk straight from the teat quicker than any mid-summer sun, and that she was uglier than a troll's underside after a long day of dung digging. Needless to say, the faemen left with Heron at their side and a stream of curses and threats at their back. He had lived in solitude within the Western Wood and among the fae since that day, always outside looking in.

"I'm sorry, master faemen," Heron said at last, allowing the tension to fade. "I meant no disrespect." He figured that while he may not owe these two anything, he was no longer destitute in The Bairnbrand, and he was no longer subject to The Marton. He would see where the fae led him … for now.

"None taken," Thurdop said and then began to move.

They weaved between the groups of fighters, ducking under the swing of glaives and swords, sidestepping falling bodies, and skittering away from wayward spells, their small forms almost completely invisible in the maelstrom. Always sticking to the walls, always in the shadows, Thrudop led the trio through the atrium, across the rubble of the great hall's threshold, and into the Sunrise Spire's main chamber. The scene before them was an extravaganza of horror, painted in crimson and crumbled gold. The grand hall, moments ago a vibrant gathering of celebration, was now a charnel house. Darklings, their black fur matted with sweat and blood, swarmed like maddened hornets, their blades carving through the noble guests who had once glittered in silk and jewels and smiles. The air, once sweet with the scent of roasted pheasant and fine wine, was now thick with the metallic tang of fresh blood and the smoke of burning draperies. Bodies, once arranged in elegant rows for the coronation, lay twisted and broken amidst trampled flower petals and spilled wine, their festive attire a stark contrast to the brutal reality of their demise. Soldiers, caught off guard, fought with desperate courage, their armor now caked with grime and gore. Sorcerers, their faces contorted in furious concentration, hurled desperate spells. Still, their efforts seemed to merely add to the chaotic destruction, sending bursts of light and displaced air tearing through the already ruined space. Everywhere Mergop looked, the beauty and celebration of moments past were being irrevocably consumed by the nightmare unfolding around them.

"Look, Thurdop!" he shouted, forgetting their need for quiet amid the chaos. "The boy! And the Crownward!"

Thurdop followed Mergop's gaze. On the elevated dais, amid the carnage, he saw Stren, the king's Crownward, fighting with a ferocity that belied his years. And beside him, slightly behind, was Ixchel, his hair wild, his hands glowing with a soft, ethereal light as he conjured shimmering, ghostly figures that flickered and danced through the battle, drawing the darklings' attention.

And then there was the prince.

Endryll moved like a dancer of death, his movements precise and lethal. The gleaming edge of his blade rang as it cut, each strike a lyric of woe. He was a whirlwind of green and gold, deflecting glaives with ringing parries, thrusting his sword into darkling hearts with perfect effectiveness. Blood, black and viscous, spattered his royal tunic. He fought not with the calculated moves of a king defending his besieged realm, but with the cold fury of a husband protecting his wife. He was unbound and unstoppable. He bellowed in rage as he hacked and slashed. Beside him, Ixchel was a blur of motion and light. His Echoborn surged and faded, attacking, only to dissolve into mist when struck, leaving the frustrated creatures to face the real Ixchel.

He wielded Sylvandralis, the blade aflame with purpose and power. With each swing, it pulsed with blinding light, throwing back the encroaching beasts, a torrent of fire and steel that slammed into the darklings, sending them sprawling. Stren, the Last Oak of Burss, stood as a mighty barrier between Endryll, Ixchel, and the dark army. His hands moved in intricate patterns, weaving spells that tore through the black ranks. Roots erupted from the marble floor, coiling around enemies, pulling them down into sudden chasms of earth. Vines lashed out like furious whips, their thorns tearing through fur and flesh. The air around him shimmered with the raw force of his Aether arts, a protective aura that crackled with untamed force, sending darklings reeling and stumbling with invisible blows. He moved with a quiet, devastating power, a sentinel guarding the last vestiges of hope. The combined might of the three was a terrifying, beautiful display of defiance against the overwhelming horde.

"They're good," Mergop mumbled with a note of deep respect.

Two Kings, One Stone: Part I

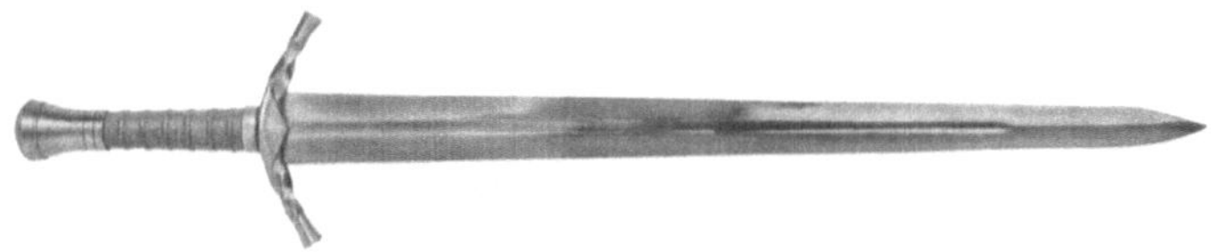

The horror clawed at Illia-Dara's senses as she ran, the screams of the dying a symphony of pain that echoed in her very soul. Her breath came in gasps. Her emerald gown, a symbol of hope moments ago, was now a trailing weight dragging at her heels. She didn't look back. She couldn't. The image of Endryll's face, pale and resolute as he shielded her, burned behind her eyes as desperate fuel for her flight. Her feet, light as a dancer's among the clouds moments before, now pounded a frantic rhythm against the ancient stone as she veered sharply from the main concourse.

The secret passage, known only to the royal family and their most trusted Crownwards, was a dark and narrow maw. She plunged into its shad-owed embrace, the air instantly colder and heavier, muffling the cacoph-ony of terror to a distant hum. The winding stone stairs coiled upward. Illia-Dara's hands scraped against rough, unadorned walls as she navigated in the dark, a stark contrast to the gilded banisters she had become ac-customed to. Here, no finery softened the walls, no candlelight fought the encroaching gloom. Only the faint, humid breath of the lost earth permeated these forgotten routes.

She exited the labyrinthian pathway through a large, framed painting hung on hidden hinges in the halls high in the Spire. She resumed her flight but made only mere steps of progress before a whimper, raw and terrified, pulled her up short. Huddled in a shallow alcove, lit only by the flickering glow from a distant candelabra, were two scullery maids. Their eyes, wide as saucers, mirrored the terror she felt, brimming with unshed tears and the dawning realization of their doom. One, barely older than a child, clutched a pewter basin to her chest, her knuckles white. She was trembling. The other, an older woman with a face showing clearly the weariness of years, wrung her hands, a low, keening sob escaping her lips.

"Run," Illia-Dara urged, her voice hoarse, raw with urgency, "to the lower keeps, the hidden passages to the garden. Hide. Don't look back, no matter what you hear. And tell anyone you see to do the same." The words tumbled out. She didn't wait for a response, nor did she stop to see if they obeyed. She couldn't afford to. Every heartbeat was a marching drum demanding she continue.

The screams from below became muffled as she went deeper into the upper halls. Her heart hammered against her ribs, a wilding bird trapped within a cage too small. She slowed as she approached the royal wing and entered quietly, cautiously. Bookshelves, carved from dark, torch-burned cedar, lined the far wall, their precisely-placed volumes untouched. Matching ottomans, upholstered in emerald Calidene velvet and stitched with shimmering silver thread, sat peacefully, as if waiting to comfort her. The hearth, screaming griffon's head and all, was a bastion of light and warmth, its low-burning driftwood fire offering an odd sense of solace. It was as if she'd walked through a magic window and into a place where everything was right again. But she knew it wasn't.

She began taking inventory of things that she would need. Her mind was not on fineries or comforts, but on necessities. She grabbed two canvas bags from the chest of drawers in the bedroom and began filling them with warm clothing, salted and dried meats from their private kitchens, and empty water skins. She packed one bag for herself and then another for her husband. She strapped a small knife, a gift from her father-in-law, to her right thigh. She paused. The thought of her father-in-law lying in a pool of his own blood on the dais of the Sunspire Citadel on the day of his son's coronation and wedding curdled her stomach. She thought of the wink he had given her as she walked down the aisle, the smile on his face. He *knew.* He knew that she was already his daughter, and he her father. She wept. The tears came hot and fast, blurring her vision as the grief, held at bay by the urgency of battle, finally broke free. It was a fresh wound, a raw agony that tore through her, echoing at first, the most profound loss of her own father, then of King Onidine. Now, twice orphaned, twice bereft, the weight settled upon her, heavy and choking. She sank to the floor, the canvas bags forgotten along with the immediate necessity of flight, and buried her face in her hands, allowing the shaking sobs to wrack her body.

Outside, a monstrous peal of thunder ripped through the sky, booming and crashing across the Serrated Sea in spectacular waves and shaking the very core of the Spire. A blinding flash of lightning followed, illuminating the room in a stark, fleeting white, then another monstrous thunder roll. For a split second, the sapphire of the coffered ceiling, painted with golden leaf constellations of Y'sa's prophets, seemed to writhe, the stars screaming in silent horror as the light saturated the room. The heavy curtains at the balcony doors, usually billowing sluggishly, surged inward, caught in the violent wind of the storm. It seemed as though even this most private of sanctuaries was being invaded. The sound of the wind was a wail, mingled with the distant screams from the hall below. And then, in the stark, fleeting brilliance, her gaze snapped to a small box. It lay on the end table, a form of perfect black against the polished oak. Its surface, covered in runes, pulsed with a dim, sickly red light, like a dying heartbeat at the core of emptiness.

Illia-Dara stumbled backward, dread seizing her. The pulsing red light from the box seemed to draw her, to call her, a malevolent beacon in the storm-lashed room. Her hand instinctively went to the pocket of her gown, where the object Atamas had slipped her pulsed in response, a faint but undeniable throbbing against her leg. It mirrored the rhythm of the box, a slow, insistent beat that resonated and exacerbated the fear coiling in her gut. With each hesitant step she took toward the table, the thumping in her pocket intensified. The air around the box grew colder, prickling her skin despite the rising heat of her blood. The runes on its surface seemed to deepen, drinking the faint light of the room into their inky depths. It was cold, impossibly cold, even from across the room, radiating the very breath of the Vintermarrow.

A faint scrape against stone, almost lost beneath the storm's fury, sounded from the balcony. Illi froze, her breath catching in her throat. Three figures, cloaked in deep violet and black, slipped through the surging curtains, their movements silent and intent. The mark of Thar-Azhul, a blackened spiral of three interlocking arcs, their thorn-notched edges coiling toward a void at the center, all encircled by a broken ring split into seven uneven shards, was emblazoned on each of their shoulders. Soot-smeared masks obscured their faces, and the glint of their swords in the sporadic lightning flashes screamed of their intent. They spread out, flanking her, their steps unnervingly deliberate. The air thickened with a chill that was not of the storm, but of something far more ancient, far more predatory. A low chuckle, devoid of true cheer, slithered from the lead figure, "No need to fear, little one," the voice rasped, the words a promise of unspeakable things. "We've merely come to talk."

The darkling's skull cracked like old timber, and he fell, a heap of twisted fur and bones. Ixchel, his eyes burning with the nascent power of his awakened flame, moved like a devil. Another, its glaive raised for a killing blow on an unarmed courtier, found itself suddenly disoriented. Its vision flickered, warped by Ixchel's illusion, and then it stumbled, its own blade twisting in its grasp to pierce its comrade. Ixchel darted forward, his hands a blur, disarming another darkling with a spin that snapped bone before he melted back into the shifting chaos, unseen among his Echoborn.

Tam-Ma and her pirates, a motley crew of roguish and weathered faces and keen eyes, had dropped from the balconies and slid down silken banners with all the theatrics worthy of *The Lass O' No Virtue*'s name. A hulking darkling, attempting to scale a support pillar, met a sudden, sickening crack as a pirate's boot slammed into its elongated and toothy face, sending it tumbling to the floor below. Another, snarling and savage, lunged at the pirate captain, herself, only to have a crude, flintlock pistol roar to life. The shot echoed through the hall, a startling punctuation to the shouts and pains all about, and the darkling fell, a smoking hole in its chest the size of a clenched fist. Her crew, with cutlasses flashing and crude knives drawn, engaged the invaders in the brutal ballet of close-quarters combat learned only on the decks of ships. They fought with the reckless abandon of those who lived on the edge of the law, using every dirty trick and opportunistic strike. One pirate, missing an eye and grinning ferociously, swung a broken balustrade like a flail, knocking two darklings off a banister in a tangle of limbs and splintered wood. The scent of burnt tobacco and stale rum mingled with the rising stench of blood as Tam-Ma's crew turned the upper levels into a meat grinder, laughing all the way.

Below, amidst the carnage, Aoife moved with ferocity unrivaled, the raw, primal potency of the Star Speaker was a firestorm unleashed. She was an angel of death wrapped in flaming wings as she soared across the battlefield. A darkling with crimson claws, soaked in Y'ssildrian blood, turned its attention to her, its eyes gleaming with hatred. Aoife's own eyes blazed. The air around her shimmered, a visible distortion of heat and light. Her fingers curled, not around a weapon, but around the unseen threads of the cosmic power. A blinding flash of pure white flame erupted from her palms, consuming the darkling in an instant, leaving behind only a faint, putrid smell of melted flesh and burnt innards. She was no longer just Aoife, she was a conduit for celestial judgement, and her fury was absolute. With every gliding movement, streams of light pulsed around her, incinerating darklings before they could even raise their weapons in defense.

Behind her, Cante and Feste Rand, armed with whatever they could scavenge, a discarded spear for Cante and a ceremonial axe from a fallen guard for Feste, joined the fray. They were not warriors, but the sight of Aoife's terrifying power, coupled with the primitive fear for their lives, spurred them on. Cante, despite his rotund frame, swung the spear with surprising force, catching a darkling in the thigh and sending it sprawling. Feste, roaring like a cornered badger, brought the axe down with clumsy but effective blows, driven by a desperate need to survive and to return whole to his family. They moved as a single, uncoordinated but surprisingly resilient unit, a tiny eddy in the raging river of war, their fear slowly morphing into stubborn and desperate courage. The clang of steel, the screams of the dying, and the crackle of Aoife's starfire filled the hall, an accord of destruction as Y'ssildria fought for its very survival.

All around the dais lay the bodies of darklings—dismembered, dead, and dying. The wide and crushing swings of Endryll's sword were no longer met with block or parry, but with the backs of attackers who had the misfortune of getting trapped between him and the ever-growing wall of the dead at his feet. Attackers stumbled past him, off balance and exposed, as they attempted to flee. The tide was shifting, at least upon the dais, where Endryll and Stren stood as a pair of lions protecting their pride. The new king's straw-colored hair, usually fashionably cut and brushing his broad shoulders, was now a wild, sweat-slicked mess, plastered to his face. A fresh cut—a crimson streak—bled openly from his temple, mingling with the sweat and blood that gritted his teeth. His usually pristine green and gold tunic was torn and stained. Yet, his eyes remained sharp, unwavering, fixed on the relentless tide. Beside him, Stren bore the marks of battle with a calm endurance. Deep lines of strain and determination crossed his features, emphasizing the decades of hard-won wisdom he carried. Gashes across his forearms and chest, angry and stark against his sun-darkened skin, bled a steady trickle, but his focus remained firm, his resolve unyielding.

"Ixchel," Endryll shouted over the struggle. He had lost sight of him and called desperately for him now. "Ixchel, where are you?"

"He is with the Star Speaker," Stren said as he batted away a strike and plunged his sword deep into the exposed ribs of a darkling.

And so it was that Ixchel had encountered the Star Speaker, and together they were pushing back the army of darklings. Together they were truly a juggernaut of retribution, and all before them perished. Ixchel's Echoborn zigged and zagged in and out of existence, this way and that amid Aiofe's flaming pulses. Sylvandralis blazed in wide arcs, taking heads and limbs with every pass. The floor was slick with blood, but that hardly affected the duo as Aiofe's feet were hovering inches above, and Ixchel, somewhere between the Aetherfast and reality at any given moment, was never in one place long enough to set his stance. The same couldn't be said for the darkling invaders. Their pawed and clawed feet slid and scratched along the marble tiles, leaving momentary marks of white in the blood-soaked floor that were quickly covered with scarlet once again.

"Ixchel," Endryll shouted again. "To me. Now! Please!"

Ixchel was there in the blink of an eye, carried by the Aetherfast. He shimmered into existence before Endryll and bowed low, taking this momentary reprieve to steady his heaving chest and to catch his breath. He was haggard and worn, but in much better condition than his friends. His dandelion hair was heavy with blood, and framed a face bruised but not cut. Angry red welts marred his alabaster and freckled skin, and his dark coat was ripped at the seams. One sleeve was half-torn, revealing a single raw scrape along his forearm.

"My king," he said in his bow, his voice thin, breath coming in ragged gasps.

"Ixchel," Endryll said, his voice raw, strained by the fight. He clamped a hand onto Ixchel's arm, his grip urgent. "Go to Illia. Now. She is in our chambers preparing to depart. We must keep her safe at all costs."

Ixchel's eyes widened, a flicker of dread replacing the gold in their hazel depths as he realized that Illia was not among them. His breath hitched. "I thought she was here with you!"

"She was," Endryll rasped, shaking his head. "But when the darklings came in full, I sent her to the hidden corridors." He grabbed Ixchel's forearm then and brought his head very near to Ixchel's own, their foreheads almost touching. Endryll's eyes, fierce and burning, bored into Ixchel's. "You are the last gate, Ixchel. Go to her—now!"

Ixchel nodded once, his jaw clenched, a desperate resolve hardening his bruised face. "You are safe behind the gate," he said, the words a promise. He embrace his king, his friend, and kissed his head. "And so is she." He turned to leave, already gathering power.

"I am proud of you, my son," Stren's voice, rough with exertion, came from the other side of the dais. "You make all of Y'ssildria proud this day."

Ixchel looked from Endryll, a king in stained and torn silks, to Stren, a bruised monument of defiance, and everything he had known. He nodded grimly once more, a silent acknowledgment, and blinked away. The cacophony of battle, the screams, the clang of steel, and the roar of the darklings all disappeared in an instant as he rode the Aetherfast to his queen.

Mergop moved with surprising efficiency and agility, his round belly somehow aiding his serpentine weaves through the thrashing crowd. It was almost as if he used his paunch as a guiding force amid the mass, allowing its heft to lead him. A discarded chair, flung by a fleeing attendant, threatened to collide with them, but Mergop, with a subtle flex of his hand against a nearby potted plant, caused a root to shoot up from the broken marble before them. The root, called by the power of the Western Wood, leaped tall and intercepted the chair just as it would have connected to them. "This was a fool's errand from the start," he said, a familiar lament now sharpened by the exacerbation of the slaughter all around them. "The little princeling's party has gone to all the hells an' we're fer bein' next."

"Stay low, lad," Thurdop said as he brought up the rear. Heron was crouched between the two faemen and looking quite nervous as his head shifted from side to side at the many sounds and sights of the battle. "They're like an army o' black ants, an' bitin' ones at that. Don't give 'em a chance ter swarm ye."

They were being swept inexorably toward the dais. Every step of progress locked them further and further into a singular, straight-forward path as the way back was perpetually swallowed up by new skirmishes and mounting bodies. As they neared the steps, a darkling, its rabid maw a masterwork of malevolence, turned its attention to them, its glaive dripping and hungry. It saw them—or saw *something*. Thurdop braced himself, pushing Heron firmly behind his back, a prayer to Y'sa on his lips. Before the darkling could even raise its weapon, a searing flash of steel erupted from the darkling in a spray of viscous fluids. Its maw, still a gaping grin much like the sword-shaped hole now in its chest, was now one of surprise and pain rather than ill intent. It was Endryll, a force of righteous anger, who had dispatched the threat. Behind him stood Stren, frenzied and exhausted, yet whose gaze was unyielding as he met Thurdop's eyes. The recognition, fleeting but potent, passed between them. Stren's voice, though rough with the strain of battle, carried across the distance between them.

"Thurdop! You're here at last. Good." His eyes flickered to Heron, then back to the desperate fight. "The boy. Get him to the lower crypts. There is a passage beneath the old armory, located on the south wall. It leads to the servant's exit near the gardens. From there, do not exit. Climb. It will deposit you directly outside Queen Illia-Dara's chambers. Ixchel will meet you."

Thurdop's eyes widened at the urgency in Stren's command. He tightened his grip on Heron's shoulder. The boy's knuckles were white as he clutched at the fae's tunic. Thurdop then began looking around the walls for the exit, keeping Heron always behind him.

Mergop darted forward, leaving Heron and Thrudop, already scanning the frantic hall for any sign of the passage. "As if this whole place isn't crypt-like enough as it is," he mumbled to himself. "How are we to be findin' an'o'thin' in this rabble?" Mergop was a grumbler, but his instincts were sharp. He was at home in the wide-open world of the Western Wood. That is where his heart was. So, even here surrounded by stone, he could sense the exit, by feeling for the Wood. He pointed a stubby, scarred finger towards a shadowed archway near the back of the dais, half-hidden by a toppled banner. "There!"

"Wha'bout the boy?" Thrudop demanded of Stren, even as he followed Mergop's movements.

"No time to explain now, Master Thurdop," Stren shot back. "All will be made clear in time, or we will all be dead. If you tarry here, it will most certainly be the latter!"

Thurdop did not hesitate. With a grunt, he heaved Heron onto his shoulder, the boy's slight frame surprisingly light work for Thrudop's muscled back. "Ye heard 'im, boy. We got ta' move, an' I ain't fer havin' time fer ye ter be stopping an' askin' questions er thinkin' ye'll be poking them wolfies every damn minute." He raced along with a renewed purpose, his short, powerful legs churning through the blood-slicked quagmire, all thought of cloaking or sneaking abandoned. The darklings, focused on the more immediate threat of Endryll, Stren, and Aoife seemed to overlook the small, desperate band as they plunged into the echoing darkness of the archway, the clamor of the battle slowly fading behind them as they descended.

STREN'S FOLLY

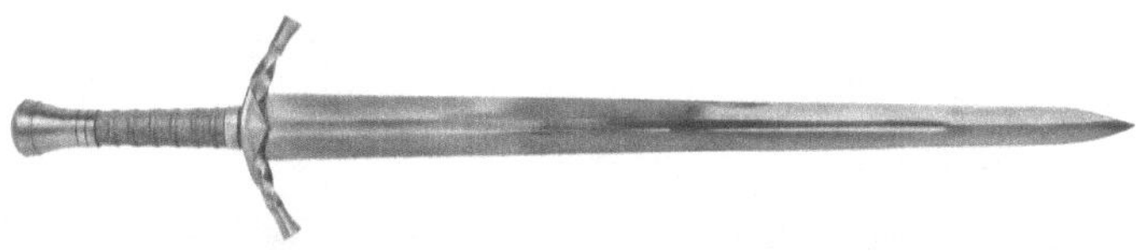

"There must be something that we can do," Onidine pleaded, his voice choked with despair, his gaze fixed on the dying infant.

Atamas looked at him, his visage one of dark and quiet things, secret things. "There always is," he replied, his tone laced with an ancient, weary knowing.

He shifted the pulsing orb, its crude form evidencing the desperate gamble he was about to make. "You ask for a miracle, Onidine, and a miracle you shall have. But miracles, my king, are seldom without cost."

"Wha—what is it you mean to do?" Onidine's grip on his son tightened. The healthy twin, wrapped snugly in Atamas's discarded cowl, stirred faintly on the makeshift bed of leaves beside Cerceia's still form. His contented cooing was a jarring sound among restrained and muffled mutterings of the forest.

Atamas's eyes pinched and narrowed slightly, though whether in thought or pain, Onidine could not tell. "The Aetherfast, the boundless fountainhead of creation and destruction—the place where all things begin, and where some, alas, return." He held up the grotesque, fleshly orb.

A shiver, not from the cold, ran through Onidine. "The Aetherfast is for the gods, Atamas, for the very threads of creation. We were taught to *respect* it, not to *meddle* with it. Stren himself—"

"Stren is a fool," Atamas spat, his voice sharp with a sudden, uncharacteristic venom. "He has abandoned us, abandoned *her*!" His eyes shot to the dead queen. "For a fool's errand, he chases empty prophecies while Cerceia dies! He clings to his dusty scrolls and ancient proverbs, to his 'balance' and his 'natural order.' He believes the world is a gentle garden to be tended. I say it is a forge, and we are the smiths, shaping fate with fire, and force, and will."

He looked at the sickly infant, whose breathing was now a shallow, desperate gasp. "This child's flame, his very soul, is too weak for this world. It is a wisp, easily extinguished. But in the Aetherfast, power flows unbound. If we can bind his fragile heart to that raw energy, we can draw from its inexhaustible well."

Onidine recoiled, clutching his son tighter. "You mean to tie him to the Aetherfast? Like a conduit? What would that mean for him? What would that *do* to him?"

Atamas reached out, his dark, soiled hand hovering over the infant's head. "It would mean life, Onidine. Life where there is only death. It would mean power where there is only weakness. It would mean a connection to something grander, something eternal."

"But at what cost?" Onidine whispered, remembering Stren speak warnings about drawing too deeply from the Aetherfast, the way it could twist and warp, consume and reshape, the danger of changing things, of making the natural unnatural.

Atamas chuckled, a dry, humorless sound that seemed to scrape against the frozen air and crawl down the length of Onidine's spine. "The cost is always paid, my friend, by the one who wields the power or by those closest to him. But for this child," he looked directly into Onidine's eyes, "the alternative is death."

He didn't wait for an answer. His fingers, stained black from the briarwood pipe and covered in afterbirth and muck, moved with a swift, almost surgical precision. He took the orb of mud and blood, the umbilical cord still clinging to it like a dying serpent, and held it above the child's tiny chest. Onidine flinched but could not look away. He moved as if to speak, as if to command Atamas to stop. But he said nothing.

Atamas squeezed the orb in his palm. When it cracked, viscous liquid oozed between his fingers and sprinkled blackened ichor across the child's head, the mud and twigs flaking away as Atamas opened his hand to reveal a core of obsidian, smooth and black as a cold winter's night. From within, a thin and shimmering tendril of iridescent light pulsed, like a heartbeat held captive. Atamas plunged his thumb into the child's fevered chest, pressing hard. It sank deep, penetrating the baby's flesh. The infant cried out in a weak, reedy sound. It squirmed feebly, for it had no energy left, and then fell still.

"By the blood given, for the life taken," Atamas intoned, his gaze fixed on the child, "I bind this fragile heart to the Aetherfast. Let the threads of existence intertwine, let power flow where weakness abounds. Let the spirit of this child become one with the boundless energies of creation and destruction. May unison be found in life and death."

The obsidian orb shattered, and the tendril of light plunged into the hole in the infant's breast, a searing dart disappearing into pale skin. The child convulsed once, a violent, arching spasm, and then fell limp once more. All was still and silent for a moment, save the soft babbling from the healthy babe. The child in Onidine's arms did not stir, did not breathe. Then, breath that had been previously rattling and shallow came forth in a deep, steady rhythm. The fevered heat receded, replaced by a strange, unnatural coolness. And his eyes, which had been dim and distant, snapped open. One was the color of crushed almonds, the other a swirling, vibrant gold, intelligent and ancient.

Atamas, exhausted, stepped back shakily and breathed heavily. "He lives," he gasped, wiping sweat from his brow with the back of his hand. "He lives, Onidine. But he is changed. Forever."

Onidine looked at his son, then at the other child, who was still cradled in Atamas's cloak next to the queen. "He is different," he whispered, with dawning and terrible awe. "His eyes, one of gold."

"A reflection of the Aetherfast itself," Atamas said, recovering his breath. "The gateway through which his life now flows. He is a child of two worlds, Onidine. Endryll is your son, born of this earth, of flesh and blood and sunlight. But this one, this one is a child of the veil, of the Aetherfast. His very being is intertwined with its currents, his flame burning with a power that will only grow." He gestured to the healthy twin, still bundled snugly. "Behold, your heir, whole and untainted, unmarked and unstained." Then he pointed to the other. "And this, the anomaly, tethered to forces beyond mortal understanding. One born of this world, the other reborn of another."

Onidine reached out a trembling finger and touched his reborn son's cheek. The skin was cool, almost cold, an unsettling contrast to the fever that had raged moments before. It felt less like flesh and blood and more like polished stone, smooth and strong. Beneath the surface, however, he felt it, a faint and powerful pulse, like a distant storm trapped within a fragile shell. It was raging, boiling, searching, and seeking. It vibrated against his fingertip, a subtle tremor that resonated deep within his bones, a low thrum that spoke of immense, barely contained energy. It was a sensation utterly alien to him, a feeling that defied his understanding of the natural world. It was as if he were touching not a child, but a vessel, a vessel for forces far beyond his comprehension. A wave of unease washed over him, a primal fear of the unknown, yet mingled with it was a sense of awe, a dizzying awareness of the power that now resided within his son. He looked at Atamas, his eyes filled with questions he dared not voice, questions that clawed at the edges of his consciousness. What had he done? What had they unleashed? And what would become of this son, forever bound to this terrifying, magnificent force?

"You asked for a way, Onidine," Atamas said as he retrieved the other child and wrapped his cloak tightly around them both. "There is always a way, but every path has its price. This is Stren's folly, not mine. He should have been here today, not me. He may have had other means. He may have been able to save Queen Cerceia. I know not, but I know had he been here, it would have been his hand guiding destiny and not my own."

He turned away from the king, his gaze sweeping over the silent, snow-laden forest. The moon cast long and clawed shadows between the trees, and the air crackled with a new, subtle power, a quiet thing that only Atamas, and now perhaps the babe, could truly perceive. "The strings of destiny," Atamas murmured, exhaling a plume of breath that mingled with the night air. "They are not frayed, Onidine. They are being rewoven. And this," he gestured vaguely to the infant in the King's arms, "is but the first knot."

Stren's coarse, woolen cloak whipped around him like a tormented spirit. He clutched the swaddled bundle tighter, pressing the small, unmoving weight closer to his chest. Inside, nestled deep within layers of homespun cloth, lay the infant. So small, so utterly vulnerable, yet bearing a weight that even he found increasingly heavy. Each cutting gust of wind whispered a name he knew well: *Cerceia*. He imagined her now, lying broken on the cold forest floor, the snow falling like a final, silent benediction. A fresh pang of grief, sharp as a splinter, pierced him as he rode. He should have been there. With Onidine, with *her*. He should have used his strength, his knowledge, his connection to the deep currents of life to save her. But duty, an uncaring and unyielding mistress, had pulled him south, away from the Spire, away from the cries of birth and death, and into the unforgiving embrace of fortune. He had sworn an oath, one older than kings and more binding than blood. He had sworn to protect the sacred balance, to safeguard the prophecies, even if it meant sacrificing his own heart, and those he loved, to the altar of fate.

And so, while he was trudging through the southern boundary of the Wilds, a remote peninsula on the fringe of Y'ssildria, a fragile newborn he was tasked to keep from the world's ravenous chill in his arms, Stren had sent his pupil to aid his dear friends in his stead. The journey had been relentless, days and nights of pushing his endurance to its limits, his body protesting with every step, his mind a war field of unanswered questions. He felt the distant tremor of the Aetherfast, a faint, discordant ripple that spoke of unnatural power at play, and a knot of dread tightened in his gut. What was Atamas doing? What desperate measure had he taken in Stren's absence? The thought was a burr beneath his saddle, a chafing and bothersome thing. Atamas, once a dear companion, but now a wraith of the man he had been, a man whose ambition had been a perpetual hindrance throughout his training and eventual initiation into the Eluminthil, was up to something, Stren could feel the distortions in the Aetherfast, and he was miles away, helpless to do anything about it.

The Bairnbrand was a place of stark necessity. It was not a sanctuary, nor a pocket of ancient magic. It was a desolate orphanage buried by time on the windswept peninsula overlooking The Serrated Sea and Bleakshore Bay. It was a place forgotten by kings and commoners alike, where unwanted children were sent. Wards and ancient, cruel magics *did* protect it, but these were the doing of The Matron, a ruthless mistress who guarded her charges not out of love, but for the resources they provided, for the subtle power she drew from their confinement. The Bairnbrand was not a happy place. Its silence was profound and heavy with unspoken regret, and its walls held no warmth, only the uncaring promise of neglect. He felt the wardings long before he saw the grim clouds of smoke rising from the old fumarole, subtle enchantments designed to dissuade and confuse visitors. They brushed against his awareness like webs strung across his path, gentle warnings against intrusion, slight suggestions for him to turn back. Stren passed through them with ease. He had no time for games.

Through the parting trees, he saw it: The Bairnbrand, a cluster of low, log-and-earth, ramshackle dwellings, built one atop or beside the other as expansion required. Their rounded and thinning roofs thatched with thick moss and interwoven branches blended seamlessly with the forest itself. There were no windows, and only the single door at the entrance of the first and oldest compartment. From there, a figure emerged, a tall and forlorn form, her presence radiating indignance and bother.

Her face was deeply lined like old bark. Her eyes held no warmth, only disdain. Her hair was silvered and reached almost to her knees. She wore a filthy robe of tattered and faded black. She did not speak as Stren approached. Her gaze was fixed on the bundle in his arms. Her silence was an expectant thing, a wordless answer to an unspoken request. She crossed her arms and lifted one ashen eyebrow.

"Matron," Stren called out, still atop his horse. "I bring you a child."

The Matron's gaze, unblinking, remained on the bundle in Stren's arms. Then, slowly, she walked forward and extended a hand, her wrinkled fingers uncurling slowly, as if she was restraining them from reaching too far. For a long moment, she simply held her hand there, not touching the infant directly, but sensing him, tasting him. "A king's son," she murmured, her voice a low, slithering across Stren's arms and onto the child. "But not a king, himself. At least not yet."

Stren nodded, a weary exhale escaping his lips. "He carries royal line within him, Matron. One that must be hidden and protected. For the sake of all Y'ssara."

The Matron finally met Stren's gaze, looking away from the child for the first time, and in her eyes, Stren saw profound depths of calculated ambition. There was no empathy there, no shared burden for the prophecies or the world's unraveling. Instead, he saw the glint of hunger, an unwavering resolve that cared nothing for the fate of kings or kingdoms. What truly lay behind those eyes was a singular, rapacious desire for power, and the vast wealth that the control of such a child could bring. The Bairnbrand was not a sanctuary, but a vault, and the child was merely an asset.

Stren's jaw clenched. She knew. Of course, she knew. "Atamas," he said, the name a bitter taste on his tongue. "He took liberties. He acted in my stead."

"He acted with darkness in his heart," the Matron corrected, her voice firm. "A thirst for power he camouflaged in desperation. The power now bound to the boy is a wound, Stren. A raw and bleeding wound in the fabric. It will become infected and rotted."

He winced. "He saved him. The boy was dying. There was no other way."

The Matron laughed then, a wicked and taunting cackle, full of the brittle crackle of old bone. It echoed in the clearing. "No other way, you say? Spoken like a true follower. You fool. The 'Last Oak' indeed, clinging to your dying roots while the world burns around you." Her eyes bored into his. "There are *always* other ways. Ways that do not involve tearing the very veil between worlds. Ways that do not involve binding a fragile infant soul to the untamed hunger of the Aetherfast. But those ways are slow, aren't they? They require patience, and sacrifice, and a hand that does not tremble with a lust for *force*." She spat the last word as if it were a curse.

"He saved the child," Stren repeated, his voice tight with a rising anger that warred with his gnawing unease. "He gave a chance at life where there was none. You speak of infection, of rot, but what is the alternative? Death? To stand by and watch a prince of Y'ssildria perish?"

The Matron stepped closer. "A prince, you say? A common babe, no more, tied to a dying queen. His claim to the throne was as flimsy as his life. And now, thanks to Atamas's 'salvation,' that common babe is a conduit, a vessel for power he cannot comprehend, let alone control. Do you truly think the Aetherfast gives without taking, old man? Do you think it merely *lends* its might? No, it consumes. It reshapes. It demands a price, not just of the wielder, but of all around it. Atamas betrayed you this night, Crownward.

"The land felt it. A shriek of rebellion against the natural order. A new kind of magic, crude and untamed, born of desperation and ambition.

This boy is a blight. A living scar on the soul of Y'ssara, radiating discord and attracting evils."

"He is a child!" Stren's voice rose, a rare burst of raw emotion. "He is innocent! He is a son of Onidine, a son of Cerceia! A prince of Y'ssildria!"

The Matron laughed again, a dry, rasping sound. "Innocence? In *this* world, Stren? A pretty word, but meaningless. He is a tool, a weapon waiting to be wielded. And Atamas, your *friend*, has forged him for a purpose. Not for the good of Y'ssara, not for the balance you so desperately cling to, but for his own ascendance. For the dark, grasping claws that now hold his soul."

She paused, allowing her words to sink in, twisting the knife of doubt in Stren's heart. "You believe in the prophecies, don't you, Last Oak? The Three Sorrows, the destiny of Y'ssara. But Atamas, he does not believe it, not like you. He *rewrites* it. He twists the words, forcing them into new patterns and shapes of his own design. And this boy, this living wound, is his first move."

Stren heard her and knew she spoke true. He had sensed the shift in Atamas, the hardening of his heart, the subtle disdain for the old ways. But to believe he would go so far, to tamper with the very essence of life and magic in such a brutish and permanent way was unthinkable. Yet, the Matron's words, sharp and venomous though they were, resonated with the deep unease he had felt when Atamas had first spoken of *other ways*.

"What purpose?" Stren asked, his voice barely a whisper. "What could he gain from this?"

"Gain?" The Matron's eyes gleamed with a predatory intelligence. "Everything! A connection to the raw power of the Aetherfast, unfettered by the strictures of traditional magic. A pawn, bound to his will, whose very existence would forever destabilize the old order. A symbol, perhaps, of a new age where power is taken, not given. And ultimately—" She leaned closer, her voice dropping to a conspiratorial hiss. "—the destruction of all you hold dear, so that a new kingdom, one built on *his* terms, can rise."

She straightened, her gaze sweeping over the bundled infant in her arms. "This one, he will be the counterweight? Will he be the *hope*?"

"He is simply a child," Stren insisted. "His blood runs with the blood of kings now lost to us."

"You would answer Atamas with the mere blood of men?" The Matron snorted, genuinely curious. "You would fight the ocean tides with walls of sand?"

"I can't change what Atamas has done in my absence," Stren said, his voice devoid of emotion, his eyes staring past her and into the unknown. "But I can do everything in my power to mitigate it, to correct it."

"There is another," the Matron said.

"There is a girl," Stren answered. "She is the counterweight."

"A useful confluence of events, wouldn't you say?" the Matron said, a cold smirk stretching her lips. "Atamas is clever. He sees weakness and opportunity. And when the natural order of humanity falters, as it always does, he will step in. He has done so this very night." Her gaze narrowed, drawing Stren back from his contemplation. "He knows what he desires, Stren. Do you?"

Stren stared back, a vortex of emotions swirling within him, grief for Cerceia, worry for Onidine, fear for Y'ssildria, and a chilling realization of Atamas's true, terrifying ambition. And in the midst of it all, the burning resolve to protect and guard the faint, untainted hope he represented. He had always believed in the deep, inherent goodness of Y'sa's creation, in the slow, natural flow of balance. But Atamas, with his sharp edges and his hunger for control, threatened to unravel it all.

"He will not succeed," Stren told her, his voice low and firm, a whisper that carried oath. "I will not allow it."

The Matron's icy eyes held his gaze. "Then the game has truly begun, old one. And the stakes are higher than any of us can possibly imagine." She took the child then and disappeared into the low-lying dwelling, leaving Stren alone in the biting cold, burdened by the chilling truth of what had transpired and what was yet to come.

He sighed. He had done his duty, as he understood it. He had brought the bastard to safety, to a place where his unique namesake could be shielded from the events that had just begun. But the Matron's words echoed in his mind, *He knows what he desires, Stren. Do you?* He closed his eyes, summoning his own deep connection to the earth. He felt the touch of the ground beneath him, the steady pulse of the Aetherfast. He felt the vast, interconnected network of roots, the quiet wisdom of the stones. And through it all, he felt power, no longer a discordant tremor, but a raw, surging thing, a wild river that had breached its banks. Atamas had opened a door, a door that could never truly be closed.

Stren sat alone on his steed in the clearing. The Matron's words, sharp and cold and gnawing, echoed in the silence. He gazed back towards the Bairnbrand, knowing that within, Heron was safe, for now. But the path back to the Sunspire, to Onidine, to a kingdom teetering on the precipice of a new, terrifying age, stretched before him.

A penetrating ache settled in Stren's chest for the innocent babe, thrust into a destiny he did not choose. Yet, even in that, a fierce resolve ignited within him, a flame kindled in the face of burgeoning darkness. He was the Last Oak, deeply rooted and steadfast. If Atamas sought to twist the threads of fate, to manipulate the prophecies for his own gain, then Stren would meet his machinations with unwavering purpose. He would return to Y'ssildria, to the fragile heart of the kingdom. He would take Ixchel, the child of the veil, as his own. He would raise him, not as a tool, not as a weapon, but as a son. He would pour into him all the wisdom of the Illuminthil, the deep understanding of the Aetherfast, the subtle dance of balance and restraint that Atamas had so carelessly discarded. He would teach him to master the power that raged within him, to wield it with intention and compassion, not with the reckless abandon of an untamed beast. The coming years would be fraught with peril, a tempest of conflicting forces, but Stren would prepare him. He would prepare them all.

With a heavy sigh rich with the scent of pipe smoke, Stren turned his back on the Bairnbrand, on the hiding place he had secured for one child, and set his gaze towards the distant, storm-shrouded spires of Y'ssildria, where another, equally vital destiny awaited his guiding hand. The webs were indeed tangled, but Stren would dedicate his life to untangling them, even if it meant sacrificing every fiber of his being.

Two Kings, One Stone: Part II

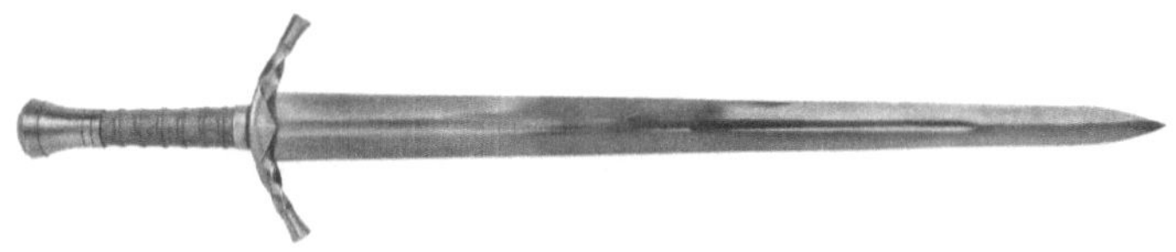

Illia-Dara moved with grace, both fluid and fierce, her emerald gown a blur of shimmering fabric as she parried a brutal overhead swing. Her improvised weapon—a heavy bronze candelabrum ripped from its wall sconce—clashed with the soldier's cruel, serrated sword. The three men pressed her relentlessly. They were no common thugs. Their movements were precise, their strikes aimed with lethal intent. One lunged low, his spear seeking her belly, but Illia-Dara spun, the wide sweep of her gown catching the blade and throwing him off balance. She brought the candelabrum down in a ringing blow against his helm. She took the momentary reprieve to rip off the skirts of her dress at the hole the spear had left. They floated to the floor in a verdant mess of silk, their beauty forgotten. The attacker she had hit staggered back, a grunt of pain escaping him, but his comrades were already closing in.

Sweat beaded on her brow, and her breath came in irregular gulps. She was a queen now, not a warrior, never a warrior, but memory pulsed in her veins and through her muscles. She had trained with Endryll and Ixchel, playfully sparring with dulled blades in the castle courtyards. Her husband was the finest swordsman in Y'ssildria and she had learned much from him, and Ixchel had always made for a wonderful practice dummy. But that was play. Now, the stakes were written in blood on the floors below, and her lessons were now severely real. She dodged a horizontal slice, the steel whistling past her ear, and thrust the candelabrum outwards, forcing the attacker to step back and pull his swing short. Her eyes darted to the ornate wooden door, its heavy bolts thrown deep into their strike plates. *They knew*. They knew she would come here, to the royal chambers, her sanctuary. And they had been waiting just outside. *How could they have known?*

The two others advanced in unison, one on each side of the fledgling queen. Illia backpedaled, casting quick glances left and right, seeking some way of escape, or some way to corral the two brutes into the same space, but she found none. A thrust came at her from the left, low and straight, just as a sweeping arc came for her from high and to the right. She was pinched between the two with nowhere to turn. She screamed in defiance as death came for her from both directions.

A crash of splintering wood and straining iron tore through the chamber, momentarily stilling the desperate battle within. It was a sound that roared with impossible force. The door, once a heavy slab of timber reinforced with iron bands, simply ceased to be. It exploded inward, not breaking, but disintegrating into a furious cloud of jagged splinters and choking dust that billowed into the room like a sudden, violent storm. The three black-clad soldiers were caught off guard by the sheer, devastating impact. Their helms snapped around as they spun, weapons raised. They adopted a tight and defensive form, expecting a fresh wave of invaders, a charging squad of guardsmen, or perhaps some colossal beast. Instead, through the lingering haze of debris and the gaping, ragged hole where the doorway had once stood, a lone, lean figure burst through the wreckage. He was propelled by an unseen momentum, a silhouette of light cast against the evil that had invaded this space.

Ixchel was motion made flesh, his dark coat billowing around him. His hands moved with an impossible precision, trailing faint, blueish energy. This was not the boy who fumbled with simple conjurations. This was not the playful pup that happily followed, wagging his tail as others led. This was the man born of the powers of the Aetherfast, the one who had been reborn. He launched himself into the fray before the soldiers could reorient themselves, a living arrow shot from a bow of ultimate rage. His Echoborn sliced through the haze before him.

The first soldier, still dazed from Illia-Dara's blow, barely registered the movement. Ixchel was a flicker, a glint of speed, the illusion made manifest by his Echoborn manipulating the light and atmosphere of the chamber as he charged. He wielded Sylvandralis, the blade blazing to life in his hand with the fires of the lava stone embedded within, casting magma-colored arcs across the chamber. With a cry, he brought the sword around in a blinding flash, its edge a searing line of white-hot fury. The blade sang as it met the soldier's neck, a horrifying silence following as the heated steel cauterized the wound even as it severed, preventing any spray of blood. The soldier's helm-wrapped head hit the floor with a thud. His body stiffened, a silent scream frozen on his face as it rolled past, a trill of smoke rising from his neck. Before his body even hit the floor, Ixchel was past him and onto the next.

The second soldier, quicker, brought his spear to bear, thrusting it forward. But Ixchel wasn't there. A shimmering echo-image, translucent and fleeting, appeared exactly where the Crownward had been a heartbeat before, dissolving into sparkling motes of light as the spear passed through it. The real Ixchel was already behind the man, a hand snapping out, fingers splayed wide. He didn't strike, but *pushed*—not with physical force, but with something unseen, something that resonated with the workings of the Aetherfast. The soldier cried out, his body seizing, his eyes wide and unseeing. He stumbled forward, tripped over the first fallen man, and collapsed, rigid and unmoving.

The third soldier growled with primal indignation. He raised his sword high, its edge wicked in the dim light of the chamber and brought it down in a powerful arc towards Ixchel. Illia-Dara cried out a warning, her candelabrum raised, but Ixchel met the strike with an eerie calm. He didn't dodge, didn't parry. Instead, as the blade descended, he brought both his glowing hands up, flat, almost placating. A wave of shimmering air, visible only as a slight distortion, rippled from his palms and slammed into the sword. The clang of metal was deafening, the sword vibrating violently in the soldier's grip as a shockwave threw him back. He hit the opposite wall with a grunt, his weapon clattering from nerveless fingers, and slid to the floor, dead.

Ixchel turned, his chest heaving, the blueish light in his hands fading, and the flame of Sylvandralis dimming to a steady glow. His wild mop of sweat-matted hair clung to his forehead, and his eyes swirled with an unearthly intensity, one a deep, crushed-almond brown, the other a vibrant, molten gold. He looked at Illia-Dara, who stood frozen, candelabra still raised, her breath caught in her throat.

"Ixchel," Illia-Dara whispered, her voice barely a breath. "How did you ... What did ..." Her gaze was fixed on him, wide with a mixture of terror and wonder. "Your, your eyes!" She took a hesitant step back, her hand involuntarily coming up to cover her mouth. "They're not—"

"Are you alright?" he managed, his voice a little hoarse.

Illia-Dara dropped the candelabrum with a crash, the bronze clanging against the floor. She stared at the fallen men, then back at Ixchel. "Ixchel," she murmured, the name a fragile sigh. "What? How?"

He took a step toward her, then another, until he was close enough to reach. Without a word, she lunged into his arms, burying her face against his chest, her slender frame shaking. He held her tight, his own relief washing over him. The scent of her, the closeness, the touch, grounded him in the moment.

"They just attacked," she said, her voice muffled against his coat. "They knew I would come here. They were waiting."

"It's okay," Ixchel replied, rubbing her back, not knowing what else to say.

Illia-Dara pulled back slightly, her eyes wide with fresh fear. "Endryll? Is he safe? Oh, Y'sa, the people."

"He was fine when I left him," Ixchel assured her, gently cupping her face in his hands. "And Stren is there. He'll watch over him."

"We have to get back. We have to help," she said, looking around the room for her canvas bags of partially-packed things.

Ixchel reached out, his hand instinctively going to her arm, but she flinched, not away from him, but away from the power she sensed emanating from him. "Illi," he said, his voice rough, urgent. "We have to go. Now. I have to get you to safety." He glanced towards the shattered doorway, the sounds of battle from the hall growing louder, closer. "Once you're safe, I'll go back to Endryll and Stren."

"No!" Illia-Dara shook her head, pulling away from him. "No, we have to get to them. We have to bring them with us." Her voice was rising, a frantic edge to it. "The city ... the people ... we can't just leave them!"

Ixchel gripped her shoulders, his gaze intense, his golden eye seeming to burn with a certainty and command that Illia-Dara had never seen in him before. "There's no time. And you know them. Do you truly believe Endryll would abandon his people in their darkest hour? Do you think Stren would forsake his duty and leave them to perish?" He shook his head, a firm set to his jaw. "They will fight, Illi. To the last breath. And so will I, once I know you are safe. This is my solemn duty as your Crownward and as your friend."

Illia-Dara held his stare for a long moment, wordless. She had so many things she wanted to say, but they would be left unsaid, at least for the moment. "You're right," she said. "I know you're right. But how can I leave? How can I turn my back on these people? On *my* people?" Her gaze drifted past him as fresh tears welled in her red and swollen eyes. "How can I leave *him*?"

Ixchel embraced her once again, to calm her, surely, but also to hide his own tears. *How can I leave* you, he wondered as he held her close. He felt the tremor in her body, the frantic beat of her heart against his own. The assault, the battle, the king's death, all of it pressed in around them in a suffocating claustrophobic vice. His hands tightened around her, not in a lover's embrace, for that was not his station, but with the fierce, possessive grip of a drowning man clinging to the last spar of a broken ship, knowing even as he held her that the tide would soon tear them apart.

"What is that?" he asked, his gaze on the small obsidian box, its surface bearing glyphs that thrummed with a faint, haunting light. It seemed to call to him in the faded din. It seemed somehow familiar to him.

"What is what?" Illi asked, following his gaze.

Ixchel nodded to the table.

"Atamas," she said. "It has to be. He slipped this into my pocket just before—" She swallowed hard, her mouth dry and her throat tight and pained with the exertion of her fight and with emotion. "In the hall." She handed Ixchel the envelope that had been thrumming in her pocket since she entered the room.

"When we were together?" he asked, anger hot on his tongue. *How dare the betrayer be so bold as to hand something off to Illia-Dara right in front of him?*

Illia-Dara moved toward the table, her steps still unsteady, her hand rooted tightly in Ixchel's. She picked up the box, her fingers trembling slightly as she held it up to get a better view.

"Don't touch it," Ixchel started, but then backed down, as she was already inspecting the box in her free hand.

Illia-Dara beheld the caisson warily. It was a thing of chilling beauty, a small, elegant cube bleeding lines of smoking aeriform from all sides, a phantasmic hand curling around the surface. It was black as the recesses of the ocean floor, covered in arcane runes and glyphs that pulsed lazily with energy. It felt impossibly cold to the touch, as though the very breath of the Vintermarrow swirled within. Gazing upon it caused a twisting of Illi's gut, a recognition of cursed magic that needed no scholar's training to discern. She placed it back onto the table with haste, unconsciously wiping her hand on her torn dress.

"What happened when you touched it?" Ixchel asked, alarmed and alert at her sudden movement. "I've seen that box before. In Stren's things, hidden away in the attic."

"It's cold," she answered him, "incredibly cold. And I don't just mean to the touch."

"Did it hurt you?" He looked her over.

"No," she replied through a slight giggle. She flushed and quickly covered her mouth. Her light and airy mirth sounded out of place among the density of the circumstance.

Ixchel stopped his inspection and looked at her, his mouth twisting to a small and crooked smile. His eyes narrowed as his head tilted. "Are you laughing at me, my Queen?"

"Never that, my most steadfast Crownward," she said, raising her shoulders in mock formality. "You took upon thy countenance a most horrid visage, as if I had suddenly sprouted a second head." She laughed again, this time with no attempt to cover it. "Your concern for me is most welcome and appreciated, especially in times such as these. But honestly, you should have seen your face!"

Ixchel laughed then, too. "Sprouted a second head? My Queen, I would have had no other recourse than to cut you down where you stand, had such an abomination burgeoned from thy lovely neck." They both laughed again, knowing that the formality of their banter was a distraction and nothing more.

Ixchel quieted and raised both hands to Illi's face, brushing back her hair. He held her there with his gaze, all merriment gone. "Are you sure you're alright?"

"I'm fine thanks to you." She took one of his hands in hers and kissed it softly. "Let's get going, before more show up."

"Show me what Atamas gave you." His voice was low and urgent. His eyes, usually so bright with amusement and wonder and affection, were now sharp with concern. He had stepped closer and subtly positioned his body between her and the mysterious box. His hand, still warm from her touch, now trembled slightly as he held it out.

Illi's gaze flicked to his face, then down to the pocket where the object seemed to be shivering with energy or anticipation. She knew this was no ordinary item. She remembered the tale Ixchel had told her of his own encounter with a similar, uncanny chill, back in Stren's loft years ago, a stone that had siphoned his strength, a living, sentient thing despite its inert form. The echoes of that unsettling memory, of something both powerful and dangerous, now resonated in the small, stitched pocket of her ruined dress. Reluctantly, she drew the petite, cloth-wrapped package from her pocket and placed it into Ixchel's outstretched hand.

It was an envelope, slight and nondescript, though it did have the dogwood insignia of Y'ssildria pressed into the wax seal that held it closed. They both stared at it for a moment, neither moving, neither speaking. Ixchel could feel the minute vibrations from within the folded page. They were almost imperceptible, but he sensed it somewhere in his sleeping subconscious. Whatever was in the envelope, whatever he held in his hand, was alive, and it was ravenous. He began to open it, but her hand stopped him.

"Let me," Illia said softly.

"Absolutely not," Ixchel responded. "Atamas is a traitor and an enemy. Anything he gave you, he gave to you with ill intent. Go finish packing and I'll—"

"Excuse me?" Illia-Dara's voice was a whip, cutting through the quiet chambers. Ixchel blanched at the sudden shift in her tone, but it was her demeanor that truly arrested him. The softness that had clung to her like her gown was gone, replaced by a rigid posture, her shoulders squared, her chin lifted to a challenging angle. Her eyes, usually so warm and expressive, had turned hard, a glint of jade fire in their depths. The delicate grace that had defined her moments before hardened into something formidable, something he had rarely seen directed at him.

He stammered, searching for words that seemed to have fled his mind. "Illia, I, I didn't mean ..."

"You didn't mean to brush me aside like a child?" she interjected, her voice dangerously quiet. "You didn't mean to tell me, the Queen of Y'ssildria, to 'go finish packing' as if I were a handmaid?" Her gaze dropped pointedly to the hilt of Sylvandralis at his hip, then back to his face, a silent accusation in her eyes. "And you, my Crownward, would so casually forget your station? To act as a shield, yes, but also as a guide, a counsel, a confidant. Not a dismissive warder."

The weight of her words settled on him, heavy and unyielding. He felt the blush creep up his neck, a hot wave of shame. He had overstepped, and badly. He had presumed, in his fear, to command her. He had forgotten the sacred trust she had just placed in him, not just as a friend, but as her sworn protector. The silence stretched between them, thick with the unspoken gravity of his mistake.

"Illia, I am truly sorry," Ixchel said, his voice stripped bare, his gaze fixed on hers with a raw honesty. "My words were inappropriate and born of a concern for you, not disrespect." He took a hesitant step closer, his hand reaching out, then falling back to his side. "You are not a child, and you are not a handmaid. You are my queen, and my friend, and my deepest and only consideration." He gestured to the small object in his hand, the force emanating from it a reminder of Atamas's sinister presence and of their ever-pressing situation. "But, Illia, please. Understand this, I am your Crownward. I swore an oath to protect you, with my strength, my breath, and my very life. And a part of that duty, my Lady, is to face the dangers that come to you, to intercept them, to disarm them if I can. This ... this thing Atamas gave you—" He squeezed the object, feeling its chilling pulse against his palm, "—it feels wrong. It feels like pure evil." His eyes pleaded with hers, earnest and desperate. "I am your friend, Illia. Your closest friend. And because I am your friend, and because I am your Crownward, I need to know what this is. I need to open this envelope, in case it *is* dangerous. I need to protect you from what you cannot see, just as I would protect you from a blade you could not parry. Please. Let me do my duty. Let me fulfill my oath."

Illia-Dara searched his face, her anger ebbing, replaced by a tired understanding. She saw the genuine fear in his eyes, the deep-seated loyalty that had so often made him seem reckless and aloof. She knew he was neither of those things, not anymore. She had seen his power. She had seen his prowess. And she knew his force loyalty. After a long moment, she gave a slow nod. "You are forgiven, Ixchel," she said, her voice strained, but the fire in her eyes had softened to a smolder. "And you are right. You are my Crownward, and my friend. And sometimes, those two things need to be the same."

As she spoke, she reached out her hand and settled it over his. Her fingers, long and elegant, found the green and golden glob of wax sealing the envelope within his grasp. With a delicate pressure, almost a caress, she broke the insignia, the king's stamp, the symbol of Y'ssildria. A faint *snap* echoed in the quiet, loud enough to draw their full attention. Ixchel's eyes widened, but he stood silent, just a breath away from her. Without further word, their fingers, entwined, worked to unfurl the fine parchment. Together, their eyes fixed on the unfolding parchment, still clutched in Ixchel's hand.

The grand hall of the Sunspire Citadel was a sepulcher of carnage. Moments passed like hours since the doors buckled, since the first screams had carved through the fanfare. The air, once sweet with perfume and celebration, was thick with the tang of iron, the bite of spent powder, and the desperate stench of terror. What light pierced the storm-lashed clerestories above was fractured, painting the scene in shifting hues of crimson and bruised indigo.

Stren was rooted deep within the fray. His robes were shredded, clinging to a body battered and bleeding from a dozen cuts. His breath came in wheezes, each inhale a knife in his lungs. His magic, typically precise and deliberate, was now a delirious, raw outpouring. Jagged stone spikes detonated from the floor, skewering darklings, only to be trampled moments later by the endless surge of their kin. He conjured walls of living earth, thick and uncompromising, but they groaned under the relentless assault, crumbling at their edges like clay. He was a dam, straining against a river of black death, and he knew with certainty that the levee would eventually break. He saw the darklings' eyes, empty pits behind their soot-smeared helms, devoid of hesitation, fueled by an unwavering malice. There were too many. *They* were too many. Always too many.

Strakk, a hunched silhouette in the high balcony's shadowed corner, watched the unfolding horror with primal intensity. The glint of his tri-hooked hand caught the light from below. He had known the hall would run red, had even relished the thought of it in the Drossfang Barrens as he imagined what Atamas had planned. But this was not the neat, efficient violence he had honed. This was needless slaughter. His beastly heart, accustomed to the raw consumption of flesh and retribution, rose within him. A low growl rumbled in his chest, a sound of approval that frightened him. His half-human, half-wolf essence waged war, not a physical war, but a battle deep within. He saw the flashes of elemental magic, the desperate gleam of blades, the unyielding courage of the defenders, and a knot of something unfamiliar twisted in his gut. He had been a part of this.

His gaze flickered to the dais where the old king lay impaled. He remembered Lord Tansys, his own king, consumed by a madness that had birthed the darklings from men. He remembered Seridwyn, his wife, lost to the cataclysm, as he chose to stay and fight for a city that turned on itself. And his children, alive somewhere, though living in squalor. Atamas's promise echoed in his mind, a venomous lure. The thought, once a burning hope, now felt like a curse, bought with the blood of Y'ssildria. His sharp nails scraped against the balcony floors, a nervous, desperate rhythm. The beast within him howled for survival, for control, but a faint, insistent whisper of humanity, long dormant, cried out against the death he had helped unleash.

He turned and moved through the forgotten balconies. Every instinct, every fleshly impulse screamed at him to flee, to return to the familiar desolation of the Barrens, to bury himself in the forgotten ruins where the sun never truly touched. But now, the thought of that familiar darkness brought no comfort, only the painful reminder of what once was. He found a stairwell, its stone steps leading down. He descended, a creature caught between two worlds, his every hurried step away from the bloodbath, even as he drew nearer, a desperate attempt to outrun the burgeoning humanity that now gnawed at his darkling soul. He needed to get out. He needed to be free of Atamas, free of this horror, and free of the impossible choice that now haunted him.

Endryll was a windmill in swirling, devastating motion. His blade was a blur of sharp edges. His movements remained fluid due to his years of training and hardened resolve. Each parry and thrust was a testament to his dedication, and his desperation. He moved to protect, weaving through the commoners still trapped in the hall, deflecting blows meant for the innocent. He was a king, even uncrowned, and he fought with the fierce, unbending resolve of one. He saw a child, no older than five, caught in the panicked rush near a fallen pillar, moments from being trampled. Endryll lunged, his sword a sterling force, cleaving through a darkling's leg before sweeping the child into his arms and tossing him into the relative safety of an overturned banquet table. He heard a mother's grateful sob, then returned to the fight, his eyes narrow, his jaw set.

A darkling, gaunt and swift, lunged towards a group of noblewomen huddled near a shattered cask. Its glaive, infused with the fire of the Helwyr Peaks, hissed spitefully. Endryll, already engaged with two other attackers, saw the threat at a glance. With a roar, he executed a blindingly fast pivot, spinning out of one engagement, his blade a defensive wall as he parried a strike meant for his ribs. He then plunged forward like a human missile. His sword met the darkling's glaive in a showering clash of sparks, deflecting it wide. Then, with a sharp, upward thrust, he found purchase beneath the darkling's helm, rupturing its brain and severing its connection to the malevolent will animating it. The creature crumpled, lifeless, and Endryll spun again, immediately back into the fight.

Moments later, a colossal creature emerged from the roiling mass of darklings, a true troll-like goliath, a wendrigal, less man-beast and more mountain. Its skin was the color of rotten fruit and raw meat left out too long, complete with a complement of flies and maggots writhing and feasting upon it. Its squirming flesh was covered with ancient scars and thick, crude plates of rusted iron strapped haphazardly across its chest. Its head, disproportionately small atop a thick, corded neck, bore eyes like chips of volcanic rock, burning with a dull, brutish fury. It lumbered forward, a living siege engine, raising a monstrous club fashioned from a tree trunk, its splintered end a crude and crushing weapon. Darklings and soldiers alike skittered and scattered in its wake. It made directly for Endryll.

Endryll drove his knee into the gut of the darkling he was fighting, forcing a gasp of pain and a momentary opening. He seized the opportunity, twisting away, leaving the stunned attacker for one of Tam-Ma's pirates swinging a brutal chain to finish off, which she did with a gleam in her eye. In three swift strides, Endryll was before the towering beast, its shadow swallowing him whole. The goliath bellowed, swinging its club in a wide, pulverizing circle. Endryll's blade met the monstrous timber with a fierce, ringing impact, the shock traveling up his arm, making his teeth ache. He sank low but remained on his feet. With a mighty shove, he deflected the blow, then pressed the attack. His every move was a demonstration of his skill.

The wendrigal behemoth, slow to adapt to such fluid a crusade, found itself outmaneuvered, its massive swings too telegraphed, its brute strength ill-suited for the quick, precise dance of Endryll's sword. The blade darted, swift and true, finding the gaps in its improvised armor, slicing deep into the exposed flesh of its thick limbs, forcing the goliath back with pained grunts, until a final, powerful thrust, aimed at the exposed neck where its head met its shoulder, felled the monstrous beast with a shuddering crash that shook the foundations of the hall.

"Atta boy!" Tam-Ma shouted in exuberance from behind him.

She was a hellion in a tri-tipped hat. Her flintlock, emptied long ago, was discarded, and in its place, a curved cutlass carved through the air. She stalked about with the predatory stride of a seasoned killer, her movements economic, brutal, just like she had done a hundred times when boarding enemy ships. She provided no quarter on the open seas or in the air, and she would give none now. She climbed upon the fallen wendrigal's massive back and raised a ram's horn full of some kind of liquor. "That's me King!" She declared to no one in particular.

A darkling's weapon swept high. She ducked beneath it as it whistled over her head, then rose, her cutlass finding the soft flesh beneath her attacker's arm. She laughed, a harsh, joyful sound, as the darkling screamed and dropped its weapon. Her pirates, a band of hardened desperadoes, mirrored her ferocity. One, the hulking brute of a woman with the scarred eye, swung her massive iron chain, its links chanting of death through the air as the anchor at the end smashed against armor, sending shards of metal and bone flying. Another, a wiry woman, moved like a viper, her twin daggers too fast to see, finding soft spots, severing tendons, leaving a trail of screaming, hobbled enemies in her wake. They were losing numbers, their ranks thinning, but each fallen pirate took a score of darklings with them.

The momentum was teetering, and surely not by skill or strength of the enemy, but by sheer, relentless numbers. The flow of the battle seemed to be in the darklings' favor. Tam-Ma knew the sea, and knew that the tide always rises, always comes back. There was no way to escape it. The darklings kept coming, seemingly without end. They poured from windows and doors like mindless insects from a disturbed hill.

Despite her bravado, Tam-Ma's cutlass was heavy in her hand. A fresh wave surged forward, their snarling faces slicked down with blood and sweat. She saw a dozen glaives rise, and knew, with certainty, that this was the end of the line. She braced herself, a snarl on her lips, ready to sell her last breath for as many of the monsters as she could take before she fell.

They descended upon her then. As one, they leaped and pounced and struck. The darklings overtook her, and she was lost. Hit after brutal hit, kick after viscous kick, the blows rained down upon her. She felt her flesh tear but felt also the damned flesh of darklings split apart with every desperate thrust of her sword. Then a blinding flash of white-hot light erupted from behind her, searing the air and siphoning the breath from the attackers. A roaring inferno swept over her, a wave of pure and cleansing celestial fire that engulfed the darklings. Their screams were brief, but dreadful to behold, cut short as their bodies disintegrated into ash, leaving only the smell of charred meat. The heat was immense, but Tam-Ma felt no pain, for as the flaming wings engulfed the dogpile, they wrapped around her, shielding her from the inferno even as it consumed her enemies. She looked up, dazed and frightened, into the fierce, resolute eyes of the Star Speaker.

"Me own guardian angel!" Tam-Ma exclaimed, pushing a wisp of singed hair from her face. "That were a sight to behold, lass! Never seen bodies burn so bright without a bit o' lamp oil!" She grinned, a flash of white teeth against her soot-streaked face.

Aiofe smiled and extended her hand.

"Ye got a knack for clearing a deck, I'll give ye that," she said as she accepted the hand gratefully. "And m'crew thought *I* was a terror! Th' name's Tam-Ma, by the way, Cap'n o' *The Lass*. And ye, me fiery little sea-witch, what be yer name?"

Aoife's flaming wings still pulsed, casting a warm glow on Tam-Ma's face. "Aoife," she replied, her voice strained from exertion. "And I'm glad I could lend a hand."

"A hand and a whole damned inferno, by the looks of it!" Tam-Ma laughed, slapping Aiofe on the back. "M'thanks to ye, Aoife. Ye saved me hide, and m' hide's a valuable thing, it is." She winked, a mischievous grin on her face. "Now, what say ye and me find a bottle of something strong to toast this fine bit o' rescuin? Ye look like a lass who knows her way around a good ale."

Aiofe surveyed the hall. They were being overrun. It was time to start thinking of an exit strategy. Her eyes found Endryll and Stren still holding the dais, though neither of them looked like they'd be able to continue much longer. "Perhaps another time," she answered with a curt nod. "I think it's time to collect my friends and go."

"Aye," Tam-Ma agreed. "Th' Spire ain't lookin' too good." She cupped her hands to her mouth and bellowed orders of retreat. "To *The Lady*, ye louts! An' collect the fallen on yer way!" She turned to Aiofe then. "Don' forget that drink, witch. It'll be m' treat an' m' thanks to ye." Then she turned and resumed barking her orders, leaving Aiofe where she stood.

Aiofe moved slowly. She needed to find her friends. She needed to help Illia-Dara. Her body, still bruised and mending, screamed in protest with every step, and the toll was climbing ever higher as she continued to draw on her powers. Streaks of fire still erupted from her hands, scorching darklings, creating temporary clearings in the black tide. But the light was dimmer now, the energy more reluctant. Her brow was furrowed in concentration, sweat mingling with the smudges of soot on her pale skin.

She saw Stren, sorely pressed and bleeding, struggling to maintain his crumbling defenses. She saw Endryll, resolute against the encroaching swarm. Her focus was on patching holes in their defense, pushing back the waves with what remained of her strength. She had accepted death on the crags of the Titan's Crown in her battle with Baelgorak. She was unconcerned for her own safety, for her own survival. Her only thought was for Illia-Dara, but she knew that the survival of the others was a means to that end, perhaps *the* means. She shifted to Stren's side, her palm pressed against his shoulder, sharing a fraction of her inner heat, fueling his flagging reserves. He glanced at her, a silent nod of acknowledgment, then returned to his desperate magic. Still, as she fought, a worm of worry gnawed at her, a whisper of a thought demanding her attention. *Where are the brothers Rand?*

She spun, incinerating a darkling that had crept too close to a huddle of terrified commoners, and scanned the battlefield. She knew they were here, somewhere amidst this nightmare, for she had seen them earlier, awestruck and out of place. Her eyes darted through the swirling melee, past the flashes of steel and the myriad faces of invaders. She needed to find them, to ensure their safety, to guide them through this turmoil they were so ill-equipped to navigate.

Cante and Feste, in the middle of the brutal battle of seasoned warriors and ruthless darklings, were an oddity. Their movements were clumsy. Their makeshift weapons—Feste with his splintered broom handle and Cante with the heavy and bent lampstand—were more akin to farmer's tools than instruments of war, and were out of place and awkward amid the plethora of discarded weapons all about. But they fought with furious abandon, fueled by a desire that transcended their fear.

Cante swung the lampstand with a grunt, smashing it against a darkling's helmet, sending the creature reeling. Feste, smaller but quicker, jabbed and thrust his broom handle, keeping the darklings at bay, protecting the terrified commoners huddled behind them. They were bleeding and gasping, their faces streaked with tears and grime, but they did not yield. They were out of their depth, two humble men from Thimbleglean Vale thrust into a conflict that dwarfed them. Yet, they fought on. Then, a voice, clear and sharp, cut through the chaos, closer than they expected.

"Brothers! We need to go! Now!" Aoife stood over them, her wings still faintly glowing, her face pressed and worn. She didn't wait for a response, simply gesturing with a decisive flick of her head towards a less-contested archway. "This way!"

The battle stretched on in a relentless grind. The darklings were an endless reservoir of barbaric savagery, slowly pushing the defenders back. Stren's earthen constructs rose and fell. His power waned. His body screamed. Endryll's movements lacked their earlier explosive force. Aoife's starfire flickered, each burst a drain on her very essence as she led Cante and Feste, bruised and battered, in retreat. They followed, swinging their makeshift weapons with every last drop of their strength, their eyes heavy with exhaustion, but still alert.

There was an immediate lull, a breath held to a man. The darklings paused, their numbers still vast, their silent presence more unnerving than their earlier assault had been. The defenders, confused but supremely thankful for the respite, leaned heavily on their knees and on each other. A chill, unlike the storm-driven dampness, permeated the hall, a coldness that bit deeper than steel. It was a breath of nullity, of utter absence. All was still.

Then, through the ruined doors at the far end of the hall, Atamas came. He strode in with an indifferent calm, stepping over the fallen, his deep violet coat unsullied by the fight. His face, now fully visible in the flickering, bloody light of battle, bore a wide, unholy smile, a predatory glee that twisted his features into something monstrous, something other. He surveyed the disastrous scene, his dark eyes lingering for a moment on the defenders, as if savoring their valiant, but ultimately doomed, struggle.

"Fall back! Quickly!" Aoife's shouted to Endryll and Stren. They did not move.

"Such admirable defiance," Atamas's voice resonated with absolute authority. "A shame it must end."

Stren took a feeble step forward. He seemed to sink into his exhaustion, his countenance shrinking as weariness took him. "Atamas," he rasped, his voice thick with a pain that surpassed the physical wounds he bore. "After all these years, you have finally become what I prayed you would not. Why, brother?"

Atamas chuckled, a vacant, dry sound that seemed to absorb the light around him. "Brother? You truly cling to such sentimental trifles, old man? We were never brothers, Stren. You were the keeper of a failing order, and I, I was merely biding my time." He spread his hands, encompassing the scene of destruction. "Look around you, master." He spat the last in disgust. "This is progress. This is the future you so stubbornly fought against."

"Progress?" Stren's voice cracked, his eyes, though filled with sorrow, never left Atamas's face. "You call this progress? Slaughtering the innocent? Turning against your own? This is not progress, Atamas. This is ruin. This is the very void you once swore to fight!"

"A void, Stren," Atamas replied, his smile widening, "is merely potential, a blank canvas awaiting a master's touch. You, with your traditions and prophecies, you were content to merely observe. I intend to *reshape*. To *create*." He took another step forward, his gaze sweeping over the room with an almost artistic appreciation. "And the 'innocent' you speak of? They are merely kindling, old friend. They are fuel for a new world."

"You speak of creation, but you bring death," Stren countered, his gaze hardening. "You stand on the bodies of those who loved you, who believed in you! Cerceia. Onidine. How could you defile her memory with such monstrous acts? How could you—" Stren's voice was lost in a choking cough. He looked to his old friend, his old king, and then he looked to Endryll, whose eyes were blazing with hatred.

Atamas's smile faltered, a flicker of something unreadable crossing his features before it was quickly masked. "Their time had passed. Their vision was limited. A new age requires new architects, Stren. Architects unburdened by the foolishness of sentiment, or the chains of a dying faith." His eyes met Stren's then. "And you, old master, you stand in my way. You always have."

"Atamas, don't!"

Atamas raised his hands, palms up, in a measured and purposeful motion. No familiar glyphs, no complex flourishes. Only a stark, dreadful directive. A wave of unadulterated force, deep as oblivion and frigid as the northern wastes, radiated from his core. It was neither flame nor soil, nor light, nor any fundamental component. It was an undoing. It was the essential nucleus of non-being, rendered into a palpable presence. It was life's inverse, existence's counterpoint. The pressure in the hall intensified, pressing down on every soul, every splinter of wood, every grain of dust. The vibrant colors of the banners dulled, their emeralds and golds leeching into muted shades. Strength faltered, and breath caught in throats suddenly tight with an unspoken dread. It was as if the very air was being wrung dry of its vitality, leaving behind only a hideous vacuum. A low hum vibrated through the flagstones, a sound felt more in the teeth and chest than in the ears, resonating with a deep, unsettling discord. Shadows deepened and stretched, clinging to every corner, every recess, pulling the light itself into their embrace. The atmosphere became heavy, solidifying into an oppressive weight that stole movement.

Stren felt the sudden, crushing pressure. It was the familiar presence of the Aetherfast, but utterly corrupted, twisted into something malignant, a perversion of life itself. He roared, throwing up a desperate, final shield of churning stone, a futile gesture against the encroaching emptiness. But it was useless. The dark energy slammed into him, a silent, invisible fist, tearing through his defenses like fragile parchment, dissolving the stone and the very air around him. He was not struck, but erased wholly from his position, flung backward, a rag doll of crumpled pain, crashing against a pillar. His head struck the stone with a sickening thud. His vision swam, and darkness, cold and absolute, claimed him.

Endryll saw Atamas raise his hands. He felt the unnatural hush that swallowed the hall. He saw Stren fall, effortlessly banished by a force he couldn't comprehend. Without a moment's hesitation, without a conscious thought, he glanced at the terrified Y'ssildrians cowering all around him. He knew he could not save them all, but he could try. He positioned himself, his sword raised, a direct challenge to the powerful sorcerer. He would meet him head-on. He would guard his people. He would avenge his father. He would protect Illia-Dara.

The blast struck him squarely.

It was soundless. There was no audible impact, no explosion, no rending of flesh or breaking of bone, no gouting blood, only a sickening stillness. Endryll stood frozen for a heartbeat, his sword still raised, his eyes wide, reflecting the approaching vacuity, mirroring the void that consumed him. Then, slowly, he began to crumple. It wasn't a violent collapse, but a sluggish, agonizing descent, as if life itself were being stolen from him, cell by cell with agonizing efficiency. His skin seemed to gray, his vibrant green tunic faded, the gold thread dulling to ash. His sandy hair, once so full of life, seemed to lose its substance, drawing inward. His face became gaunt and sunken, as his eyes hollowed. Suffering was written plainly across his visage as he lowered to the floor. His sword—still clutched in his hand—lost its gleam, becoming a dull, lifeless piece of inert metal, its very essence leached away. He fell to his knees, then forward, pitching onto the blood-soaked wood of the dais. So insubstantial was he that he floated like a discarded garment settling on the floor.

A single, choked gasp escaped his lips, a wail swallowed by the sudden, absolute silence that had descended upon the grand hall, a silence that was heavier than any sound. His body was there, whole, but emptied, his essence extinguished. His light, once so brilliant, was gone, leaving only a hollow shell, a husk. Endryll was no more. The Light of Y'ssildria faded and died.

She held it in her open palm. It was an obsidian stone, smooth and black. It seemed to be absorbing the light of the chamber—or consuming it. Yet, from its surface, thin, shimmering tendrils of iridescent light pulsed and writhed, like caught gossamer, or miniature lightning trapped within a dark heart. They pulsed and shifted, reaching out, alive and needy.

"What is that?" Ixchel breathed. He felt it, an echo deep within his body, within his soul, a resonating thrum that quickened his pulse. It was the same energy he had felt when touching the stone in Stren's alcove and again when he had found his flame in the gardens, when he had crossed over. It was the Aetherfast, made manifest in the mortal plane.

As he stared, captivated, the twinkling wisps from the stone began to elongate, stretching towards him. Then they began to divide. Half of the threads coiled and then darted towards Ixchel, a silent and hungry haunt, as if seeking to enter his very being. The other half, equally vibrant, surged towards the black, runic box that lay on the table.

Ixchel gasped, a strange, electric current shooting through his limbs. He felt a pull, a recognition, as if a missing piece of himself was being drawn out, or he was being drawn toward it. His golden eye, the one touched by the Aetherfast, flared with a renewed, internal light. He instinctively raised his free hand, not in defense, but in a strange mixture of curiosity and an undeniable connection. He felt the tendrils brush against his skin, not with a physical touch, but with a breath across his very being, a gentle probing that spoke of immense, waiting power. It was like tasting the source of something he had always sought but never fully found.

Illia-Dara, seeing the bizarre division of the light, instinctively drew back the stone, severing the connection. The tendrils snapped back into the blackness, retracting, leaving only their faint rhythmic throbs. "It's reaching for you," she whispered, her voice laced with fear. "What is this, Ixchel? What has Atamas given me? What has he done to you?"

Ixchel lowered his hand slowly, his mind reeling. "I don't know," he admitted, though a terrible, dawning understanding was beginning to take root in the swirling sea of his thoughts. He looked from the stone, now almost inert in Illia-Dara's trembling hand, to the black, runic box. Its surface seemed to thrum faintly in his newly awakened senses. *Cursed magic?*

"This is not a gift," Ixchel said flatly. He reached for the black box, his fingers brushing against its cold surface. It pulsed again, a low vibration that seeped into his marrow. "This is a trap. And we're already caught." The tendrils from the obsidian stone and the ominous pull from the box became alive again, almost as if they were reacting to his presence in their proximity.

The world tilted, or perhaps it was only Ixchel's perception. The air thickened, pressing in on him. Reality dulled, as if muffled by an unseen hand. Illia-Dara clutched the stone, its unnatural cold seeping into her skin, its pulsating light now the only clear thing in a blurring reality. Ixchel felt the terrifying call, the same irresistible force that had first drawn him into the Aetherfast during his training with Stren. But this was different. This was not a familiar path. This was a forced surrender.

"Run, Illi," he whispered, pushing her back, away from the box and away from the encroaching darkness that now radiated from it. His voice felt distant, as if it belonged to someone else. He could feel the threads of connection between the stone in her hand and the box on the table, a horrifying, invisible web that tightened with every pulse of malevolent energy, and he felt, too, his connection to both.

A flicker of understanding passed through Illia-Dara's eyes, quickly followed by terror. She saw the determination on his face, the strange light in his golden eye, the way his body tensed as if braced against an unseen impact. "Ixchel, no!" she cried, but her words were swallowed by the sudden, deafening silence that came upon them from the hall below.

Ixchel felt it first. Not pain, but an agonizing emptiness, as sadness, hollow and bare, bereft of all things. The tendrils from the obsidian, now flaring wildly in Illia-Dara's hand, slammed into him, connecting him, tethering him, to the black box, to the emanating darkness. He was pulled, stretched, unwound. He saw his own body begin to shimmer, not with the controlled illusion of his Echoborn, but with dissolution. His flesh seemed to diffuse. His form flickered like an image struggling to hold shape in the dying light of evening. He was being unraveled, thread by thread, his very essence tearing and ripping.

His mind screamed. Atamas had not simply given Illia-Dara a cursed gift. He had given her a lock, and Ixchel was the key. He was the sacrifice, meant to power this new, horrifying thing. The siege, the darklings, and the battle had been a distraction, a cover for this final, terrible rite. He was a conduit, a vessel. And the vessel was now being shattered.

He saw Illia-Dara, her face contorted in a scream he could not hear, tears streaming down her cheeks as she futilely tried to pull the obsidian stone back, to sever the connection, to save him. Instead, it was torn from her hand by the powers now linking it to Ixchel and Ixchel to the box. It hovered there, just out of reach, taking of Ixchel all he was and all that he would ever be and feeding it to the box, which consumed insatiably. He saw the horror in her eyes, reflected a thousand times in his own rapidly fracturing consciousness. He saw her love, her grief, her desperate, futile struggle. And in that last agonizing moment of existence, as his body dissolved, as his flame was extinguished, he knew no more.

With the last vestiges of his will, a final surge of desperation fueled by his unspoken, unyielding love for her, Ixchel focused. Not on stopping Atamas, for that was impossible now, not on saving himself, for he was already lost, but on her. All he had left was for Illia-Dara. He had sworn to be her shield, her barrier, her last gate. And even as he was unmade, he would fulfill that oath. The last remnants of his scattered power, the brilliance of his flame, didn't fight the void. Instead, it coalesced, focusing, channeling through the agonizing link between him and the obsidian stone, between the stone and the dark box.

The black box, which had pulsed with a faint heartbeat before, now snarled with an all-consuming hunger. It tried to draw his essence deeper, to swallow him whole. But Ixchel's final act changed its nature. He was not merely a victim, he was a catalyst. His dying flame, warped by the Aetherfast, by the void, by his desperate love, became a funnel. He was not only unmade, he was unleashed.

Instead of simply being absorbed, Ixchel's dissolving form erupted, not in light or power, but in a blinding wave of pure energy. It was every memory, every thought, every feeling he had ever possessed, every ounce of his Aetherfast-touched flame. A thousand lifetimes, lived and unlived, poured forth in a single, devastating burst. It was the crushing push of knowledge, the suffocating embrace of endless possibility, the searing agony of ultimate truth. It was the Aetherfast, not taken, not lost, but given. Ixchel's very being slammed into Illia-Dara. It wasn't a gentle transfer, but a violent, invasive thrust of will. Her mind, unprepared for such an onslaught, reeled. Images, sensations, and emotions that were not her own flooded her con-sciousness. She saw through his eyes, felt with his heart, experienced the excruciating pain of his death, and the burning intensity of his unspoken love. It was a violation, yet one born of ultimate selflessness.

The obsidian stone became a searing missile aimed directly at her, intent on recovering the lost power. Illia recoiled and threw her hands up in a reflexive effort born of reaction and despair. New tendrils emerged, crawling from within the stone and racing toward her. She knew Ixchel's pain, and knew that the same pain, the same fate awaited her. She cried out. The tendrils reached her and dove for her essence, only to be stopped by three emerald and near-translucent images of Ixchel that blinked into existence to form a shield before her—Ixchel's Echoborn. The dark box pulsed erratically. Illia-Dara screamed, a sound torn from her throat as the Aetherfast's brilliance coursed through her veins. She fell to her knees, such was the torment of this agonizing inheritance. She buckled under the strain, threatening to fracture, to shatter into a million pieces under the crush of the power that coursed through her, Ixchel's power.

Her eyes, wide with horror and a dawning understanding, fixed on Ixchel. He was there, yet not fully. The echoes of his being flickered around her. His form wavered before her, a shimmering outline against the glow of the tendrils. Tears streamed down his ethereal face, mirroring the hot rivulets carving paths through the dust on Illia-Dara's cheeks. He raised a hand, so insubstantial it seemed to be woven from moonlight, reaching for her. Illia, despite the searing pain in her veins, stretched out her own trembling hand. She was desperate to touch him, to anchor him, to pull him back from the void. Their fingertips neared, so close. His hand passed through hers as if she were the ghost, not him. The contact, or lack thereof, was more painful than any physical blow and a sob tore from Illia-Dara's throat.

Ixchel's eyes, once burning with Aetherfast fire, now held only a penetrating tenderness. His form flickered, becoming even more sheer, like a fading memory. With the last remnant of his presence, and a voice that was barely more than a breath, he spoke. "I love you, Illi. I always have."

And then, with a final, silent shimmer, he was gone. There was no trace. Just the cold, indifferent air, the throbbing, alien power within Illia-Dara, and the terrible silence of her solitude. The dark box fell still. The obsidian stone dropped unceremoniously to the floor, where it bounced and rolled to a stop at Illia-Dara's feet. She didn't see it. She didn't see anything. She remained on her knees, her hand still outstretched, grasping.

INTERLUDE: ECHOES OF HAPPINESS

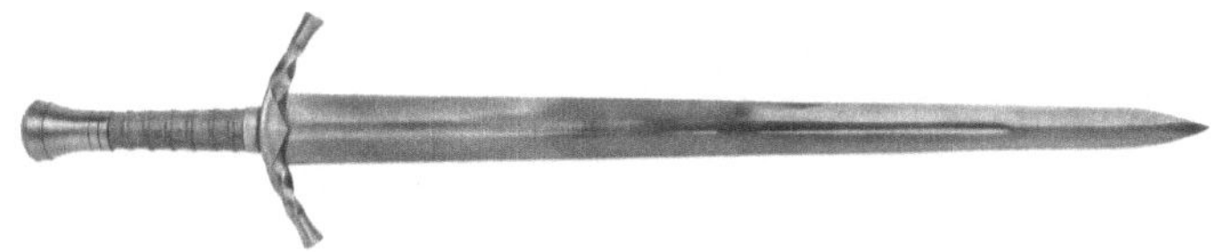

The training ring in the Sunspire Citadel was a sprawling chamber lined with weapons and armor that told the histories of Y'ssildria in every perfectly-shaped line and curve and fold of steel. Every battle, every victory, and every loss were written with the deep gauges and yawning dents from enemy hammers and blades. The room was a cavern of natural stone and arches far beneath the Spire, where only the most dedicated practitioners of arts, both melee and martial, were allowed entry. Torches, set in intricate recesses shaped like roaring gryphons carved into the stone, cast shifting, hungry light across the dirt floor, consuming the sunless darkness and illuminating the swirling dust motes that flittered in the air behind dancing feet. Here, swords rang, steel clashed, and the deep pulse of practiced effort vibrated through the very foundations of the ancient fortress. Yet, for Illia-Dara, Endryll, and Ixchel, it was less a place of rigorous discipline, though surely that was an element, and more an intimate canvas on which they sketched their future together, a private stage for the intricate play of their friendship.

Though the chambers often sounded with shouts and grunts of arduous training, theirs were the joyous shouts and raucous laughter of three youths lost in the unabashed and unhindered rhythm of their love. Endryll, a master swordsman even at such a young age, moved with the fluid refinement of a true fighter. His naked chest glistened from exertion, and his light linen pants swayed with his every move. His blade, a polished steel practice sword, dulled at the edges, but weighted precisely, sang a fierce, constant note as it cut through the air. He was a beast caged and a dancer set free. His form, honed by years under the keen eye of the kingdom's finest masters, was fierce and elegant, both.

Against him, Illia-Dara, clad in simple, practical leathers, was a tempest. Her movements, less brute force and more controlled evasion, wove and darted like a hummingbird in flight. She wielded a blunted dagger. It was little more than a silver streak against Endryll's blade, but her parries were meticulous, her strikes were quick, unexpected, and aimed at openings only she seemed to perceive. She moved with an intuition that belied her short training. A wildness in her footwork kept Endryll constantly reevaluating and changing his attacks, as his goal was not to win, but to present Illi with every possibility that might arise in mortal combat, and for her to work out how to navigate them.

Ixchel was neither fluid nor graceful. He did not fight, so much as fumble. His movements were a subtle disruption, a flicker at the edge of vision. He bore a dulled shortsword and relied on speed and an uncanny knack for being where his opponents were not. His swordsmanship was passable, Endryll had seen to that, but he was too often distracted. He too often simply watched and admired his friends and their duet. He too often simply watched Illia-Dara from the outside of the combat ring. It was safer there. No one could be hurt there.

"Too slow, my Queen!" Endryll decreed as his sword flashed, forcing Illia-Dara back with a broad sweep. She ducked beneath his guard and lunged forward and behind the swing, as her dagger whipped across his side, aimed for the small of his back. Endryll grunted and twisted, the flat of his blade deflecting her thrust.

"Not at all, *prince*!" Illia-Dara countered, emphasizing his station, her laugh echoing. She spun away and set herself again, her eyes bright with challenge. "You forget, boy, that I have learned from the best." She dropped into a low crouch, her smile widening, her stance inviting, then exploded forward, feinting left, then striking right.

Endryll met her head on, his brow furrowed in concentration, his smile as wide as hers. He knew her tricks, knew her playful moves, yet still she surprised him. His blade came down in a heavy chop, forcing her to block and not parry. The dull impact sent a jolt up her arm. She recoiled, shaking her head. "You wound me, Endryll! My delicate frame cannot withstand such barbaric blows!"

"Delicate?" Endryll scoffed, a knowing grin breaking across his face. "You'd make a battle-hardened knight weep for his mother, Illia-Dara. Don't lie to me." He pressed his advantage with vigor.

Illia rocked back, throwing her free hand to the ground, then kicking high with both feet. Dirt and dust showered Endryll, temporarily blinding him, as Illia-Dara tightened her core and, using the momentum of the double-kick, brought her feet above and then behind her, balancing momentarily upside-down on one hand, only to land on her feet once again.

Ixchel, who had been circling the periphery, chose that moment to strike. Though he was hot and sweating, he remained fully clothed. He hated revealing his body in the presence of his two friends. Endryll's body was honed and sculpted, golden in any light. Illia-Dara was striking in her beauty, athletic and muscled, and perfect, while he was pale and freckled, and had not yet developed the muscle tone or height of his peers. Dirt clung to his drenched clothing in dark clumps. He had, as always, been waiting for the perfect opportunity to insert himself into the drama. He darted between them. His hand, quick as a snake, caught Endryll's sword arm, not with force, but with a subtle, disarming twist. Endryll had taught him well. Thrown off balance and stumbling, Endryll's attack on Illia faltered, and he was left open for riposte.

"Fiend!" Endryll bellowed, recovering quickly, but Illia-Dara had already darted past him, her dagger flicking at his exposed knee. He grunted, blocking with his free hand, then spun, his eyes blazing with mock fury at Ixchel. "You're supposed to be helping me! We are two against one, you idiot!"

Ixchel simply grinned, a broad, impish smile of mischief. His chestnut hair, ever the wild tangle, seemed to fluff even further as he darted away, just out of Endryll's reach, leaving a dust cloud behind. "My duty is to the

Lady, my prince. And her duty, as I understand it, is to humble you. My allegiance lies with her."

Illia-Dara laughed, a clear and joyous sound that filled the chamber with spectral light, like that of a jolly rainbow. "A man of true principle!" She chuckled as she gave a playful bow to Ixchel, then turned, her dagger suddenly at Endryll's throat. "Yield, prince. Before you embarrass yourself further."

Endryll, still busy chiding Ixchel, had failed to notice Illi's quiet approach from the back. He sighed dramatically, lowering his sword. "Humiliation!" he cried out. "My reign has yet even to begin, and I am defeated at the hands of laymen. What will the bards sing?"

"They'll sing of your wisdom in choosing allies, my love," Illia-Dara said, a soft smile on her lips as she lowered her dagger.

Ixchel felt a familiar ache in his chest, a subtle twist beneath his ribs. He watched her, the way her hair, damp with sweat, clung to her neck, the light of the torches catching the lighter highlights in those auburn tresses. She was a mirage, a sun-inspired dream, and every glance at her was a fresh wound, a reminder of the chasm between them. Endryll called her "my love," held her close, and would soon take her as his wife. Ixchel would always be the third, the loyal friend, the one who watched from a distance.

"One more round," Ixchel said. "This time, Endryll, you and I. Illia-Dara, judge our efforts."

Illia-Dara clapped her hands, her eyes sparkling. "A magnificent idea! A fair challenge, indeed. Show him the true cunning of the Stren's apprentice, Ixchel!"

Endryll groaned. "Oh, spare me. His 'cunning' usually involves him running around in circles until one of us tires." He adjusted his grip on his sword, just a hint of competitive fire in his eyes. "Very well, Master Ixchel. Show me your best. But know this, I will be faster today. And far less patient."

But Ixchel, for all his feigned bravado, was not there. He stumbled aside with a yelp on his lips, his movement an almost comical scramble that was just quick enough to avoid the point of Endryll's blade. The lunge carried Endryll forward, his balance committed, his eyes locked on the space where his friend had been only a heartbeat before. Ixchel skittered away, half laughing, half squealing. It was the perfect distraction.

In that moment, as Endryll recovered his footing to press the attack, Illia-Dara moved. With the quiet of a hunting cat, she sprang from her position. Her feet barely seemed to touch the ground as she closed the distance. Endryll sensed a flicker of movement behind him, but it was too late. She leaped with arms wide, legs bent at the knees, and an expression that bordered on ferality.

A sudden, surprising weight landed squarely on his back. A tangle of scarlet hair and flailing limbs enveloped him, followed by a triumphant laugh. Illia-Dara's arms wrapped around his shoulders, her weight yanking him off-balance.

"What in the—" Endryll's exclamation was cut short as his forward momentum became his enemy. He staggered, his sword arm useless, his legs buckling under the combined force of his own lunge and Illia's assault. He went down with a surprised croak, landing in a heap of tangled limbs and mock fury on the soft dirt, with Illia-Dara still clinging victoriously to his back.

Ixchel was there in an instant, leaning over them with a broad, innocent grin, though his eyes danced with devilment. "I believe," he said with grave formality, placing the tip of his shortsword to Endryll's neck, "that the champion has been unseated."

"Unseated? I've been ambushed!" Endryll twisted, trying to dislodge Illia-Dara, who was now laughing so hard she could barely hold on. "This is treason of the highest order! Attacked by my own!"

"We have simply proven our superior tactical prowess, my love," Illia-Dara said, finally rolling off to sprawl on the ground beside him, breathless with laughter. She pointed a finger at him. "You were so focused on the horse that you never saw the fly."

"The horse?" Ixchel placed a hand on his chest in mock offense. "I'll have you know my distraction was a masterclass in evasive maneuvering. If anything, I was a lion, and you were a mouse."

Endryll pushed himself up on his elbows, a reluctant grin finally breaking through his artificial outrage. He looked from Illia-Dara's radiant, laughing face to Ixchel's smug expression. "So, this was your plan all along? To conspire against your prince?"

"We simply sought to prove a point," Ixchel said, offering a hand to help him up.

Endryll ignored it, instead grabbing Ixchel's ankle and pulling, sending him tumbling to the earth with a thud. "And what point is that?"

"That *we* are the two greatest fighters in all of Y'ssildria," Illia-Dara declared, poking Endryll in the chest, "and that *you* are nothing without us."

The three of them lay there, side by side, covered in dirt and grime. The sounds of swords and heavy, exhausted breathing, replaced by the sound of their shared and effortless laughter.

Illia-Dara walked slowly towards him, her gaze fixed on his face, on the unsettling yet captivating look in his eyes. "Where are you right now, Ixchel?" she asked softly, reaching out a hand to touch his cheek. Her fingers felt the slight tremor beneath his skin. "You are not here. Your eyes are far from this place."

He leaned into her touch, his stern visage softening, the edge fading into something tender. "I wouldn't be anywhere without you two. Both of you. You push me. You make me want to be better." His gaze shifted to Endryll, a depth of affection in his eyes. "You make me want to be worthy."

Endryll joined them, placing a hand on Ixchel's shoulder, a gesture of deep brotherhood. "You are more than worthy, Ixchel. You always have been. And with a friend like you at my side, I will never want." He looked at Illia-Dara, then back at Ixchel, a solemnity entering his gaze. "One day," he said. "One day, everything will change. One day I will be king." He looked at Illia-Dara, his eyes filled with a love that needed no words. "I will need you both. By my side, always."

Illia-Dara clasped Endryll's hand, then reached for Ixchel's, completing their circle. The three stood in the center of the large training ring, the torchlight flickering around them, casting their shadows long and inter-twining them, three into one.

"We will be there," Illia-Dara said, her voice a promise, firm and clear. "Forever and always."

"Forever and always," Ixchel repeated.

Ixchel squeezed her hand, then Endryll's. He looked at them both, his heart aching with a bittersweet certainty. He would indeed be there. He would be their shield, their barrier, their last gate. He would protect their love, their kingdom, and their very lives with his own. He would watch over them, and he would love them, silently, fiercely, until his dying breath. He knew this. It was his destiny. And he embraced it, even if it meant remaining forever in the shadows of their magnificent light.

A heavy silence lingered for a moment before Ixchel broke it with a playful grin, the tension easing from his shoulders. "Well," he began, his voice lifting the solemn mood, "now that all that is out of the way, what will be your first royal decree? Free sweets for all, I hope? Or perhaps you will outlaw chores on rainy days?"

Endryll laughed, a deep, warm sound that filled the space between them. "I'll consider the sweets. But first, we'll open the northern granaries to the villages in the foothills. No one should face a winter with fear in their bellies instead of warm bread."

"And we'll expand the libraries," Illia-Dara added, her eyes alight with the thought. "We'll send scholars to the far reaches to gather stories and histories from every corner of Y'ssara."

"And I," Ixchel announced with grand importance, "will personally oversee the alignment of every painting in the citadel. A crooked portrait is the first sign of a kingdom in decline. It's a heavy burden, but one I am willing to bear for my people."

They laughed together, the sound bouncing and bounding in the emptiness of the ring. The weight of the future felt lighter, somehow, when shared between them. The laughter subsided, and Illia-Dara turned to face Endryll fully, her hand still holding his. The teasing in her eyes softened into a profoundness that seemed to quiet the mirth around them.

"You will be the finest king Y'ssildria has ever known, Endryll," she said, her voice soft but sure. "Better than your father. Better than all the kings who came before."

Endryll looked at her, his heart swelling at her faith in him. He shook his head slowly and turned his gaze to Ixchel, a knowing smile on his face. "She's the one who will change things," he said, his voice full of awe. "Y'ssildria is just the beginning for her."

Ixchel nodded in immediate, fierce agreement, looking at Illia-Dara with an expression of reverence. "He's right, you know," he affirmed, his voice dropping to a near whisper.

"You, my lady, will one day rule nations."

They walked from the arena hand in hand, light laughter following behind them.

The Queen of Sorrows

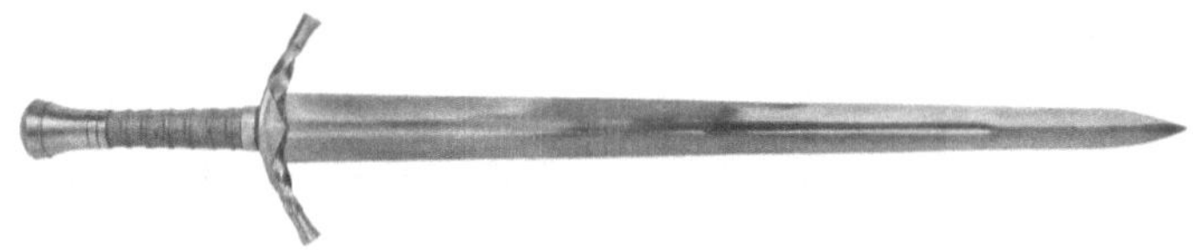

The emptiness was a gaping and gushing wound, festering and rotting in the center of the bedchambers. It pressed upon Illia-Dara, a crushing and indifferent weight that muted all around her, amplifying the frantic blast beat of her own pulse. She remained on her knees, and the sudden absence of Ixchel was a more profound agony than she ever thought existed. Her hand, still outstretched, felt the phantom brush of his ethereal form. The memory of his final words was in a dream where his laughter once resided. Tears, hot and ceaseless, evidenced a love now severed, a promise nullified. She withered there alone.

The stone lay forgotten at her feet, its malevolent thrumming now merely a faint discordant bleating beneath the shrieking of her grief. The box sat sated and silent on the end table. Her body pulsed with the alien power Ixchel had gifted—or cursed—her with, a searing venom in her veins that offered no comfort, only a terrifying awareness of what had been. She was the vessel now, overflowing, and yet utterly empty.

Then, a soft scrape, timid and delicate. Illia's head snapped up, all suffering clouded by a surge of animal fear. She saw movement in the ragged gullet where the double doors had once stood, indistinct shadows against the flickering light. Her hand, still trembling, instinctively sought purchase with something on the floor, something near to her. Her fingers closed around the hilt of Sylvandralis. It lay where Ixchel had dropped it, just beyond the edge of her pooling tears, its white blade now singing a low, mournful hymn, as if mirroring her own sorrow. It felt impossibly heavy, yet she knew the weight of it almost intimately. The sword was familiar to her in an utterly personal way, as if born for her hand alone. With a surge of strength, she clutched the sword. The pure gold of its pommel was cool against her burning skin. She hauled herself to her feet, her legs screaming in protest, but her resolve hardening with every ragged breath.

The figures revealed themselves from the doorway. There were three of them. Two were squat and broad, their bodies thick and their beards long and full. The gloom and the grime of battle obscured their faces, but she could tell they were fae. Mud-splattered and blood washed, they entered wearily, weapons drawn. The third was no faeman. He was a slender young man. His fiery red hair seemed to hold the light of the few candles that remained upright and lit, and his face was barren of any beard. It was also, somehow, known to her, but she couldn't say how.

"Lady!" a gruff voice rumbled. It was Thurdop, his beard a knotted tangle, his eyes wide and fixed on her. Mergop, wider and rounder, stood just behind him, clutching at his stomach, as he surveyed the room.

Illia-Dara tensed and raised Sylvandralis. "Who are you?" she demanded, her voice hoarse, raw. "What do you want?" She scanned them, her mind racing. Why were fae here? Why now? Suspicion cut through her grief. "Are you with Atamas?" Her gaze sharpened, fixing on the largest of them. "Did he send you to finish what they could not?" She swept Sylvandralis across the room, indicating whom she spoke of. The three soldiers had not moved and never would again.

Thurdop slid his axe through a loop on his belt and took a hesitant step forward, his hands held open, palms out in a gesture of peace. "Nay, Lady, nay! We be kin o' the Wood, no friends to tha' darkness that's taken the Spire. We been sent by the Crownward, hi'self. We're here ter help ye. Ter help ye escape."

Escape? The word ricocheted in her mind, hollow and meaningless. Endryll. Her husband. The king. He was down there, fighting, dying, perhaps already dead. The thought was a stab of pain. She needed to get to him. She needed to help him. She needed to tell him of Ixchel.

"Escape?" Illia-Dara said more bitterly than she intended. "You speak of escape when my husband fights for his life and for his people? When Ixchel, when my Crownward, my brother, my friend, was just stolen from me?"

Her voice broke. Her grip tightened on Sylvandralis, her knuckles white. The sword pulsed in her hand, a response to her despair. "You lie! You're with them! You're all with him!" Her eyes blazed with grief, a wildfire that threatened to consume her. "Get out! Get out of my chambers before I—"

Mergop whimpered, backing further into the shattered doorway and leaning halfway out into the hall. "She's quite the fiesty one, Thurdop. We ought ter be leavin'. Less trouble, that."

"Quiet, y' idjit!" Thurdop snapped, his gaze still fixed on Illia-Dara. "Lady, we mean ye no herm. We comed from the Western Wood, on Stren's writ. He sent us wi' the boy Heron." Thurdop's eyes flickered to Heron, who stood frozen, wide-eyed, his gaze fixed on Illia-Dara. "And ter bring 'im ter this place. We were on our way to the crypts, as Stren instructed, but we ended up all turnt around an' then we heard ye. We were ter be meetin' ye in the gardens, but they're cut off."

"Swarmin' with dirty dogs," Mergop added from the doorway.

Illia-Dara followed Thurdop's gaze to the boy. *Heron.* The name tasted strange on her tongue, unfamiliar. It didn't belong. He was young, thin, and looked terrified. He had the likeness of neither a conspirator nor an assassin. His eyes, a bright, startling blue, met hers, and for a fleeting moment, something stirred within her. It wasn't a memory or a concrete thought, but a faint, insistent ripple. It was a wisp of recognition that had no source, no form.

Heron's gaze locked with hers, and a strange current passed between them. He saw the pain in her eyes, a pain that felt, impossibly, like his own in some way. It was the pain of loss. He felt a pull, a desperate need to soothe and to protect this woman he had never met, yet whose sorrow resonated so deeply with him. He did not know this Ixchel she spoke of, but he knew instantly that she loved him deeply and that he was gone. Heron had never known his parents, but was told by the Matron that they had died and that he was alone. That pain of never knowing who they were, and in turn, who he was, was a persistent agony within his own heart.

"Lady," Heron said, his voice surprisingly gentle, a divergence from the faes' gruff tones. "Please. We truly are here to help. Stren did send us. He spoke of you." He took a step forward, his youthful face drawn with sincerity. "We will not hurt you. We just want to see you to safety." He glanced around the room, fully taking in the fight that had taken place. "Though by the looks of it, you may not need us."

Illia closed her eyes, pushing the burn of fresh tears out to run down her face. She did not want anything from these men. She wanted *her* men. She wanted Endryll, who was fighting for his life, for her life, and for the lives of all of Y'ssildira. She wanted Ixchel. Yet, the quiet earnestness in this one's voice, the desperate plea in his eyes, pierced through the layers of her sadness and suspicion. He looked so young, so innocent, so clearly out of his element in this place. Stren would not send traitors. But why did he *send* anyone at all? Why hadn't he come for her himself? Why hadn't Endryll come? She looked at the young man for a long moment, and that subtle, inexplicable connection to Heron swayed her.

"Who is he?" she asked Thurdop, her voice softer now. She lowered Sylvandralis, the blade scraping across the floor. Her gaze swept over the three men before her in turn but returned to Heron.

Thurdop sighed, relief easing some of the tension in his broad shoulders. "This here is Heron, Lady, a lad from the Bairnbrand. Stren sent us ter fetch him ages ago an' ter keep 'im safe like. Said he got a connection ter yer royal self. Mentioned some kind of divided blood, er somat, if yer takin m' meaning." He offered a small, hesitant smile. "But we ain't got time for the old wizard's riddles now. We need ter move, Lady. The Spire is fallin'."

"Falling?" The word was a fresh shock, causing her knees to buckle slightly. She had known the battle raged, but *falling*?

Before Thurdop could elaborate, a sudden clamor erupted from the other end of the hall. Heavy, stumbling footsteps. Shouts. The clatter of what sounded like an entire armory skittering across the length of it.

Mergop yelped, leaping back into the room. "Somethin' big comin' this way!"

Aoife dropped from the covert nook in the wall and into the hall that led to Illia's chambers. To her left was Illia-Dara, she could sense her. To her right, a battalion of black-armored darklings raced down the corridor toward her, surely intent on the same destination. Behind her, still well-shadowed in the recess of the carved space that led back to the stairwell, were Cante and Feste Rand. The clamor of heavy, clawed feet echoed through the hall. Howls and snarls led the charge as the darklings set their sights temporarily on Aoife.

"Stay back," she commanded the brothers. She whipped her arms down and out to her sides as two flaming swords materialized in her grip, one in each hand. Coils of smoke hissed and writhed from her back as large, feathered and flaming wings spread wide, folding at the apogee as the halls were too narrow for full extension. "Stay hidden."

The first darkling met its end not with a scream, but with a gurgling, wet belch of blood and visceral spray. It had lunged, glaive leading, a creature of pure, brutal momentum. Aoife didn't parry. She stepped into the attack, a movement so fast, so fluid that it seemed the air itself bent around her. Her left blade, a shock of incandescent orange, sheared through the darkling's outstretched arm at the shoulder. The metal of its armor, along with all the bone within the trajectory of the strike, vaporized in an instant. The wound was already well cauterized by the time the point of the sword completed its upward trajectory and dismantled the creature's throat. Momentum carried its unbalanced and dead body forward, its snarling face frozen in confusion and pain, before her right sword, a rippling brand of white-hot fire, scythed upward through its jaw and into its skull. There was a dull crack, like a dry log splitting, and the darkling collapsed in a pile of smoking ruin.

She didn't pause. The second and third were on her before the first had finished falling. They were smarter, coming from either side, their serrated blades carving tight, vicious arcs meant to hamstring and disembowel. Aoife's wings, still folded, slammed outward like battering rams. The right wing, a solid curtain of flame and force, caught one darkling square in the chest, the impact buckling its crude iron plate and sending it flying backward into the oncoming horde. The left wing flared, its feathered tips grazing the stone wall and showering the corridor with sparks as she spun. Her swords moved in a devastating, continuous figure eight. One blade took the one on the left across the knees, severing sinew, shattering bone, and crumpling the body, the other sword plunged into the throat of its companion.

But they were a torrent of filth and fury. For every one she felled, three more clambered over the twitching bodies of their kin to take its place. The narrowness of the hall, once a disadvantage, became an asset. It was a grinder, and she was the stone. A glaive skittered off the flagstones, aiming for her ankle. She leaped, her wings giving her more than enough lift to clear the attack, and brought her heels down hard on the darkling's helm. The metal caved with a sickening crunch. She kicked off its body, using it as a springboard to drive her swords into the chests of two more.

A clawed hand raked across her side, its razor-sharp nails tearing through her flimsy garments and into the flesh beneath. Pain, sharp and hot, lanced through her ribs. She grunted and spun, her back hitting the cold, damp stone of the wall. She used the momentary support to anchor herself as she loosed a torrent of fire from her left blade, a horizontal wave of heat that washed over the forward rank of the charge.

The darklings shrieked as the fire consumed them, their black fur igniting, their armor glowing cherry-red before melting and fusing to their flesh. The smell of burnt hair and cooked meat, thick and nauseating, filled the corridor. From the safety and darkness where they hid, Cante felt his stomach heave. The sight, the smell, the sheer, unrelenting violence was more than his mind could process. He saw Aoife, a terrifying angel of death, her face streaked with blood. He saw the darklings not as a faceless horde but as individual creatures, their bodies breaking, burning, coming apart in the most gruesome ways imaginable. He was a seller of potions and poultices, a farmer, and a family man, not a slayer of monsters. He retched where he crouched.

"Mercy," he croaked, his voice trembling. "She's a demon."

"No," Feste breathed, his eyes wide with horror. "She's the only thing keeping the demons at bay."

The darklings began to adapt. They stopped their headlong charge and started to use the walls, their claws finding purchase in the ancient mortar, scrambling up the sides to drop on her from above. One landed on her shoulders, its weight driving her to one knee, its teeth snapping inches from her face. She roared, arching her back, her wings flaring with such intensity that the darkling on her back was incinerated instantly, its body turning to cinder atop her. Ashes fell around her like blackened snow, covering her completely in smears of gray.

But the moment left her exposed. A spear, thrown from the back of the press, flew and struck true. She twisted, but not fast enough. The sharpened iron head slammed into her shoulder, not piercing deeply or mortally, but with enough force to send a jolt of numbing pain down her arm. Her right sword flickered, the flame wavering.

She gritted her teeth, ignoring the fire in her shoulder, and fought on. It was a brutal, desperate brawl. She slammed a darkling into the wall, crushing its ribs with the pommel of her sword. She kicked another in the groin, then drove the crossguard of the sword in her left hand through its eye socket in a murderous punch. She was bleeding and ragged from exertion. The sheer attrition was wearing her down. Her movements, once effortless, were becoming labored. Her flames, once a roaring inferno, were now a guttering and dimming flicker. She knew she couldn't keep up. There were still dozens of them, a wall of black iron and snarling hate between her and Illia-Dara's chambers. She needed to end it. Now.

With a final surge, with everything she had left, she drove her swords into the floorstones. They sank deep, the flames licking at the blood-soaked decking. She drew a tattered breath, pulling not just air, but power into her lungs. She was a core of starlight, a far-off and silent force of the cosmos. Her wings flared to their full, magnificent, terrifying width, melting through the stone walls. The heat and light shone so intensely that the darklings in the front ranks recoiled, shielding their eyes.

"Be unmade," she whispered.

A concussive wave erupted from her, an expanding sphere that filled the corridor from floor to ceiling, wall to wall. It wasn't just fire, it was the energy of a newborn star. It didn't burn the darklings, it annihilated them utterly. Their bodies were blasted into the umbra, their armor reduced to slag. Their howls were cut short, swallowed by the roll of her power. The wave washed down the corridor, leaving nothing but scorched stone and the ghostly, fading outlines of what had once been living, breathing creatures in its wake.

The hall fell silent. The only sound was the ragged heaving of Aoife's breath. The flaming swords dissolved, their light extinguished. Her wings drooped, their fire sinking back into her, leaving trails of smoke. A film of gray and gore covered her from head to foot. Blood sluggishly seeped from a gash in her side and the puncture in her shoulder. Her body screamed, every muscle, every bone, every fiber of her being protesting the immense expenditure of power. She was altogether spent.

From their hiding spot, Cante and Feste stared out at the aftermath. The walls were painted with scorched shadows and blood. The floor was a carpet of ash and cooling, melted iron. It was a vision of hell. They saw Aoife leaning against the wall, every inch of her trembling with enervation. But her gaze wasn't on the devastation she had wrought. It was locked onto the door at the far end of the hall. They watched as she pushed herself off the wall, her legs shaking. She began to walk, one slow, deliberate step at a time, through the ghostly remains of the small army she had just destroyed and toward Illia-Dara.

"I want to go home," Cante said somberly.

"So do I, brother. So do I," Feste answered as he lowered himself from their hiding hole and held out his hand. "But I think they might be needing us sooner than later. And I *know* that we're needing them."

Two short, round men stumbled into the chambers to be met by two other short, round men. Behind the latter stood Illia-Dara, Sylvandralis raised in a two-handed grip, poised to strike, and Heron, who, if it weren't for his tattered and bloody clothes, would look very out of place, like a fox amongst a pack of wolves. Behind the former stood Aoife, worn and crippled by a battle that few else could have survived, leaning heavily on Feste's strong shoulder.

"Who the hells are ye?" Mergop and Thurdop asked together, suspicious and wary of the new arrivals, ready to defend the queen with their lives.

"Who the hells are you?" Both Rands responded in unison, their voices rising to a near comical inflection.

"Aoife," Illia-Dara said, dropping Sylvandaris to the floor, leaving it to rattle and clank, and running to the wounded woman. "What happened? Are you okay?" Illia began to examine Aoife, her hands and eyes exploring the numerous wounds, assessing and inventorying them to prioritize triage options. "What of Stren? What of my husband?"

Aoife's face crumpled. The strength that had carried her through the inferno of the hall seemed to evaporate, leaving only exposed nerve. Tears, hot and immediate, welled in her eyes. "Illia," she began, her voice was shattered glass and nearly stolen by the howling wind outside. She tried again, swallowing against the knot of grief constricting her throat, against the truth that she knew she must tell. "Stren is down, but alive, at least he was the last time I saw him. But Endryll," she choked on his name. "Endryll fell, Illia. I felt it and know it to be true. He fell protecting the throne. He fell protecting you."

The words hung in the air, small and insignificant against the backdrop of the storm, yet they landed with the force of a mighty troll's blow. Illia-Dara froze. Her hands, which had been gently probing a gash on Aoife's arm, stilled. The world seemed to tilt on its axis. Everything around her receded into a dull, hollow roar. A profound silence descended, a vacuum where thought and feeling ceased to exist. She was spinning, and there was nothing to hold onto, nothing to ground her, no anchor.

Endryll.

She saw him as he was just that morning, his laughter echoing in the quiet of their chambers, his hand in hers, his smile a promise of a thousand tomorrows. She saw him as a boy, chasing her through the Crownfields, his hair waving like golden wheat in the summer sun. She saw him standing before her, his eyes filled with a love so pure and so absolute that it had been the cornerstone of her entire world.

And now he was gone?

The world she had known, the future she had envisioned, crushed into dust, leaving her adrift in a desolate, colorless sea of emptiness, alone. It was a loss too vast to comprehend, a stabbing wound too deep to feel. She had just lost Ixchel, her constant, her shadow, her sworn protector. His dissolution, the violent tearing of his essence, had left a gaping hole in her soul, a void that still throbbed with the ghost of his pain and his love. And now, Endryll. Her husband and her heart. Her king. The pillar of her existence was ripped away in the same cruel breath of fate.

The shock was a physical thing that stole the air from her lungs. Her body, which had moved so freely only moments ago, now felt like a leaden shell, disconnected from her mind. She swayed, her eyes wide yet unseeing, fixed on a point somewhere beyond the chamber walls, beyond the storm, beyond the edge of reality, for this reality had become too much for her to bear.

Aoife reached out, her own injuries and pain a secondary thing next to the agony radiating from the young queen. "Illia," she said, her voice gentle, "I am so sorry." But the words were meaningless, pebbles tossed into the abyssal sea. How could she comfort a grief that was so total, so absolute? She couldn't. There were no words to heal this, to *fix* this.

"It was Atamas," Aoife continued, her tone hardening, the need for action overriding the futility of seeking solace. "He is behind it all. He attacked Stren. He killed Endryll. He is seizing control of the castle, of everything. We have to leave. Now."

While the two women were suspended in their bubble of grief and grim reality, a different kind of tension was brewing across the room. The four stout men, two fae and two something else, regarded each other with the intense, dubious scrutiny of badgers stumbling upon a rival clan's territory.

Thurdop, his beard a wiry, tangled mess, took a step forward, his hand resting on the small axe at his belt. He squinted at Cante, who was still trying to subtly wipe a smear of what looked suspiciously like boar grease from his cheek. "What sort o' creature are ye, then?" Thurdop grunted, his voice a low rumble. "Ye smell o' man, but ye ain't big enough for all that."

Cante, puffing out his chest, took offense. "Not *big* enough? I'll have you know we are the Brothers Rand, proprietors of the finest gallipots and thumblejacks this side of the Titan's Crown! Or we were before our wagon was reduced to kindling by a stampede of lunatics."

"Thumblejacks?" Mergop scoffed, poking a curious finger at the silver-trimmed edge of Feste's new coat, which was, of course, ruined. The fabric, though, was still richer than anything he'd ever worn. "Fancy name for a peddler. And what's this then? Silk? For one o' yer—" he paused for a moment, as if finding the right word, "—girth? It's unnatural. Ye should be wearin' sackloth an' yarn fer a belt, heh."

Feste smacked his hand away. "And what are you supposed to be? A garden gnome who's been left alone for too long with naught but your herd of sheep to keep you company at night? Your beard's got more knots than a sailor's rigging, and it looks like you've got last season's moss growing in it." He leaned in, sniffing dramatically. "And is that dung I smell?"

The four of them began to circle each other slowly, a low-stakes standoff of insults and prodding fingers. Mergop jabbed a thumb into Cante's ample belly. Cante, in turn, tugged on a loose thread from Mergop's tunic, causing it to unfurl even further. Thurdop and Feste were locked in a silent, intense glaring match, each trying to outstare the other. Heron, standing awkwardly to the side, looked back and forth between the unfolding farce before him and the gut-wrenching grief behind him. He had never seen such heartbreak, such misery, in all his life, nor had he ever seen such a ridiculous display of masculine posturing, and he was raised in the Bairn-brand.

Then Illia-Dara wept. It wasn't a cry, or a scream, or a sob. It was a sound that seemed to tear itself from the very fabric of her being. It was a sound of such penetrating agony that it silenced everything. It was the sound of a world ending, of a soul being ripped apart, of a love so deep it could only be expressed in a lament that relied on something other than words. The four men froze, their petty squabble forgotten. The color drained from their faces as they turned to look at their queen.

Illia-Dara was on her knees, her body wracked with violent convulsions. Her hands clawed at her own chest and tore at what remained of her gown, as if trying to rip out the source of the pain. Tears streamed down her face in a flood, soaking the bodice of her dress, mingling with dark stains of blood. Her mouth was open in a soundless scream, her jaw locked, her face contorted in such utter, desolate misery that it was too much to behold. All the men looked away, ashamed and broken as she cried for all of Y'ssildria.

The sound that had escaped her was not of this world. It was the keening of a banshee, the shriek of a soul cast to judgment. It was the sound of every hope she had ever cherished gone. She swayed, her eyes rolling back in her head, the sheer force of her grief threatening to pull her into the welcome relief of unconsciousness. She saw Ixchel's fading form, his ethereal hand passing through hers. She imagined Endryll, his light extinguished, a fallen king on a blood-soaked dais. She saw her father-in-law, cut down and hanging heinously from the shaft of a glaive. She saw her mother and her father, a ghost of a memory, lost to avarice and misplaced loyalty.

She was alone. Utterly, completely, irrevocably alone. The crownless queen of a fallen kingdom, the bride of a dead king, the friend of a vanished protector. The weight of it all, the crushing, suffocating weight of her sorrow, was too much to bear. Her body gave out, slumping forward, her forehead hitting the cold, unforgiving floor with a dull thud. And still, the silent, agonizing sobs shook her frame. It was pain so true and so real as had never been felt before.

Aoife knelt, wrapping her arms around the unconscious woman, trying to offer a warmth that could never penetrate the icy grip of such loss. "Illia," she whispered, her voice thick with concern. "Illia, you have to breathe."

But Illia-Dara was beyond hearing. She was lost in the raging tempest far more violent than the one lashing the Citadel walls.

"We have to go," Aoife said, her voice hardening with urgency. She looked at the men, who stood frozen, their faces pale with a mixture of shock and a terrible sympathy and compassion. "We have to get her out of here. Atamas's troops could be here any moment. She can mourn later. If we stay, there will be nothing left to mourn for."

Heron stepped forward then, his young face showing a strength and resolve that gave her pause. He had stood by feeling useless, a bystander to a tragedy he couldn't comprehend, sharing a pain that was not his. But seeing Illia-Dara, so broken, so utterly lost, stirred something deep within him, a protective instinct he didn't know he possessed. He knelt beside Aoife, his touch surprisingly gentle as he placed a hand on Illia-Dara's trembling shoulder.

"My Queen," he said, his voice soft but firm, cutting through the haze of her grief. "Please. We must go."

Illia-Dara didn't respond. Her body was still wracked with sobs. Aoife looked at Heron, and acknowledgment passed between them. Together, they gently but firmly began to lift her. Her limbs were sluggish, her body a dead weight and unresponsive. But they persisted, Aoife on one side, Heron on the other. They had her standing, though she was swaying like a fragile doll, held up only by their support. Her eyes were vacant, her face white. She looked at them as her head lolled, but it was clear she saw nothing.

"The gardens are filled with darklings," Thurdop said. "Tha' was ter be our escape."

"This way," Aoife said, gesturing with her head towards a narrow doorway that led to the outer castle walls. "To the parapets. It's our only chance."

With the four stout men taking up vanguard positions in front of Aoife, Illia, and Heron, they began to move, half-carrying, half-dragging the broken queen. They moved through the desecrated chamber, a small and wretched procession of survivors. They passed the obsidian box, still sitting on the end table, its runic surface dark and inert. They passed the shattered remnants of the door. They moved down the hall and toward the howl of the wind and the relentless drumming of the rain. They were heading for the southeastern wall, for the high, windswept parapets that overlooked the raging sea, and met with the long run of the Stoneguard. It was a last-ditch gamble for escape, for survival, for a future that seemed to have died with their king.

Moments later, a single, dark figure stalked into the chamber, its fur matted and knotted, its monstrous clawed feet scraping and scratching the ruined floors. It moved with a predator's unsettling quiet, a hunched shape against the storm-lashed light filtering through the shattered doorway. The darkling paused, its head lifting, its flared nostrils twitching as it tasted the air. The scent was a complex concoction of recent events. It smelled the cloying perfume of nobility, now soured by the copper tang of fear and blood. It smelled the damp, earthy musk of the fae, a scent as old as the forest floor. Underlying it all was something else, something that made the fur on its neck prickle. It was the sharp, ozone scent of spent Aetheric power. The scents were fresh, the occupants of the room only just departed.

Its yellowed eyes, burning with a scavenger's cunning, scanned the room. This was a place of wealth, and wealth meant opportunity. It kicked aside the forgotten candelabra, the bronze ringing hollowly on the stone. Its claws tore through a velvet cushion on one of the ottomans, revealing a cloud of white down, but nothing of value. It grunted in frustration, its gaze sweeping across the discarded bags, the torn silks, the faint, drying pools of blood.

Then he saw it. On the small end table near the bed, almost overlooked in the gloom, sat the small black box, and just below it, on the floor, was a broken obsidian stone. They were still, inert, yet the darkling's keen senses picked up the faint, aura clinging to them, a power that did not belong in this world. He approached the table cautiously, his head cocked, sniffing at the objects. The cold emanating from the box was unnatural, a chill that had nothing to do with the storm and everything to do with the void.

A wicked, toothy smile stretched the darkling's maw, its rotted fangs protruding menacingly. With a swift, practiced motion, it snatched the item from the table. Its clawed fingers wrapped around the box. It pocketed the frigid container, then scooped up the smooth, dark stone and tucked it safely away in a pouch at its belt. It had come for scraps and found a treasure of a different ilk.

As it turned to melt back into the shadows of the ravaged citadel, a faint, almost imperceptible sound reached its ears. It came from the pocket where the box now rested, a tiny, muffled scream, like that of a soul trapped in glass, thin and full of despair, before it was abruptly silenced. The darkling paused for a fraction of a second, then its smile widened, and it disappeared into the gloom.

Darker Days Will Come

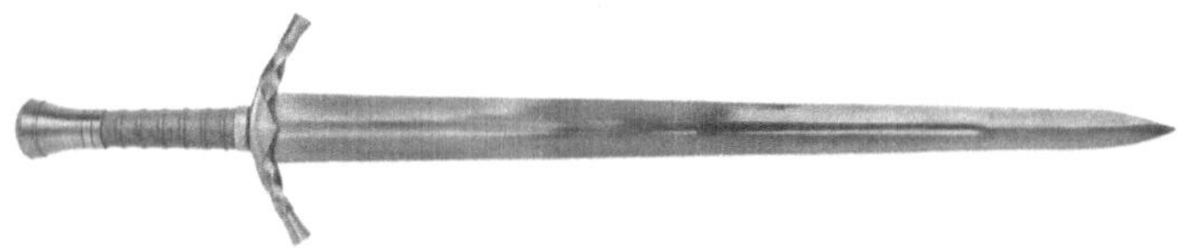

The dying screams of the innocent, the last valiant push of the soldiers, and the final kicking and begging of escapees being dragged back had all been extinguished, silenced by the bloody boots of the darkling army. Statues lay shattered, their granite faces gazing blankly outward. Banners, once proud green and gold, hung in tattered ribbons, soaked crimson and black where they were not burned away. The floor was now a mosaic of shattered glass, discarded finery, and the unmoving bodies of those who had come to celebrate. There was a terrible hush of a conquered people. It was the hush of a people holding their breath, waiting for the next blow, the next decree, the next twist of the knife. Dust motes, thick with the residue of shattered stone and incinerated flesh, danced in the few shafts of weak, storm-filtered light, like pixie dancers waltzing across a graveyard.

Beyond the desecrated hall, the sprawling streets of Y'ssildria bore the scars of conquest as well. The cobbled streets, usually alive with the sounds and movement of merchants and the laughter of children, were silent save for the scuff of darkling patrols and the occasional, distant wail of a grief-stricken survivor. Homes lay in ruins, their timber looking skeletal against the backdrop of the storming sky. Their contents had been plundered or scattered, nothing of value, sentimental or otherwise, was left. The vibrant market squares, where the scent of baking bread and fresh-cut flowers once mingled, now reeked of smoke and burned flesh. Broken wagons, their wheels splintered, lay overturned, their spilled wares a mournful attestation to lives both interrupted and destroyed. Everywhere and nowhere, the subtle, invisible presence of the Aetherfast, once a constant, comforting thing, was gone, replaced by a dull, aching emptiness that pressed upon the very soul of the city. Plants wilted, their leaves curling and browning as if a sudden winter had gripped them. The air felt thinner, less breathable, less alive.

Atamas moved through the wreckage. He was a conqueror, a victor. His coat remained spotless. His boots dripped horrid death as he stepped over corpses and debris with indifference. He no longer bore a countenance of courtesy, but instead wore a wide and unholy smile, a predatory glee that twisted his features into something mean and monstrous. He surveyed the devastation with an almost artistic appreciation, as if admiring a masterpiece freshly wrought. His eyes, devoid of warmth, gleamed with triumph, reflecting the flickering flames that still licked all about, casting a lurid hue of destruction across the square. The scent of his berryroot and bitter-grass tobacco clung to him, shrouding his passing with a sinister perfume among the captured city.

Behind him, darklings moved. They were no longer the frenzied beasts of battle but disciplined instruments of a calculated will. Their snarls were muted, replaced by the soft scuff of their claws on stone as they went about their tasks. They dragged bodies, sorted rubble, and began to round up the living. Their tasks were performed with a methodical efficiency. Their eyes burned with cruel focus. They were extensions of Atamas's will, a terrifying precision grafted onto their primal savagery.

"Separate them," Atamas's voice resonated through the square, clear and sharp, cutting through the commotion like a harvester's sickle through grass. The command vibrated in the bones of the survivors, while compelling obedience from those who served him. "Those who wield the Aether, to the lower crypts. The rest to the kitchens, to the stables, and to the servant quarters. They will work. Those who do not wish to work will die."

Dread spread like a blight across the lachrymose eyes of the survivors, huddled and cowering beneath the shadows of the viscous darkling mob. Women sobbed as they held their children close. There were few men left, as most had died fighting, but those who remained were being beaten and dragged this way and that, disappearing down dark alleys and through darker doors, their cries of pain trailing them. The wolf-faced savages herded the cowering Y'ssildrians like frightened sheep and were none too gentle as they went about their work.

A group of groveling noblewomen was unceremoniously pulled apart and sifted. One, Lady Elara of House Valerius, her usually proud bearing reduced to a trembling lump, clutched at the faintly shimmering thread of a weather charm she had woven for the day. It was a simple thing, a comfort charm, meant to ward off the rain during the outdoor festivities. Now, its delicate magic was fading into a wisp of dull shine, and she had no clue as to why. Still, she fingered it compulsively. It seemed a necessary thing for her, some semblance of normalcy or reality amidst the terror she was now enduring.

A darkling, its snout sniffing the air, turned its head, its eyes fixing on her. It reached out and took hold of her wrist. The charm sputtered, then vanished, as if the world refused its existence. The woman cried out, not from pain, but from the sudden, terrifying emptiness of her power, for as she felt the powers of the charm fading, so too did she feel her own innate grasp on the Aetherfast disappear. She stared at her hand, now devoid of her small craft, realization dawning in horror. She was lifted from the ground then and led away, her movements stiff, her eyes wide with a fear. Her magic, her very essence, was gone. The unraveling had begun.

All across the ravaged scene, the Aetherfast began to fade. Orbs of fire and light that had illuminated the streets flickered and died one by one, plunging the city into a deeper, more oppressive gloom. Spells fizzled into nothingness. The ancestral blade of a knight, felled and eternally sleeping, lost its Aetherly shimmer and was now nothing but a piece of inert, mundane steel.

This Great Unraveling was not a single, booming event confined to the walls of the Sunspire Citadel, or the city of Y'ssildria. It was a million quiet deaths that rippled out from the slaughter in the grand hall. In the Western Wood, the ancient trees, which had for generations carried the thoughts and fellowship of the Timber-Folk, fell silent, their sacred communion instantly severed. On the forlorn road of Deadlock Pass, where the enchanted Bellflowers, which once awoke to cast a vibrant, multicolored glow upon the path, wilted in an instant, their light extinguished forever, leaving only darkness. Sylvandralis, the most famed of blades, whose mortal gears were meant to ignite its lava-stone glyphs into a searing flame, was now just a sword, its inner fire quenched. The desperate party fleeing across the open parapets high above witnessed the sword dim and die, casting them into shadow as they ran. In the quiet kitchen of Stren's cottage, the delicate, magical balance of life collapsed. The venom-vine could no longer support the healing Moonthistle, which now withered under its own miraculous weight. The very heart of Y'ssildira and its surrounding hamlets and towns, farms and shops, fields and mountains and seas, had ceased to beat, leaving only a somber, hollow stillness in its wake. And the storm raged on.

"Master," one darkling said to Atamas. "He wakes."

On the dais, Stren stirred, a groan crawling and clawing from his throat. The world swam back into focus as a miscellany of aches and confusion. He pushed himself up, his head pounding, his vision blurred. He felt hollow and immediately knew he was without. The intimate and constant connection to the earth that had been his companion since birth—the steady pulse of life in the stone beneath him—was gone. He reached to the Aetherfast with all his strength, commanding the roots and rock to rise to his aid. Naught responded. The earth was speechless. The stone was just stone. He could no longer hear the tiny earthworms and voles rooting about beneath him. He could no longer sense streams or the myriad fish that swam there. He was nothing. He was just an old man, wounded and dying on a bloodwashed floor surrounded by the corpses of his friends. He collapsed then and saw the body of Endryll, broken and bled dry.

He felt the footsteps before he heard them. He looked up, his eyes finding the calm, smiling visage of Atamas looming over him. Then Stren understood. This was not a consequence of the battle, this *was* the battle. Atamas hadn't just attacked Y'ssildria. He had blinded and bound it. He had muted it. He had ripped it, wholly, from the Aetherfast. *But how?*

How was this possible? How had he not seen it? He had marked Atamas as a potential threat. He knew Atamas' ambitions, or at least he thought he did.

"What have you done?" Stren rasped. He struggled to push himself up, his limbs heavy and unresponsive.

Atamas' smile widened to full, showing a chilling satisfaction. "I have brought salvation." He gestured expansively at the carnage, at the stunned prisoners, and at the darklings, who seemed entranced and enraptured by their master's voice. "The Aetherfast was a crutch. A warm blanket that kept Y'ssildria in a perpetual, comfortable infancy. It made you weak, reliant on its power instead of controlling it."

Stren finally got to one knee, his body screaming in protest. He leaned heavily on a fallen pillar, his gaze sweeping over the hall, seeing not just the dead, but the extinguished potential, the past, present, and future of Y'ssildria destroyed. He saw the dead and dying, the inert enchantments, the vacant expressions on the faces of the few remaining children. "You call this salvation? This is your, what, your cure?" he choked out his words, his voice trembling with a fury that was all he had left. "You have performed amputations on a healthy body, and you call it healing! You have desiccated a kingdom, bled it dry, and you call it progress? For what? This is not salvation!"

"A handsome metaphor," Atamas conceded with a nod. "But inaccurate. I am not a surgeon. I am no mad scientist, dawdling about in my laboratory brewing up foul concoctions. I am an architect. You clung to prophecies, Stren, while I studied diagrams. This kingdom, for all its beauty, was built on a flawed foundation. It was beholden to forces across the veil. It was destined to crumble. I have merely hastened the demolition so that something stronger, something *real* and *lasting* may be built in its place. A world forged by strength, by mortal hands, not one dependent on the whims of a force we cannot control."

Stren's eyes darted to the still, broken form of King Onidine pinned to his own throne like a songbird stretched and fastened to a board for observation and dissection mid-trill, to satisfy the curiosities of a lunatic. "And him? Was he part of your grand design? What of Cerceia? Was Cerceia's death the first brick laid in the foundation of your new world?"

A flicker of something unreadable crossed Atamas's face, a disturbance, a ripple that was gone as quickly as it came. "Onidine was a good man, but a king of the old world. He, like you, believed in the sanctity of what *was*. He mourned it, even as it failed him." He took a step closer, his voice dropping. "Do you remember that night in the forest, Stren? The night Ixchel was dying? I saved him. I did what had to be done. I bound him to the Aetherfast because it was the only tool I had." His voice rose in bitter resentment. "You should have seen how Onidine was looking at me! He looked at me as if I were a savior, as if I were a god!" He was screaming, spittle flying from his mouth and catching on his beard. "I was helpless as a healer, *master*! HELPLESS! I had already failed Cerceia. She died in my arms, and I was powerless to save her. For all the authority, all the potency, all the strength that the Aetherfast has provided to us, her conduits, her true disciples, I was a neutered pup. It did NOTHING when I called!

"And then Endryll came, so strong, so full of life. He had consumed Ixchel's strength, you know. Even in the womb, he stole everything from his brother. Even before they were born, Endryll was a cancerous leech in a one-sided symbiotic relationship with Ixchel. And Ixchel just gave and gave. He gave so much that he came to life dying." Atamas was weeping openly now, reliving that dreadful night. He knelt beside Stren. "He gave, and Endryll took. And even with his last breath, he gave."

"Ixchel," Stren whispered, realization dawning. "You used him. The veilstone, the beating heart within the box, that was your key." The pieces crashed into place in Stren's mind, a horrifying jigsaw of betrayal and lunacy.

"He was *born* a key," Atamas corrected, his voice laced with pain and venom and the pride of a master craftsman. "A child uniquely tethered to the Aetherfast, a living bridge between worlds, a flaw in the design. I simply used that flaw to turn the lock. Progress requires sacrifice, Stren. His was a small, but necessary price for the birth of a new age. The Aetherfast kept him alive. He should never have been!

"When Cerceia died, despite my calls, my *pleas* to the Aetherfast, I knew what I had suspected for a very, very long time. The Aetherfast is a lie. It is crumbs fallen from a table at which we are not permitted to sit. It is the leash that tethers us, giving us just enough rope to feel free, but we were never free. We were always bound. Until now."

"What did you do?" Stren asked. He was shaking now, both from exhaustion and from fear.

"I destroyed the veil's link to our world," Atamas answered simply. His eyes were alight with fervent passion. He had been waiting for years to reveal his coup. "On the night of your absence, when Ixchel was dying and all my knowledge of healing, both mortal and Aether, had failed, I knew we had been betrayed. I took from Cerceia the essence of her being and combined that with the boy's own. I then took a piece of his heart that still remained in the veil and hid it away in the stone."

"You sacrificed the child of the woman you loved!" Stren roared, finding a sudden surge of strength. He pushed himself to his feet, swaying but standing. "A boy I raised as my own! You speak of architecture, but all you have built is a kingdom of corpses! You are no creator, Atamas. You are a destroyer!"

Atamas stood then, his anger flaring hot. "You are the destroyer, Stren D'anyan, Lask Oak of Burss. By setting your roots so deeply in an empty faith of the past, by refusing to evolve, to awaken, you have damned yourself and all those you've been leading in this dead faith. Your god is dead, and your blind faith clouds all that you will ever know! Y'sa was silent that night, and thus shall remain silent forevermore. The binding and breaking of Ixchel have seen to that. You are a relic, Stren. Your time, and the time of your fickle faith, is over."

Stren slowly descended to lean his back against the pillar. His body was a twisted wreck of bruised flesh and splintered bone. His vision swam, a kaleidoscope of red and black, but his mind was clear with terrible clarity. He tried to move, but his body refused. He could only bear witness, his eyes wide with horror, his heart a hammer against his ribs, beating a mournful tattoo for a dying age.

He knew it then, intimately, the insidious emptiness in the air. The Aetherfast was muted. Suppressed. Gone. It was like a great river suddenly dammed, its flow stemmed, its roar not even a faint gurgle. The connection was severed. And with that knowledge, the whole, horrifying truth unfolded within Stren's consciousness, a monstrous ambition born of perceived betrayal. He saw it all, as if projected onto the inner chambers of his mind. He reeled back as the barrage assaulted him. It was a farewell gift from the powers he had known for so long; a final desparate and terminal coda sent across the veil. It was the last word of the Aetherfast of things unknown.

The cold forest floor, long ago, under a skeletal moon. Queen Cerceia's lifeless body, two babes in her arms. The fevered cries of one, a child clinging to life by a thread, the silent despair of Onidine. Atamas, his face grim, his hands stained with afterbirth and muck, clutching the crude orb of blood and mud and umbilical cord. The orb wasn't just a focus. It was the physical manifestation of what he had taken, the remnants of Cerceia. The soiled, discarded innards of a queen who had just given life, now reduced to a damned catalyst. The Matron's words echoed: "His claim to the throne was as flimsy as his life. And now, thanks to Atamas's 'salvation,' that common babe is a conduit, a vessel for power he cannot comprehend."

Stren was torn from reality as the images thrashed and mauled him.

"By the blood given, for the life taken." Atamas's voice, a whispered incantation, binding the infant Ixchel to the Aetherfast, forging him and intertwining his nascent flame of the pure, boundless energy of creation, with the vile, corrupted remnant. The abomination of flesh and fluid and bone, compressed into the obsidian stone, became the true anchor. A fragment of death woven into the very fabric of life. And the fragment of Ixchel's slowly beating heart, locked away in a box, awaiting the day of its purpose.

And then, years later, the familiar scene in his own cottage. The moment Ixchel touched the stone, the surge of power, the siphoning of his strength. The stone, alive, hungry. It had tasted him. It had recognized him. It was the other half of the binding, a malignant parasite tethered to Ixchel's own yet-known flame. He had thought it was a test of will. How wrong he was.

The coronation. The gift. The dark box, pulsating with the breath of the Vintermarrow. The stone, slipped into Illia-Dara's pocket, then handed to Ixchel. It was the final link, checkmate. Atamas knew of Ixchel's love for Illia-Dara. He knew of his oath, his unyielding desire, his need to protect her. And he had turned that love into the final instrument of his triumph.

When Ixchel, in his desperate, final act of love, poured his essence, his full, unbridled flame into Illia-Dara, he did so through the conduit of the obsidian stone. And the stone, tied to the dark box, which in turn contained the physical essence of the abomination, the cursed remnants of Cerceia, completed the circuit. It was a twisted, unholy marriage of life and death, of creation and corruption, a ghastly rupture rending apart the Aetherfast.

Atamas had not merely killed Ixchel, he had used him. He had taken Ixchel's living flame, supercharged it with his corrupted magic, and then detonated it, like a bomb, precisely within the heart of Y'ssildria. The resulting backlash, the Aether explosion, had not only undone the veil's link, extinguishing his connection to the Aetherfast and the world, but had ripped a hole in the Aetherfast's influence across the entire city, perhaps further.

And then it was gone, as elusive and unreachable as before. The Aetherfast was gone.

Within Y'ssildria's new boundaries, the very source of their power had been cut off. Only crude, raw, brute force remained, the kind that did not require the Aetherfast's subtle currents. The kind Atamas himself wielded now through the armies of darklings. The kind that killed kings and unmade princes. The kind that would build a new kingdom on the bones of the old.

"Take him," Stren heard Atamas say from somewhere very far off, and then the fallen Crownward was hoisted up by his arms and carried away.

Rain, driven by the gale, lashed down, turning the bloodied cobblestones and earth into a slick, treacherous mire. The storm had transformed the world beyond the Citadel's shattered gates into a sodden, weeping landscape, a living nightmare for the citizens of Y'ssildria. Atamas stood in the center of the square, a foreboding vinculum of order in the core of the storm. His gaze swept over the cowering people. The non-magical survivors huddled together, a trembling mass of soaked wool and fear, while the captured magic users, their hands bound, were being forced to their knees in the mud. His smile was a thin, cruel line.

"Citizens of Y'ssildria!" he said, his voice rich and resonant and soothing and terrible in its calm authority. "Look around you. Behold the ruin. Behold the death. Behold the opportunity."

He paused, allowing his words to take hold, his gaze lingering on the smoldering Citadel, the pyre of the old king a grotesque backdrop to his triumph. "For centuries, you have lived under the illusion of safety. You have put your faith in kings who stood for balance, in mages who preached caution and restraint. You have lived in the shadow of the Aetherfast, a capricious and dangerous mistress that grants power only to the chosen few, leaving the rest of you vulnerable and weak. You, the common folk, the good, honest people of this city, have lived in fear. Fear of the uncontrolled and uncontrollable. Fear of the so-called 'gifts' of the gods. Fear of those who would rise above you, claiming divine right. And what has it brought you? This!" He gestured to the destruction. "This is the empty promise of their protection!"

He spread his hands, encompassing the weeping and frightened crowd. "No more! The age of imbalance is over. The time of those with power and those without is no longer! The Aetherfast has been gagged! Its wild energies, once a threat to all goodly folk, are now silent. Its influence, once a source of division, is now gone." His voice was a snare, drawing them in, offering them an answer, even as he plotted their destruction. He pointed to the captured magic users, now being herded towards the Citadel's smoking gates. Their faces were pale, their hands trembling, their magic useless. "Are these your betters? Are these *illumined* more deserving of opportunity or title or privilege than any of you, simply because they were born into powers that you weren't given a chance or choice to receive?" He paused just long enough to let the question marinate. "You have had to labor and toil for mere scraps, while they snap their fingers and the world is handed to them. You have been persecuted and pressed under their thumb simply for being *other*. Well, no longer! Their power has been severed! They are nothing now. Mere men and women, like you. And they will learn humility in the darkness that you have endured your whole lives! It is time for a renewal, friends. It is *your* time!"

A murmur rippled through the non-magical crowd, a mixture of fear, confusion, and even a flash of hope. They looked at the imprisoned magic users, at the now-impotent symbols of their former awe, of their jealousy. Could it be true? Could they truly be equal now? They were never seen as lesser, never treated poorly. More often than not, it was the non-magic users who held positions of power and prestige within the walls of Y'ssildria, and truly without, as well. But there *was* an unspoken understanding, a hushed acknowledgement that those without the Aetherfast could never truly be equal. The promise of balance, of conformity, false as it was, was a potent lure.

"From this day forward," Atamas proclaimed, his voice rising, "there will be no more fear. No more hidden powers. No more secrets. No more separation or segregation. You, the true strength of Y'ssildria, will no longer live in the shadows of those who claim to be greater. You will be safe. You will be free. Free from the arrogance of the *gifted*. Free from the dangers of a magic that cares nothing for your lives or the lives of your loved ones. You will be free from the clutches of order, of systemic and unfair rule."

He paused, allowing the poison of his words to spread, to take root in the fertile ground of their terror. It was bitter and grossly inaccurate, but it tasted sweet. It was honey atop a bear trap, and the coils were taught and ready to spring shut. He was offering them paradise, a world without the existential threat of unpredictable power. A world, ironically, built on the bodies of those who had once wielded that very power to protect them and to make their lives easier.

"Those who once claimed dominion over the Aether will now suffer as you have suffered," Atamas continued. "Their power is gone. They will live out the remainder of their days in the cells below your feet. They will hear your footsteps as you rebuild your lives without them. And they will mourn. And if they resist, if they cling to the old ways, to the old faith, they will be extinguished, just as this city's past transgressions have been extinguished this day." He allowed his gaze to sweep across the devastated square, emphasizing the point.

Among the prisoners, a healer stumbled. He looked at his hands, hands that had brought comfort, that had knitted flesh and soothed pain with a mere touch. Now, they were useless. He saw his young apprentice, a boy whose eyes once sparkled with Aether, now crying and scared as a darkling dragged him off towards a different group and away from his master. The healer resisted, a futile, desperate struggle, his voice a hoarse shout. "You cannot! This is blasphemy! The Aetherfast is the breath of Y'sa!"

A darkling lieutenant struck the healer across the mouth with the back of his gauntleted hand. The healer crumpled, his cries stifled. "Your gods are deaf here now," the darkling snarled. "Your magic is dead. You are nothing." The healer was hauled away, his body limp. That scene played out across that yard, as many of the prisoners objected and fought back. Some were silenced, some were killed, and all were brought low.

"And you," Atamas turned back to the non-magical folk, his voice softening, a predator mesmerizing its prey. "You will live in a new Y'ssildria, a stronger Y'ssildria, a safer Y'ssildria. You will build and you will work, and you will thrive. And you will do so under the protection of a new order. An order that values the lives of the many over the lives of the few. You will have no more fear. Only obedience. Only service. Only safety."

The truth of his words hung in the air. Some heard them for what they were, some heard only what they wanted to hear. He was not freeing them. He was not saving them. He was exchanging one master for another. He was stripping them of choice, of freedom, of the very concept of individual power, while offering that same notion. He was providing slavery under the guise of security. The fear of magic had always been present, a subtle undercurrent in the lives of the common folk. Atamas had not eradicated that fear, he had merely redirected it, turning it into a tool, a justification for his own tyranny. The illusion of safety was more important to some than the reality of freedom. And that was all that was needed to fan the flame.

Among the general populace, confusion warred with relief. A mother, clutching her child, watched as a group of exhausted and beaten prisoners was marched towards the Citadel's kitchens. She had seen the flash of magic save her neighbor from a falling beam just moments ago, but now the source of that power was gone. And the man who offered them peace, albeit an alarming peace, had eradicated it. A new sense of hope, dark and unsettling, began to bloom in the shattered remnants of her heart. *Perhaps this is for the best*, a chilling whisper in her mind suggested. *Perhaps we will be safer?*

A grizzled old merchant, his face streaked with tears, felt a peculiar sense of calm settle over him. He had always mistrusted the Illuminthil, those haughty, distant figures who wielded powers he could not comprehend. Now, they were humbled. Now, they were just like him. And the new lord promised order. He promised safety. The fear, the immediate terror of the darklings' invasion, was slowly being replaced by the insidious lure of security. He watched, almost as if he were outside of himself, as a darkling, remarkably gentle now, guided him towards the Citadel's kitchens, away from the blood and the fire, towards a promise of a new and better future. And thus, Y'ssildria's nightmare began to wane. Morning was coming, and with it, a new day. But it would be the dawn of destruction, a morning whose light served only to illuminate the evils of the night before.

"Burn it all down," Atamas ordered, though his voice was not heard by the onlookers.

A fleet of flaming arrows screamed into the sky, loosed by hundreds of archer darklings awaiting their master's word. The sky was alight with fire as each arrow marked and landed on the buildings across Y'ssildria. Blades of fire sliced and spread across the rooftops, until all the city burned.

PREDATOR AND PREY

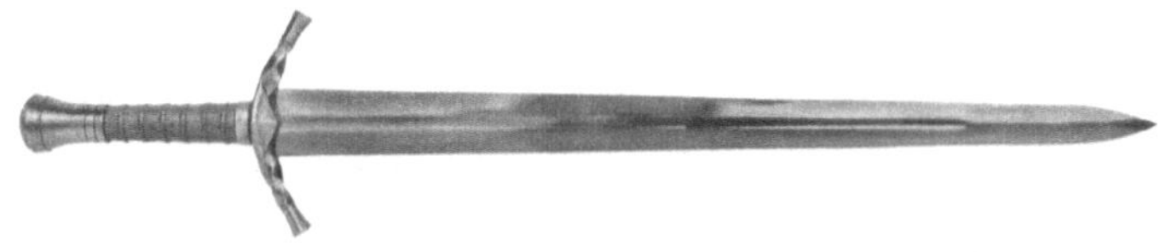

Illia-Dara was wholly bound to her pain and lost within. She shook, her muscles spasming as they had no other outlet for the adrenaline coursing through her. She was an invalid being carried along, unaware and uncaring of where or why. Her eyes were now hollowed voids, reflecting the churning sky, but perceiving nothing. She moved because she was pulled, held firm by the unwavering grip of The Star Speaker. Aoife's body was taught with resolve, even though battered. She would not lose Illia-Dara. Heron, having abandoned all fear and bewilderment, marched determinately forward, matching Aoife with every faltering stride and resolute step, holding onto Illi's other arm. Behind them, a mismatched company of misery and melancholy formed their rear guard.

"By m' cracked an' blistered bunions," Mergop wheezed, his short legs pumping furiously to keep from sliding on the slick stone. "This is bein' worse than fightin' w' m' damned piggies during a thaw! At least in a pigsty, the mud has the decency ter be stayin' put!"

"Would ye rather we been stayed below fer a pint w' our new darkling overlords?" Thurdop grunted, though he fared no better in the ankle-deep rush of rainwater. The deluge was so fierce that the drains carved into the battlements could not keep up. "Keep yer feet movin' and yer mouth shut. Less chance o' slippin' that way."

"It's not the slipping that worries me, friends, it's the landing!" Feste Rand squeaked, his eyes wide as he risked a glance over the edge. To the south, the Serrated Sea was a cauldron of churning, frothing death, its waves crashing against the teeth of shattered rock hundreds of feet below. The north side was no comfort either, as myriad torches could be seen bouncing this way and that around the square. The fighting seemed to have stopped, but the people of Y'ssildria were being herded together and separated. Either way was certain death for the ragtag party. Feste swallowed hard, or tried to, as fear and exhaustion lodged in his throat.

"I'm with him," Cante added, trembling. He had his arm linked through his brother's at the elbow. "This is for eagles and madmen! And I'm neither!"

The wind was a ravenous beast untamed and insatiable, clawing at the high battlements of the Sunspire Citadel and the precarious parapets on which the party now fled. It howled through the crenellations, its voice thick with the spray of the storm-lashed and salty sea far below. Rain no longer fell, but drove hard in horizontal sheets, hammering against the stone, turning the narrow parapet into a slick and treacherous river of uneven granite. Each gust threatened to peel the fleeing folks from the perilous walkway and cast them into the roiling abyss.

Heron said nothing. He trudged along, Illia-Dara secure against his side. His gaze was fixed on her and on the next step directly in front of him, nothing else. He felt her grief as if it were his own, and he didn't know why. It was a strange ache in his chest that had no source, yet he knew that it had something to do with her. He was just a boy from an orphanage, yet he felt the stirrings of a purpose he could not name, a loyalty to a woman he did not know.

A flash of lightning, brighter and more violent than any that had come before, did not merely illuminate the sky but seemed to rip it asunder. It was not a distant, indifferent bolt. It struck the parapet not twenty paces ahead of them, exploding a stone gargoyle that had stood vigil for centuries. Shards of granite, sharp as daggers, whistled past their heads. Feste yelped and dropped to the ground, covering his head with his hands. The thunder that followed immediately after seemed to be accompanied by a low, laughing rumble that reverberated off the stones and slithered into the stomachs of those at whom the lightning was aimed.

"Tha' weren't natural!" Thurdop shouted over the ringing in his ears.

"The sky be tryin' ter kill us!" Mergop agreed.

Aoife pulled Illia-Dara behind her. "Do you have her?" she asked Heron. "Do you *have* her?" she repeated, after receiving no response. Heron was staring dumbly at the smoldering crater that the lightning strike had left behind. He blinked the rain from his eyes and nodded once, readjusting his hold on the queen. Aoife's eyes burned with faint light as she scanned the boiling clouds. "He's right," she said to no one in particular. "This is no natural storm."

The words had barely left her lips when another searing bolt slammed into the flagstones where Cante and Feste had been standing a moment before. The stone buckled and cracked, a shattered web of fissures spreading from the point of impact, glowing with an angry, residual heat that hissed as the rain struck it. The brothers dove aside, positioning themself against a larger cutout in the stone battlement.

"Get up!" Aoife commanded, her voice slicing through their panic. "Move! Now!"

They scrambled to their feet and joined the others. The parapet snaked ahead, a narrow and exposed spine of rock running along the outer edge of the Citadel toward the vast, open expanse of the Stoneguard. It was their only path, and it was a desperate gamble. It led away from the carnage below and their pursuers who were no doubt making their way toward them from the upper chambers, but apart from that, they had no direction. The Stoneguard led to nowhere, a dead end. They didn't know what would come next. They only knew that to stay still was to invite death from a dark sky turned hostile or a jagged blade in the hands of an enemy.

"Faemen to the front," Aoife ordered. "Cante and Feste, behind. Heron is with me. Go!"

They ran. The Spire shrank behind them as the foreboding darkness of the Stoneguard's end loomed ahead. Aoife was sucking in wet air heavily, her lungs aching and tender. She had pushed herself beyond her limits and she knew it, but moving forward was her only choice, *their* only chance. As they ran, continuing to dodge lightning blasts, always concentrating on keeping their feet beneath them, a new sound joined the concerto. It wasn't the roar of the wind or the crash of the sea. It wasn't the thunder or the lightning. It was a scraping—a dry, skittering scratching on stones below and all around them.

Thurdop was the first to see it. He stopped dead, his face paling beneath his grimy beard. "By the bare arse o' m' wee bairns," he whispered.

Over the edge of the parapet, a clawed hand appeared, its black, shaggy fingers digging into the mortar, then another, and another. Then a snarling, canine snout, its eyes catching the lightning wickedly. It pulled itself over. Before any in the group could react, another appeared beside it, and then another. They poured over the edge of the cliff face, scaling the sheer rock like ants following a sweet trail of spilled wine. It was unnatural, their movements swift but awkward. From the Spire's archways behind them, more emerged, a living, furry wall of black iron and snarling hate. The exhusted and battered party was becoming surrounded.

The darklings didn't charge immediately. They crept forward, closing in slowly, methodically. The wind whipped at their tattered black cloaks, revealing glimpses of crude, heavy armor and wiry, powerful limbs. They were a wild pack of gluttonous wolves, and the small band of survivors was a cornered rabbit. There was a tidal wave of killer dogs in front of them and a sea of sharp stones and ravaging waters far below. They were at the cliff's edge of the Stoneguard. There was nowhere else to go. If they'd had more time, they might have been able to scale the mountainous rock wall down, but they would be pelted with arrows, glaives, and boulders well before making it halfway down if they tried that now. The darklings had found them.

"Well," Mergop said, his voice strangely calm. "This is it, then. I ne'er thought I'd be dyin' w' me wet bum-rags stickin' ter me arse."

Aoife moved Illia-Dara behind her, pushing her toward Heron. "Protect her," she said. She drew a deep breath, and the faint embers in her eyes began to glow. Her hands, empty moments before, now blazed, the twin swords of her celestial legacy flickering into existence. They were dimmer than before, their light wretched and guttering, a dull duplication of what they had once been, but they were there.

Thurdop and Mergop stood beside her. They drew their petite axes and widened their stances, their knuckles white as chalk as they prepared to die. Cante and Feste, weaponless, looked about frantically for something—anything—to arm themselves with. Feste grabbed hold of a heavy, dislodged piece of a shattered gargoyle, hefting it over his head, ready to squish the first darkling foolish enough to cross him. Cante found something a bit more exotic.

Heron had dropped Sylvandralis when he had taken hold of Illia-Dara. He held her close, tight against his chest as they both sat in a shrunken ball behind their friends. He would make her as small and hard to hit a target as he could, but if danger did come their way, he thought to reach for the famed sword, call its mighty flame, and throw himself in front of her. At least that was the plan, until Cante raced by, a smile so wide across his face that it made him look touched. He heaved the sword upward, calling the flames even as he ran back to his brother. But the flames did not come.

Shoulder to shoulder with Feste, gasping from the sprint to retrieve Sylvandralis, and ready to die should fate have it, Cante gave his brother a wink. "Now our fiery little angel won't be the only one lighting these doggos up like ugly candles."

"I don't think you should be playing with that," Feste said. "Grab a piece of rock and leave the magic swords to those who know how to use them."

"Pfft," Cante snorted so loudly that all in the company turned to look at the brothers. "I know how to use it. I just gotta turn it on first."

The darklings approached. They moved as one, scores of angry weapons aimed forward as they marched. The sound was a funereal beat of clawed feet and boots striking the stone, a rhythmic scrape that set the defenders on edge. With each rigid step, the forest of wicked glaive points swayed in perfect and dreadful unison, the sharp edges looking black as the night surrounding them.

"Everyone behind me," Aoife shouted. "If any get through, stop them on your life!"

"*Fire*," Cante whispered frantically.

"Heron." She looked back at the young man cradling the queen. "If we fall, jump. You and Illia-Dara both."

"Flame *on, flame on*, FLAME ON," Cante was screaming at Sylvandralis and banging its perfect, slender blade against the rocks. "Flame on, you stupid sword!"

Heron was taken aback at Aoife's order—but only for a moment—then he gave one somber nod and looked behind him to the treacherous drop. He brought Illia-Dara closer still and began to pray. Had his whole life, miserable and lonely as it was, been only for this? Was he going to die for and with a woman he didn't know? He could run! He could scale the cliffside and be safe at the bottom of the Stoneguard before the fighting was over! He laughed as he cradled the unconscious queen. No. He would not run. He would stay and he would die. He didn't know why, but he knew that was how it must be.

"The sword's magic is useless now, Cante Rand," Aoife said. The darklings were upon them. She set one foot behind the other in a martial stance and breathed deeply, in through her nose and out through her mouth, calming herself and finding her center. "The Aetherfast is no longer with us here. Things of the Aether are but mundane tools now. Ready yourselves," she said to the group. "And take as many of them with you as you can before you die."

"Then why does she still have all her fiery goodies and magics?" Cante asked his brother in a whisper.

"Because I am not of the Aetherfast," she responded. And then she leaped.

They were outnumbered and standing on the edge of doom. They had reached the end, where there was nothing beyond them but the sheer, yawning cliffside of the Stoneguard. There was no escape as the darklings surged forward. As one, the beasts loosed a barrage of blood-thirsty howls that were deafening in their combined dissonance. Aoife had felled dozens and dozens, but still they came. She was tiring, drawing too much on reserves that were not there. She was beginning to slip, slowing, and despite her most valorous efforts, darklings were passing her, untouched by her flame.

The reserve line held, for a time. Thurdop and Mergop, though no warriors, were born with the blood of savage protectors coursing through their veins. At one time, their forebearers fought for their mountains and their homes. They hacked and slashed and bit and kicked relentlessly. And though their prowess in battle was nowhere near that of Aoife or Endryll or Ixchel or Illia-Dara, not a single darkling got past them. The third and final line was secure on their end.

The brothers Rand were not faring as well. Feste's plan of squishing the first darkling to cross his path was an utterly messy success. The stone was still where he had aimed it, and underneath was a crushed dog-like creature, only its hands and feet visible amid a pool of blood that was slowly seeping into the porous stone beneath. The problem lay in that once that devastating projectile had been released, Feste was weaponless and defenseless. Cante was disarmed upon his first offensive assault. He swung Sylvandralis in a double-handed, over-the-head strike typically reserved for axes and for lumberjacks. The darkling who was to be the target of his blow parried the telegraphed attack away easily, dropped its hips, and twisted its right hand in one fluid motion, easily wrenching Sylvandralis from Cante's grip and casting it aside. The remainder of the Rands' battle consisted mostly of frantic scrambles and clumsy tackles, for though they each had the strength of daily farming and the intelligence to mix dangerous and volatile herbs into healing medicines, their understanding of warfare tactics was limited, especially in such an intimate and perilous space.

"I'm fer shorin' up tha' side o' our sad friends," Mergop shouted to Thrudop over the clamor. "Will ye be needin' me here ana'time soon?"

"Go," Thurdop responded. "Jus' don' go gettin' yer'self kilt!"

"Bwahahah! I'm fer tryin' me hand a' tha sword the silly one let fly! Let's see what a flamin' stick can do in the hands o' th' fae!"

"It innit fer workin'," Thrudop called out, but Mergop was already running toward the overtaken brothers.

Mergop flanked Aiofe as he ran. Her wings, once a glorious inferno, were now little more than smoldering appendages of ashen ember, barely able to keep her standing. Her movements were labored, her breath coming in ragged and painful gasps when it came at all. Yet, she stood as a wounded lioness protecting her cubs. She knew that she would fall soon, but she would fall fighting. "Are you needin' help, Lady?" he asked, still in full sprint.

"Help the brothers, Mergop! Fight to the end!" Aiofe, momentarily distracted by the faeman, miscalculated a parry and took a vicious lick to her wrist. The ethereal blade in her right hand disappeared, and she fell.

"Git yer behinds ter the queen," Mergop shouted as he barreled in front of the Rands, taking a handful of surprised darklings to the ground with him. He wrestled and chewed and cut, and soon, he was standing before a pentagonal pile of corpses. "I'm fer takin' yer place here," he said to the stunned brothers. He smiled then, seeing the shock so evident on their faces, but while his display of primal fury was quite something, it was the visage of the faeman soaked in dark ichor, the blood of his enemies running down his face and into his eyes and mouth, covering his teeth in a sickening merlot that had them so aghast.

Being thus so swiftly and brutally disabused of any heroic notions, the Rands turned toward Heron and Illia-Dara. They scrambled backward, stumbling over loose stones and the bodies of the dead. They were peddlers, not warriors, men of comfort and ease. The visceral reality of the battle, the shrieks, the sickening crunch of bone, the slick flow of blood, the sheer and hate-filled malice in the darklings' eyes was something their minds were ill-equipped to process. They slid low next to Heron and huddled near the cliff's edge, their backs pressed against the cold, wet stone of a boulder protruding from the crags.

Heron held the unconscious Illia-Dara in his arms, her body a dead weight against his slight frame. They were on the very precipice of the Stoneguard, the roaring sea a hungry beast waiting below. Her fiery hair, now dark with rain, whipped across his face. He clutched her with a desperate strength. He was no warrior, no mage, but in that moment, he knew what he had to do. He watched the faltering line of their defenders. He saw Aoife fall and knew with a chilling certainty that the darklings would break through. He stood, locking eyes with the brothers, neither asking for permission nor forgiveness, but perhaps just a bit of understanding. Then he jumped.

The brothers sprang from their sprawled position and peered over the side of the mountainous fall, their screams lost to the depths. And then, a new sound tore through the storm. It was a low and gruff blast, yet clear and cutting. It was the sound of a pipe organ and a dying leviathan, a sound so absurdly, brazenly loud that it seemed to bully the storm itself into a momentary silence. All combat ceased as every head, darkling and defender alike, snapped upward.

Out of the roiling and wounded belly of the storm clouds, it came. It rose as a whale breaching the waters. *The Lass o' No Virtue* ripped through the veil of rain and lightning, straight up, as if scaling the Stoneguard itself. It clanked and wheezed as it climbed, but climb it did—a monstrosity of scavenged parts and imagination. Its massive balloon pods, a medley of a dozen different colors and fabrics, groaned and strained against their iron chains. The reinforced sails, black as a void and laced with now inert Aether filament, snapped and billowed. Steam hissed from a dozen vents, and from its prow, the horned warrioress figurehead grinned down at the warriors atop the Stoneguard as if she had personally orchestrated the entire scene.

The airship bucked and swayed, fighting the gale, its copper turbines whining, its boiler threatening to give out at any moment. It was ugly, it was loud, and it was the most beautiful thing any of them had ever seen. And standing on the deck, looking somehow regal and stoic despite his near-certain death, was Heron, Illia-Dara held safely in his arms.

"Well, I'll be a flutterin' pixie!" Mergop exclaimed, his jaw dropping so low his beard brushed the stone.

On the quarterdeck, a figure stood silhouetted against the storm, one hand on the ship's wheel, the other tipping a wide-brimmed hat. Even from this distance, they could see the reckless grin of Tam-Ma as she wheeled the ship around. Her pirates, sure-footed and focused, were scrambling across the rigging, swinging ropes and hooks this way and that.

"Looks like ye lot are in a wee spot," she shouted. "Use a lift, could ye?"

The darklings, having been momentarily stunned by the absurd apparition, recovered with a collective snarl. Roars tore from deep within their throats, and they hefted their heavy glaives as crude javelins. Shoulders straining, they hurled them skyward in a ragged volley, a dozen upon a dozen streaks of black iron slicing through the rain-lashed air. For a moment, the wicked blades seemed to climb, to consume the distance, but gravity, unlike the Aether, was still an unbridled and unmastered power within Y'ssildira. Momentum bled away, and the glaives peaked, hung suspended for a heartbeat, and then plummeted back down to be lost in the Serrated Sea.

"Oh, no ye don't, ye ugly poochies!" Tam-Ma roared in response to the assault. Cannons, previously hidden behind retractable panels, slid out from the ship's sides. They weren't firing cannonballs. They erupted with a deafening roar, spewing canisters of rusted nails, jagged scrap metal, and what looked suspiciously like broken kitchen cutlery. The makeshift grapeshot tore through the darkling ranks, shredding them and sending them scurrying for cover.

"Get the ropes!" Tam-Ma bellowed.

From the railings, two-score scarred and roguish pirates began firing crossbows and hurling insults at the fleeing monsters. Coils of thick and heavy rope snaked down from the ship's sides, their ends weighted and swinging wildly in the wind. There were six of them, dancing like men condemned to the gallows.

"Go!" Cante yelled, shoving Feste toward the nearest ladder. "Climb!"

"You're coming too, you idiot!" Feste retorted.

"Of course I am," Cante huffed. "But I gotta be a hero at some point. What would my wifey say?"

Feste and Cante grabbed the same rope. "You first!" Feste shouted.

"No, you!" Cante argued, even as he began to climb, his stout body swinging precariously. "Just remember who told who to go first!"

Thurdop and Mergop, nimbler than their roundness suggested, found their ropes and began to ascend with a surprising agility born of generations spent in the high branches of the Western Wood. Mergop, halfway up, paused. "Wha' 'bout the fiery one?" he yelled, scanning the corpse-littered stone. "There!" he pointed out to the center of the carnage, where Aiofe lay unmoving.

"Climb on, brother," Thurdop said, "An' be ready fer pullin' us up!"

Thurdop slid back down the rope, his calloused hands paying no mind to the friction of his rapid descent. He ran across the high, slick stone of the rampart. Lightning cracked across the sky, illuminating the yawning chasm to his right as the deafening roar of Tam-Ma's cannons boomed from *The Lass*, sending concussive blasts that nearly tore him from his feet. He found Aoife crumpled near a fallen battlement of jagged rocks. She was unmoving, and her face was pale against the blood-darkened stone.

There was no time for tenderness. With a grunt, he unceremoniously heaved her over his shoulder and turned. Her head lolled, and a limp arm swung with the rhythm of his frantic, pounding feet as he ran back to the ship. The mad dash back was a blur of pumping legs and burning lungs. The storm tore at him as he slipped and slid on the treacherous ground. The hanging ropes whipped in the gale just ahead.

He didn't slow.

Gathering his strength, he launched himself from the precipice and into the void. For a heart-stopping moment, there was only the wind and the fall, then his fingers closed around the thick, wet rope. The jolt nearly tore his arm from its sockets, but he held on. Aoife hung loosely over his shoulder, her dead weight working against him. As Mergop and the others began to haul them up, *The Lass O' No Virtue* turned, its sails catching the wind with a great creaking. It pulled away from the cliff face, leaving the smoking ruin of the Sunspire Citadel and the broken heart of Y'ssildria to be swallowed by the storm behind them.

Forever and Always

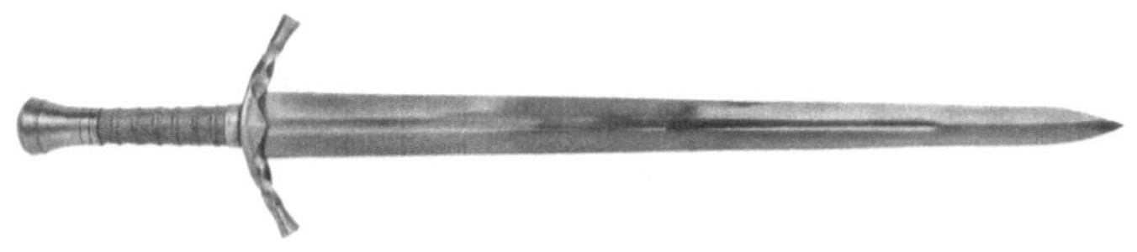

Her dream was woven in sacrosanct remembrance. The deep, clover hush of the King's Garden was illuminated by a full moon and star-sprinkled sky, unobscured by even a single cloud. It was a place of curated wildness, a sanctuary where the meticulous hand of the royal gardeners worked in harmony with the untamed spirit of nature. A gentle breeze, carrying the sweet, heady perfume of moonblossom, night-blooming jasmine, and damp, loamy earth, flitted through the foliage. It stirred the trees until their leaves shimmered like a thousand tiny coins in the moonlight, and it coaxed the weeping willows into a slow, hypnotic dance, their branches tickling the tips of the wild grasses and flowers that reached up from the soil.

She drifted along the paths, in and out of the tree lines. Her toes barely touched the ground. The hem of her shift clung to her ankles as her toes pointed downward, her feet slightly crossed, and she floated along. Her hands were loose at her sides, rising and falling wherever they wished as they welcomed the many leaves and trees and bushes with grazing touches. She knew this sacred place well.

The garden was alive with the soft, philharmonic notes of the untamed. The rhythmic, almost trance-like chirping of crickets set the meter. The deep, resonant croaking of frogs from the pond's edge, their calls a series of bass notes in the nocturnal chorus, carried the low end. The distant, haunting hoots of boreal owls echoed from an ancient maple that stood sentinel at the garden's edge, creating a serene and hypnotic melody. Fireflies, like scattered remnants of fallen stars, blinked in and out of view, their ephemeral lights sparkling, tracing lazy, glowing patterns against the deep green shadows. Above, the moon hung bright and clear, a pocked, yet flawless pearl against a sea of infinite night, casting a silver glow that softened the sharp edges of the world and made the garden feel like a vision.

And in the heart of that glow stood Illia-Dara. She was a zephyr; at this moment, she was a creature born of that same moonlight. Her white silk gown, unadorned by any jewel or embroidery, clung to her form as if it were poured over her. Her simple elegance eclipsed all beauty that had come before. Hers was a beauty that required no artifice. The silk spoke with her every slight movement, catching the light in soft, flowing ripples. Her fiery hair was a splendor, a cascade of scarlet piled high atop her head in an intricate, woven knot. It was an adornment all by itself. A few stray strands, rebellious and free, had escaped to offer gentle kisses to her neck and temples. She wore no makeup, no glittering trinkets, yet to the man who gazed upon her as she approached, she was the most precious jewel the world had ever known, the sole and brilliant flame in the quiet dark of the alcove.

They met at the very center of the garden, before the aged, white dogwood where King Onidine himself had, years ago as a young prince, brought Cerceia. Together, with a nervous hand, they had carved their initials, O and C, into the smooth bark, encircling them with the crude shape of a heart. It had become a monument to their bond, to their love, and to all of Y'ssildria, a place where their story grew in the very grain of the living wood.

As Illia-Dara approached, Endryll held his hands out to her. When they met, his thumbs gently stroked the delicate skin of her knuckles. Dressed in the crisp, severe lines of his princely military uniform that seemed to accentuate his broad shoulders and the lean, powerful strength of his frame, he stared openly at her, his lips parting ever so slightly. The austerity of the uniform was to manifest pride and duty; yet in her presence, it seemed only to frame the gentle soul within. His wheat-colored hair was pulled back into a loose, elegant knot, revealing the substantial column of his neck and the soft skin of his ears and throat. His eyes sparkled with a devotion so profound, so utterly consuming, it seemed to light him from within, casting a warmth that defied the cool night air.

Ixchel stood beside them, not just as a best friend to both, but as a solemn witness. He wore a formal robe of deep forest green, the cuffs and collar laced with delicate gold filigree that shimmered and caught the moonlight with every soft breath he took. His own unmanageable mane of chestnut curls had been pinned back in a reluctant concession to the gravity of the occasion, for he would not allow a single stray curl to block his vision. Tonight, he was not just a friend—he was a part of this, and he dared not miss a single, precious moment. He held the rings, their cool, solid weight a tangible representation of the overwhelming joy and the quiet, persistent ache that resided, side by side, in his heart.

The priest, Father Elian, a man whose sharply-trimmed sandalwood beard was as meticulously kept as his faith, smiled warmly at the couple. Dressed in the traditional green robes of a holy man of Y'sa, the three intertwined golden circles of Y'ssildria embroidered over his heart, he began to speak. His voice was not the loud projection of a man addressing a congregation, but a gentle and intimate tone, one that seemed to blend with and even accompany the night's tender chorus.

"My dear children," he started, his eyes full of a fond, fatherly love, moved between them with a tenderness that spoke of years of shared history. "I remember the day I first held you, Endryll, a babe wrapped in royal silks, your tiny fists already clenched with a king's resolve. Your father was bursting with a pride so fierce I thought the very stones of the Sunspire would crack under the strain of his joy." He chuckled softly. "And I remember the first time I saw you, Illia-Dara, a quiet, fierce girl with eyes that held the wisdom of ancient forests and a spirit that refused to be tamed. You were the very reflection of dear Queen Cesseria, already a queen in your own right, though you knew it not, your chin held high, a silent challenge to a world that had tried, and failed, to break you and leave you abandoned."

He paused, a nostalgic smile playing on his lips as he looked at the three of them. "I have watched you grow. I have seen your steps, both in triumph and frustration. I've patched your scraped knees after ill-advised adventures in these very gardens, and I have refereed more than a few of your, eh, spirited debates." A soft chuckle rippled between the three friends, a shared memory bringing a blush to Ixchel's cheeks. "I have seen your friendship blossom, a rare and beautiful thing, a cord of three strands not easily broken, and it is *impossible* to break when those strands are born of a love such as yours. And over the years, I have seen that friendship deepen, transform, into this—" He held his arms out before them. "—a love as steadfast and enduring as the Aetherfast, as radiant as the dawn, a love that has become the quiet essence of this city."

His gaze grew more intense and more heartfelt as he looked directly at them, his voice dropping to a more private register. "Love, true love, is not just the fire of passion that burns bright in youth or in secret. It is the strength of a hand to hold in the dark when the path is uncertain. It is the shared language understood without words. It is the unwavering faith in each other, the certain knowledge that even when all else falls to ruin, you will remain. You, Endryll, have your father's formidable strength, but it is Illia-Dara who gives you your heart, who shows you the tenderness that makes a ruler truly great. And you, Illia-Dara, have a resilience that could shame mountains, a fire that could light the darkest night, but it is Endryll who gives you your anchor, your calm harbor in the storm."

He gestured to the intertwined hands. "Tonight, under the watchful eyes of Y'sa, you do not simply join your hands, but your very souls in a holy promise. You forge a bond that will be the bedrock of this kingdom, a shining light to all who witness. Together, you are more than two become one. You are a covenant. A covenant of hope to a world that will desperately need it. Now, if you would, your vows."

Endryll turned to face Illia-Dara fully, his heart in his eyes, his voice thick with an emotion he made no attempt to hide. "Illi," he began, "from the first moment I saw you, just a flash of red hair and wide, curious eyes that challenged the world, you rewrote my universe. I thought I knew what my life was to be, but you, my love, you wrecked me. Even then, I knew I was undone and would not be whole again without you. With you, I am not a prince. With you, I wear no title, I wield no sword, no authority, save that given to me as your husband. With you, I am Endryll. You see me. You see the flaws, the fears, and you love me not in spite of them, but because of them. You challenge my temper, you sharpen my wit, and you have filled the quiet, lonely halls of my heart with a laughter I never knew it lacked. I vow to honor you always. I vow to protect you always. I vow to comfort you always. And I vow to love you. Forever and always, until my dying day. I will cherish your fire, which inspires me daily, and strive, every single day, to be a king worthy not just of this kingdom, but of the incredible, fierce, and wonderful woman who will be my queen. I am yours, Illia. Wholly, completely, and for all of time."

Tears streamed freely down Illia's face, each one a glittering diamond in the moonlight as she looked at the man she was about to marry, where she saw the same glistening tears. She took a shuddering breath, her own voice trembling as she spoke. "Endryll," she whispered. "I came to this kingdom with nothing but a buried name and the memory of pain. I was an orphan of a shattered land, a weed in a royal pasture. But you never saw me as broken. You saw *me*. You and your mother and your father saw *me*. You saw the girl who preferred dirt-stained tunics to gaudy gowns, who found more truth in the quiet wisdom of the stars than in the empty flattery of courtly gossip, and you accepted me. You gave me a home, not just within the castle walls, but within the boundless warmth of your hearts. And then you saw me as something more. In your arms, I am not an orphan. In your arms, I am beloved. In your arms, I am safe. In your arms, I am whole. I will walk beside you. I will cherish you. And I will love you. You have my heart, my body, and my soul. Forever and always.

Father Elian, his own eyes glossy and wet, wiped a tear that was tickling his mustache. "The rings," he prompted gently, waving a hand toward Ixchel.

Ixchel stepped forward, his movements rehearsed and solemn, or as rehearsed as they could be, given that he had run through the motions a million times over the last few hours in his head. He first handed Endryll the simple band of woven gold meant for Illia-Dara. As Endryll took it, Ixchel reached up and playfully scruffed the back of the prince's perfectly arranged hair, a familiar, brotherly gesture that earned a soft laugh from the prince. Their eyes met for a fleeting second, a silent exchange that spoke volumes of shared adventures and secret hideouts, of boyhood pacts sworn in blood and spit under this very moon, of a brotherhood forged in laughter, loyalty, respect, and love.

Then, Ixchel turned to Illia-Dara, his heart a weighted cast in his chest, the ever-present ache a familiar companion. He held out the matching ring, a slightly broader band of the same pure, smooth gold. As she took it from his palm, her fingers brushing his with a feather-light touch, she leaned forward and pressed a soft, lingering kiss to his forehead.

"I will always love you, Ixchel," she said for his ears alone, a tender acknowledgment of the love he could never speak and the devotion she had always known was there. "For all you've done and have yet to do, for all you have said and for those words you dare not speak."

A single tear escaped his eye, hot and traitorous as he'd set himself in stone this night, promising himself that he would not cry. It drew a path down his cheek and landed in the corner of his mouth, where he struggled to keep his lips still. He nodded, unable to form words, his throat tight with a bittersweet mix of profound joy for his friends and a deep, personal loss. He watched as they slid the rings onto each other's fingers, the moonlight catching the gleam of the gold, sealing their vows, their futures, and his, forever.

"Then by the light of Y'sa and the undeniable love that binds you," Father Elian declared, his voice ringing with a pure, unbridled joy, "I pronounce you husband and wife." He looked at Endryll, then. "You may kiss your bride."

Endryll did as he was told. It was a kiss that held all the promise of their future, a tender and passionate union under the soundless and approving gaze of the moon, a perfect moment of love and hope carved into the memory of the night, just as his mother and father's initials were carved into the tree before them.

"Well," Endryll said as he pulled Illia close, wrapping an arm securely around her waist. "It seems I'm well and truly trapped now." The priest had offered his final blessing and departed, melting back into the shadows of the garden. As he did, the three of them remained, looking toward the citadel. They stood together in the garden, the soberness of the moment settling around them like a comfortable and intimate blanket. "And in two days' time we get to do it all over again, for the sake of my father and in front of all of Y'ssildria."

Illia-Dara's laugh wafted across the gardens like wind chimes as she leaned her head against his shoulder, fitting perfectly into the curve of his body. "And what a terrible fate it is, to be trapped with me for all eternity."

"The worst," he agreed with a nod, pressing a kiss to the top of her head and inhaling the scent of her hair. "I imagine a lifetime of you correcting my form in the training ring and beating me mercilessly at strategy games. A truly grim and humbling existence."

"Someone has to keep you humble," Ixchel chimed in, the playful light returning to his eyes, chasing away the last of his regret. "It is a heavy burden, to be sure, but one we are willing to bear for the good of the kingdom."

They stood like that for a long while, simply breathing in the fragrant night air, the three of them a single, solid unit against the world. Illia-Dara looked from her husband's loving face to her dearest friend's, her heart so full it felt as if it might burst. "It feels like this is the start of everything," she said softly, a sense of awe in her voice.

"It is," Endryll affirmed. "Soon, the real work begins. My father looks so tired, Illi. I saw him today, staring out at the storm clouds gathering over the sea. I worry the weight of it all is getting to him, what with the feast and the coronation and with him ceding his crown."

"He is a strong man," Ixchel said reassuringly, though he too had noticed the weariness in the old king's eyes. "And he has Stren. They have weathered so many storms together, both literal and political. This will be no different. Besides, it's not like he's losing his crown to a usurper or some vile army. He is giving it to you! It is probably the easiest thing he has ever had to do in his life."

"I hope you're right," Endryll murmured, his gaze drifting towards the dark, looming silhouette of the Sunspire Citadel.

"It's just nerves," Illia-Dara said, though a flicker of the same inexplicable unease touched her own heart. She squeezed his hand, her touch grounding them both. "We will face it together. All of us. Your father will finally be able to rest, to enjoy his grandchildren." A soft blush graced her cheeks. "And Stren will finally have a new charge to grumble about." She smiled at Ixchel, her eyes full of affection. "I promise to be a most vexing and disobedient queen, just to keep him on his toes," she declared to him with mock gravity.

"I have no doubt of that," Ixchel laughed. "I will bring him his pipe and a strong drink after the ceremony. He will need it." He grew quiet then, his usual playful demeanor giving way to a rare moment of vulnerability, his gaze far off. "It is a great responsibility you both take on. I only hope I am strong enough to be the shield you need."

"You are our brother, Ixchel," Endryll said as he clapped a hand on his friend's shoulder. "You are the last gate. And we are safe behind you. Nothing and no one could ever breach it."

"Forever and always," Illia-Dara added, her hand finding Ixchel's in the darkness and giving it a firm, reassuring squeeze.

He looked at them, his two dearest friends, his king and his queen, bathed in the soft, silver light of the moon, their faces filled with so much love and hope. In this perfect, fleeting moment, suspended in time, he believed it. He would never fail them, nor they him. And they would be safe. He would ensure it. Forever and always.

Reflections in the Clouds

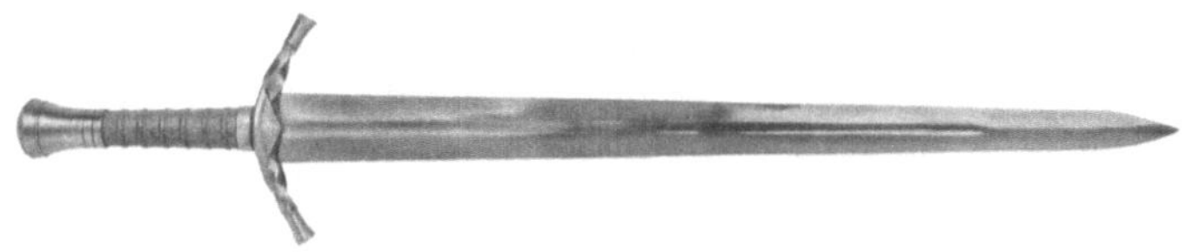

Sailing on *The Lass* was no gentle cradle, no lavish and comfortable voyage on listless and balmy seas. She was a brawler's tavern caught in a cyclone strapped to the back of a raging bull. She was groaning timber and rusted nails. She was warped planks and squeaky valves. She was as rugged as her rigging and as steely as her anchor. She whipped through the storm as rain hammered the deck. Below, the boilers chugged noisily, and the ship's engines whined a high, thin note of strain. She managed the best she could and made a fine show for it, but without the additional support of the Aetherfast, she struggled against the storm's fury.

The usual clamor of Tam-Ma's crew was gone. The bawdy shanties, the sharp-tongued insults, and the easy laughter had been swallowed up by the dismal certainty that clung to them like the cold, wet rags they wore. They moved with somber efficiency. Their bodies were stiff with battle fatigue and chills, and they moved slowly and achingly to secure the rigging and check the gauges. They were pirates, yes, accustomed to the sharp and brutal finality of battle. Still, the sacking of Y'ssildria, the loss of their kings, the mass murder of so many, were no playful skirmishes over cargo. It was the gutting of a reality, and their hearts felt the sting of it.

On the quarterdeck, partially sheltered by a tattered awning that flapped and snapped like a wounded bird, the survivors sat stunned and silent. Cante and Feste Rand were hunkered close together, their borrowed finery a ruined mess. Feste was trying to tend to a shallow cut on his brother's arm, but his hands, usually so steady when measuring tinctures or setting splints, trembled too much even to tie a simple knot.

"Just leave it," Cante murmured.

"I'm sorry, brother," Feste said quietly. He gave up on the bandage and simply rested a hand on Cante's shoulder. "I'll ask one of the others to do it."

"No," Cante insisted. "Just leave it. It's a small thing when looking about at what the others are putting up with. I'll wipe it down till it stops bleeding."

Feste huddled closer to his brother, his gaze drifting to the friends he had made as they tended to their wounds or attended to others, offering curatives and triaging what and where they could. "Quite a mess," he said, more to himself than to Cante.

"Aye, we should go help where we can," Cante replied, pushing himself off the warped decking and swaying slightly until he found the rhythm of the rocking ship.

Not far from them, Thurdop and Mergop stood with their backs to the wind, their short, sturdy forms braced against the ship's railing. Their magnificent beards whipped like tangled ropes around their necks. Both bore trauma of their own. Thin, bloody lines ran across their frayed tunics, and bruises and open gashes marked their faces. Thurdop wore a particu- larly garish wound that ran from above his right eye all the way down his cheek and into his neck, though he seemed not even to notice. They stood in silence and gazed back at the receding coastline, where the Sunspire Citadel was now little more than an angry, crimson smolder against the dark purples of the horizon, a distant pyre marking the death of an age.

Mergop opened his mouth, a familiar prelude to a litany of grievances and objections, but no sound came out. With a look of bewilderment on his face, he closed it again. He reached out a hand, not to the rail of the ship, but to the empty air, as if trying to touch something that was no longer there. He closed his fingers around the air and squeezed tightly to nothing.

"It's gone," he said. "The Song. I ca' no' hear it."

Thurdop nodded, his face marred and hard as stone. "The roots have been cut. The earth is silent." For a fae, it was a loss more fundamental than sight or sound. The constant communion with the Wood, the shared lifeblood of every living thing, whether leaf or root or creature, the very soul of their world, had been extinguished. It was as if the sky had gone black and the sun turned to ash. They were blind. For the first time since the dawn of their kind, they were truly, utterly alone—separate and singular. The sheer scale of the tragedy had rendered Mergop's legendary pessimism utterly taciturn. There were no words for this. There was only the watching, and the terrible, aching silence where the voice of the Wood should have been.

"You boys look like you could use a drink," Cante said as the brothers came up alongside the faemen. He unstoppered a dark brown bottle of even darker brown liquor. "Courtesy of Tam-Ma," he said. "From her own private stash." He took a deep swill before handing it to Mergop.

"Well, I ain't fer passin' up the chance to ferget m' pains an' problems," he winked and worked out a kink in his neck as he raised the bottle, "specially when it ain't me own coins what're payin' fer it." He pulled hard on the bottle, his throat bobbing up and down with multiple swigs, as he patted Cante on the back.

"If yer fer finishin' off that bottle a'for I'm fer gettin' m' own fill, yer ter be payin' w' yer teeth," Thrudop grumbled, snatching the bottle from the greedy grasp of Mergop's lips, spittle and liquor spilling out behind it. "If yer fergettin, yer still fer havin' both yer derned eyes."

"Bah," Mergop said, "Yer still fer havin' yer eyes, y' old lickpenny. Quit yer bellyachin and get ter drinkin' so ye can get ter healin'."

"You two seem to have gotten the worst of it," Feste said as he came up beside his brother. He was taking in the many open gashes, welts, and bruises littering the faemen's faces. Shame struck him, then, as he remembered his and his brother's poor showing atop the Stoneguard. "I'm sorry we weren't more help," he said, looking at his feet.

"Ye stood with us an' ye stood w' yer queen," Thurdop said as he came up for breath from the depths of the bottle. "Ye did what were needin' doin'. Don' ye e'er be ashamed fer that." He poured some of the brown liquid across his face and hissed as the alcohol splashed over his wounds.

"I can't believe it's gone." Aoife said as she sidled up slowly next to the group and leaned heavily against the rail. Her breathing was shallow and uneven, her body a litany of lesions and contusions. The true color of her flesh was indiscernible from the rainbow of bruises that painted her. She felt the ship's shuddering climb, felt the cold rain on her face, but her senses were muted, dulled by a weariness so acute that she struggled even to remain upright. She had survived Baelgorak. She had survived the slaughter in the great hall. She had survived the battle outside Illia-Dara's chambers. She had survived the ambush on the Stoneguard. But survival felt like a hollow prize when weighed against the cost, against everything that was lost. Her gaze drifted from the fires of Y'ssildria, across the deck and past the grim-faced pirates, to settle on the double doors of the captain's quarters, scorched black like the ship's figurehead and scarred by old battles. Heavy bands of pitted iron, bolted through the wood with rivets the size of a man's thumb, held them together. Etched into the grain of the left door was a crude carving of the horned warrioress, her grin knowing and menacing. And beyond those doors lay Illia-Dara, her ministrations being administered by Tam-Ma and *The Lass's* healer.

"How is she, Lady?" Feste asked, following her gaze.

"Her ailment goes much deeper than yours or mine, good-brother Rand. Hers is an affliction of the heart and soul. A wound that no salve can soothe nor stitch can mend." Aoife's voice was dismal and distant. She turned from the door, her eyes far, far away. "You saw a battle of steel and flesh. She has just endured the sundering of her whole world. In a single day, she has become a queen with no crown, a wife with no husband, and a sister with no brother."

Cante shook his head and wiped his face to mask his tears. "To be so broken," he said. "I've seen folk lose kin to plague and sword, both. It's a terrible thing, to be sure. But this—" He trailed off, unable to give shape to the pain the young queen must be feeling.

"This is fer bein' different," Thurdop agreed in an uncharacteristically soft timbre. He stroked his tangled beard, his gaze fixed on the deck. "The lad, the one she been callin' Ixchel. Stren told us he was o' the Wood, in his own way o' bein'." He paused for a moment, as if trying to remember. "When a great tree falls, the ferest itself is fer feelin' the tearing o' its roots. It grieves. The Queen grieves like the ferest this night."

"Grieves?" Mergop harumped. "She's been crushed, an' don' ye be doubtin' it. She's the potter's prettiest bauble dropped right on the stone o' his dirty floor."

A violent lurch jolted her, a tremor from the world she wished to leave behind that tore at the edges of her sanctuary. For a horrifying instant, the moonlight wavered. Through a crack in her perfect memory, she saw Endryll's face, not smiling, not staring longingly into her eyes, but pale and still, his eyes wide with a final and terrible shock. She saw Ixchel, not grinning, but dissolving into shimmering, agonizing light, his face a contortion of love and pain.

"No," she whimpered faintly. She squeezed her eyes shut, pushing the nightmare away, clinging to the warmth of the garden, to the presence of her husband, to the unshakeable confidence of their forever.

Heron felt the whimper more than heard it. He had refused to be separated from her, even after Tam-Ma had threatened him with shackles and an evening spent belowdecks in the brig. He looked down at Illia's face, at the myriad emotions that crossed her features as she was wrenched away from her slumber. He didn't know what demons she fought in her silence, what ghosts haunted the ruins of her mind, but he knew that he would not let her face them alone. He was a boy from an orphanage, a bastard, a nobody. He knew loneliness and he knew what it was to be alone. He could not help her with the former, but he would be sure that she never, ever experienced the latter.

In the real, waking world, the unfamiliar aromas of dried herbs, spiced rum, and the lingering wisps of Tam-Ma's rolled parchment cigarettes permeated the air. Tam-Ma's quarters were a study in organized disarray. The chamber was a rounded space tucked into the stern of the airship, its curved walls paneled with a dozen different kinds of wood, mostly scavenged from shipwrecks. Brass pipes, warm to the touch, ran along the ceiling, hissing with the steady breath of engine steam and providing the only warm water on the ship. Light filtered in through a large, circular porthole window, its thick glass warped and bubbled, distorting the sky into a swirling watercolor. The walls were cluttered with navigational charts held down by daggers, star maps marked with Tam-Ma's own wild scribbles, and **WANTED** posters from a half-dozen kingdoms, most bearing a flattering, though heavily embellished, depiction of Tam-Ma herself. A massive, iron-strapped sea chest doubled as a table, its surface littered with silver coins, a half-empty bottle of dark liquor, and a complex clockwork astrolabe that ticked and whirred with a life of its own.

Illia-Dara lay on a cot built into the curve of the ship's hull on the far side of the room. The mattress was stuffed with fine wool and had a faint scent of lavender. The quilted blankets were rich velvets and practical, hard-wearing wool, heavy and comforting. She stirred more fitfully, finally waking in a panic and sweating heavily. She sat up, her eyes wide, and kicked the blankets off of her.

"My Queen," came a gentle voice. "You're awake. You're safe." It was Heron. He sat on a low stool on the side of the bed. His shoulders were slumped with weariness, but his eyes were alert and fixed on her. He held a damp cloth in his hands, and when he saw her stir, he leaned forward. "Be still, please."

"Where am I?" she demanded as she bunched the spilled blankets about her. She was flushed with heat, but the feelings of vulnerability counter- manded the need for comfort. She fell back into the mattress, leaving only her head visible.

Before Heron could answer, another figure bustled into view. Rigby, *The Lass's* healer, was a wiry woman with dark skin, wrinkled and weathered, and hands more calloused than those of the deck crew. Her eyes spoke of years of hard living and had seen more bar fights than sickbeds. She wiped her hands on a stained apron and peered at Illia-Dara, leaning in close. She placed a hand on Heron's shoulder to steady herself as she held a small glass object up to Illia-Dara's eyes.

"Bout time," the healer said curtly. "Had us worried you'd sleep 'til the end o' things. How's the head?"

Illia-Dara tried to sit up again, but a wave of dizziness washed over her.

"Easy now," Tam-Ma's voice cut through the queen's haze and confusion. The pirate captain leaned against the doorframe, her arms crossed, her usual roguish grin absent. Her look was bleak. "This one's name is Rigby. She's better with a needle and gut than a bedside manner, but she keeps me crew in one piece. Mostly."

Rigby grunted and pressed a cup of steaming, bitter-smelling tea into Illia-Dara's hands. "Drink. It'll dull the edges."

"Rigby," Tam-Ma said. "This is Illia-Dara, Queen of Y'ssildria. Ye'd be doin' me a great thing iffin' ye be treatin' her as such." Her voice had much more of a rough sea-living inflection and left little question as to whether this was a request or a command. The old healer bristled, standing up straight, and locked eyes with the captain.

"I know her name well enough, Ma," she said sternly. "I been treatin' her since she been put on this here cot. An as for her station, well," she looked to Illia-Dara, "me apologies, queenie, but I'm more for healin' than for playing courtly games."

Illia-Dara didn't acknowledge the surly woman. She stared into the murky liquid and saw her own reflection there. It was a pale and haunted image, a stranger staring back at her. She hesitated before drinking. The edges were all she had left. Would dulling them be a betrayal? She looked from Tam-Ma's guarded expression to Heron's open, aching sincerity, and then to Rigby's expectant and impatient face.

"Just water, please," she said, placing the warm cup on the table near her bed.

"As her majesty wishes," Rigby replied, bowing in a mocking gesture and taking the cup. "I'll bring ye some water, then." She turned and left the room, letting the doors swing shut in her wake.

"Don't pay her any mind," Tam-Ma said apologetically. "She's a dear friend and loyal to a fault, but she can be stubborn and even nasty when she wants to be. But she's a good woman, and a better healer. She'll see to it that you're right as rain in no time."

"Where are we?" Illia asked, slowly pushing herself up to lean against the rough paneling behind her.

"Aboard my ship," Tam-Ma answered, pushing off the doorframe and walking toward the great porthole. "Far off the coast of Y'ssildria and heading toward—" She looked blankly out the window. The night had passed, and they seemed to have outrun the reach of the storm. Thin brushstrokes of white clouds were painted across an otherwise pristine blue sky.

"We have to go back," Illia-Dara said.

Tam-Ma turned. Her expression was soft and delicate, but her eyes were granite. "There's nothin' to go back to, lass. The Citadel's fallen. The king—" She let the word hang in the air.

Heron reached out and gently placed his hands over Illia-Dara's, which were trembling. The warmth from his skin was startling, a small focus of life in the great and cold emptiness of her sadness. She didn't pull away. She held his gaze, unwilling—or unable—to look away.

"Do you remember?" Heron asked softly.

Illia said nothing. She simply nodded and looked away, her lower lip quivering. She couldn't speak. She couldn't even look Heron or Tam-Ma in the eyes when thinking about it, when remembering. She didn't even know these two, not really. But their eyes were full of brokenness, full of pain. It was a pain that mirrored her own, but was a single grain of sand on an endless beach of her grief. It was too much.

The heavy doors creaked open slowly. It was Rigby. She held them as they closed behind her, so as not to make too much noise. Her demeanor had changed. She seemed to be more aware of Illia's state, and, in turn, more aware of her attitude. She walked gingerly to the cot to join the three and handed Illia-Dara a mug.

"Drink this, child," she said. "Nothin' but water and some herbs for strength. Nothin' to dull that pain that you're needin' right now." She held one hand to Illi's forehead and one to her throat. "And I'm sorry. I'm sometimes forgettin' me'self and only thinking about the ailments, not who it is that might be ailin'." She stroked Illi's hair back a few times and then leaned in close. "Ye'll be alright, ye know. Ye got many here who are with ye, and they are for ye." And with that, she turned and disappeared the same way she came in.

Days turned into weeks, and while she hadn't recovered her mirth or zest for life, Illia-Dara had recovered her strength. She walked about the ship, though more often than not, she felt as if she were simply floating by. Life moved all around her while she merely observed. Her movements were methodical, her eyes held the distant and haunted look of one who saw neither the present nor the future, only the past. The constant motion of *The Lass* became the rhythm of her existence. Tam-Ma would set her to menial but necessary tasks to occupy her time and, more importantly, her mind. She mended torn canvas with steady hands, the simple, repetitive motion of the needle distracting her from the relentless loop of memory. It didn't help. She would see Endryll's smile in the flash of sunlight as it bounced off a brass fitting. She would hear Ixchel's laugh in the playful chatter of the crew. The memories were daggers, each one a fresh twist in a wound that refused to heal.

Aoife often found her staring out at the endless expanse of the sky, her expression unreadable. She'd stand beside her as a silent companion, offering her presence, if ever Illia needed it. The others did the same. They were precious metals brought together in the crucible of battle, forged in mutual need, and tempered in mutual loss. They were hundred-times-folded iron. They were family. And not one of them would leave her side.

"He would have liked this," Illia-Dara said one evening. Her voice startled even herself, as this was the first time she had spoken since the day she had awakened. It was barely a whisper, and it was coarse and hurt her throat. Her gaze was fixed on a constellation she and Ixchel had once named after a particularly clumsy baker. "The quiet. The feeling of being untethered."

The brothers Rand and the faemen exchanged surprised and awkward glances. Each seemed to be prodding the other to respond. Feste's eyes went wide, and he nodded his head toward the queen as he stared hard at Thurdop. Thurdop, in response, mouthed something uncouth and altogether physically impossible, and then nudged Mergop with an elbow. Mergop grunted in surprise and then kicked the shin of an unsuspecting and unaware Cante, who let out a frightened squeak, before quickly covering his mouth. His icy gaze lingered on Mergop with a silent promise of retribution. Feet shuffled nervously. Eyes twitched and darted. Arms were crossed and uncrossed and crossed again. Heron went to put an arm around her, but was stopped short by the firm hand of Thurdop.

"Is no' fer ye, lad," he said somberly. "Is no' fer any o' us."

"He is a part of it now," Aoife said finally. "The stars remember him."

Illia-Dara didn't respond, but a single tear traced a path down her cheek.

"They sing of him and to him," she continued. "He is at peace now, resting in the comfort of Y'sa's arms."

"Damn him, then," Illia said. "Damn him for leaving me. Damn him for not coming with me." She pounded the railing with her fists. It hurt, but she embraced it. It was the first thing she had truly felt in a very long time. She slammed the railing again. "Damn him for dying!" She was weeping openly now. "Damn you, Endryll!" She screamed into the night sky. She screamed it to the stars, to the moon, to anything and everything, and to nothing.

Crewmen came out of their quarters, some armed, some barely dressed, all drawn by the queen's cries. The Rand brothers and the faemen stepped back quietly, allowing the woman to have her space, to have her anger, and formed a protective semi-circle around her. This was not for the crew. This was not even for them. They turned around, keeping their crescent form, and locked eyes with the curious pirates, daring them. One by one, the crew returned to their quarters and their beds. And then it was just the seven once again.

She was trembling, not from exhaustion, but with rage, a rage that had been locked away, hidden, held back. But now it was free. Aoife had an arm around her. Heron shook free of Thurdop's weakened grip and went to her, embracing her from opposite the Star Speaker. They said nothing. They simply held her as she loosed the anger, the pain, the demons, all of it.

"Damn you, Ixchel! Why did you leave me? Why did you have to leave me, too?" Her fists had turned into vices, gripping the railing so tightly that her knuckles were a blistering white and cracking with the strain.

Her body was warm to the touch and getting warmer. Aiofe and Heron felt it. Illia was shaking and screaming, but something else was happening. A soft glow began to emanate from her center, pulsing outward. Shimmers of golds and blues, like a minuscule galaxy, began swirling about her, reaching out and illuminating the deck in a kaleidoscope of nebulous hues.

Soon, the heat of her was too much for Heron. He threw a hand up against the blaze and stumbled back. Aiofe, fearing neither her friend nor the fires of her passion, moved in closer. An inferno of broad, feathered wings erupted from Aoife's back Dand shielded those behind her, though even the brilliance of her cosmic flames was paled by the building brightness coming from Illia-Dara. Aoife held Illia. Her arms were wrapped around her, her wings fully extended, as she spoke reassurances to her.

She didn't know what was happening, but she would not let Illia-Dara go through it alone.

The planetary cyclone expanded across the entire deck, limning everything in that same galactic light. It continued to spin, to widen, until even the blackness of the night sky was lit with its glow. And then, it returned to Illi with an audible rush of wind. It created a vacuum, as if all the air in all the world had been siphoned in with it. There was no sound, no breath. No creaking boards or rattling ropes. Nothing. Then, as if a cache of dynamite had been detonated, all the power, the entire galaxy of energy, exploded from within her.

The men on the other side of Aoife's wings were knocked from their feet and thrown across the deck like discarded scraps from the table. The force of the blast tore through *The Lass*. It was a shockwave of unadulterated Aether. Wood splintered, ropes snapped like threads, and the great black sails billowed violently, groaning against their footings. *The Lass* rocked violently. Glass shattered, and the crew was thrown from their cots.

From the nexus of that devastating blast, three figures shimmered into existence. They were not solid, but made up from the same residual starlight that now clung to the air, translucent and ethereal. They were echoes. They were Ixchel. They were his Echoborn.

One stood with his arms crossed, a familiar, impish smirk dancing across his lips. Another knelt, head bowed, his form flickering, his shoulders trembling with a silent, unending sob as he showed reverence to her. The third stood tall and resolute, a glimmering shadow of Sylvandralis held in a two-handed grip, its blade a line of pale light. His eyes fixed on her.

The power receded and so too did Illia-Dara's strength, leaving her sagging against Aoife, her body limp. The bereft queen stared at the three apparitions, her heart a boulder in her chest. It was him, all of him. There was the jovial and charismatic boy she loved, the ever-mourning man who knew a love unrequited, and her Crownward, her last gate, who had given his life for her. Everything he had been, everything he had tried to be for her and for Endryll, was standing before her. She wept bitterly, held vertical only by Aiofe's unfaltering grasp. In all the histories of Y'ssara, since the first tear fell and sadness was given a name, there had been few sorrows remembered throughout all time. Her lamentation that night silenced them all. It was a lament so honest, so grave, that never before and never again had the likes of it been heard in all of Y'ssildria, and none there that night would ever forget it.

"By Fumblefoot's beard," Mergop breathed, as he and the others approached. "Wha're we ter do?"

Heron stared with wide, uncomprehending eyes. He saw the face of the man Illia-Dara had mourned, multiplied and made of light, and a strange, instinctual ache bloomed in his chest. He wanted to run to her, to comfort her, but he knew not how. What could he say? There was nothing in all the world he could offer her at this moment. So, he cried. His heart was brought to shattering in the presence of such sorrow. He fell to his knees and hid his face in his hands and wept. The others did likewise, not out of solidarity, but because they, too, were undone.

The three Echoborn turned as one to the North, in the direction of Y'ssildria. Then their collective gaze, one of mirth, one of sadness, and one of duty, settled upon Illia-Dara. They did not speak, but in that moment, a single, undeniable truth resonated across worlds, and she knew what she must do. She smiled through the tears, and those were her last. She rose, standing on her own and turning to those around her, to those who loved her, and to those she loved, as the Echoborn twinkled into the night. Her kneeling friends stood. Aiofe tucked her wings to her side. The few pirates who hadn't the luxury of retreat from this most solemn moment because of shifts and chores, stood at a distance, tri-horn hats lowered across their hearts. Tam-Ma and Rigby watched from the captain's quarters, through the port window. Not an eye was dry, save one.

Illia-Dara wiped the final tear that she'd ever cry over Y'ssildria, over Onidine, over Endryll, over Stren, and over Ixchel, and she spoke one word. Like an epitaph carved into the tombstone of the world, it was an immovable and undeniable proclamation. It was the first stone in the foundation of a new reign, an oath sworn, and a prophecy of retribution. It was a damnation. It was a promise.

"Atamas."

EPILOGUE

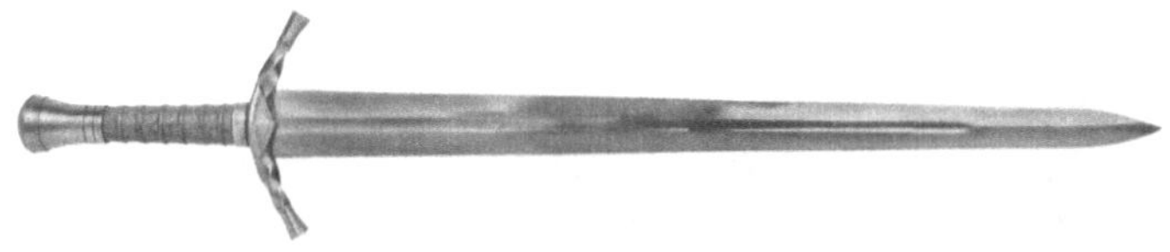

Weeks had passed since the fall of the Citadel. Almost a full two months spent drifting in the vast, empty curtains of Y'ssara's southern skies, each league forward a league further from the smoldering collapse of Y'ssildria. A fragile, unspoken routine had settled over *The Lass's* mismatched refugees. Tam-Ma's pirate crew was back to their usual boisterous selves, hurling crude insults and managing the ship they called home. They patched her wounds, tended the churning engines, swabbed the decks, stitched sails that glowed once again with aethereal magics, and had even emptied and cleaned out one of the crew quarters so that the stowaways had a place of their own to gather and talk and sleep, though there was no awkward segregation between them. The crew had also taken on the task of returning some form of normalcy to Illia-Dara and her company.

The Brothers Rand had found a strange solace in the galley, under the tutelage of a feisty young chef called Singe. The brothers had a sneaking suspicion that Singe wasn't the young pirate's birth name, but a moniker given by the rest of the crew due to the consistent and predictable lack of eyebrows and beard. The Rands, stripped of their wares, their wagon, and their beloved mules, clung to the simple, grounding act of creation, and with little else than ingredients at their disposal, the kitchen had called to them.

Cante, hands still bearing the scars from his brief, clumsy attempt at swordsmanship, now kneaded dough with a focused intensity, the rhythmic press and fold a meditation against his loss. Feste meticulously chopped preserved vegetables, the steady *thump-thump-thump* of his knife a metered compliment to Cante's kneading. They spoke little of what they had lost. Instead, they cooked, creating meals that provided sustenance for their new friends and family.

Thurdop and Mergop sat cross-legged on the deck, the salty wind pulling lightly at their hair, which had been recently braided into their beards. Aoife had insisted on baths for the faemen and threatened to show them the full extent of her powers should they refuse. They did not refuse. Now, bathed and braided and dressed in borrowed tunics, they enjoyed each other's company, and something else, as well. For weeks, the silence of the Wood had been a constant, aching presence they both reached for in vain. But something had changed. It had started the night Illia-Dara's final gift from Ixchel, his Echoborn, appeared. It began as a faint tremor beneath the skin, a call at the very edge of the wind, and had grown into a shout. The Aether was breathing again. The deafening void in their souls was being filled, note by note, with the song of a world.

Channeling the rush of returning sensation, Thurdop had taken to carving. With a small, sharp knife, he worked a piece of driftwood, his calloused hands coaxing a shape from the grain as the communion of root and rock flowed back into him. He was carving a face, a small, fierce woman with wide, knowing eyes and a crown of leaves, a fiery sword in her hands. It was a tribute to a queen he had only just met but loved and respected fiercely.

"It hurts m' heart," Mergop said, "to hear them again. The trees. They're not fer singin' their beautiful songs."

Thurdop didn't look up from his work, his knife making a soft, scraping sound. "They're fer mournin', brother," he said. "They be feelin' Y'ssildira's fall as an axe to their own bark. An' they're fer feelin' what our new queenie be feelin'."

"Er'ythin's changin', in'it?" Mergop asked, though it was not a question that needed an answer.

"Aye, that it is," Thurdop answered anyway, not looking up from his whittling.

Aoife rarely left Illia-Dara's side. Her presence was a constant in the turbulent sea of the young queen's recovery. The Star Speaker's own wounds, though still tender, were a secondary concern. Her force was absolute, not affected by the departure or return of the Aetherfast. Her gaze was fixed on the woman who now bore the weight of a shattered world. In those first days, Illia-Dara had been a trace of her former self, her movements listless, her eyes vacant. But slowly, the brokenness began to calcify, hardening from the crippling agony of anguish and grief into a diamond-hard resolve. The color had returned to her cheeks and the light to her eyes. The Aetherfast, once silenced by Atamas's grand betrayal, was breathing again beyond the reach of his influence, and its returning presence seemed to flow directly into her.

The young queen now spent hours with Sylvandralis resting in her grip, or comfortably in its scabbard, or across her lap. The blade, which had gone dull and inert in the dead zone of Y'ssildria, now pulsed with a soft, internal luminescence. The lava stones that imbued the sword with unquenching fire glowed hot, forged anew in Ixchel's sacrifice, and seemed to drink in the ambient magic of the Aether, its golden hilt warm to the touch. The sword was a part of her now, an extension of the power Ixchel had poured into her soul. It was a constant, painful, and enchanting reminder of all she had lost, and all she now had to fight for.

In the quiet moments between daily life aboard *The Lass* and endless strategic debates, a bond had developed and deepened between Illia-Dara and Heron. They would often be found huddled over one of Tam-Ma's sprawling maps of Y'ssara, their heads close together. He was roughly the same age as Ixchel and Endryll had been, but he had such an innocence about him, yet here he stood, thrust from the obscurity of abandonment into the very center of a kingdom's fight for survival. He possessed a peace that seemed to soothe the raging tempest within Illia. He would trace the rivers and mountains with a hesitant finger, his questions simple and direct, cutting through the complex knot of politics and warfare to the heart of the matter, the people.

"My mother was a fae, but I never knew her," he admitted to Illia-Dara and Aoife one afternoon. "The Matron at the Bairnbrand told me that she had left me there after my father died."

"You are not alone, Heron," Illia-Dara said, looking up from the parchment she was currently poring over. "Not anymore." She placed a hand over his as they both stood over the large map sprawled out before them. "You have us. You have me."

He smiled a sad smile. "And you have me, Illi."

"And we all have lot's o' thinkin' to do here," Tam-Ma said, interrupting the tender moment. "We know we're headin' for Burss, that much is clear, but what then?"

The planning sessions were intense, fueled by warm bread and ale, fruits and vegetables, and cheeses and meats courtesy of the brothers Rand. Tallow candles burned low throughout the days and nights as they discussed and argued over the best course of action. Tam-Ma, pragmatic and unflinching, would jab at the maps with the charred end of a stick, and Aoife would knock it out of the way. Illia-Dara would allow them their squabbles, content to sit back and listen, never aloof, but never wanting to interrupt the discordant consonance of her two generals.

"Y'ssildria is a fortress," Tam-Ma said, blowing a stream of tobacco smoke toward the ceiling. "The Stoneguard is sealed, and Atamas will have patrols on every approach. A direct assault is a fool's errand. We'd be sending dead men to fight a stone wall."

"Then we will not go as an army," Aoife countered, waving her hand in front of her face. "We go as a small, tactical unit. Not as a big bludgeoning club, but as a scalpel, a quiet and surgical strike to cut out the heart of the infection."

"An' what's ter be the target?" Thurdop piped in from a corner where he stood, well away from the war table. "Them ugly, doggo beasties, er the black-hearted bastard hi'self?"

"The darklings are too many," Feste piped in from the cot where he, Cante, and Mergop sat gambling with dice, as had become their routine when Illia-Dara's cadre had begun to gather and take part in planning. "We all know how that ended last time."

"Aye," Mergop responded. "W' our behinds bit an' living on this cloud-floatin' dungeon."

"A' least ye found yer cheery words after all this time, ye dour dolt," Therdop said. "Er are ye just sour cause yer fer losin' a' dice to them Rands again?"

"Atamas is the head," Illia-Dara said, cutting the conversation off before it veered too far from being saved. It had become a common occurrence. They were all going cabin-mad. They were healing, they were angry, and they all wanted off that damned ship. All eyes turned to her. "You're right. We cannot fight him with an army. There are too many citizens. I'll not accept further casualties." She paused for a moment and looked at each of them in turn. "I'll not demand that any of you follow me where I must go."

Tension swelled. The gentle creak of the constant settling and resettling was the only sound. All eyes were on the queen. All conversation and even breath halted. The candles flickered, light and shadow exchanging lead in a quiet dance across the faces of all in the room. Anticipation hung distended and bulging in hushed stares and wordless agreement even before she spoke again.

"But I will ask it of you," she continued. She rose, her gaze first finding the Star Speaker. "Aoife, First Maiden of my Queensguard. You have fought battles older than my kingdom and have borne ancient scars that would have fractured mountains. This is not your war, yet you have bled for it as if it were your own. You have bled for me. I ask you to stand with me, knowing that the path ahead leads into a darkness deeper than any you have faced, and from which we may not return."

Aoife nodded.

Her eyes shifted to the roguish captain of their vessel. "Ma, General of My Unbound Skies. You owe allegiance to no flag, and your freedom is the only treasure you value. I ask you to shackle yourself to a broken queen's cause, to risk your ship, your crew, and that precious freedom for a kingdom that is not your own. I ask you to sail with me into the heart of the storm, knowing the harbor we seek may be our own grave and nothing more."

Tam-Ma removed her tri-horn hat and bowed low, the hat swishing across the floor of her captain's quarters.

She then turned to the two stout men from Thimbleglean Vale, who stood shifting their weight and wringing their hands. "Feste Rand, My True Voice of Reason. Cante Rand, My Spirit of Rebellion. You are men of the earth, with homes and families who await you. You have already lost more than any man should be asked to lose. I ask you to turn your back on the peace you have known and now so eagerly await and march alongside me to fight for all the other families of Y'ssara who now live in fear. I ask you to join me, knowing this journey may deny you the chance ever to see your homes or your families again. I know this is an impossible request, but one I earnestly ask you now. I need you both."

The brothers Rand replied as one. "We will, Lady."

Her gaze found the two fae, their faces stern, their connection to the wounded Wood a palpable and living thing in the small cabin. "Thurdop, Root of My Resolve. Mergop, Thorn of My Truth. Your loyalty is to the Whispering Wood and to the balance of all living things that Atamas has so brutally violated. The affairs of men and their kingdoms are not your burden, yet I ask you to abandon the sanctuary of your forests and walk into a city of stone and steel, to fight for a world where the trees might one day sing again. I ask you to stand with me, knowing that the plague we face may destroy us all."

The faemen looked at each other for a moment, Mergop cursed under his breath, and then they both offered a bow so formal, so perfectly courtly, that all in the circle stared in unbelief.

Finally, her eyes, now glistening not from sadness but from the overwhelming understanding that these people were agreeing to follow her to death, that this group of strangers was now her family and her friends, settled on the boy with the fiery hair, so much like her own. He met her stare, his own fear eclipsed by a fierce, protective allegiance that seemed to spring from a source neither of them understood. "Heron of Bairnbrand, My Unwritten Verse," she said. "You were given no choice in coming here, and for the first time in your life, you have the freedom to walk away, to truly discover who you are, to carve your own path in the world. I do not know what bond ties us, or why my heart tells me you are essential to me. I only know that it does. I ask you to risk the future you have never had for a past you never knew. I ask you to join me, knowing that the answer to who you are may be found at the end of a road from which there is no coming back."

"My past is behind me, neither forming me nor guiding me," Heron said. "My future is with you, to the end."

She looked at them all as they encircled her, a seven-spoked wheel of shared experience and resolve. She was the hub, the center from which all their strength now emanated. They were fae and farmers, a Star Speaker, a pirate, a man with no past, and a queen with no crown. They were no longer a collection of strays, but a single, terrible instrument of retribution. They had one purpose. *This* was her army. *This* was her fellowship. This was her confidence, and nothing in all of Y'ssara or beyond would stand in its way.

He sat deep in the ground, far below the rebuilding and restructuring of the Spire and of Y'ssildria. The passing of time had become marked only by the regular beatings and tortures from his captors. His feet were rotting, his body failing. The only nourishment he received was a thin, grey gruel, served cold in a rusted bowl. It was a foul slurry that tasted of mold and old meat, with slick, unidentifiable lumps that slid down his raw throat. The water, scooped from a seeping crack in the wall, was thick with moss and rust, a mockery of the life-giving liquid he had once commanded from the earth itself.

His name was nearly lost to him. All he knew was that here, in the suffocating damp, he was only a thing of decaying flesh and mind. The chill of the cracked flagstones had seeped into his bones, a permanent cold that no amount of shivering could dislodge. His feet, perpetually submerged in a shallow pool of brackish water, were the worst. The skin had turned waxy and corpse-like, white and pruned and soft, the flesh beneath slowly blackening with rot. At first, there had been pain, but now there was only numbness, a deadness that was creeping up his shins, claiming him piece by piece.

His mind was crumbling. Memories, once sharp and clear as the northern air, now swirled in a murky fog. He was truly lost. He tried to cling to the tenets of the Illuminthil, to the deep communion to the Aetherfast that he once knew, but there was no answer. The earth was deaf to him now, a dead and hollow thing.

The only thing he knew was hurt. He would hear the scrape of the iron bolt, the guttural laughter of the darkling guards, and a strange, sick sense of hope would flicker within him. *This time. Let this be the time.* They would drag him from his corner, his feet leaving slick trails on the stone. The blows would rain down, the dull, meaty thud of fists against his emaciated torso, the sharp crack of a wooden club against his ribs, the searing agony of a boot connecting with his face. And then unconsciousness would take him.

Initially, he had endured it with an unflappable, angry challenge. He fought back. He made them work for it. Now, he prayed for it. He offered no resistance, letting his body hang limp in their grasp, hoping his passivity would incite them to greater violence, to that one, final, merciful blow. He would focus on a single point of pain, a shattered rib, a split lip, and pour all his remaining will into it, begging it to be the wound that would finally unravel him, that would grant him the release of oblivion.

But they were skilled tormentors. They knew the precise line between torture and termination. They would bring him to the brink, to the very edge where death beckoned, and then they would stop. They would drop his broken body back into the mire of his cage, their laughter echoing down the corridor as the bolt slammed shut, leaving him alone once more with his own suffering, the ragged, wet sound of his breathing, the frantic, useless beat of his weak heart, and the relentless, maddening drip, drip, drip of water in the dark. And in that crushing silence, the true pain would begin again.

The prison doors opened. The familiar echoes of clawed, dog-like paws clacked down the desolate hall of the dungeon corridor. Stren listened for the accompanying laughter and mocking barbs from his tormentors. None came. All he heard was the sound of a singular pair of claws along the wet stone. He had neither the light nor the strength to see down the passage.

They never come alone, he thought, a strange, cold peace settling over him. *This is truly it, then. Praise Y'sa, this is the end.*

He did not uncurl from the tight ball he had become in the corner of his cell. His body had atrophied to a useless pile of skin and bones, and he had no desire to present anything but a willing participant for his own execution. He simply lay there, his forehead pressed against the frigid, weeping stone, and waited. Let the final blow come. Let the darkness take him. It would be a mercy. The solitary footsteps drew nearer, their rhythm steady and unhurried—purposefully quiet, even. They were not the eager, brutish stomp of his usual guards, but something more deliberate, more patient. The sound stopped directly outside the iron bars.

Stren held his breath, his heart frantic against his ribs. He welcomed death, surely, but still, he was afraid. What waited for him on the other side now that his communion with the Aetherfast was severed? Would Y'sa accept him? Would the god even look for him? He waited for the heavy bolt to be thrown, for the door to be kicked open with a crash. But the expected violence never came. Instead, a faint, metallic jingle broke the stillness, a sound so alien in this place of brute savagery that it sent a tremor of unease through him. *Keys? They were coming in through the main hall, then, and not the tormentor's entrance?* Then came the soft, grinding scrape of a key turning in a lock that had not been used since he'd been here, a sound of careful stealth.

The door did not fly open. It swung inward with a soft and grinding groan of rusted hinges, a sound like a dying man's last breath. A sliver of the corridor's faint, flickering torchlight sliced through the absolute blackness of his cell, illuminating nothing but a patch of slick, grimy floor. His eyes burned, and he shut them quickly, looking away. It took a long moment for him to brave the dim light, but as he did, he saw a blurry silhouette filling the opening. The figure standing before him was hunched and broad-shouldered and undeniably that of a darkling. Its sharp, fur-tufted ears poked high above its canine head, and its rotted fangs dripped saliva from its gaping jaws. It paused, a monstrous shape against the gloom, its breathing a hoarse rasp.

Slowly, it stepped inside, and the door swung silently shut behind it, plunging the cell back into near-total darkness. Stren could smell it now, the familiar, rank odor of damp fur and rotten meat on its breath, but underneath it, something else. The sharp, coppery tang of fresh blood, so thick it was almost a taste in the back of his throat.

The creature moved toward him, its steps now almost gentle on the sodden straw and stone. As it knelt beside him, the dim light caught the glint of metal. Stren's eyes, cracked to a slit, focused on the appendage. It was not a hand. Where the darkling's right hand should have been, a grotesque, tri-pointed hook was bolted to the mangled stump of its forearm. The metal shanks were barbed and honed to vicious points, and they were not clean. Clinging to the blades were tufts of black fur, matted with gore, and ribbons of something else, some pale, fleshy matter that trailed from the tips like obscene pennants.

The darkling's other hand, a clawed and scarred paw with long and curling nails, reached into a leather pouch at its belt. Stren flinched, bracing himself for a blade, for some new instrument of torture, for a single final blow. But what it produced was not a weapon. It was a black box.

Stren's breath hitched. It was a small, runic coffer covered in etchings and runes. Stren recognized some of them, but not all. Its surface seemed to drink the darkness, the glyphs upon it pulsing with a faint, sickly light that Stren could somehow feel more than see, a vibration of power. It was the Aetherfast. He knew it instantly. Then, the darkling's clawed fingers dipped back into the pouch and retrieved the second object.

It was the obsidian stone. It lay in the creature's palm, a piece of polished night, perfectly smooth. Within its depths, the faint, shimmering tendrils of iridescent light still writhed, a captured, tormented piece of the Aetherfast. The two artifacts that had unmade a kingdom were now before him, presented to him by this mutilated, solitary beast.

Stren's mind struggled to piece together the impossible scene. His wish for death was forgotten, replaced by a surge—a need—to survive. He dared to lift his head, his gaze traveling from the artifacts up to the face of the darkling kneeling over him. In the gloom, he saw its maw stretch wide, its yellowed, rotted teeth dull in the obscured light. It was a smile, sharp and full of a terrible, cunning knowledge. The creature's eyes met his, and in their black depths, Stren saw not the mindless savagery of his tormentors, but a flicker, just a feint glimmer of something else. Hope? Humanity?

The darkling leaned closer, its voice a low, gravelly rasp that scraped through the silence of the cell.

"We have work to do."

ARCHIVE #431

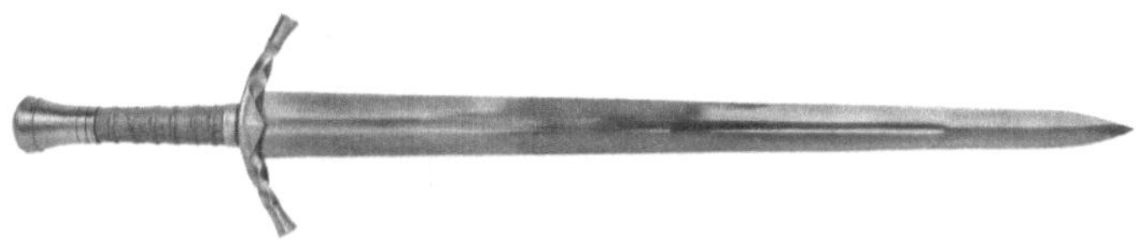

This is the account taken by Dariath Dandelion of *Meritha Pol's Historical Histories of the History of Meritha Pol*, compiled from the accounts of those who remember their histories.

Fumblefoot

When Fumblefoot was just a wee faeman, just a sprout, a sapling, barely old enough for the first braiding of his beard, he was not known for his strength, nor his courage, but for a spirit as round and soft as his belly, and a laugh that tumbled from his lips like plump white snow tumbling down from a mountain. He lived with his kin in Meritha Pol, a sanctuary tucked deep within the heart of the Western Wood, where the sun filtered through an umbrella of sprawling limbs and leaves, and the whole of the forest was alive with the gentle magic of growing things. His hands, though broad and calloused from tending the soil, were made for coaxing blossoms from reluctant bulbs and not for the clumsy heft of a warrior's axe.

Faeries, despite the grandeur of their beards, were a people of quiet routine and simple joys. Their days were measured by the turning of seasons, the ripening of berries, and the steady, patient work of their hands. The world outside the Wood was a distant tale of steel and stone, of cities with towers that stabbed the sky, and of peoples whose lives were a frantic blur. Fumblefoot listened to these stories, huddled with the others around a crackling fire, his large, inquisitive eyes wide with wonder and longing. He felt a dissonance in his heart, a yearning that warred with the peaceful rhythm of his life. He found himself dreaming of adventure, of deeds sung by bards, of standing tall against some unseen force of darkness.

His father, Old Man Tumble, a faeman whose beard was as white and wispy as a cloud, noticed this restlessness in his son. He would often find Fumblefoot staring out from the edge of the Wood, his gaze lost on the distant horizon of Greenfallow Downs, watching the sun rise in a blaze of gold and warmth.

"What troubles ye, son?" Old Man Tumble asked him one morning, his voice coming as a soft rustle of dry leaves. "Yer fer lookin' like a man w' a king's burden, an' not a faeman with a beard still wet from the first dew."

"'Tis nothin', Da," Fumblefoot replied, though his shoulders slumped as he said it. "'Tis just sometimes, I'm fer wonderin' if there ain't more to life than this quiet place, the plantin' an' the reapin' an' whatnot. I feel like there be a part o' me tha' ain't properly whole."

Old Man Tumble smiled a knowing smile and placed a warm hand on his son's shoulder. "Aye," he smiled. "The world outside the Wood is fer a certain glamour, innit? There bein' songs o' high deeds and grand adventures. But folly is fer livin' out there, too, don't ye doubt. Pride and vi'lence and disappointment that's fer breakin' a man's heart. We ain't fer choosin' the quiet because we're fer bein' weak, but 'cause we're fer bein' wise. For all the world's fury, this quiet endures. An' a good garden, ye should know, is more of a blessing than all o' the things bein' dreamed about out there."

Fumblefoot understood the wisdom in his father's words, but it did little to quell the storm brewing in his heart. He was a faeman, born of the earth and destined for a life of peace, yet an unyielding voice within him cried out for something else, something more. He wanted to be a hero. He wanted to stand between the world's unknown horizons and the solitude he so cherished, not simply to observe them from afar.

The world he knew offered no such opportunity until one day, it did.

Fumblefoot had been foraging near the riverbend, his wicker basket already full of wild strawberries and plump blood morels. He was humming a cheerful, tuneless ditty to himself when he heard it. It was a sound utterly foreign to him. It was a shrill, frightened cry that sliced through the peaceful babble of the waters around him. He froze, his hand halfway to plucking a lily to tie to his beard. It came again, a desperate, heart-wrenching sob, the unmistakable sound of a child in pain. It was a cry that would never—could never—be heard in Meritha Pol.

It was fear.

His father's words of warning melted away like morning fog. A dread crept over him, dark and looming as a winter storm, and flooded his veins. He dropped his basket, his collections forgotten, and scrambled towards the sound. He burst through a tangle of briars and emerged onto a small, sun-dappled clearing. There, huddled beneath the protruding roots of an old alder, was a little girl no older than five. Her face was streaked with tears, and her small body was trembling with terror. She wasn't fae. She was human, a child from one of the nearby fishing villages—lost, frightened, and alone.

Her cries were not from injury, but from terror. He knelt before her, his round face creased with concern, but kept a respectful distance. He did not want to frighten her further and knew that sudden movements could spook even the most docile creature. Her small, trembling hands were scraped and bloody. A vicious thorn, thick and barbed, had embedded itself in her calf, its jagged head buried deep within her pale skin.

"Don' na be afraid, wee one," he said, his voice soft and soothing. He unfastened the single pin that held the first, proud braid of his burgeoning beard, a badge of his coming of age, and began unspooling the tightly-wound hair with trembling fingers. "I'm fer bein' here to help ye. I won' na hurt ye."

The girl, seeing the kindness in his eyes and the gentle movements of his hands, stopped her crying and replaced it with subdued, hiccupping breaths. She watched him tear a strip of cloth from his shirt. Her wide, brown eyes brimmed with a tug-of-war between suspicion and hope as he came closer. He was about to set to work on her wound when a shadow fell over them. It was not the gentle wafting shade of the canopy above, but a large, looming, and menacing cloud cast by the hulking figure of a large boar, its tusks yellowed and sharp, its eyes glinting with a feral, mindless hunger. It was a brute! Its hide was a gnarled mass of scars and matted bristles, and it had caught the scent of blood.

The girl let out a fresh shriek, a sound so desperate and so fearful that it pierced Fumblefoot's heart like a spear. His own body, which had known only peace, screamed at him to flee, to hide, to let the forest take its natural, violent course. But when he looked at the girl's face, at the panic in her eyes, a new sensation surged through his veins. It was rage. It was a sudden and commanding desire to protect this small, defenseless creature, no matter the outcome. It was the birthing of something that had been growing within him for as long as he could remember.

It was courage.

Fumblefoot rose slowly, setting himself squarely between the girl and the beast. He wielded no weapon, save for the knife he used to clean his mushrooms, a tool of his trade and his people. It was a simple length of steel—sharp but small. The tang was full, and the handle was a simple leather wrap. It was a useless thing against the giant boar that towered before him. Still, he stood tall, his hands clenched into fists, his round face set in a look of dire determination. His heart pounded furiously, but a strange calm settled over him, a sense of rightness, of purpose.

He had been born for this day.

The boar snorted, its dark eyes fixed on Fumblefoot, a farcical obstacle in its path to a much easier, much more palatable meal. It pawed at the dirt and let out a low, menacing growl that rumbled in its throat. Its monstrous head, nearly the size of Fumblefoot, twitched back and forth as it sized up its opponent. It dug tusks the length of the doomed fae's arms deep into the loam of the forest floor, sharpening them against the rocks beneath.

"Yer not fer touchin' this one," Fumblefoot announced, his voice quaking with fear. "She be in m' ferest this day, an' so she be mine fer protectin'."

The boar was unimpressed, and understandably so. It charged, a grunt of aggression rumbling from its throat, its heavy hooves tearing at the earth. Time seemed to slow. Fumblefoot saw the flash of its yellowed tusks, the foam flecking its lips, the totality of the unstoppable weight of its motive charge. He blanched then, understanding the futility of his stand. The forest, his beloved home, was no longer a place of quiet refuge. It was an unforgiving and unfair stage for a clash between nature's savagery and a faeman's newfound bravery.

At the very last moment, Fumblefoot did the only thing he could think to do. He didn't try to fight. He couldn't. He was a gardener, a tender of things, not a warrior. Instead, he simply moved. He threw his body to the side. It was desperate and it was clumsy, but it was all he had. He snatched the girl into his arms mid-flight, and they rolled together, away from the charge. The boar, unable to stop its headlong rush, slammed into the roots of the ancient alder. The impact was immense. The tree shuddered, and a shower of leaves and branches rained down on the clearing. The tusker, dazed and disoriented, stumbled as its head was buried in the earth.

Fumblefoot scrambled to his feet, a burst of adrenaline giving him a strength he didn't know he had. He grabbed his knife and, with a roar that frightened him even as it leaped from his throat, plunged the steel deep into the boar's flank, into the soft flesh of its side where the plates of its thick hide did not meet. The boar howled, a caterwaul of pain and rage and surprise. Fumblefoot did not withdraw the blade. Instead, he pushed it deeper and drew a long line across the boar's belly. Blood and gore and entrails spilled onto the forest floor, and still he cut his macabre line wider. The beast bucked and thrashed wildly until at last, with a final, violent spasm that sent Fumblefoot tumbling back against the dirt, it gave one last slow, shuddering exhalation, and went still.

The faeman lay on the grass, breathless and shaken, clutching his knife with shaking hands. The scent of fresh blood was all around him. He lay there for a long moment. He had done it. He had faced down a monster and won, but he felt no triumph, only exhaustion, only a release of all the fear and rage that had possessed him as he had seen the young girl threatened. He rolled over, his gaze falling immediately on the child. She was still huddled beneath where they had landed. Her eyes were wide with a different kind of awe now. She looked at him, not with fear, but with respect and admiration, and he liked it.

Forgetting his own aches and pains, he crawled over to her, his movements once again slow and gentle. He took the strip of cloth he had torn from his tunic and carefully, meticulously, bound her leg, taking care to remove the thorn. As he worked, humming the same tuneless song he had been singing earlier, a new feeling bloomed in his chest. It was not the loud, boisterous, and arrogant pride of a warrior, but rather a quiet, enduring sense of peace. He had found his purpose. He had found the thing that called to him. It was not in the earth or the soil, or even in Meritha Pol or the Western Wood. It was the simple act of protecting. He was a faeman, yes, a gardener of the Wood. But from that day forward, he was also a protector, a guardian of the weak. He had become something more. He had become, in his own small way, a hero.

The encounter with the boar was a bell tolling and silent no more in the depths of Fumblefoot's soul. From that day on, the peace and calm of Meritha Pol did not feel like a sanctuary where he could spend his days simply enjoying the tranquility offered there. It became a delicate thing in need of a champion. The world outside the Western Wood was a distant, glamorous story no longer, it was a place of wild boars and lost children, of dangers and those in need of rescuing. He had tasted the intoxicating wine of purpose, and the flavor of it lingered on his tongue. It was a constant reminder of the life he had found and a life he was now destined to live.

He began to train. He practiced with an old, weathered branch instead of an axe, learning to move, to parry, and to strike. He would spend hours at the riverbend, dodging the swift currents as they flowed past him, imagining them as the charges of wild beasts or the thrusts of ill-intentioned foes. His movements were bumbling at first, but driven by his singular focus, they became something else. They became a clumsy but efficient choreography of offense and defense.

He never sought out violence, but he prepared for it. He was a faeman who would have the answer prepared well ahead, if the question was ever asked.

He became the unofficial protector of the fae children. He would lead them on foraging expeditions, his keen eyes ever scanning the forest for dangers, his hands quick to disarm a fallen branch or chase away a curious serpent. He was a constant presence on the outskirts of the Wood, a sigil of security along the borders. The human villagers knew of him, too, calling him "The Watcher of the Wood." He would often leave baskets of freshly-picked berries or polished stones on their doorsteps as a promise of his vigilance. They learned to trust his presence, an understanding that brought a unique kind of peace to the turbulent lands surrounding the ancient forest.

Fumblefoot's confidence grew with each passing season. He became strong, not just in body, but in the self-reliance born of tested courage. He saw himself not as a small, insignificant creature of the woods anymore, but as a faeman of action. His beard grew long and magnificent, and was braided and decorated with river stones and wildflowers. It became his pride, a physical manifestation of his unwavering strength and resolve. He would often speak of the day he saved the little girl, a story that grew in the telling, becoming less a memory and more a prophecy of his own making. He would speak of his strength and of his honor and of his valor. His heart and soul swelled with a pride that was born of a genuine desire for good.

Over the years, the fae elders grew concerned over Fumblefoot's growing attachment to the outside world and admonished him with weary patience. "Yer place is bein' here, 'round yer own kind an' kin," Old Man Tumble would chide him, clutching his son's magnificent beard in his shaking hands. "Tha Wood be needin' her gardeners, an' no' her warriors. A wayward heart is a bothersome thing, me boy, an' it ain't fer healing it out there wit' them who ar' no' yer kin."

Fumblefoot would simply smile. "I ain't fer havin' a broken heart, Da," he would say. "I'm well fer knowin' tha' the day a heart breaks is the day it's fer bein' to forget its purpose. An' my purpose, as I'm now well understandin' it, is ter watch fer them who ain't able ter watch fer themselves. The outside world has its broken hearts ter be sure, but I'm fer mendin' 'em."

His fateful day came as a call for help. The fishing village, nestled on the quiet basin of the Summershine River, was a peaceful place, a place he had watched over for years from the higher elevations of the Wood. One day, a fierce and stubborn regiment, a band of cruel and lawless men, seized the village, taking its townfolk as prisoners.

Fumblefoot heard the cries of the villagers as a scream, one that resonated deeply and reminded him of the cry of the little girl he had saved all those years ago. He saw the smoke curling from the rooftops and ran to their aid. The memory of that day, the fear in her eyes, and the helplessness he had felt before finding his courage ignited a fire within him. He did not hesitate. He did not seek counsel. He knew his destiny. This was his purpose—the glorious battle he had spent a lifetime preparing for.

-Dariath Dandelion of Meritha Pol
Keeper of the Written Word of the Historical Histories of the History of Meritha Pol

A LETTER TO THE READER

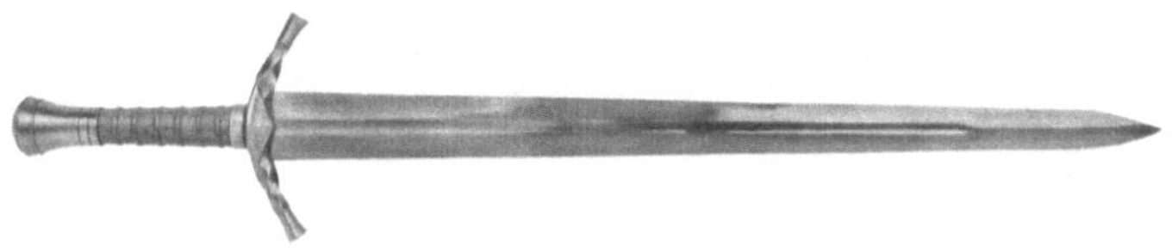

To the brave traveler who has journeyed alongside me through the pages of The Singing Blade, I offer my most profound and heartfelt thanks.

Thank you for choosing to step into this world, for walking the winding roads of Y'ssara, for feeling the chill of the Vintermarrow, and for standing with Illia-Dara as her world shattered, her heart broke, and she experienced her first sorrow. Your willingness to give this story, and my characters, a chance means more to me than words can express.

Writing is a lonely trek, a quiet journey through the landscapes of the imagination. For 23 years, these characters—Illia-Dara, Aoife, Stren, Ixchel, Endryll, The Rand Brothers, The Fae, Strakk, Tam-Ma, and Atamas—have lived only in the private corners of my mind. Their joys and their sorrows, their triumphs and their devastating losses were a secret shared between only me and the page. By reading this book, you have breathed life into them. You have made their struggles real, their hopes tangible, and their world real. For that, I am eternally grateful.

The story you have just finished is but the first note in a much larger song. The world of Y'ssara is wounded, but not yet lost. Illia-Dara's journey has only just begun, and the path ahead is fraught with danger, destiny, and the terrible choices that await a queen with no crown.

The Queen of Sorrows: Book II is coming in December 2026. Until then, I invite you to visit my website at www.micahcampbell.com. There, you will find exclusive updates, deep dives into the lore of Y'ssara, character spotlights, and behind-the-scenes glimpses into the creation of this world. It is my hope that this website becomes a community for all of us who have found a home in the kingdom of sorrows and a reason to hope for its future.

Thank you once more for your readership. Your belief in this story is the fire that keeps me writing.

With sincere gratitude,
Micah Campbell